Rock the Boat

A Novel

We Were The Puget Sound Series

Book 1

Danielle Bailey

Daughters of Gwenneth
Publishing, LLC

First Edition

Cover art: Sarah Rain Johnson

Cover design: Danielle Bailey

Editor: Macy Giunti

USS Puget Sound AD -38 Name and Insignia © Permission Granted by US Navy Trademark Division

Published by: Daughters Of Gwenneth Publishing LLC

[ISBN] 978-1-7372583-3-9

Library of Congress Cataloging-in-Publication has been applied for.

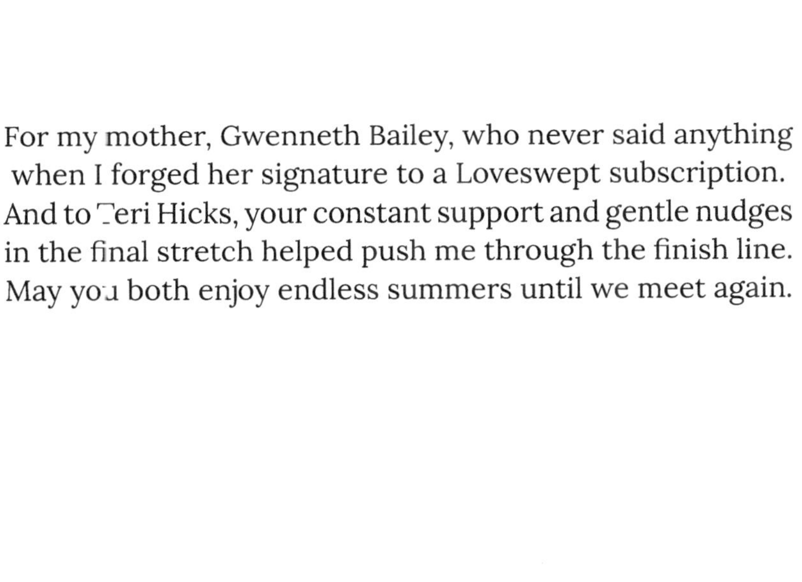

For my mother, Gwenneth Bailey, who never said anything when I forged her signature to a Loveswept subscription. And to Teri Hicks, your constant support and gentle nudges in the final stretch helped push me through the finish line. May you both enjoy endless summers until we meet again.

Acknowledgments

I just want to take a moment to thank my first critique partners, Morag McKendrick and Diane Blackman. They were here in 2002 when I first started RTB and in 2021 when I finished it. And Teri Hicks, who I knew for a short time but significantly impacted my writing. She drilled into my brain that every chapter needed to leave her wanting her more, and to my dismay, some of them weren't.

And to the rest of my amazing, marvelous, super patient beta readers—Andrew Scott, Barb Desmarais, Breanna Wiggins, Bilqis Mansur, Ester Noguera, Olga Alicea, Tiffany Lowe, Tricia Daley, and Quinn Blaiklock, who managed to push through all the grammatical errors because I forgot to put on the Grammarly app that I paid for. Ya'll are the real ones!

Introduction

From the moment BM2 Meadows rolled a trash can down the middle of the berthing in boot camp at 0319, I've had a love/hate relationship with the Navy, probably because I had undiagnosed ADHD and was so rebellious. I grew up in the South Bronx—what do you expect yo? I went to Captain's Mast a month after being on the ship, but that wasn't my fault, I swear. I didn't even know what the fire party was, and I wasn't doing it. And I got kicked out of the DOD Photography School twice y'all for the most randomness of reasons before they finally let me graduate. But after six months of living in Pensacola, I had a bangin' tan. So it wasn't all in vain.

Despite my complaints and grumbles about the Navy, I cannot ignore the fact that the Navy finished raising me from the last month of my 17th birthday until I was 23 years old. To this day, I still look at civilians who cry at work with mild disgust. Family emergencies notwithstanding, I'm not a monster. But if it didn't come in your seabag, is it really that important? I still don't have the answer to that question.

However, what the Navy gave me that *didn't* come in my seabag were terrific, long-lasting friendships, great loves, and memories that have stood the test of time. At 18 years old, I walked through the bazaars alone in Souda Bay, Crete, looped arms in Rota, Spain, with my best friend Ester, which I dragged to the Navy with me and was transfixed by the enormous moon sitting low in the night sky as we walked around on base. I ate at the Pizza Hut in Palma Majorca, Spain, because we were so happy to see American food. My cruise girlfriend and I got followed by two men in Naples, probably because they saw us in the adult theater across the street from McDonald's, wondered why the hell was Sigonella, Sicily, so boring and quiet, and where was the mafia? Almost went to the naked beach in Corfu, Greece (I wish I had gone, but I wasn't going with Ewing), ate yogurt with honey for the first time. Fell in love with Antalya, Turkey, because our tour guide had the kitchen make me a drink that calmed my upset tummy. I wished he was in Marmara when we ate those mussels that sent us directly to the head when we got back to the ship. I got lost in Marseilles, France, trying to find black hair products, and froze while waiting for the bus because I failed to pack a fall jacket and rode the train in Monte Carlo, unimpressed by the ordinary experience. I guess I was expecting rich people to be riding public transportation. My only bonafide regret of Med Cruise '94 was that my dramatic ass didn't leave the ship in Lisbon, Portugal. I was too busy being sorry for myself because my cruise girlfriend was going back to *her* real girlfriend when the ship pulled back in. First loves are the absolute worst...

It's been twenty-nine years since that first wave of sea-sickness had me doubting my decision to join the Navy, and my memories of some parts of the ship are not as sharp as I'd like them to be, especially if they weren't my skating destinations. So if something isn't accurate, slide into my DM's, don't be out there tryna put me out on blast, please, *and* thank you. Also, the characters in this story are very fictional—I repeat fictional as in made, as in not real. If you think I'm talking about you—I'm not. So don't ask me.

Also, I'm trying to keep things as authentic as possible, so the characters will switch back and forth between first and last names while on the ship. Each chapter is titled with the character's name and rank to hopefully lessen the confusion, Navy terminology is in the footnotes, and of course, there is a glossary.

Rock the Boat is the first book in the *We Were The Puget Sound* series set in the Navy during the 1990s because we all know the '90s were dope. So pack up your seabag, stock up on Cup O'Noodles and those little tuna fish kits, kiss your family goodbye, secure your cruise boo and join the USS Puget Sound AD-38 and the rest of the Sixth Fleet as they prepare to set sail to the Mediterranean Sea.

Word of Caution (Again): This book is set in the Navy, not only will Navy terminology be used, but first and last names will also be used interchangeably when the characters are onboard the ship. So pay attention to last names so you don't get lost.

<u>**Naval Terminology**</u>

1MC/Main circuit: loudspeakers.

Aft: rear of the ship or a space.

Aft Lookout: covered section extending from the rear of the ship.

A School: where sailors go to receive their specialized rate (job) training.

AT Land/Apprentice Training School: a general training for undesignated sailors by their rating—airmen, firemen, seamen, and seabee (construction battalion).

Berthing: living quarters aboard a ship.

BM/Boatswain's Mate: train, direct, and supervise personnel in ship maintenance and boat seamanship.

Boatswain's locker: various secured spaces throughout the ship where Boatswains store deck gear and hang out in.

Boondockers: steel toed boot.

Brow: the temporary bridge that connects the ship's quarterdeck to the pier.

Bridge: room or platform of a ship from which the ship can be commanded.

Bulkhead: wall.

Captain's Mast: a low-level and relatively informal forum for handling minor misconduct.

Chit: refers to almost every piece of paper, from an official form to a special request.

Chow: to sit and eat.

Coffin rack: beds that are stacked three high with a locker underneath the mattress, and when the top that housed the mattress was propped open, it resembled a coffin. Think Murphy bed.

Deck Department: consists of two divisions. 1st division maintains the outward appearance of the ship and specific areas throughout the ship, and 3rd division runs the boat deck. Together they are responsible for the safe navigation and operation of the vessel, both at sea and in port.

EN/Enginemen: operate, maintain, and repair engines, main propulsion machinery, refrigeration, air conditioning.

ESWS/Enlisted Surface Warfare Specialist: Personnel trained and qualified to perform duties aboard surface warships.

XO/Executive officer: second in command.

FC/Fire Controlman: provide system employment recommendations, perform organizational and intermediate maintenance on digital computer equipment and subsystems and operate and maintain compact and weapons direction systems.

Fat Boy Program: the stigmatized weight-control program of nutritional counseling, exercise, and humiliating monthly weigh-ins.

Forward: the front of the ship or a space.

Damage Control & Damage Controlman: the ship's fireman, maintaining and repairing damage control equipment and systems, the ship's stability, firefighting, fire prevention, etc.

Deck Department: consists of two divisions; 1st that maintains the outward appearance of the ship and 3rd division that runs the boat deck. Together they are responsible for the safe navigation and operation of the vessel, both at sea and in port.

Designated Striker: a person in paygrade E-1, E-2, E-3 who has been designated (appointed or specified) as technically qualified for a particular job/rating.

Dog: to close or "dog down" a watertight hatch.

Don't ask/Don't tell: a set of policies, laws, and regulations governing how the U.S. Military dealt with gay, lesbian, and bisexual service members.

Draftsman: create original art, technical illustrations, graphics for briefings, visual aids, and publications for the Navy.

Duty: responsibilities given to a group of people for 24 hours.

Duty Section: the group of sailors assigned to 24-hour duty at a command.

Hatch: a watertight opening to a deck. If it goes through a bulkhead, it's a regular door.

HM/Hospital Corpsman: assist health care professionals in providing care to Navy personnel.

General Quarters: announcement made aboard a naval warship to signal all hands must go to their assigned battle stations as quickly as possible.

GM/Gunner's Mate: are responsible for the operation and maintenance of the missile launch systems, underwater explosives, gun mounts, and other ordinance equipment.

Indoc or Indoctrination: orientation to a new command.

IS/Intelligence Specialist: they collect all types of intel about everything and everyone.

Ladder: stairs.

Leave: authorized absence from a place of duty. i.e., vacation.

Liberty/Liberty Call: authorized absence granted for short periods to provide respite from the working environment.

Lithographer: they run the print shops and produce printed material used by the Navy.

Machinist Mate: are responsible for operating and maintaining ship propulsion machinery and outside machinery.

Main Control: controls the propulsion system of the ship.

Manning the rails: sailors at parade rest, spaced evenly on port and starboard the wing walls, and the aft lookout while the ship leaves the pier and when it returns.

Master-At-Arms: a petty officer appointed to carry out or supervise police duties on the ship.

Mess Cranking/Crankers: sailors who are not mess specialists by training but are sent by their divisions to help out in the mess aboard the ship or command.

Mess or Mess Deck: a designated area where military personnel eat and socialize.

Muster: taking attendance of the members in a division or department.

NOB: Naval Station Norfolk is a United States Navy base in Norfolk, Virginia, that is the headquarters and home port of the U.S. Navy's Fleet Forces Command.

Naval Medical Center Portsmouth: based in Portsmouth, Virginia.

Nuke: Navy's Nuclear Program consisting of various rates/jobs.

OJT: on-the-job training.

Ombudsman: a sailor's spouse at the Command who serves as the liaison between the Command and the families.

Overhead: ceiling

Passageway: hallway of a ship.

Personnel Man: human resources folks.

Photographer's Mate: in charge of filming and recording operations that occur during Navy operations.

POD/Plan of the Day: command's schedule for the day.

Port: left side.

PRT/Physical Readiness Test: physical fitness test done twice a year for all hands.

Rate or Rating: an enlisted sailor's job or job description.

Red Cross message: confidential emergency communication via the American Red Cross to service members who are on deployment.

Quarterdeck: the shipboard area connected to the brow where personnel arrive and depart the ship.

Quarters: a meeting with the sailors of a division or department, usually happens in the morning.

Sea and Anchor Detail: sailors are assigned to specific areas throughout the ship so they can attach and release the mooring lines to the pier safely and also pick up and drop the anchor safely as well.

Seabag: duffel bag.

SH/Ship Serviceman: manages all shipboard retail and service activities, such as the barbershop, laundry, and commissary.

Starboard: right side

SK/Storekeeper: are responsible for maintaining a ship or company military supply store

Striker: non-designated personnel. Usually refers to sailors who are attempting to learn a rate by doing on-the-job training.

Taps: signal and announcement for the end of the day.

Torpedoman: are in charge of everything from torpedoes and missiles to small arms and ammunition.

TSP/Thrift saving plans: a retirement plan for military

personnel

Twilight Tour: when a sailor is approaching their last years in service.

UCMJ/Uniform Code of Military Judgment: federal law, enacted by Congress, defines the military justice system and lists criminal offenses under military law.

Underway: laymen's terms: the ship is out to sea. Nautical definition: the vessel is not at anchor, aground, or secured to the shore or dock.

USS Dwight D. Eisenhower (CVN-69) (known informally as "Ike") is a nuclear-powered aircraft carrier currently in service with the United States Navy.

USS Puget Sound (AD-38): was designated to perform repairs and maintenance of the U.S. Navy's shore and seagoing equipment.

USS John F. Kennedy (CV 67): was the fourth and final ship of the Kitty Hawk-class of aircraft carriers.

Warrant Officer: highly skilled, single-track specialty officers.

Watch: the time an individual is assigned a specific, detailed responsibility.

YN/Yeoman: administrative and clerical worker.

<u>Enlisted</u>

Seaman Recruit (SR/E-1)
 Seaman Apprentice (SA/E-2)
Seaman (SN/E-3)
Petty Officer 3rd Class (PO3/E-4)
Petty Officer 2nd Class (PO2/E-5)
Petty Officer 1st Class (PO1/E-6)
Chief Petty Officer (CPO/E-7)
Senior Chief Petty Officer (SCPO/E-8)
 Master Chief Petty Officer (MCPO/E-9)

Chief Warrant Officer (CWO-1)

<u>Officer</u>

Ensign (ENS, O1)
Lieutenant, Junior Grade (LTJG, O2)
Lieutenant (LT, O3)
Lieutenant Commander (LCDR, O4)
Commander (CDR, O5)
Captain (CAPT, O6)
Rear Admiral Lower Half (RDML,O7)
Rear Admiral Upper Half (RADM, O8)
Vice Admiral (VADM, O9)
Admiral (ADM, O10)

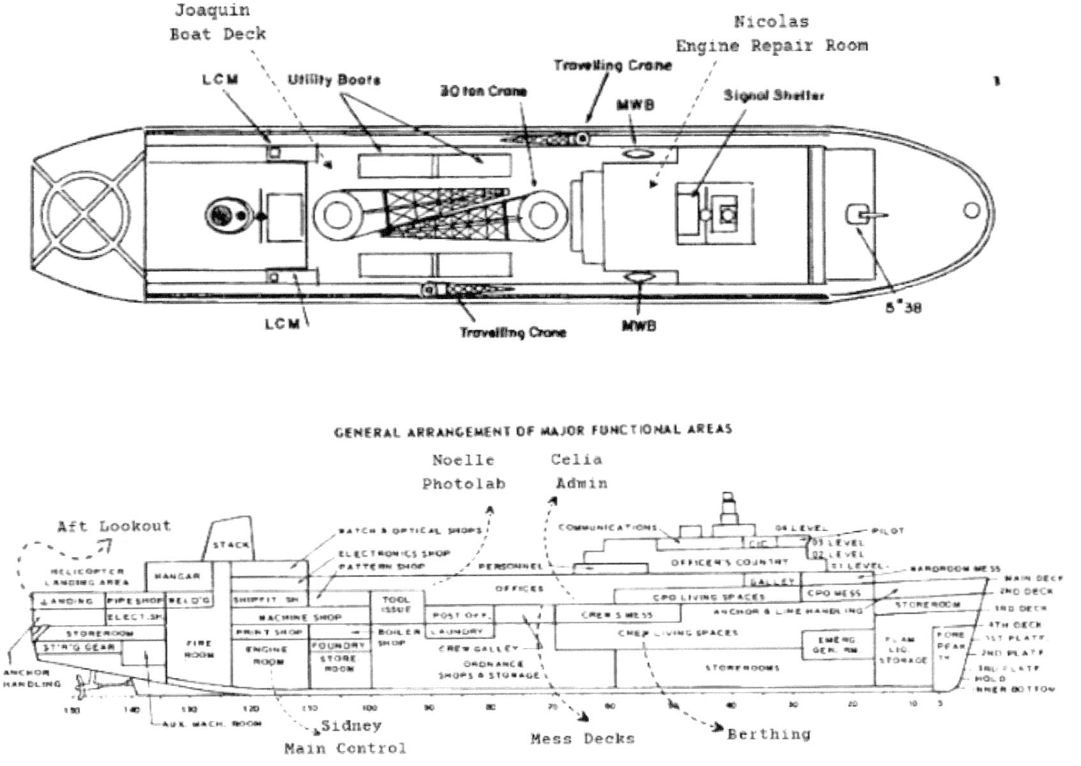

USS Puget Sound AD-38

Author's Note

Please be aware that this story discusses parental death and grieving, adultery, undiagnosed ADHD, unspecified generalized anxiety in adults, brief mention of abortion, and mentions of physical violence.

April 4th, 1994

Eight Weeks Before
Deployment

Chapter One

PHI Noelle Bentley

Gluttony will be my downfall, Noelle thought after reaching across the passenger's seat to grab her bookbag but instead finding a box of girl scout cookies in its place. Funny, she always thought pride would be her downfall; however, this morning it was definitely greed. It wasn't even the good kind of greed that made you rich. It was the kind that gave you the sugars and left you stranded at the gas station on E.

With the crystal-clear hindsight that only seemed reserved for mistakes, Noelle saw herself pat her grumbling stomach, then set the black bookbag that doubled as her purse on the floor instead of slinging it on her shoulder and reaching for the box in the cabinet. The same box her roommate Celia ordered her not to touch since Noelle inhaled the last two boxes. The forbidden taste of minty chocolate hit her tastebuds the exact moment her eyes widened at the time on the stove clock. She grabbed the box because she needed a snack for the drive and ran out the door. And where was her bookbag now? On the damn kitchen floor...with her purse inside! She sucked her teeth. Thank goodness she kept her keys and ID on her lanyard with her pager clipped to it, or else she would've locked herself out of the house. Celia was going to have a field day with this shit.

Frustration didn't stop Noelle from popping one of the cookies in her mouth as she contemplated what to do. She had fifty cents in her ashtray, she usually kept a twenty in her glove compartment for emergencies but she spent it on lunch yesterday. She could use a quarter to call a cab and meet Celia at the pier to pay for the cab. But there was still the issue of getting her Jeep to a parking space; scary thought since she felt like she glided in on fumes.

Noelle shook her head. She stopped trying to understand where her aversion to getting gas came from long ago. It was just a part of her now, like her prematurely creaky knees. There wasn't a week that her gas tank wasn't hovering precariously over E as she passed by gas station after gas station, telling herself she'd get gas later. And later had been during yesterday's lunch run. She then further exacerbated the issue by putting it off again for the morning, forgetting that time was never on her side because the Gods were always conspiring against her and not for her.

Sighing, Noelle glanced at her *Swatch*. It was 0728. She groaned, also realizing she'd grabbed the wrong watch. This one had the bright, multi-colored wristband, and she needed the basic black one while in uniform. She had to remember to take it off before muster, unlike the last time when she forgot and got called out for it.

Noelle was a Photographer's Mate[1] First Class, stationed

aboard the USS Puget Sound [2] at Naval Station Norfolk[3]. Liberty[4] on the ship was secured at 0800. If you crossed the quarterdeck after that, your ID card would be confiscated by the Master-at-Arms[5]. It wasn't like a civilian job where you could just go ahead and get some breakfast since you were already late and then mosey on in whenever with some random excuse. During the almost three years she'd been stationed aboard the Sound, her perpetually late ass somehow managed to avoid the shame of asking her Chief to retrieve her ID card from the MA's. Her luck might run out today, though, because she was still 20 minutes away, and all the close parking stops were probably already taken, so who knows how far away from the ship she'd have to park. This was a nightmare. There was no way not to make a scene trying to join muster.

One of these days, she was going to...*Do what? A whole lotta nuthin', that's what!* She was a goddamn mess of an adult. Noelle sucked her teeth and shook her head, shaking the thought away. She got out of the Jeep to close her gas tank cover and was about to slide back in when a low,

---

2. USS Puget Sound AD-38: a ship designated for repair and maintenance of the U.S. Navy's shore and seagoing equipment serving the Atlantic Fleet.

3. Naval Station Norfolk: is a United States Navy base in Norfolk, Virginia, that is the headquarters and home port of the U.S. Navy's Fleet Forces Command.

4. Liberty/Liberty Call: authorized absence granted for short periods to provide respite from the working environment.

5. Master-At-Arms (MA): Naval police force

smooth voice stopped her. "Do you need some help?"

"Huh?" Hand on the door rim, Noelle turned to look between the gas pumps at a tall man in a black suit on the other side. How in the hell did she miss *him*? Granted, the pumps were in the way, and she was too engrossed in the consequences of her bad choices, but this man was fine as hell. He was tall, maybe 6'1" or so. At 5'7", she'd have to look up to him, which she never really liked because it made her feel small and powerless. Then again, he was *fine*. She'd push aside her ego this one time.

He was also a bit broad in the shoulders, which stoked her inner Food-Shelter-Water man craving. He looked like he could BBQ, paint the house, chop some wood for the fireplace and carry buckets of water to put out the inferno she would undoubtedly make while trying to start a fire, and then proceed to lay the wood. His nose, unlike hers, harkened from the Motherland. His Caesar fade was nicely shaped up, highlighting his short waves on top, and his deep mahogany skin had a red undertone that had not a pore to be seen.

He must use the whole Noxzema product line.

And his lips...mmmmm. Noelle bit the inside of her bottom lip in response. They were full and topped with a prominent angel shush that she wanted to trace her fingers over and then her tongue. However, his warm, brown eyes sealed the deal. He had those pretty eyeliner eyes that only seemed reserved for men, with thick lashes to boot. She had a thing for pretty eyes. Shit, she had a thing for pretty ass men, which he most definitely was.

But pump the brakes! Was that a patois she heard? She wasn't familiar enough with all the island accents to pinpoint his, but he was West Indian. That pretty face might not make up for that. She had a complicated relationship with men from the Islands. She loved them, yet at the same time, she wanted to throat-punch them. She blamed her Caribbean family dynamic for that confusion.

Realizing she was staring, Noelle blinked, grinning sheepishly. "No, I'm good, thanks—unless you want to pay for my gas since I managed to leave the house without my wallet." Shaking her head, she started to get into her truck.

"Is that all you need?" He chuckled as he came around to her side of the pump. "I can take care of that for you."

"Ummm, take care of wha— Oh, okay, I guess...." Noelle's voice trailed off as she watched him head inside the store. She stood there awkwardly, trying to ignore the car that pulled up behind her as she waited for him to return. Good googly moogly, was she really about to let a stranger pay for her gas?

"What's your gas type?" He asked when he returned.

Noelle grimaced. "Ummm, you really don't have to do this."

"It's cool. It's already done." He picked up the nozzle as those lips twitched with just the slightest smirk on one side. "Go ahead and pop open your tank cover again. Gas type?"

Umph, girl, you don't know this man. Are you supposed to pay him back? And with what exactly? I don't like it, a voice inside her head said.

Kaboom! Constance, the Control Freak, has stepped in the room!

Constance was the voice that tried to interject common sense into any situation. Noelle had about four voices that represented her mental state. Some might call them personalities, but they weren't. Her mind was just constantly on. It was filled with so many ideas—both abstract and concrete, stories, fears, and random ass shit that should be sorted and categorized on *Jeopardy!* Giving her mental states names helped to provide structure and organization to her brain so she didn't get overwhelmed. It worked 95% of the time; that remaining 5% was an absolute shitshow. While she was fairly certain that everyone had that little voice in their head, she kept the fact that she named her private. Celia and Sidney only ever found out because they heard her talking to herself one day. Thank goodness they knew her well enough not to report her to medical. Because honey, she was constantly having full-ass conversations with herself.

But Constance was right this time. She didn't know this man from Adam, and he probably was gonna want something from her in return. Except for her daddy and her brothers, no man had ever paid for her gas. Correction: she never *allowed* any man to pay for gas; occasionally, she let them pump it when it was raining or freezing, though. She didn't want them to get too familiar with her. Her ridiculous control issues were not, however, going to get her to the ship on time.

Noelle, you in danger, girl, Constance warned.

Hush. You don't have to walk. I do. I mean, you do, but I am literally doing the footwork. Noelle reached inside the truck and pulled the lever for the gas cover. "87." He nodded, and he put the nozzle in the tank. "Well, this is really sweet of you. I would have been pushing my car over there in a minute." She pointed to a parking space in front of the 7-Eleven. "Boy, I tell you, procrastination is the devil's work. It gets me every time."

"So then why do you keep on doing it?" Her Good Samaritan asked.

Noelle clutched her imaginary pearls. "Did you really just ask me that?" She waved her hand at him. "I dunno. I just hate getting gas. I know I need it but I will wait until the last minute. Maybe something happened to me in a past life. The gas station exploded or something, and now my soul knows it's on borrowed time. So, light a candle for me, say a prayer, throw some bones down, read the tea leaves so I can find out the reason."

"You forgot to sacrifice a chicken," he added.

Noelle snapped her fingers. "I sure did! That's a standard. Thank you. And that just might be the one to do it too. You're just so helpful this morning. Gas, offering to sacrifice a chicken—"

He held up his hand. "Didn't say I'd sacrifice it for you. I just added it to the list of options."

"But you were so quick with it." Studying him, Noelle tilted her head to the side. "Something tells me you've killed a chicken before."

"Because I have an accent?" He raised his brows.

"Yes." Noelle wrinkled her nose. "I mean, I know it's bad to say out loud, but you have haven't you?"

"Yes." Grinning, he shrugged his shoulders.

"I knew it! Listen, sometimes those stereotypes are right. And since you've done it before, you can totally do it for me now. I'm just throwing it out there," Noelle said.

"If it would make you stop asking me to do it, I would."

"Again, it's not a request if you made the suggestion. I am just taking you up on the offer."

"This is the weirdest conversation I've ever had," he said with a light chuckle.

"You're welcome. Intriguing and unusual conversations are what I do best," Noelle said. He did look a bit puzzled; her chitter chatter be like that sometimes.

"I didn't say thank you." But her Good Samaritan's smile contradicted his words.

Noelle's pulse accelerated the sight of those white teeth. Jesus, take all dem wheels! Even the spare and the jack. Just leave her on flats! His smile was absolutely divine. Like his eyes, it was warm and welcoming but also sexy and confident. But not in a smug asshole way. In the "just relax girl, I got this" way, that made her want to sit on his face and then climb on his back like a baby howler monkey so he could haul her around with him, only putting her down so he could have his way with her...and feed her. He definitely knows how to make some jerk chicken.

Meanwhile, she looked like an extra from the "Save the Children" campaign. She hadn't started tanning yet, so her pilot light wasn't on. Over the mild winter months of Virginia, her melanin had faded from the rich toffee of her dreams to a dusty-ass beige. Basically, she was out here in these streets looking like she needed a new liver. Earlier, she had thrown on her Navy sweatpants that she'd been hanging on to since boot camp. The waistband string got lost years ago, and the large white N was fading and peeling in places; she even had little bleach spots splattered down one leg. They were also a bit snug because she had gained almost twenty pounds since boot camp, which wasn't too bad considering it had been seventeen years since. She scooped up the wrinkled *Ocean Pacific* t-shirt from the bedroom floor. Was it clean? Probably not. But after an exploratory sniff, the pits smelled okayish, and it wasn't like she was planning to wear it all day, so on it went.

Oooh, and speaketh not of her hair! Her tapered afro was a bushy mess. She had glanced at her Indian Hemp grease when she rushed around the bathroom and foolishly decided against it since she'd be in her coveralls and ballcap after muster. So her usually well-defined and moisturized curls were so dry that they looked more like the wood shavings used for starting fires. Now she wished she had at least wet it. She was lucky she was under the awning, or the Virginia morning sun would indeed light her hair up. Self-consciously, she patted her hair with both hands. She was pleasantly surprised that pieces of it didn't break off in her hands.

At that exact moment, a strong breeze decided that it was the perfect time to plaster her T-shirt to her breasts. She usually wore a tight tank top instead of bras underneath her shirts, but they were all still wet in the washing machine because she forgot to transfer them to the dryer last night before going to bed. She thought she'd get up early enough to do it in the morning. She'd contemplated wearing it while still wet but decided against it. Goddammit, she needed to get her life together.

His eyes flickered down to her breasts. Noelle wasn't sure if it was the breeze or the heat of his gaze, but her skin started prickling like crazy. Is this what being tasered felt like? It took everything in her not to fidget. She fought the urge to inhale and puff her chest out as if she were sporting 34 DDs instead of 34 A's while simultaneously feeling awkward and overexposed and wanting to cover herself up. Unsure of what to do, she held her breath, and when he looked back up, he caught her exhaling.

Fuck! She dropped her hands to her hips and immediately regretted her decision when the cotton pulled against her nipples, drawing his eyes back down again. *Nope.* Flustered, she finally crossed her arms over her chest.

Noelle almost did a little cheer when her Good Samaritan's gas pump stopped, and he went around to his car. This modesty level—or shit, it might be insecurity—was a new feeling for her. He wasn't leering at her; it was just a quick 'Oh you got titties' glance, so she didn't know where this bashfulness was coming from. And she damn sure didn't like it.

At thirty-four years old, Noelle was quite pleased with her body. By the grace of birth control pills and a quick trip to the clinic that one time, she had managed to stay childless. As a proud card-carrying member of the itty bitty tittie committee, she was particularly fond of her small breasts. At least she had great nipples, or so she'd been told. There was a little texture in the back of her thighs that no squats or running had ever been able to smooth out, but she couldn't see it, so she didn't care. Every year, she looked forward to hitting the nude beach in Corfu, Greece, during the Sound's yearly Mediterranean cruise.

While he took care of his car, Noelle peeked between the pumps to get an uninterrupted look at him. Even from behind, the fit of his suit was perfect. Oh, and he had a nice grabbable butt too. Surreptitiously, she leaned forward to look at his shoes. *Humph*, they looked expensive. Her high school teacher, Mr. Grossman, told her that you can tell everything about a man from his shoes. He was probably thinking more in line with how he took care of himself and his finances, not the size of his penis. His feet were huge! Yikes, and yes Lord, were both in order.

Noelle leaned back, her gaze automatically rising to his hips as she speculated. This man was indeed a beautiful Mandingo Warrior. *Daayuum!* But he might need an advisory sticker for that thing if the old saying turned out to be true for him. She threw up a small prayer for whatever woman he had to be dating because he was too fine not to have a slew of women trailing behind him. She hoped their cervixes were okay. A big dick was a dangerous weapon in inexperienced and/or careless hands. She could be a poster girl for that public safety warning. Her tummy tightened, and her thighs squeezed reflectively in sympathy at the memory of her last year's cruise boo. BM2 Corey Harrison was a handsome man—not as handsome as her Mandingo Warrior—and his dick had been a fantastic sight to behold. But his stroke game was a travesty, and he took going deep to a whole 'nother level. His gift became her curse. Her cervix might never be the same. Never again.

Well, maybe not "never again" because this man was fucking gorgeous! Being the glutton for punishment that she was, he was definitely getting them digits if he asked it! And her brand-new pager number too. Heck, she might even throw in her AOL email address to have all her bases covered. All she could do was send up a protection prayer to the heavens for her Precious. She stole the nickname from Sidney, who made up all these random names for her private parts because she wouldn't say the word vagina or use any other anatomically correct language. But Noelle did love the nickname, Precious. It made her vagina feel so....precious...except when she was telling someone to eat it. Back to pussy it was—'Eat my Precious' was just too much for her. She wondered if Sidney told her boyfriend, who was just as much of a weirdo prude as she was, to do that. *Gross,* she shuddered.

That disturbing thought and her nozzle clicking off snapped her back to attention. Her mind always picked the wrong time to go on a walkabout. "Oh! I didn't mean for you to fill up my tank. I am so sorry. My mind just wandered off."

He quickly came back around and took the nozzle out before she could, setting it back in the mount, twisting her gas cap close, and shutting the tank door. "To where?" He smiled again and held her gaze.

"Umph humph." Mesmerized, Noelle wanted to look away, but she couldn't. Did she just sway? Was he a vampire? She felt heat pool in her belly, and a flush replaced the prickling this time. She wanted to fan her face, then spread her legs and fan her crotch. Better yet, grab his head and bury his face in it. Woah! Was she ovulating? There had to be a reason for all *this*. Damn, she wished she were darker because she knew her cheeks were on fire. Another moment passed before she realized that she had just mumbled rather than answered him. Dude had her speaking gibberish with his smile. He's definitely a vampire—one of those old ones that can come out in the daylight.

"Oh, nowhere. Everywhere. It does that sometimes," Noelle finally managed to say.

"Have you seen a doctor for that?" His brows furrowed slightly.

"For being distracted? No, should I? Is that a thing?"

"It could be."

"Oh really?" Noelle's brows rose. "Am I having a stroke?"

"No. Why would you think that you're having a stroke?" He chuckled. "But really, it's a thing."

Noelle gave him the side-eye. "Umph, you seem real sure about that. Are you a doctor? Because I have been struggling with brain busyness for years. My mother insists I have *something*. She's a nurse, so she's always sayin' something's wrong with me. So you got some treatment options for whatever this is? Will it solve my math block? Will it help me finish sweeping a room in one go and not leave little dirt piles everywhere when I start something else? Will it help me stop making right turns when they are clearly not needed and put away the laundry after folding it? And for the love of God, help me get everything that's on my grocery list the first time around?"

He looked startled for a second before recovering. Then nodding thoughtfully, he said, "It's sorta your lucky day. I am a doctor—an obstetrician, to be more specific. But I do know a little bit about mental health. Which is not as bad as it sounds," he said quickly when Noelle squinted her eyes at the words: mental health. "So I can maybe do some preliminary diagnosing. I would recommend that we do some *extensive* testing. Some of them might be intense, but the results would definitely be worth it. We can get started anytime you're ready." He stared down at her, his expression filled with quiet confidence.

"Extensive huh?" Nibbling on her bottom lip, Noelle stared back at him. Right then and there, Noelle decided she was going to sleep with him. As if he knew what she was thinking, he smiled slowly. Bedazzled, she blinked a couple of times before regaining her composure. "But you're an ob/gyn though. I don't think that has anything to do with my brain exactly. However, I wouldn't mind being part of a scientific study..."

...and can we start the fuck right now? Another voice, this one light and flirty, finished in her head.

We most certainly can! Noelle almost did a little two-step dance. When Reckless Rhonda, Noelle's faithful, chaotic sidekick, came to the party, all common sense was about to fly out the window.

Well then, let's get this party started right! Rhonda sang out.

Indeed, they were about to set it off. Noelle's mind whirled, and her imagination went into overdrive as she considered all the possibilities. Yes, she was on her way to work, but she could figure out an excuse for her lateness to avoid getting in trouble. He looked like he was on his way to the office as well, but that was his problem. His car was too small to get comfortable in, but her Jeep was—

Woah, woah, WOAH! No, ma'am, we're not doing that!

Constance shrieked. *"What is wrong with you?"*

Shit! Noelle's gaze dropped to the cement as reality kicked back in. Woah is right! What the fuck is wrong with her? She hasn't felt this level of impulsiveness and, quite frankly, irresponsibility in donkey years. It bordered on that fresh-out-of-boot-camp feeling when sailors went wild in AT Land[6] and humped everything they could get their hands on. She had a different guy for three out of the four weeks she was there.

But you're not eighteen, you're thirty-four. We don't have sex with strangers. We don't do it after the club. Or in the club for that matter. We don't do it on vacation. We definitely don't do it with men we meet at the gas station. Scientific study, my ass. You better study them roads on the way to work, Constance said.

"All this talk about donating your body to science, and we haven't even properly introduced ourselves, have we?" He held out his hand. "My name is Quentin."

"I'm Ben—Noelle." Noelle almost gave him her last name Bentley. Military conditioning had her sometimes forgetting her first name. His hand engulfed her,s and a zing went up her arm when he squeezed her hand just a teeny-tiny little bit. The roughness of his palm against hers was precisely what she liked. He definitely be building shit. Oh yeah, this was going to be so wonderful. Maybe not today—

Definitely not today, Constance said.

—but she was going to have them hands on her body in the near future.

A movement out of the corner of her eye caught her

---

6. AT Land/Apprentice Training: A general training for undesignated sailors by their rating- airmen, firemen, seamen, and seabee (construction battalion).

attention. A woman was walking by, glaring at her. What in the hell was that mean muggin' for? Then from between the pumps, she saw the woman open the passenger side door to Quentin's silver Maxima, get in, and slam it so hard the sound echoed through the parking lot. Stunned, she glanced around in search of no one in particular and caught the eye of the man sitting in the car behind hers. He was totally engrossed in the scene playing out before him. She would be, too if she wasn't in the damn starring role. She was a voyeur of drama, not an active participant in it.

Umph, now look at you, Constance said.

Right? Ain't this about a bitch? Noelle swung her eyes back to Quentin. She frowned at him as he clenched his jaw before glancing between the pumps in annoyance. Boo, get off the stage! Where's the Sandman when you need him? What did he have to be annoyed about? Did he forget he had a woman in his car already? She sucked her teeth. *She* was the one who should be pissy and offended. Her plans were completely ruined. Got her all hot and bothered for nothing. He had her contemplating car sex in broad daylight, for cryin' out loud! She was so glad she hadn't said anything. She couldn't imagine having to walk that statement back.

Stifling a sigh, she gently but firmly pulled her hand from his and ignored the empty feeling that settled over her. Gosh, what was it about this man? Unfortunate as the interruption was, maybe it was a good thing they got interrupted. He had her acting all out of sorts with just his smile and a handshake. What that D goan do? Probably wreck her damn life. Did she really need that before the cruise started? No siree, she did not! Yeah, it was time to go. Impatiently, she glanced at her *Swatch*. All of this took three and a half minutes. It felt like a goddamned eternity.

Did this man know how to stop time? If she hurried, she could still make it across the quarterdeck.

"Well, Quentin, I gotta get going. Thank you for the gas. I will totally pay it forward." Noelle couldn't stop the regret from tinging her voice. Because, dammit, this was a sad and disappointing situation. She grabbed her door handle.

Still frowning, Quentin held his hands up, palm out. "I promise you this is not what it looks like."

Awww, he looked so cute frowning like that. Maybe it wasn't like that. Maybe there was a valid reason that a woman was throwing eyeball fists at her so early in the morning. Noelle hesitated, her resolve almost faltering.

I would hear the man out, Rhona said.

Seriously? I can't even. Just get in the car, Constance said.

But I don't think it's gonna hurt to listen, Noelle hedged.

If you don't get your fast ass in the car NOW! Constance yelled.

Fine. Noelle huffed. She pressed her palm over her heart. "You might be right, but this is just too confusing."

"If you just give me a second to explain," Quentin said.

Noelle shook her head. "I really do have to get to work. And I think this man is about to fight me." Or pull out a camcorder to record the gas station brawl and send it to Murray. She gestured over her shoulder with her thumb at the man eyeing them down. She offered him a small smile and even threw the raised shoulders in for an extra apologetic measure before sliding into the driver's seat. "Thank you again. Take care, and God bless."

Quentin stood there looking at her through her window for a split second before shaking his head and exhaling, furrowing his brows, and deepening his frown. Still fine in all his triflingness. Her still riled-up state almost had her rolling down her window to tell him to just take her damn number. She sighed in relief when he turned and went back to his car. If he only knew that asking three times was her breaking point. Thank God for little favors. She made eye contact in the review mirror with the man in the car behind her. He shrugged his shoulders and threw his hands up. Shaking her head, she cranked the engine.

Exactly, Noelle thought as she waved at him over her shoulder and put her car in drive. She cursed her luck when she realized she had to drive around Quentin's pump to get into the exit lane. And the passenger side was facing her and not her Good Samaritan.

Try as she might, Noelle couldn't resist looking as she went by. The other woman *actually* rolled down her window and gave her another blistering look as though the glass was somehow preventing Noelle from seeing her facial expression. No, that crazy was Windex approved. Man, she better go somewhere with that shit and save all that attitude for that man sitting next to her.

Noelle rolled her eyes and turned up her radio. Heavy D and The Boyz 'Is it Good to You?' blasted from her speakers. Damn, that could have been their background music while he rubbed her down. She was pretty sure they had whipped cream in the refrigerated section at this station. Ugh!

As Noelle waited for an opening in the traffic, the Maxima pulled up behind her. She made eye contact with Quentin in her rearview mirror. His face was still except for his pursed lips, and she could tell his nostrils were flared. Oh my God, he was really fucking gorgeous. All that repressed anger somehow made him glow. Something was wrong with her for reals forreals-forreals because anger should not be a turn-on. But yet, here she was lusting after a man because his nostrils were flaring. That ain't nothing but the Devil! Only the Devil would give a man enough audacity to have him out here trying to pick up a woman while his girlfriend was in the store like it was nothing. Or he must think he got it like that because ole girl got in the car without a word.

Shit, *did* he have it like that? Noelle sucked her teeth. Probably. If she were five seconds slower, he most definitely would've had *her* like that. Absolutely positively. Wife, girlfriend be damned.

Quentin looked like he had that good, strong D. And that was some powerful stuff. It didn't come around too often, and when you got that shit, you tried to hold to it by any means necessary. That's why women act the fool over a man. It ain't because she loves him. Nope, it's because that dick done found every spot and ones she didn't even know she had. Orgasms were just as addictive as crack. But you didn't hear Nancy Regan telling people to say no to that. Even though Quentin held the promise of addiction, disappointment at the missed opportunity still had her shaking her head.

Oh well, dem be the brakes. Noelle stole one last glance at Quentin before merging into traffic.

Chapter Two

LT Quentin Jacobs

Fucking Cynthia. Quentin ground his teeth as a tension headache began to form at the base of his skull. He rolled his shoulders, trying to relax, before getting back to his car, where his ex-wife waited inside.

After seeing Noelle and getting caught up in her crazy conversation, he totally forgot Cynthia had run into the store for coffee. Dammit, he knew it was a bad idea to take her to work this morning. Her car was in the shop, and she asked after they had sex yesterday, so he felt obligated. Now he wished he had just called her a cab. Or better yet, just said no when she crept into his room after coming by his parent's house for dinner like they were teenagers again. He'd been back for only two days, and he was already starting this foolishness up with her again. Whenever he came home to visit, he found himself back in the same pattern with Cynthia. They would sleep together no matter if they were in relationships or not. Messy couldn't begin to explain their relationship.

"Cynthia, what have I told you about slamming my car door?" Quentin asked tightly, sliding behind the wheel.

Cynthia studied her French manicure. "It slipped."

Quentin sucked his teeth and started up the car. He felt the base of his neck tighten up, and he tilted his head from side to side to loosen the muscles. He refused to let her agitate him this morning. He had his second interview for an obstetrician-gynecologist position at Bon Secours Hospital, so he needed to be cool, calm, and collected. It was hard enough getting an interview; he didn't want to mess it up by giving off angry Black man vibes. Cynthia cut her eyes at him and made a show of settling back in the bucket leather seat as if it belonged to her. "Was that someone you knew?"

Quentin ignored her and tapped his fingers on the steering wheel to Aaliyah's "Back and Forth" as it played on the radio. The title was more fitting to their situation than the actual song lyrics. He continued on his way to the Navy Federal Credit Union, where she worked as an executive loan officer. There better not be any accidents on the way. He wanted her out of his car as soon as possible.

"You weren't trying to get *that* woman's number, were you? She looked like a welfare queen. Did she have snotty nose pickneys in the back seat?" Cynthia continued to press when Quentin didn't answer.

No, she didn't have kids, or at least any that needed car seats. Quentin did a quick peek inside her Jeep when he put the nozzle in her tank. Not that he wouldn't date a woman with kids; he just didn't like hollerin' at one while their kids looked on. He ignored Cynthia and continued to hum the song.

Undeterred, she turned in her seat and looked at him. "Umph, Quentin, I heard that California living was laid back, but I didn't think it would lower your standards."

Mi rass. This woman irritated the hell out of him. Quentin's lips pursed. He wouldn't give her the pleasure of knowing that she got under his skin. She seemed to thrive off of negative attention.

When they hit a red light, he glanced at her. "No, I can't blame San Diego; they have been low for about twenty years or so." The light turned green, and he started driving again. He heard her sharp inhale. They first met twenty-one years ago during Christmas break. He felt the anger rolling off her. It filled every crevice in the car, but wisely, she didn't speak again. He didn't enjoy belittling remarks or trading barbs with Cynthia, but he was not above it.

But Quentin was tired of it. He was tired of many things. His obligation to the Navy was one of them, which was why he was getting out this summer. His fellow officers thought he was crazy since he was up for Lieutenant Commander in the next advancement cycle, but he was just mentally done with the Navy.

Burnout aside, he also needed to help care for his aging parents. After his father's retirement five years ago from the postal service, they moved here from Brooklyn to be closer to their grandchildren. His twin sister Vanessa and her family lived only two houses away from their parents. But he couldn't trust her to keep an eye on them. Her husband was also an officer in the Navy, and she was too busy being an Ombudsman[1] for his command at Little Creek and the PTA. He also suspected Vanessa didn't want to be bothered by their parents, as they took turns being difficult. Their mother, Jocelyne, just let her husband, Quentin Sr. do whatever he wanted. He didn't know if they were both in denial that they were getting older or if his mother secretly wanted his father dead.

A few weeks ago, Quentin Sr. tripped over a paint buck-

---

1. Ombudsman: A sailor's spouse at the Command who serves as the liaison between the Command and the families.

et while the kitchen was being painted. Luckily, he didn't break anything, but the incident was even more vexing because Quentin had paid someone else to paint, and his father just couldn't stay out of the way and let the painting team do their job. The next project was replacing the roof before hurricane season started in July. Quentin was already preparing himself for the battle of keeping his father off the roof and out of the contractors' way. He didn't need to add his and Cynthia's relationship to the mix.

To add another layer to their already complicated situation, Cynthia has been Vanessa's best friend since their freshman year in college. That was how they met, and his parents still loved her. Like him, her family also came from St. Croix and was prominent with good connections. Per his father, she stayed "nice and slim", so what more did he want? Cynthia saw his parents more than he did, and he knew she was still on their emergency contact list. They were more devastated than him when they divorced, and his father still got on him about correcting his mistake. If they got wind that they were still involved, he wouldn't hear the end of it. He also didn't want their sixteen-year-old son Tre to find out that his parents were creeping around behind his back while barely saying two words to each other in front of him. This needed to end.

When he pulled up in the parking lot of the Navy Federal, he parked the car. Taking a deep breath, he turned to look at her again. There was no question that Cynthia was gorgeous. She reminded him of Phylicia Rashad, complete with the sultry eyes that often flashed him with hate and discontent. During one of their good years, they had dressed up as Cliff and Clair Huxtable for Halloween. He still had the picture somewhere. They had a normal relationship with its ups and downs before everything fell apart.

"I apologize for that, Cynthia. I shouldn't have said it. But we also shouldn't be having a conversation about who I want to get involved with. And if we weren't having sex, you wouldn't have asked. You hardly speak to me outside of the bedroom. When we do talk, if it's not about Tre, we're arguing about some random nonsense. I don't even know why we fuck Cynthia. Do you know? Because I don't." Quentin sighed. "We just need to stop whatever this is that we're doing. It's not healthy for both of us. Our marriage ended years ago because we weren't good together. We haven't been since before Tre. As a matter of fact, I think for whatever reason you might just hate me—"

Cynthia whipped around to face him. "If I hated you, Quentin, I wouldn't have let you come in my mouth. And your memory is a bit skewed. We were *very* good together."

"No." Quentin shook his head. "When we were in college, yeah. But the day I got accepted to medical school, things changed between us. When I allow myself to think back on it, I am amazed that I did as well as I did because you weren't supportive at all. And then you got pregnant."

"I got pregnant? So I did all that by myself? Did medical school teach you that?" Cynthia snapped.

"No, of course not. But since you wanna go there, I asked you to get on birth control, just wait until I was done with school. We were still young, and we could've started a family during my residency. I just needed to get through school. So let me tell you what I did learn in school: abstinence is the only sure form of protection. But if you take your pills, there's at least a 90% chance you can prevent pregnancy. But you gotta take those pills every day. You took *one* pill, Cynthia. One pill. After you told me you were pregnant with Tre, I found your three-month supply, sans the one pill, in a basket underneath the bathroom sink."

Cynthia froze but kept her expression neutral. Her only tell was her rapid eye blinking. "Why didn't you say anything?"

Quentin leaned forward, pinning her with his eyes. "What was I supposed to say? Get an abortion? I really didn't want to know if the woman I had loved since I was eighteen was intentionally trying to sabotage my dreams of becoming a doctor for no damn reason at all. What would that have solved? Nothing. So what would have been the point of bringing it up?"

Cynthia's eyes dropped to his chest at the accusation. Quentin felt almost lightheaded as the burden of carrying around her secret lifted. He'd been holding on to it for sixteen years. He loved his son with all his heart, but he always harbored resentment against Cynthia because of her selfish choice. No matter how much he tried, he couldn't let it go. He missed so much of Tre's childhood because of medical school. He missed his first roll-over, his first words, his first steps; he rarely got a chance to put him to bed. Tre was usually asleep before he got home from his study group. He didn't even get to take him to his first day of kindergarten because he also had a class that morning. Bitterness was behind every interaction he had with her.

"I always wondered if you knew." Cynthia's shoulders slumped as she collapsed into her seat. "I wasn't trying to sabotage you. I don't know how to explain the panic and fear I felt when you got accepted into medical school. I was still trying to figure out what I wanted to do with my life, and you always had a plan, and everything just seemed to come so easily for you." She held up a hand when Quentin opened his mouth. "I know you busted your ass, and you have always pushed yourself harder than anyone I have ever known. You set these standards for yourself and damn near everyone else around you. I always loved and hated that about you. But since we're being honest, I guess I can finally admit, I was afraid of not being the center of your attention. I didn't think I could compete with your dreams, and I didn't have any of my own. So I got pregnant. At least I could have something that was mine. It sounds sad, pathetic, and selfish now that I'm saying it aloud, but that's how I felt back then."

Stunned, Quentin also slumped in his seat and stared out the windshield. Out of all the possibilities he'd come up with, he never considered Cynthia's fear of being forgotten to be the reason.

"I know I fucked up. I don't regret having Trevor, but it fucked up what we had. I felt you pull away, but I couldn't do or say anything without admitting what I had done. But even though we fought like cats and dogs, I was so angry when you asked me for a divorce because that meant you would never forgive me. When someone wrongs you, well lemme just say ya nuh easy ah'tall. So for all these years, before and after the divorce, I've wanted your forgiveness but I couldn't bring myself to tell you why I needed it."

Quentin stared at Cynthia. He wanted to say she was lying about him and how he would have treated her, but she wasn't. He had no illusions about himself. He knew he could be an extremely cold-hearted man when the circumstances called for it. His sense of integrity and righteous indignation was so strong; there was almost no placating him when his trust was breached or when he felt maligned. He could count the number of people that he had forgiven on one hand. The disillusionment he got from people had a lot to do with his decision to become an obstetrician. There was nothing more satisfying to him than delivering babies. Hearing a child's first cry softened his soul and gave him hope in an often unjust world.

"I should have said something when I found out. Then maybe—"

Cynthia cut Quentin off. "We just would have gotten divorced sooner. In hindsight, that might not have been a bad thing."

Turning to look at her, Quentin sighed. She was right about that too. "So what do we do now? I don't know about you, but I'm just exhausted from all of this."

"I don't know either. We're not going to solve all our problems in the Navy Federal parking lot," Cynthia said.

"Do you want me to pick you up from work?" Quentin asked as she opened her door.

"Noooo, I think we've had enough of each other for the rest of the week. Maybe longer. Lata." Cynthia got out of the car, and this time she didn't slam the door.

Chapter Three

YN1 Celia Navarro

What the hell? Celia frowned at the phone ringing on her desk. She glanced at the clock on the bulkhead next to the mounted TV. It was 0645. The double ring informed her that it was a call from inside the ship. Dammit, she wasn't going to answer it. Admin didn't open for another forty-five minutes. She picked up her mug. This yeoman[1] was at breakfast, even if it was only coffee. Blowing on her coffee to cool it, she stared at the phone until it finally stopped ringing. No sooner had it stopped, it started again. Another inside call.

Shit. Celia had an idea who it was, and she didn't want to be bothered. But if she didn't answer it, she wouldn't get to drink her coffee in peace because, no doubt, there would be a knock on her door soon. She picked up the receiver with a resigned sigh before the next ring.

"Admin Office, YN1 Navarro speaking. How may I help you, sir or ma'am?" Celia's husky, slightly nasal voice still held distinct traces of the South Bronx, although she hadn't lived there in almost eighteen years.

"You can help me by telling me where you were last

---

1. YN/Yeoman: administrative and clerical worker.

night," Kendrick barked into the phone.

Celia bit back a groan. It was way too early for this. *Fuck*, she should have let it ring. "First of all, lower your voice. Secondly, I was on the ship. I had duty, remember?"

Kendrick sucked her teeth. "I know. But I called the office, and no one answered. Then I called the berthing[2], and no one could find you. So I stopped by around eight, and I couldn't find you anywhere."

"You came by? Really? Why?" Celia rolled her eyes. "Did you think I was missing?"

Around 1900 last night, Celia was standing on the starboard weather deck when she saw Kendrick walking up the brow and ran back to Admin. She was almost certain Kendrick wasn't coming to visit her, but better to be safe than sorry. She was sitting in Admin with the lights off and the TV muted when Kendrick knocked five minutes later.

"Yes, *really*. And I wanted to see you, that's why. What—I'm not supposed to want to see you?"

"Did you look in the berthing?" Celia asked.

"That was the first place I looked," Kendrick replied.

"In Admin?"

"The second place."

"What about the DC classroom? Did you look there?" Celia's tone was light and breezy belying the storm she was causing.

After hiding out in Admin for an hour and a half watching *Living Single*, and an episode of *New York Undercover* for good measure, Celia took a calculated risk and headed down to the berthing via the forward mess decks. Halfway down the ladder, she peeked around and saw Kendrick

---

2. Berthing: living quarters aboard a ship.

entering the damage control classroom with DC2[3] Tamika Allen.

Not even a week ago, Celia asked Kendrick if she had something going on with Allen. It was merely out of sheer curiosity because they didn't have a relationship per se, just some casual, 'My laundry's done, I ain't got shit else to do so I might as well fuck you' sex-tionship. Kendrick vehemently denied it. What made this conversation even more perplexing was that she explicitly told Kendrick on multiple occasions—earlier that day, to be precise—that she could go be with someone else whenever she wanted. So why she felt the need to pretend to visit her when she actually went to see Allen was beyond Celia's comprehension. The only weird thing was that she and Allen were in the same duty section, so Kendrick could have just waited until the next day to see her, but whatever.

What Celia *did* know was that this shit was going to be cleared up today. She didn't want any miscommunications that would cause drama when the cruise started. They would all be trapped together for six months, with their only escape being when liberty was called. Being stationed on a ship was interesting, to say the least. Sailors somehow managed to form intimate, yet at the same time, casual relationships with each other during cruises. Depending on where you fell on the spectrum would determine if your cruise would be fun and exciting or tedious and dreadful. Celia imagined it would be the latter for her if she didn't end things with Kendrick today.

There was a slight pause before Kendrick spoke carefully.

---

3. Damage Controlman: the ship's fireman, maintains and repairs damage control equipment and systems, the ship's stability, firefighting, fire prevention, etc.

"What are you talking about?"

Celia took note of her change of tone and smiled. *That's more like it.* "I asked, was that *before* or *after* you left the DC classroom? Right before they called taps. Last night. After you gave up looking for me, I assume." She let her statement resonate while she took a sip of her coffee. "You know what? Never mind. I'll see you after quarters[4]."

Kendrick hesitated again before answering. "Yeah." Then mumbled bye and hung up.

Bitch. That ought to give you something to think about. Celia smiled as she hung up the phone. While she sipped her coffee, her co-worker, YN2 Martin Howard, came into the office with a dozen warm Krispy Kreme doughnuts.

"God bless you, sailor. You are a true service to this country," Celia said as she opened the box, and the smell of freshly baked doughnuts wafted to her nose. If a person didn't like Krispy Kremes, something had to be wrong with them. Almost reverently, she picked a doughnut and moaned when she sank her teeth into its warm gooeyness. It was like biting into a piece of heaven.

"I actually need to have a chit[5] approved." Howard went and sat at his small desk across from Celia.

"Are all these doughnuts mine?" She asked through a mouthful of doughnut. They had seven other yeomen in the office and the chief, and she didn't want to share.

"If I say no, will you deny my request?" Howard asked.

"Maybe." Celia squinted at him.

---

4. Quarters: A meeting with the sailors of a division or department, usually happens in the morning.

5. Chit: Refers to almost every piece of paper, from an official form to a special request.

"Then they are all yours." Howard gestured to the box.

"*Muchas gracias.*" Celia was his first class, and she had to approve his request before it went up the chain of command. She had no reason to deny it, but if she could get a dozen Krispy Kremes to herself, why not? She was on her second one when the rest of the office staff arrived.

As her chief spoke during quarters, Celia's mind wandered off. Her current dilemma was all Noelle's fault. If she hadn't damn near ordered her *not* to mess with Kendrick, she never would've done it. Noelle had been her best friend since the 10th grade, and unsolicited opinions and advice were her main form of communication; she just said there was something about Kendrick that she found funny acting, and then she wouldn't shut up about it. So Celia ended up dealing with Kendrick out of spite just to piss Noelle off. It didn't help that Kendrick was jealous of Celia and Noelle's friendship, no matter how many times she reminded her that *one*, they weren't in a relationship, and *two*, Noelle was her best friend. Now, she was going to have to hear the I-told-you-so's from Noelle until she threatened to shake the shit out of her. The only woman Celia dated over the years that Noelle actually liked was Julia.

Julia Peron. Celia sighed softly. Julia had been the instructor of the dementia education class Celia attended. Her mother had something called Lewy Body dementia brought on by the stroke she had a year prior. Celia offered to give her sister Monica a break from caregiving while she was on her neutral duty rotation, but first, she had to learn about her mother's condition.

From the moment the tall Latina stepped in front of the class and briefly made eye contact with Celia, a spark ignited inside her, and she knew they would be something. Her skin reminded her of Noelle's homemade caramel sauce.

She would burn it ever so slightly, so it had a bit of bitterness to temper the sweetness. Celia wondered if Julia had that same complex flavor. For the entirety of the two-day training, she was mesmerized by Julia's soft and compassionate voice, her knowledge and passion for elder care, and its effect on caregivers. She was simply amazing.

Not to mention, she had a banging body. Julia's curves were on display even with her conservative slacks and blouses. Unlike Celia, who was slim and petite, Julia's body looked like a soft pillow you just wanted to lay on and wrap your whole body around. Her full and heavy breasts led to a softly rounded belly evened out by the width of her hips. Celia imagined if she freed her thick and curly dark brown hair from its discreet top bun, Julia would be transformed into a lush fertility goddess with scores of adoring mortals worshiping at her feet. She spent most of her time in class fantasizing over her like a lovesick teenager.

After class, Celia lingered while gathering her stuff as Julia made her rounds to the other people in attendance. By the time Julia got her, they were alone in the room. When both of Julia's warm hands covered hers as they shook hands, Celia resisted the urge to pull her closer so she could inhale more of the perfume that teased her nose. She later found out that the fragrance was aptly named *Tabu*, and it was Julia's signature scent ever since her favorite aunt gifted her with a vintage bottle as a teenager. Celia didn't know how long they stood with Julia holding her hand comfortingly; just how bereft she felt when Julia let go to pass along her business card. Her empty feeling was replaced with intrigue and delight at Julia's emphasis on calling if she needed *anything at all.* Which ended up being much sooner than she thought, and not for the reason she intended.

That Monday after class, Celia's phone rang at 6 A.M. She rolled over and stared warily at the phone on her nightstand. Nothing good comes from phone calls before 8 A.M., and today was no exception. The inhale she heard before her sister spoke told her everything she needed to know. Together they called their youngest sister to tell her that their mother had died in her sleep. The nurse wasn't sure what had happened. She could've had another stroke that had gone undetected or a heart attack. Celia believed she was just tired and wanted to go home. She had so many people waiting for her, and in her current condition, Celia couldn't blame her for leaving. After handing her younger sister over to her husband's care and ensuring her other sister was okay, Celia called her Chief to start emergency leave[6].

Celia hung up the phone and made her way into the kitchen when it was done. On autopilot, she started to make her coffee. Turning the kettle on, she leaned against the counter and stared at nothing while waiting for the whistle. It wasn't until she held the coffee up to her lips and the smell of Cafe Bustelo filled her nose, did she lose it. Cafe Bustelo was her mother's favorite coffee, and all the memories of watching her mother make it in their tiny South Bronx apartment kitchen overwhelmed her. Mother always took so long, fussing at the sweetness, the perfect color—it had to be just right. It was her ritual, and it made the coffee taste better, she told Celia when she teased her about it. There would be no more teasing. No more extra spoonfuls of rice and beans, translating everything into

---

6. Leave: Authorized absence from a place of duty. i.e., vacation.

Spanish for her because she never learned how to speak English. There would be no more of anything. Her mother was gone.

Torn between sobbing and hyperventilating, Celia managed to set the mug on the counter but not without spilling half of it on her hand.

Her mother was dead. Her mother was dead. Her mother was dead. The sentence looped over in her head as she paced the kitchen, wringing her hands. She needed to call someone. This was too much to deal with on her own. Snatching her purse from the coat rack, she frantically searched through it for a minute before she got frustrated and shook all the contents out onto the table. *Where is it?* Her sob of relief took precedence over her grief when she found Julia's card.

Inhaling a shaky breath, she tried to calm herself down as she dialed Julia's number. However, the second she heard Julia's voice, she started crying again. Somehow through the tears, she managed to give Julia her address. Hanging up the phone, she went into the living room and curled up on the couch. She didn't know why she called Julia. She barely knew her. But she, not Noelle, was the first person that came to mind, and she didn't seem surprised that a stranger was calling her, bawling on the phone. Julia was a hospice nurse, so she was probably used to this behavior, and for that, Celia was grateful.

Celia's doorbell rang thirty minutes later, and she dragged herself off the couch and flung open the door without asking who it was. Julia stood on the side wearing a long red sundress and flip-flops. Her skin glowed like rich maple syrup in the soft morning sun, and her face was scrubbed clean of makeup; her still-damp hair curled wildly around her face and shoulders. She looked so gentle and welcoming, and when she held out her arms, Celia stepped into them. Her sigh came from her soul when Julia's arms tightened around her.

"I am so sorry, neña," Julia said as she rocked her.

Somehow, they made it back to the couch without Julia letting her go. She made soft cooing noises while Celia cried against her shoulder. Never once did Julia interrupt her tears. When Celia's body started to slump, she coaxed her head down to her lap, combing her fingers through her hair and lightly massaging her scalp.

In the back of her mind, Celia knew she should be embarrassed about dissolving into nothing all over Julia's lap. The feel of the wet cotton fabric underneath her cheek made her tears flow harder and faster because they were a tangible sign of her grief, made heavier because Celia didn't get to see her before she died. Correction, she didn't make time to see her. She ignored that feeling in her gut, telling her time was running out. Instead, she channeled her anxiety into ensuring everything was set for her mother's move. It was all for nothing, though—her mother was dead. She buried her face in Julia's lap and cried until only watery hiccups were left.

"What was your mother like?" Julia asked.

Celia sighed. "She was very protective of me and my sisters; she made sure we were safe and overly fed. Her beans and rice were the best. There would always be one more spoonful piled on your plate. Some of my best memories were when she and my dad would go to Orchard Beach and sell soda and beer. It was their summer-time hustle. We'd be at the beach all day. She loved to swim, and I would admire her for that. Sometimes we'd be in the grassy area, and she'd put up a tent and a hammock, and we would all take turns laying in it. I remember the smell of the ocean and the sound of the waves. We'd always be at the park or doing something fun. Mother didn't like to sit in the house. She was always on the move. Even when my parents divorced, she didn't let that bring her down. She kept it moving. She was caring and generous and funny—just the sweetest woman."

"She knows you love her," Julia said, running her hand over Celia's hair.

Celia's eyes welled up again at the use of the present tense, and she forced herself to sit up. "I should have seen her." She leaned back and pressed the heels of her hands against her eyes in an attempt to stem the fresh flow of tears. They leaked out anyway. She felt Julia move, and then her hands were gently pulled away from her face. She opened her eyes to find Julia kneeling before her.

"You did what you thought was the right thing at the time. There will be a million shoulda, coulda, wouldas, and there will never be a right answer. I can promise you that." Julia cupped Celia's face and used her thumbs to wipe the tears running down her face.

Celia stared at Julia. "I don't know what to do with all of this."

"You just sit with it and allow all the feelings to come up so they can pass through you. The only thing you have to do is let yourself grieve, mami," Julia said.

"But what about everything else? Her hospital bed, the supplies in the garage, her ramp is being installed tomorrow..." Celia's voice trailed into a deep sigh.

"Give me the number. I'll call for you." Julia stopped rubbing Celia's cheeks so she could beckon with one hand.

"Oh no, you don't have to do that." Celia's protest sounded weak even to her ears. She was already exhausted at the thought of making the call. "You've already let me cry all over you. I think that's more than enough." She took Julia's hand and gave it a squeeze.

"Don't worry about me. I'll let you know when I've had enough," Julia said with a soft smile. Her eyes searched Celia's face as she rubbed her thumb over Celia's knuckles.

A sharp awareness prickled inside Celia through the fog of her pain, making her jittery. Her breath quickened as her mind tried to catch up with the sensations running through her. Unable to resist the urge to move, she tried to pull her hand away, but Julia held it tight.

"*Respira*," Julia whispered. Then she lifted their joined hands and lightly brushed her lips back and forth against Celia's knuckles. "*Respira*."

Celia closed her eyes and focused on the feel of Julia's lips against her skin. *This* is why she called Julia despite only talking to her for five minutes. *This* is why Celia knew she would come. It had nothing to do with her being a hospice nurse. No, Julia was coming for her. She just got here a little sooner than either one of them expected. But she was always coming for her.

When the realization finished settling over Celia, she took a deep breath and exhaled slowly before opening her eyes to find Julia staring intently at her.

"Give me the number, Celia," Julia said.

Celia gave her the number and everything else she asked for.

Julia was magnetic. Celia was lost from the first taste, and she couldn't get enough of her. Their relationship was like a wildfire, flash flood, and tornado, all mixed into one. All of Celia's emotions were intensified with the knowledge that she could never keep Julia. She was happily married and loved her husband and their kids. She wasn't a late-in-life lesbian, secretly exploring her newly found sexuality. No,

Julia was faithful. To her, cheating was cheating, and it didn't matter if it was a woman. And that resolve held until Celia.

Ironically, her happy marriage made it easier for them to be together as much as they were. Her husband trusted her completely and never questioned her movements, even when she was out late. Celia never knew what Julia told him, and she didn't ask. The only thing that mattered was that she had her time with Julia. Celia knew it wasn't healthy to have such a deep need for Julia. A woman that she could not claim nor who could claim her had quickly become a vital part of life. She gave her air when she was suffocating in her grief and soon it felt impossible to take even a small breath without her. And when Julia ended the relationship...

Okay, no more of this! Celia mentally clapped her hands. This was a pointless and dangerous path for her to be on. Quarters secured, she waved the chief over, frowning a little when he grabbed one of her doughnuts. He might have asked her for one, but she hadn't been paying attention to anything that was said. Howard would fill her in later.

Howard opened the helpdesk window as Celia grabbed her third doughnut and bit into it. It was still warm, but it didn't quite hit the spot this time. Thinking of Julia never boded well for her. She blamed Noelle for that too; she didn't know how, but somehow it was her fault. Shoving another piece of the doughnut in her mouth, she chewed it with the same intensity as a dry piece of steak. The second anniversary of their breakup, or rather, memorial, was coming up soon. She'd have more than enough time to fall down that rabbit hole then, but right now, she had to start her fine, fine Navy day and then jettison[7] a bitch.

---

7. Jettison: to throw or drop (something) from an aircraft or ship.

Chapter Four

PHI Noelle Bentley

Breathing heavily, Noelle raced up the Puget Sound's enlisted personnel brow[1]. Her foot slipped off one of the rungs, and she almost fell flat on her face before catching hold of the handrail. *Sonovabitch!*

Besides the food, the people, and life in general aboard a ship, the enlisted bow was another thing she hated. Why couldn't it have actual stairs like the officer's bow? There was probably a stupid outdated, historical reason for it that she didn't have the time or energy to research.

Huffing and puffing, Noelle crossed the quarterdeck[2] a split second before liberty was secured and immediately followed by muster for all hands. Wiping the light sweat from her brow, she held up her ID card to the officer of the deck. "Respectfully request permission to come aboard."

"Permission granted." The 1st class saluted her. "You just made it."

---

1. Brow: temporary bridge that connects the ship's quarterdeck to the pier.

2. Quarterdeck: the shipboard area connected to the brow where personnel arrive and depart the ship.

"I know." Noelle glanced over at the Master-At-Arms[3] BT2 Sampson, who was waiting to confiscate the ID cards from unlucky sailors who came aboard late. Remembering their little secret, Samson blushed as he always did when he saw Noelle. He saw her boobies last year when he let her into the seabag locker to get her dress blue uniform pants. It wasn't intentional, she was digging around her seabag, and her shirt gaped open, and because she hardly wore a bra, her titties were just front and center. She saw it as a thank you for letting her in after-hours, and he blushed profusely every time he saw her after that. It was so adorable.

Noelle winked at the flustered Samson before taking off to the female berthing. She had five minutes to change into her uniform and make it in time for quarters[4]. It could be done; she'd done it many times before.

Crossing the aft[5] and forward mess decks in a power walk that became a light jog; she waved at sailors she knew who were actually on their way to quarters. When she passed the MA shack across from the female lower berthing hatch, the MA on duty, SH Raymond[6], tapped at his watch and shook his head at her. Shooting him an innocent grin,

---

3. Master-At-Arms (MA): a naval petty officer appointed to carry out or supervise police duties on the ship.

4. Quarters: meeting with the sailors of a division or department, usually happens in the morning.

5. Aft: rear of the ship.

6. SH/Ship Serviceman: manages all shipboard retail and service activities, such as the barbershop, laundry, and commissary.

she shrugged her shoulders before starting down the first ladder. When she got to the second ladder, she grabbed the metal handrails, lifted her feet, and slid down the last few steps. Her feet hit the speckled blue linoleum deck, and she took off running through the maze of cubicles.

All berthing[7] spaces aboard a ship were built like a Tetris game. The main goal was to fit as many triple-stacked coffin racks[8] as humanly possible in one space. Her berthing alone housed over three hundred women. It was a living nightmare for someone who didn't even like working with women because of their sheer messiness, much less being trapped with them for six months at a time. Luckily, her rack[9] was in a back corner section occupied by the Engineering division. She was determined to be as far away from the front of the berthing where the deck females lived. The majority of the deck crew—male and female—were young, dumb, and full of come, as the saying went. Being sent to Captain's Mast[10] was in the fine print of their rate description.

Noelle was already lifting her T-shirt over her head when she got to her rack, checking at the time as she did so. She had four minutes. She hoped her uniform didn't look too

---

7. Berthing: living quarters aboard a ship.

8. Coffin rack: beds that are stacked three high with a locker underneath the mattress, and when the top that housed the mattress was propped open, it resembled a coffin. Think Murphy bed.

9. Rack: bed.

10. Captain's Mast: a low-level and relatively informal forum for handling minor misconduct.

wrinkled, not that it mattered because she didn't have time to iron it. To her surprise, her uniform was hanging up on her standup locker, perfectly ironed; she even had a pair of clean socks stuffed in her boots.

Good looking out, Celia. Unlike Noelle, Celia took pride in her uniforms, taking extra care to have sharp military creases on all her uniform tops. Celia was like that even back in boot camp. She was assigned to the shoe-shining team because she could put a reflection on the tip of her boots shiny enough to put her lipstick on with it. Meanwhile, Noelle hid her extra uniforms in her pillowcase for eight weeks so she didn't have to fold them. Celia consistently got a 4.0 on her evaluations every year and always got outstanding on her physical readiness test. Noelle was content to be a 3.0 sailor. She stopped at the minimum requirements for the PRT, seeing no need to surpass the mandatory twenty-four pushups and forty-five sit-ups. Besides, she only ran enough to finish her mile and a half in thirteen minutes. With the exception of the chief's exam, Celia also passed all her advancement exams the first time around, whereas Noelle had to take all her exams twice. The study material *actually* put her to sleep on the toilet.

Noelle quickly spun the combination on the lock securing her rack. She propped the top up with one hand while she grabbed a white t-shirt with the other. Letting it slam back down, she pulled the midriff t-shirt over her head. All of her white t-shirts were cut in half despite being out of regulation because she hated having to tuck it in along with her dungaree top. It was too damn hot for all that fabric. She forewent her bra since she never wore one and doubted she would see her executive officer[11], Commander Echert, aka Spanky, anytime soon. It was rumored that Spanky fake-patted the backs of female sailors who stood watch[12] on the bridge[13] to check if they had a bra on. He only did it to the white girls though, so she was safe to free titty it and not be undercover sexually harrassed.

Changing quickly, she stuffed her clothes in the laundry bag at the foot of her rack and, running, retraced her steps back through the berthing. At the top, she yelled to Raymond, "I'm gonna make it!" before sprinting down the passageway[14] toward the quarterdeck[15] . The torpedomen's[16] shop was right before the quarterdeck. Had she been dressed, she could have headed straight down. But for some reason, all of her uniforms were on the ship. Why? She didn't know. She made a mental note to bring at least one home.

Everyone was in group formation by the time she got down there. She discreetly slid up next to the Gunner's

---

11. Executive officer: second in command.

12. Watch: the time an individual is assigned a specific, detailed responsibility.

13. Bridge: a room or platform of a ship from which the ship can be commanded.

14. Passageway: the hallway of a ship.

15. Quarterdeck: the shipboard area connected to the brow where personnel arrive and depart the ship.

16. TM/Torpedoman: are in charge of everything from torpedoes and missiles to small arms and ammunition.

Mate[17] 1st class in front of the formation. It was times like this when she wished she was a 2nd Class or below, and then she could get lost in the mix of lithographers[18] , torpedomen, gunner's mates, draftsmen[19] , fire controlmen[20] , and a few boatswain's mates[21] .

The only person who seemed to notice her almost tardiness was her Division Officer, Lt. Tonya Atkinson, which Noelle expected since the Lieutenant watched everything

---

17. GM/Gunner's Mate: are responsible for the operation and maintenance of the guided missile launch systems, underwater explosives, gun mounts and other ordinance equipment.

18. LI/Lithographer: run the print shops and produce printed material used by the Navy.

19. DM/Draftsman: create original art, technical illustrations, graphics for briefings, visual aids, and publications for the Navy.

20. FC/Fire Controlman: provide system employment recommendations, perform organizational and intermediate maintenance on digital computer equipment, and subsystems and operate and maintain compact and weapons direction systems.

20. FC/Fire Controlman: provide system employment recommendations, perform organizational and intermediate maintenance on digital computer equipment, and subsystems and operate and maintain compact and weapons direction systems.

21. BM/Boatswain's Mates: train, direct, and supervise personnel in ship maintenance and boat seamanship.

she did, mostly out of spite and discontent. Lt. Atkins was probably planning to hold her grudge against her until one of them transferred. It wasn't her fault they unknowingly shared that man-whore Harrison. Lt. Akins wasn't even supposed to be dating him in the first since the military frowned upon that whole fraternization thing. But if she wanted to stay tight over bullshit, that was cool. As long as she kept everything professional between them and approved her request chits, Noelle didn't give a damn how she felt about her. But the moment she started buggin' out, Noelle was going to sing like a bird.

After quarters, the Lieutenant didn't approach her—just gave her the evil eye, so Noelle went up to the photo lab with the other two photomates that worked with her. Immediately upon returning, both of them grabbed their camera bags and said they'd be back before lunch. They probably told her what they had to do. She was sure it was written down somewhere, but Noelle couldn't remember. She shrugged. She trusted them to do their jobs mostly out of lack of fucks to give. Gordon and Libby were outstanding second classes; they both enjoyed doing all the grips and grins, foreign dignitary jobs, and candid shots of the sailors throughout the ship and on liberty, and they dealt with the strikers[22] . The only thing she had to do were the cruise book headshots, develop the film, and print the pictures. And that was if she felt like it. Being a first-class was great.

Noelle flopped down in the chair behind her desk, picked up the black phone receiver, and dialed Admin. Propping it between her ear and shoulder, she twirled the seat around

---

22. Strike or Striker: non-designated personnel. Usually refers to sailors who are attempting to learn a rate by doing on-the-job training.

while waiting for someone to answer. Admin was only next door, but she didn't want Howard, whose desk was right next to Celia's, eavesdropping on her shame.

"Admin office, YN1 Navarro speak—"

Noelle cut her off. "*Hola, chica. Muchos gracias mi amor* for ironing my uniform." After she got off the phone, she was going to change into her coveralls because she suddenly remembered that she told Gordon she would do maintenance on the Noritsu color printing machine. The various processing chemicals used for the color printing machine were notorious for leaving rust-colored stains on everything. This was one of the two last good tops she had left, and she didn't want to ruin it. Yes, sailors received a yearly uniform allowance, but she'd be damned if she spent it on actual uniforms.

"*Da nada,*" Celia replied. "I seriously don't know how you made it to E-6."

"Shit, your guess is as good as mine. I did have to study, though, since I just couldn't stomach sleeping my way to the top—that was a commitment I just couldn't make as much as I wanted to."

"And I also figured you'd be running late because I know you didn't get gas yesterday like you said you would. You were barely on a quarter tank yesterday morning if I remember correctly. How you haven't been stranded on the highway is an episode for *Unsolved Mysteries.* As a matter of fact, your whole life is an unsolved mystery. You'd be the only topic they'd need for at least three seasons."

Noelle sucked her teeth. "Whatever. You don't know me."

"Hmmm, but I do."

"No, you don't. I was only almost stranded at that gas station because I stole your Thin Mints and left my wallet on the counter. Not because of my lack of gas. So there."

"No, that's even worse. So how'd you get gas?" Celia said.

"Well, that's a story..." Noelle quickly told Celia how her act of thievery led to meeting Quentin, aka Mandingo Warrior.

"One serves you right. Stop stealin' shit. And two, you hit him with the Christian fuck you and go to hell? Was it that serious?" Celia asked when Noelle got to the end of her harrowing tale. When the third "selectively" Christian man Noelle dated recited the ole "take care, and God bless" after she cussed them out, she surmised that was the godly way of saying fuck you and go to hell.

"I know! That might've been a bit harsh. And no, I'm not sure the situation called for it. But it was sooo awkward. I didn't know what else to say." Noelle exhaled heavily. "Umm, did I tell you his name was Quentin? I've never had a Quentin before, and now I never will."

Celia hummed before saying, "Okay, brace yourself because I know you're not going to like what I'm about to tell you, but I don't think that was his girlfriend."

"Why?" Noelle closed her eyes and groaned. She knew Celia was going to say that. "Why do you think that?"

"You said he looked annoyed, right? There's a distinct difference between annoyed and guilty. And what woman do you know that's just gonna go sit in the car while her man hollas at another woman? I can't see that. It's possible, but I mean, it wouldn't be me, and I damn sure know it wouldn't be you." Celia laughed as Noelle let out an anguished wail. "If it makes you feel any better, I would have done the same thing because that whole scene you described was just too much drama for so early in the morning. I can't imagine what getting involved with him would have been like. You probably dodged a bullet."

"But it was a beautiful bullet that probably had a big ole

thang," Noelle whined.

"Ummmm-hmmm," Celia murmured. "Just go back to the store and see if he shows up again. Hopefully, this time without that woman in his car. That's what I would do."

"Didn't you just tell me I dodged a bullet?" Noelle asked. And Celia called *her* contrary. "You're giving me very conflicting signals, best friend."

"You're gonna do it anyway."

"No, I am not!" Noelle sure as hell was. She planned on going back after work and every morning until she got tired of doing it, but she hated being called out on her bullshit. "Just because you're a stalker doesn't mean everyone else is. This bird is not of your feather."

"*Puta,* we are the flock." Celia sucked her teeth. "We've gone over this before, Noelle. Just because I'm assertive and go after what I want does not make me a stalker. The only person I really got obsessed with was Julia. And I did not stalk her."

"You sat outside her job in my car," Noelle reminded her.

"Because I wanted to *see* her. I did not *approach* her. I was dying. So fuck you with the intensity of thousand suns. And this ain't about me, so no amount of deflecting will change the fact that you're gonna be at that damn gas station every day. There is no comparison to your up-and-coming one-woman stalking expedition of the 7-eleven of a man who tried to holla at you while his girl bought gum."

"She had a coffee in her hand. Not gum," Noelle said with a sniff.

"Shipmate, I do not have time for your tomfoolery," Celia said.

"What? Noooo, wait a minute. Where are you going? I'm not done yet." Noelle still had more whining in her—at least three more minutes.

"Kendrick's here, and I have to talk to her." Celia's tone was reluctant as she answered.

Noelle gasped. *The audacity!* How dare Celia get off the phone with her to talk to that bitch. This was really a shitty Monday. "Ohmigod, you're leaving me in my time of need to talk to that *bitch*?" She put bass in her voice for the expletive.

"Time of need?" Celia exclaimed. "*Hay Dios mío*! I'll come get you for lunch. *Ciao*."

"You're not Italian," Noelle muttered. Louder, she said, "Fine. Be like that. You know I like to hold grudges."

"I think you already have at least ten against me just from the weekend alone, bodega cat, so what's another one? Adios, chica."

"What I told you about callin' me bodega cat?" Noelle snapped. She might be mercurial and prefer to just lay around in the sun, having people serve her, and she did feel like she was always in heat, so she might be a bodega cat, but still, that was her business.

"What did I tell you about callin' me a stalker?" Celia shot back.

"But you are one!"

"And you're a goddamned bodega cat!"

"It takes one to know one."

"Really?" Celia said with a laugh.

"Yes, really. Bye, stink ass," Noelle mumbled. Celia was still laughing when she hung up the phone. Pouting, she went into the tiny black and white lab to change into her coveralls, remembering to put her belt on this time. She didn't want the male sailors to think she was advertising her availability for sex if she was beltless. God knows who started that ridiculous rumor, but the higher-ups took it seriously. It reminded Noelle of what she had heard about the story of men in jail wearing their pants hanging down, identifying them as gay and ready to get it on. Maybe that's what it reminded the Khakis of too. The military did feel a little like a prison sometimes. So far, no one had gotten written up for it, but it was only a matter of time before someone did, and she did not want to be the example.

She went back into the main lab and pulled a plastic rolling cart over to the Noritsu. Propping the rear cover open to access the processing racks, she lifted them out, letting them drip a moment before setting them inside and rolling the cart over to the deep sink. Transferring the racks to the deep sink, she grabbed the spray nozzle and turned on the water. Absent-mindedly, she sprayed the chemical residue off the individual white wheels as she replayed her last moments with her Mandingo Warrior. Specifically, the way the woman looked at her. She still looked like she wanted to beat her ass; that much didn't change, but with Celia's words overlaying the scene, she switched her focus back to Quentin's face and body language. The way his head tilted down slightly so he could look her directly in the eyes, the way his hands were splayed out—palms up, the way his tone was soft and apologetic, with a hint of desperation. And sincerity. He was full of sincerity. It rolled off of him in waves that bounced off her ever-present anti-trust shield. *Fuckity-fuck-fuck!* Celia was right. *Dammit!*

Forgetting she had the nozzle in her hand Noelle fought the air with her fists, causing chemical-laden water to spray everywhere. A couple of drops landed precariously close to her eyes. Shit, she needed to put her goggles on. She was about to fuck around and blind herself. Then how would she see Quentin again? She could feel his face like that blind girl did of Lionel Richie's clay bust in his *Hello* video. Which somehow always struck her as wrong.

Was he a high school teacher singing about a student or a college professor? Either way, she had questions about the appropriateness of that relationship.

Groaning, Noelle dropped the nozzle in the sink and grabbed the safety goggles *and* apron from the hook next to the sink. Before she could put them on, there was a knock on the door, and Seaman Diana Thomas entered. Well, damn, also forgot that Gordon told her Thomas was coming. Thomas was part of Deck's 1st Division[23], and she'd been trying to strike[24] for Photographer's Mate since last year. Noelle approved her coming to the photo lab twice a week to do OJT[25], but now she wished she had denied it. Thomas was highly annoying because she reminded Noelle of herself at nineteen. She was just so *very*—very talkative, very smart-mouthed, very hard-headed, very adorable—and she used that one to her benefit. Noelle didn't mind that one. A woman had to use every advantage given to them in the military, and men were easy to play, so why not? She also looked up to Noelle and always asked for advice she never took—again, another reminder of herself at *any* age. It was so fucking frustrating. Hopefully, this was

---

23. Deck Department: consists of two divisions. 1st that maintains the outward appearance of the ship, and 3rd division that runs the boat deck. Together they are responsible for the safe navigation and operation of the vessel, both at sea and in port.

24. Strike or Striker: non-designated personnel. Usually refers to sailors who are attempting to learn a rate by doing on-the-job training.

25. OJT: on the job training.

as close to having a child as she would get because the way her patience was set up, she'd jump straight over Claudine and turn into Mommy Dearest.

"Good, you're in your coveralls. Put these on, and I'll show you how to do this maintenance," Noelle directed, handing her a second pair of safety goggles.

"Cool. And while we do this PH1, I really have to ask your opinion about something. So I talked to Parker the other night, and he said..." Thomas began to Noelle's dismay.

Parker was the 3rd Division[26] lil seaman boy Thomas was dating, and he was allegedly dating multiple girls through-out the ship. All of which he adamantly denied with the blatant audacity that only a twenty-year-old can have. Every week there was a new allegation, and Thomas went through the motions of being angry with him and then somehow defending him by the end of the conversation. This was turning out to be a very disappointing morning indeed.

Noelle rolled her eyes and handed Thomas the sprayer after she donned her goggles. With a resigned sigh, she sat down on a stool in front of the Noritsu and pretended to listen to Thomas.

---

26. Deck Department: consists of two divisions. 1st that maintains the outward appearance of the ship and throughout, and 3rd division that runs the boat deck. Together they are responsible for the safe navigation and operation of the vessel, both at sea and in port.

Chapter Five

BM1 Joaquín Santiago

"Hey man, I thought you quit smoking."

Boatswain's Mate[1] 1st Class Joaquín Santiago looked wryly at the cigarette he was holding and then looked over to his friend, Storekeeper[2] 2nd Class Mike Ingram, who had just joined him on the aft lookout[3] smoking area.

"This is my last one. I start smoking cessation class this afternoon. I want to get it down before the cruise starts." Joaquín took a slow drag off his cigarette, and closing his eyes, he slowly exhaled. He would miss his nicotine, but he'd been trying to quit after his father, a retired sailor, was diagnosed with COPD. He didn't know if it came from smoking or simply being aboard a ship before OSHA be-

---

1. BM/Boatswain's Mates: train, direct, and supervise personnel in ship maintenance and boat seamanship.

2. SK/Storekeeper: are responsible for maintaining a ship or company military supply store.

3. Aft Lookout: covered section extending from the rear of the ship.

came a thing, but either way, he was trying to avoid the same fate.

As he patted his shirt pockets, an unlit cigarette dangled from Ingram's lips. "Man, lemme borrow your lighter." Joaquín reached into the breast pocket of his coveralls and was handing it over when he caught sight of a petite Hispanic woman stepping through the hatch, followed by a taller but equally slender Black woman. They walked off to a corner and started talking.

Celia Navarro. The only way to explain his fascination with her would be: extraordinary. At least ten times a day, he wished he had the freedom to do whatever he wanted. He wanted to drag her into Boatswain's locker[4] and fuck her until they both couldn't breathe. Get them both some oxygen and carry on. But he was married, and he couldn't bring himself to have an affair. It was commonplace aboard the ship, but he just couldn't bring himself to do it. He only thought about it. Constantly.

His fascination went unnoticed, however, because Navarro didn't even know he was alive. She was friendly enough and always had the same smile for him that she had for everyone else. He considered it a mixed blessing that she overlooked him. He was so far gone; any hint of extra attention would have him knocking people down just to get to her.

"Uh-oh, it looks like not all is well in licky-licky land," Ingram commented as he watched the two women.

Navarro and Kendrick did indeed appear to be arguing. Kendrick was gesturing wildly, puffing on her cigarette,

---

4. Boatswain's locker: various secured spaces throughout the ship where Boatswains stored deck gear and hang out in.

but Navarro was leaning back against the railing, looking relaxed in her working whites, answering back calmly.

"Man, I'd fuck the shit outta that damn girl. All she gotta do is say the word." Ingram blew a stream of smoke out the corner of his mouth.

"Which one?" Joaquín didn't know why he asked because he already knew.

"Kendrick's fine, but I don't think she's seen a dick in years—coochie's too dusty. I don't have time to stop and sweep away the cobwebs before I hit it. Navarro's the one I want."

Joaquín grunted. He really didn't want to hear about how much Ingram wanted to fuck Navarro. Ingram, as usual, didn't need any encouragement to keep talking.

"I heard Navarro used to be engaged before she came here. That guy must have fucked her over real bad to make her turn on us," Ingram said.

Joaquín nodded, although he disagreed. In his opinion, Navarro simply wanted to be with a woman. There wasn't any place better than the Puget Sound. He'd never been on a ship where there were so many lesbians out actively recruiting, even before "Don't Ask, Don't Tell[5] " was signed into law. There was so much shit going on between the walls of this ship that sometimes he felt dirty just coming aboard.

Suddenly Kendrick stormed off, and Navarro didn't even spare her a glance. She just turned around and leaned on the railing, staring at the pier.

"Now look at her sticking that tight little ass out," Ingram

---

5. Don't ask/Don't tell: a set of policies, laws and regulations governing how the U.S. Military dealt with gay, lesbian and bisexual service members.

said. "She knows I'm watching her. Always teasing a brother. I'm telling you, man, I'm gonna get that ass one day."

Joaquín nodded again. If Navarro ever showed any interest in Ingram...he didn't care if it broke the man code; he'd cock-block him with all he had. It was selfish and irrational, but he couldn't deal with her messing with his friend.

"You think she's a real redhead? I've always wondered about that. Man, I bet she got them strawberry-colored nipples. Think she got strawberry milk?" Ingram laughed at his own joke and puffed on his cigarette. "That would make a great "Got Milk" ad. You know a brother's lactose intolerant, but if I saw that ad, I'd drink more milk."

Navarro was indeed a natural redhead. While they were on the last cruise, he stumbled upon the opportunity to find out. Santiago overheard Bentley saying they were going to a nude beach in Corfu. Naturally, he followed them, and that afternoon his fascination with her went from average to extraordinary.

Any questionable thoughts he had about spying on her vanished when Navarro walked naked from the Adriatic sea. The neat V of hair at the apex of her thighs confirmed his suspicions. In the throng of scantily clothed and nude bodies, all he could see was her. Her wet hair shone like copper underneath the hot Mediterranean sun, and droplets of water sparkled like diamonds on her skin. Mesmerized, he stared as she walked back to her lounging chair next to Bentley. Before she sat down, she tilted her head to the side and squeezed the water out of her hair, closing her eyes to the sun. He was maybe five or six people away from her, but just like she didn't notice he was alive on the ship; she didn't catch him gawking at her then.

Unlike his wife, who was almost as tall as he was, with a body full of dips and curves, and places to bury yourself in, Navarro was a wisp of a woman. She barely reached his shoulders and with barely any curves to speak of. There wasn't an ounce of extra flesh on her. She only had a slight dip in her high waistline, her dangling, unauthorized navel piercing lay flat against her stomach, and she had surprisingly long and shapely legs. He knew she kept fit by doing all the latest workout fads. She was doing Tae Bo kickboxing like a madwoman and trying to convince everyone else to do it with her, as he'd overheard Bentley complain.

But it was her breasts that got his complete attention. He always considered himself an ass man, but she had what he dubbed banana-shaped breasts—-high and sloped upwards and tipped with medium size nipples that reminded him of ripe strawberries. They were perfect. He remembered how they bounced and jiggled when she reached up with both hands and fluffed her curly hair around her face and shoulders at that beach. He fought off the erection the memory brought on.

Joaquín was debating whether to leave the smoking area when someone called out to Navarro. When she sharply turned around to see who it was, the loose bun in her hair unraveled, and her long, thick, copper ponytail fell down her back. Rolling her eyes, she kneeled to retrieve the lost bobby pins off the deck. Sticking the pins in her shirt pocket, she twirled her hair back up in the bun and started repining it.

Joaquín's eyes involuntarily focused on her shirt stretching across her breasts. He was staring so hard it took him a moment to realize she was also staring at him. Their eyes locked, and his mask of indifference slipped for a second, revealing his hunger before he composed himself.

But that second was all it took. Navarro's eyes widened, a myriad of expressions sweeping over her face: surprise, confusion, suspicion, disbelief, back to confusion before finally settling on the one look he longed for and dreaded at the same time: awareness. While still pinning up her hair, her full lips painted in her signature brown lipstick curved into a small but satisfied smile, and she began to stroll leisurely towards him.

Navarro had a feline quality in the way she moved. Her heart-shaped face and slightly upturned hazel eyes added to her cat-like appearance. Her eyes stayed locked on his as if daring him to look away, inhaling deeply when she got within arm's length of him. The nostrils on her dainty nose flared as if taking in the scent of prey. He felt like she was stalking him, waiting for him to run so she could chase him. He tensed. The hairs on the back of his neck rose. He briefly considered flicking his cigarette over the side of the ship and, indeed, running, but it wouldn't accomplish anything. He had nowhere to go where she couldn't find him. Instead, he forced himself to relax and leaned back against the railing.

"*Buenos Dias*," Navarro greeted. "*Que tal?*"

Joaquín nodded. "*Bien gracias, y tú?*"

"*Muy bien gracias*," she replied. "*Estamos de acuerdo para la cita ?*"

"*Que?*" Joaquín frowned. A date? They didn't have a date. Maybe when he was dreaming, but not when he was awake.

Before Navarro could respond, Ingram said, "Now that's just plain rude. Do I look like I speak Spanish? Y'all in America and y'all need to speak American."

Laughing, Navarro turned her attention to Ingram. "Well, hello there, Storekeeper 2nd Class Michael Ingram. How are you doing on this fine, fine Navy morning? Is that better?"

Ingram rolled his eyes. "Not really. Now you sound all corny and shit."

"Men. Y'all never satisfied. That's what's wrong with y'all." Navarro's eyes twinkled.

"I'll tell you what *can* satisfy me, but we might have to take it somewhere else," Ingram said with an exaggerated wink.

"Oooh, I'm sorry, darling. As tempting as that sounds, I'm afraid I'm going to have to decline the invite. I already have a previous engagement I need to attend," Navarro said, her eyes briefly flicking over to Joaquín.

Joaquín, taking a desperate drag on his cigarette, almost choked on the smoke.

Ingram caught the look and sucked his teeth. "That's so fucked up, girl. You know I've been waiting for you. I tell you at least once a week, and you just kick a brother to the curb without even giving him a chance. That's cold-blooded."

"Awww, *aye calindo*." Navarro pinched his chin.

Ingram swatted her hand away. "Don't touch me. Well, not there. If you *really* want to make it up to me, you can touch me somewhere else."

Navarro chuckled and shook her head. "Not today, ship-mate. I already told you I'm gonna be busy."

Joaquín studied the tip of his cigarette rather than looking at Navarro. *What the fuck was going on here?* Her change of heart gave him whiplash. Five minutes ago, she was arguing with her girlfriend, and now here she was looking at him like he was something on the menu she wanted to order. He flicked the cigarette over the side of the ship. Reaching into the breast pocket of his coveralls, he took out a piece of *Doublemint* gum, popped it in his mouth, and began to chew it as if his life depended on it.

"So I'll see you in ten minutes then," Navarro told Joaquín.

"What?" His brow wrinkled. Then he remembered he wanted to talk to her about the First Class Association meeting that was being held later today. He was the President of the Association, and she was the secretary. He practically lived for the one-on-one sessions with her. She had his head spinning so much that he had forgotten about it. "Yeah, see you in a few." She left with a wink for Ingram, who waved a dismissing hand at her, and a nod for Joaquín.

"Man, lemme borrow your lighter again?" Ingram asked.

Frowning, Joaquín glanced at the half-smoked cigarette dangling between Ingram's fingers. "Why? You haven't even finished smoking that one."

"So I can burn your face with it. I'm tired of you pretty motherfuckers getting all the ladies. Damn, leave some for the average nigga," Ingram complained.

Joaquín laughed, shaking his head. "Bruh, you ain't gotta worry about all that. I ain't payin' her no mind."

"And why not?" Ingram asked in disbelief. He waved his hand. "Because of Marisol? You need to get that taken care of so you can move on with your life."

Joaquín shook his head tersely. Ingram was the only person on the ship that he confided in about his suspicion that his wife was cheating. Aboard the Puget Sound, keeping your personal business private was hard. But in a moment of weakness, he told Ingram about Marisol, and now he wouldn't let it go.

"So you're just going to let Navarro get away? Do you know how many guys want to hit that? And she's throwing it at you! Did you not see that? Mannnn, you trippin!" Ingram said.

Joaquín sighed impatiently and shrugged. He needed to go before Ingram started on how stupid he was.

"*Shee*-et yous a fool, man!" Ingram threw his hands up in the air. "I cannot believe this! Bruh, you do realize she ain't had a man in only God knows how long? That just about makes her a born-again virgin. You sure about that?"

No. "Yes." Joaquín's voice was firm, but he felt the dull ache beginning at the thought of how tight Celia probably was.

"Then put in a good word for a brother," Ingram asked.

"No, I don't think so." Joaquín pushed off the railing.

"Now that's *really* fucked up, man," Ingram said to Joaquín's back as he walked away.

That it was, Joaquín agreed silently. He flashed Ingram a peace sign over his shoulder and kept on walking. He wasn't concerning himself with his friend. He had about ten minutes to get his guard up before he saw Navarro again. For peace of mind, he needed to squash whatever she was planning.

Chapter Six

YN1 Celia Navarro

Celia's jaw dropped open the second she stepped through the hatch[1]. Grabbing the top button of her white top, she vigorously fanned her flushed skin. Hay Dios mio! Her body was on fire. The polyester cotton blend of her summer working uniform was not suitable for hot flashes. Sweat dotted the bridge of her nose, her white undershirt stuck to her lower back, the gusset of her panties was damp, and her pants were clinging to her ass as she walked. She was a hot, sticky mess, and it felt awesome! She hadn't felt this way since Julia. She didn't realize she was missing this deep, primal, hungry lust in her life until right now. She wanted to get naked in the material handling passageway[2] and run around the ship.

Ten minutes later, Celia managed to pull herself together when Santiago appeared at the helpdesk window. Gesturing for him to come inside, she studied him as he walked

---

1. Hatch: a watertight opening to a deck. If it goes through a bulkhead, it's a regular door.

2. Material Handling Passageway: a long corridor that has outside access so that large items can be brought on board.

the short distance over to her. He wasn't that tall, maybe 5'9 or so, but he was fucking gorgeous in them blue coveralls. And wait, he's bow-legged. God bless a bow-legged man.

Santiago sat in front of Celia's desk and crossed his arms. His sleeves were rolled up to his elbows. His forearms were just how she liked them: thick with a heavy dusting of hair and bulging veins—a must-have for arms *and* penises, they added delicious texture for the tongue.

Celia dragged her eyes away from his arms. "¿Entonces qué pasa?

Santiago gave her a ghost of a smile. "Same ole, same ole. I just need a couple of minutes of your time. It's about the last meeting, did you..."

His voice faded as Celia stared at Santiago. Seriously, how could she have missed how fine he was? Where the fuck had she been? Besides the meetings, she saw him at least once daily throughout the ship. But somehow, she failed to notice the smoothness of his almond-colored skin, the small crescent-shaped scar above his left eyebrow, his dark brown bedroom eyes with those incredibly long lashes, nicely-shaped lips, and the silver streaks in his thick black hair. She leaned forward slightly and inhaled the light woodsy scent she caught a whiff of earlier. He smelled so edible; she wanted to lick him all over.

"So, were you able to look into that?"

Celia blinked rapidly. She hadn't heard a word he'd said. *Oh shit.* "Ummm, well...I, ummm..."

Santiago frowned. "Were you listening to me?"

Aye, yi-yi, he even looked good frowning. "Of course I was." Celia widened her eyes and tried her best to look sincere.

"No, you weren't."

"Yes, I was."

"Then what did I ask you?"

"Humph." Celia looked down at her desk, trying to recall anything he said. "Well, you talked about wanting something and hmmmm, yeah, and a lot of other stuff."

"*Navarro.*"

"Okay, okay. I wasn't. Sorry," Celia apologized sweetly.

Santiago shook his head at her. "I don't like wasting my time, Navarro. You know I'm busy. I have a lot of things to do before we leave."

Oh, so it's like that? Then why did you walk your ass all the way down here when you could've just called me? Celia wondered. Now that she thought about it, he always had these stupid little ten-minute meetings with her when he could've just called. Or emailed her. This was 1994, after all. People didn't have to see each other unless they wanted to. And from the look on his face earlier, he definitely wanted to.

"I know, I know. I just got distracted." Celia said, licking her bottom lip. Heat flared through her when his eyes followed her tongue. Instantly, a bead of sweat formed and rolled down between her shoulder blades. What condition caused you to pass out from excess sweating? Heat stroke or heat exhaustion? Whichever one it was, if she kept up all this sweating, she was going to fall victim to one of them.

"By what?" He asked curtly.

Celia's hand went to the nape of her neck and toyed with a damp tendril of hair. She was never one to beat around the bush, so she said what was on her mind. "You know, I have seen you almost every day for the past two years, and I'm wondering when you got so fine? I must admit, it has me a little bit perplexed."

Santiago cocked his head to the side as he studied her. "Nothing's changed about me. You were always just too preoccupied with other things to take notice."

"True. I cannot argue with that." Celia chuckled. "But I'm not anymore."

Cocking one brow, Santiago leaned back in the chair. "Is that right, Navarro?"

Celia propped her elbows on the desk, folded her fingers together, and rested her chin on her clasped hands. Leaning toward him, she said, "Celia. Call me Celia. And yes, that is indeed right."

Santiago's lids dipped as he leaned forward as well. "So, where is your focus now, *Celia*?"

Celia's eyelids fluttered. A thousand tingles traveled down her spine at the way he said her name. He murmured it slowly as though he was tasting a delicacy he wanted to savor. Belatedly, she realized he had murmured everything. Even when others were loud in the meetings, he never raised his voice. He would sit patiently, waiting until everyone quieted down before speaking again. The phone on her desk rang. Maintaining eye contact with Santiago, she answered it.

"Girl, why didn't you tell me you dumped Kendrick?" Noelle's excited voice snapped her out of her sensual reverie. Gossip traveled faster than the speed of light on this ship.

"I was going to later. It just happened," Celia answered. "Who told you?"

"Girl, 'bout five different people. You know Kendrick loves ta chat, eh. That shit will probably be in the POD[3] tomorrow morning."

Celia shook her head. "Who you telling? Okay, let me holla at you later."

---

3. POD/Plan of the Day: command's schedule for the day.

"*Why?*"

"Because I'm busy."

"Busy doing what?" Noelle sing-songed.

Celia sighed again. "I'm in a meeting."

"With whom? It's no one serious 'cause you answered the phone."

Oh no, it's serious as the heart attack I'm about to have if I don't off get this damn phone! "I am at work, so that's why I answered the phone because that's part of my job." Celia paused. "And if I told you, I'd have to kill you."

"You know I'd gladly die a thousand deaths for a secret. So, try again. Actually, never mind ho, I'm coming over."

Noelle probably would. She was noisier than ten old ladies gossiping on a stoop.

"You better not." Celia heard someone in the background talking to Noelle. Then one of the machines started beeping. "Oh. My. God! This girl! You done lucked out this time. But you better bring your ass here when ya done. You hear me talkin' to ya gal?"

Noelle sometimes sounded like she was from Fort Worth instead of the South Bronx. She blamed Sidney for that mess. However, coming from Sidney, it was soft and sweet. Coming from Noelle, it was a damn abomination. "You do remember you're from the South Bronx, right? You be killin' me with that fake country accent."

"Yeah, I've been around Sidney too long, but don't change the subject. Don't make me come find you." Noelle hung up.

"Sorry about th—" Celia was cut off by the phone ringing again. Not bothering to stifle a sigh of impatience, she picked up the receiver. Santiago moved to rise, and she held up a finger, forestalling him. She was on the phone for under ten seconds, but that was long enough for the phones at the other desk to start ringing and a couple of people to appear at the helpdesk window. *What the fuck did these people want?*

"It seems your workday has begun," Santiago said after she hung up the phone. "And I need to head back to the boat deck anyway." He stood up.

Celia's eyes trailed up his body, briefly stopping at his groin, wondering what his dick looked like before traveling up to his inscrutable face. *Fuck me, he was gorgeous.* "So it seems. We'll continue this conversation another time, *si*?"

"*Si.*" Santiago's eyes darkened. "*Adios.*"

"*Adios.*" Celia's breathing went shallow, and she clenched her jaw at the intensity of his gaze. She felt it from the roots of her hair to the tips of her orchid purple-painted toenails. Light beads of sweat dotted her nose again. She wanted to climb over the desk and launch herself at him, but she could wait. They would have more than enough time for that later.

Chapter Seven

YN1 Celia Navarro

"Then what'd she say?" Noelle asked when Celia paused as she recounted her break-up with Kendrick. "Whadshesay! Why are you taking so long? C'mon! Thomas will be back soon, and I can't keep on sending her on fool's errands."

Celia leaned back in her seat and pursed her lips. She went to the photo lab as soon as Joaquín left—well, as soon as she had dealt with all the distractions that had let him get away. She was deliberately drawing out her conversation with Kendrick. She liked making Noelle wait because she had the patience of a three-year-old haggling with her parents on Christmas morning. Celia was the parent telling her to wait until Mommy had her coffee.

"YN1[1] Navarro!" Noelle snapped. She jumped from the stool she was sitting on and grabbed the nozzle hanging up above the sink, and pointed it at Celia. "You're about to get this hose."

Celia laughed. "She called me a bitch. I am thoroughly offended by that because I am not a bitch."

"Gasp." Noelle dropped the nozzle, and her hands flew to

---

1. YN/Yeoman: administrative and clerical worker.

her throat. "But I call you a bitch all the time."

"Yes, but that doesn't count. It's said with love and affection. Kendrick wanted to hurt my feelings. Can you believe that shit?" Celia clutched her chest in mock horror and then laughed.

"What? Naw! You serious?" Noelle shook her head and rolled her eyes. She held her hand up. "Now, you know I don't like that girl, right? She's a goddamn hobgoblin, but you *did* dump her on the smoke deck."

"I can't dump someone I wasn't in a relationship with in the first place." Celia shrugged. "And clearly, she is fuckin' with $DC2^2$, so what the fuck yo?"

"She just didn't want to be cut off from your *cocha* while she was munchin' on other ship *cocha*. Ain't no different from a man. Hoes have no gender. Everyone wants to have their cake and a slice of everyone else's too. But what I find really baffling is that she chose Allen, crept on y'alls duty day, and then made a scene about it. Just fuck with Allen and shut the fuck up," Noelle said, sitting back down in front of Nortisu.

"Exactly. And that's what I told her, but she was adamant that she wasn't doing anything with Allen—almost started crying and everything. I was like, *oh Jesus*, I'm walking away from her if she starts that shit," Celia said.

Noelle stopped pressing buttons on the panel before her and spun around to face Celia. "Crying. Like real tears? From her eyeballs?"

"Both eyeballs!" Celia added with a grimace.

---

2. Damage Control & Damage Controlman: the ship's fireman, maintaining and repairing damage control equipment and systems, ship's stability, firefighting, fire prevention, etc.

Noelle froze as a thought occurred to her. "Wait, do you think she was trying to make you *jealous*....like full-on fisticuffs." She punched the air, ducking and swerving like a boxer. "With the other chick jealous?"

"Eww, no, why would she do that?" Celia's face scrunched up. "That is just *disgusting*! All we did was have sex. I don't know shit about her, and she damn sure don't know shit about me, or else she would have known not to try that bullshit."

"True dat. You are quick to cut a motherfucker off. Well, I guess if she didn't know, now she knows. Good fucking riddance. She had one more time to look at me funny before I started boiling the water."

Celia inhaled and exhaled through puffed cheeks. "You and your grits. You need to stop thinking about burning people with hot grits. It's not normal that it's your go-to when you can't resolve differences. You're gonna end up in jail, 'kay? And I am not going to bail you out. I want to make it to Senior Chief, and I can't be associated with criminals."

"No ma'am, you are going to bail me out because your shenanigans are always the reason I want to burn someone. And I ain't trying to resolve differences—I'm trying to peel some flesh from your muscles."

"You need Jesus," Celia said.

Noelle sucked her teeth. "Go find him and tell him. Oh, wait, you've been excommunicated, so never mind. Anteeways, I've so been over Kendrick. On to the next new thing. Who was in the office with you when I called? You sounded awfully chipper when you answered the phone."

Celia hesitated. She wasn't sure what Noelle was going to say. Sometimes she was all "*ho is life*" and wholeheartedly partook in and endorsed the life. Other times she was your Victorian best friend and rebuked the way of the ho and reminded you of all the ways that being a ho has complicated your life. After all these years, she still hadn't figured Noelle out. With all those voices she named in her head, she doubted Noelle had either.

Noelle squinted, then snapped her fingers. "Never mind, trick, I already know you had a meeting with Santiago. You have one with him every Monday. You go over pointless minutes from the First Class meeting."

Celia's mouth dropped open. "How do you know this? You don't even come to the meetings."

"I went to one. It's a big jerk-off session. I'll pass. And don't worry about what I know, just know that I know. Is *he* the reason you're coming back on to dick rotation now?" Noelle asked.

Something about Noelle's tone made Celia eye her friend cautiously. She still wasn't sure who she was getting. She didn't need or want any lectures about fucking a crew member. After Harrison, Noelle was adamant she wouldn't do it again because there was nowhere to go if the relationship got messy, as hers did with him. Although Celia believed there was more to the relationship than Noelle said, she had yet to pry it out of her. As much as she flapped her flibberjibbers, as Sidney called them, Noelle could be notoriously close-mouthed when she chose to be.

"Uh-uh, not yet. I'm working on it." Celia said finally.

Noelle shot her a dubious look. "I don't know about that one, boo."

"Why not?" *Okay, here we go.* Pensively, Celia scratched the corner of her mouth with her out-of-regulation-length pinkie nail. Shit, wait—was Noelle about to call dibs on Santiago? Dammit, she hoped not because then she'd have to leave him alone. This is why it sometimes didn't pay to have girlfriends.

Noelle laughed at Celia's gloomy expression. "Fix your face girl, I don't want him. I thought about it for a hot minute—you know I like my Spanish guys. 'Specially if they're from New York. But I'm pretty sure he's Columbian—from Miami I think or somewhere in Florida. Anyway, I just happened to be talking to him on the mess decks one day, and then you walked by, and girl, it was like someone held that man in a damn trance. It was a wrap for him and me, I guess."

The relief in Celia was so strong it made her a little light-headed. "Oh, okay. Why didn't you say something sooner?"

"*Whyyy-yah?*" Noelle dragged the word out and then sucked her teeth. "There are multiple reasons why, but the main one was you had your face in between some broad's legs, so what would have been the point? Seriously, think before you speak, crazy girl."

"You're right. Julia messed up my rotation. I should have been on men already. It's like I skipped over it and went straight back to women after breaking up with her. I'm not sure why though. I haven't been with a man in almost two years. Now *that's* crazy," Celia said.

"Not really. Because honestly, I really do think you're a lesbian that has moments of heteronormality. Oh, wait," Noelle snapped her fingers. "You did a brief stint with that dude from the Kennedy[3] . He was the reason for the grits, lest you forget. He was a fucking asshole. I think we wiped him from our collective memories because you always be bringin' up the grits and not the reason for the grits. Anyway, back to Santiago, you being a lesbian and all was the

---

3. USS John F. Kennedy CV 67: was the fourth and final ship of the Kitty Hawk-class of aircraft carriers.

reason why I didn't tell you. You would've just fucked with his head because you could."

"Shut up." Celia rolled her eyes. "No, I wouldn't have."

"Bitch, please. All you do is fuck with men's heads. You need a part-time job or something. You have too much time on your hands."

"I am just flirtatious, I'm not to blame if men take me too seriously. What do you know about Santiago? I didn't have time to go through his records since you threatened me. Does he have a girlfriend or something?"

Noelle groaned and rolled her eyes. "I swear to God, your lack of observation is why you stay in these problematic situations. It's definitely the Libra in you." She tsked. "He doesn't have a girl, but he does have a wife. Like a whole-ass family."

"Oh!" Celia blurted, then pouted. "He wasn't wearing a ring."

"So what? A lot of sailors don't." Noelle shrugged one shoulder. "Apparently, I am the only sailor who watched *The Abyss*. That's why I started wearing a ring on my middle finger because you never know if this ring could stop a door from closing."

Noelle and that damn movie. Celia shook her head. "All of our hatches seal manually, Noelle, so just know that if you're locked behind one, it's me double dog tightening[4] it."

"But if you kill me, how will I be able to tell you the other stuff I know about Santiago?" Noelle said slyly, turning her back to the panel.

Celia pressed her lips together and mentally counted to three before asking sweetly, "What else do you know,

---

4. Dog: to close or "dog down" a water tight hatch.

Noelle?"

Noelle glanced over her shoulder and rolled her eyes. "Oh no, booger bear, I am not telling you a goddamn thing. You just threatened to kill me."

Celia bit back a groan of frustration. She would not let Noelle know how desperate she was for information. "I don't know how I've managed to stay friends with you all these years."

"Because I keep your life interesting. Without me, you'd be a ho without substance. I give you gravity."

"And a fucking migraine." Celia exhaled gustily. "What else do I need to know about him, PH1 Bentley? If you don't tell me right now, I'll leak out the real reason you stopped dating Harrison."

Noelle whipped around and narrowed her eyes at Celia. "You wouldn't dare!"

Noelle had complained about the sex with Harrison from the very beginning. He was overly endowed. The final straw was when he pinned her knees to her chest, and the position was too much for Noelle's intestines and colon to handle. She shit the bed. Celia laughed so hard at her friend's utter mortification that she thought she would vomit and piss herself at the same time. After that night, Noelle swore she wouldn't have sex if she'd even eaten an appetizer.

"Try me." Celia raised one of her thinly arched eyebrows. "Oooh, just tell me, dammit. You are such a pain in the ass!"

"I was going to tell you. There was no need to threaten me. Anyway, so last cruise—I think we were in Naples, Ingram was drunk and in between him trying to fuck me, I asked him where Santiago was because that's his homeboy, and I wanted him to come to get his drunk ass. But he just blurted that Santiago is 99.9% positive that his wife cheated on him, and he's been buggin' him to confront her about it, but he hasn't. I was shocked because I didn't even ask him all that. It was like he just couldn't keep it to himself. Since I've known him for years, I guess I was a safe person to tell." Noelle paused and pursed her lips. "And they say *women* like to gossip. Personally, I think Ingram's just miserable and wants everyone around him to be divorced like him."

"That's highly possible. He has been undercover miserable since his wife left him. Did he say why Santiago hasn't?" Celia asked.

Noelle shook her head. "Nope. You'll have to ask him that. I dare to say it wouldn't take much to get him to tell you. You've had his nose wide open like a jar of damn Vicks for a while. I don't know what kinda man he is—if he's faithful and all that or if he's just a looky-loo. However, I do think the only reason this hasn't gone down yet is that you didn't pay him no mind. Now that you have, ummm..."

"Yeah, he did sorta bring that up and we were about to really start talking when you called because you always make an appearance at the most inconvienant times. You need to list that in the skills section on your civilian resume."

"You know I have *The Shining* for bullshit, and when you good and ready, girl, you be on that bullshit. So what I need is a personal deflector shield." Noelle paused, pointing at Celia and then holding both hands around her ears before continuing. "Ima need you to put your listening ears on and pay attention to what I'm about to say. You got them on?"

Celia mimed putting on that extra set of invisible ears and cupped her hands around them. "I'm paying attention."

"Okay, you better be because I am only going to say this once. Santiago is one of those men that will put it on you, and you won't even know it until you're up in jail and they've made a Lifetime story about your tragic, tumultuous, scandalous affair. He has the same strange intensity about him that Julia did. They just ooze sexual energy. It's a little scary because they're not faking the funk, yanno. It just oozes from their damn pores. I mean, I was attracted to Julia, and you know I am strictly dickly. But she had me thinking that I needed to take a dip in the lady pond—just put my tongue in it, so to speak. I digress. Another reason I didn't make a move on him, besides the fact he was obviously smitten with you, I was also thinking I like having a soul. I think he's a soul snatcher. Again, like Julia. So I left it alone. Because you too are a soul-eater, you're attracted to people like him and Julia. I think you have a jar of souls underneath your bed. It keeps your titties high cause them bitches ain't dropped since high school. Oh, and I think he's a Scorpio. Yet another reason why I was like, nope."

"Oooh, a Scorpio? Oh, that's nice!" Celia rubbed her hands together. She wasn't into astrology as much as Noelle, but she knew firsthand the truth about Scorpios.

"Julia was also a Scorpio, lest we forget," Noelle said with a deadpan expression and then shook her head. "You didn't retain anything I said, did you? When you heard Scorpio, it just wiped the slate clean, didn't it? I hope you still have your counselor's number. I think you're going to need it."

"*Mira*, Julia is the one and only time I have lost my shit. Quit actin' like I do it every fiscal year. Damn. Have some faith in me," Celia said with a hand over her heart.

"I don't, shipmate," Noelle said gently. "Because I already know what's going to happen. The Shining, remember." She tapped one temple to emphasize her self-declared powers of prognostication.

"Just make sure you have an appointment ready the day after we pull back in for you *and* for me," Noelle added. "I'm gonna need some support. If this is anything like you and Julia, I might actually need a support *group*. The fallout of y'alls relationship was truly traumatizing. I can't imagine what you would've been like if I hadn't been here. Ass woulda been up in Bellevue somewhere, I guarantee. Now go find somewhere else to skate. Some of us don't like committing fraud, waste, and abuse of government funds. You're a bad influence."

"Says the girl who had me going to summer school every year for gym class from playing hooky."

"I haven't led you astray for almost twenty years. That's all on you boo." Noelle pointed at Celia and made a circle in the air.

Celia cut her eyes at her best friend. "You know what I think? I need counseling just to be your friend."

"Whatever, chica, just make sure you make your appointment and mark it on your calendar. Now git!" Noelle shooed her out of the lab.

Chapter Eight

MM1 Sidney Pascal

Sidney pulled up next to Noelle's Jeep in the driveway of the elegant one-story ranch-style house they shared with Celia. She turned off the ignition to her Honda Civic with a tired sigh and leaned back in her seat. Writing papers always mentally drained her. She couldn't keep track of all the papers she wrote for her master's in social psychology. She loved reading and studying the casework, but papers were a slow death.

As opposed to the quick death she'd experience if she weren't gainfully employable in the twenty-four months. That's how much time she had to prepare herself for civilian life if she didn't get picked for warrant officer or chief in the next upcoming advancement cycle. Or else this command would end up being her Twilight Tour[1]. She did pass the chief's exam last year but somehow didn't make it to the board, and her meticulously prepared chief warrant officer[2] package was passed over as well. That's when she

---

1. Twilight Tour: when a sailor is approaching their last years in service.

2. Warrant Officer: highly skilled, single-track specialty officers.

panicked and started her master's degree, thinking maybe her path was no longer a naval one. Hindsight was indeed 20/20 because it would have been so much easier to do it when she was stationed on shore duty. Even though the command made accommodations for higher learning, it was still a pain in the butt trying to complete a master's degree when the ship was out to sea for so much of the year.

Sidney blamed being stationed in the Mediterranean for the last eight years for her lack of preparation. Before transferring to the Sound, she did four years in Rota, Spain, and then hopped over to Naples, Italy, for the last four. She'd just made E-5 when transferred to Rota and made it to E-6 on time. However, Naples did her in. Everything was too dang relaxed. She fought against the leisurely way the Napoleons lived for about six months before she gave in. Her breaking point was when her stove failed, and it took over two weeks for her landlord to fix it. She already didn't like cooking, but she did want the ability to do so if needed. She thought she was going to lose her mind waiting on that man. Then one night, she ordered pizza from the family restaurant down the street and never looked back. They were on a first-name basis when she left. She still sent the Ascione family Christmas cards and looked forward to seeing them every time the Sound docked in Naples.

Once she let go of always having control, life in Naples was incredible. It was the most carefree Sidney had ever been in her life. She spent way too much money, over-ate rich food, drank more than she should, discovered her love of Black & Mild cigars and an occasional cigarette, and she ignored studying for any advancement tests. She simply was content to be an E-6. She fell off everything but her physical fitness. That was only because she didn't want to be in the Fat Boy Program[3].

Now she was paying for all that delicious freedom because she was sure she was developing an ulcer from the stress she'd put herself under trying to play catch up. And her boyfriend, Nelson, didn't make anything easier for her. He demanded so much of her time and always sulked when she didn't give it to him, regardless of whether or not she had assignments due. In response, she'd taken to going to the base library during the workday, if her Chief let her, rather than to his apartment after work whenever she had to write a paper.

Sighing again, she got out of the car and entered the garage through the side door. None of them could park in the garage since they used it to store most of Noelle's and Sidney's stuff. Sidney's boxes were neatly stacked against the wall. However, next to them were Noelle's bits and bobs scattered everywhere. One open box sat with clothes hanging out of it, a partially completed project she had started enthusiastically only to forget two weeks later was on top of another one. Noelle was a menace. Frowning, she made her way to the kitchen, where she found her little chaos demon rummaging through the freezer.

"Missed you at lunch, chica. Did you finish your paper?" Noelle asked when she saw her.

"Yes, ma'am, I sure did. I'm gonna look it over one last time before I give it to you." Sidney took off her boots, and put them on the mat beside the door, dropping her bookbag next to them. Going over to the sink, she washed her hands and looked over at Noelle, who was already in her shorts

---

3. Fat Boy Program: the stigmatized weight-control program of nutritional counseling, exercise, and humiliating monthly weigh-ins.

and tank top. She must've been home for a while. Sidney had a lot of freedom as a First Class in Main Control[4] , but Noelle had her beat. She just did whatever she wanted. She usually never made it to liberty call[5] , she just left. She said it made up for taking everyone's pictures during the cruise because she hated almost all of the crew. For the life of her, Sidney didn't know how Noelle hadn't been written up already.

Noelle found what she was looking for and sat down at the kitchen table with a half-gallon carton of Breyer's Butter Almond ice cream. "You know I'm still bitter about the way you manipulated me."

"What you call manipulation, I call successful negotiating. You know I have a hard time writing papers, and you wouldn't have given me so much as a synonym without our lucrative trade agreement," Sidney said, grabbing a spoon from the dish rack. She scooped out a spoonful, narrowly avoiding Noelle's spoon as she tried to knock the ice cream off. She was so possessive about her ice cream.

"Lucrative? For whom? That shit was pure extortion. Your ass should have taken political science instead of psychology. You have the making of a great colonizer," Noelle said.

Sidney chuckled. "I thought about it, but I like studying people more. And quit complaining; you got what you wanted. I am living with you, ain't I?"

---

4. Main Control: controls the propulsion system of the ship.

5. Liberty/Liberty Call: authorized absence granted for short periods to provide respite from the working environment.

"Yeah, but at what cost?" Noelle exclaimed.

"I think the joy of my company is worth it. Gimme some more ice cream," Sidney said, motioning with her spoon. Noelle scowled but pushed the container over.

Since Noelle's master's in journalism was gathering dust (she even refused to write anything for the ship's cruise book), and Sidney hated writing papers, she offered up a trade: Noelle would help her with all her papers—thesis included—in exchange for moving in with them. It was also payment for dealing with Noelle's over-the-top personality and lack of personal boundaries.

Noelle would really holler like a stuck pig, however, if she knew that Celia had already offered Sidney the third bedroom while she looked for a place when they got back to Norfolk. Sidney joined the Puget Sound during the 1992 deployment, and it was impossible to look for an apartment while overseas. She had been just about to tell Noelle about Celia's offer when God shut her mouth. Noelle balked and tried to counter it for the rest of the cruise, but Sidney held fast, and Noelle finally agreed.

Sidney did feel a little bit guilty about using Noelle's request against her because she knew the reason behind the proposal. Underneath all that '*I'm from the Bronx*' bravado, Noelle was sentimental, and she wanted to have her closest friends around her one more time before they went their separate ways again. Navy life manages to disperse friends and family alike to all the seven seas, but chile, she quickly got over that guilt when she got her first A from a paper Noelle edited. She'd been getting C's and B-'s on all her previous ones. Extortion paid well.

"So, did anything interesting happen while I was dying in the library?" Sidney asked.

"Oh my God, yes! That was the first thing I was going to

say, but you distracted me with your tomfoolery," Noelle said.

Sidney rolled her eyes. "Says the woman with a master's degree already."

"Potato, patato. Anyway, this has been a fantastic start to the work week. It felt like a Friday. Lemme put this back; I want some chips and salsa now." Noelle licked her spoon clean and covered the carton, and put it back in the freezer. Then, she grabbed the salsa from the fridge and tortilla chips from the pantry and set them on the table. She went back to the fridge and got a Corona for her and an O'Doul's non-alcoholic beer for Sidney. Sidney always loved how Noelle and Celia remembered that she didn't drink, but she also didn't like feeling left out. She handed Sidney her fake beer and told her what happened between Celia and Kendrick and then with Santiago.

"You think she's gonna sleep with him?" Sidney asked. She had only met Celia a couple of times before moving in with them, but she instantly liked her. Celia had the kind of sticky personality that people clung to. She superbly balanced being coy and flirtatious with evasiveness and shocking bluntness, even more so than Noelle. And she could actually bat her eyelashes, and it worked. She had never seen it done in person before Celia did it. However, hard comma, her desires were...how could Sidney put it? Complex. Chaotic. Overwhelming. She wasn't messy, per se, because it never spilled out past her onto anyone else, except for that one time with the guy from the Kennedy[6]

---

6. USS John F. Kennedy CV 67: was the fourth and final ship of the Kitty Hawk-class of aircraft carriers

. Sidney had been glad she got her finances back in order before she transferred to Norfolk because Noelle would have needed a good lawyer if she had succeeded in boiling those grits. But other than that one time Sidney knew of, Celia was her own personal hazmat suit.

"Is Celia gonna mess with Santiago? Ma'am, is rain wet? Does fire burn? Is dirt dirty? Is craze crazy?" Noelle threw her hands up. "Hell yeah, she is."

"Oh my goodness, girl! But why?" Sidney asked. By the time she had transferred to the ship, Celia had gathered herself together. But Noelle was present from almost the beginning of Celia and Juilia's relationship and from the way Noelle told it, the aftermath of the break-up was the equivalent of a hundred-car pile-up, complete with mass casualties. Everyone was left with scars and missing limbs. Why Celia would open herself up to potential pain was beyond Sidney.

"No, I was too caught by surprise." Noelle shrugged. "Then I went into damage control mode because I knew there was only the slimmest of chances that could talk her out of it. But I should get the lowdown if for nothing else but notes for her counselor. But I tell you what, he got that sexy, intense, I'm gonna fuck you to sleep and maybe lock you in a closet vibe that Julia had. You know her undercover crazy ass love that shit. People don't think she likes crazy, they think it's me but it's not. My mother, our friends. But it's *always* been her."

Nah, it's both of y'all. That's why y'all are best friends, Sidney thought. But then she considered Noelle one of her best friends, so what does that make her? Sidney dismissed the notion that she, too, liked crazy and instead focused on Julia. "Julia made me a little uncomfortable, to be honest."

"That uncomfortableness is called attraction to the same

sex!" Noelle said with a sage nod. "Yeah boo, she did that to me too."

"Noooo!" Sidney gasped, then hollered.

"Yassssss! I was so confuzzled. I do not like any vagina but my own, but Julia had me thinking maybe I can get past the texture, what I imagine the taste would be, and being smothered by lady thighs. But enough of them, let's get to the best part: what happened to *moi*."

Oh lawd, what more could've happened? Celia and Santiago were more than enough. It was already adding to Sidney's phantom ulcer.

"Okay, are you ready?" Noelle placed a hand on her heart and did a little jiggle in her seat.

"Am I ever? But go 'head." Sidney laughed and settled in to listen to Noelle's quite frankly overdramatized account of events. The more excited Noelle was, the faster she talked. It had taken her a few months to retrain her ears after not being around her every day.

Well, dang, both her roommates had something going on. Granted, Sidney was pretty sure that Celia's excitement was going to turn into turmoil later. That woman seemed to love like a Shakespearean tragedy—God bless her lil heart—and Noelle was undoubtedly going to ding-dong dash that man if she saw him again. Still, she felt a slight pang of envy at their potential going-ons.

For the most part, Sidney enjoyed her structured, calm life. She found comfort in routine and predictability, which was why the military appealed to her so much. Unless it was wartime, everything was the same, day in and day out. That was how she liked it, or at least that's what she told herself.

After her early marriage ended amicably, Sidney had one wild and outrageous relationship that wore her the heck out. She needed a six-month nap after Bernard. Noelle loved him, of course, because crazy love crazy. Despite what Noelle said about Celia, she got a few screws loose too.

Sidney figured she must've used up all her wild and crazy man points because all the men she dated after were conservative men like her current boyfriend, SH1[7] Michael Nelson, who thought titillating sex was doing it with the lights on.

"Ewww, what's that ugly look for?" Noelle said, giving her an ugly face of her own.

Oh, poop. Sidney hadn't realized she was frowning. She smoothed her brow out and relaxed her lips. She was *not* about to share her thoughts with Noelle. She was constantly launching grenades at Sidney's relationship with Nelson, and she was not about to give her more ammunition. "Nothing. I am just tired, chile."

The phone in the kitchen rang, and Noelle went over and looked at the caller ID. "Ugh, it's Nelson." The disgust was evident in her voice.

"Can you tell him I'm in the shower?" Sidney stood up and stretched. Drinking the rest of her beer, she tossed the empty bottle in the trash and headed to her bedroom over the garage. Noelle had been occupying it, but Sidney made her move out. Another part of the terms and conditions of her living with them was that she wanted her space and privacy, and the room that offered the most privacy was Noelle's. So, she had to give it up because everyone knew Noelle had boundary is-

---

7. SH/Ship Serviceman: manages all shipboard retail and service activities, such as the barbershop, laundry, and commissary.

sues. Sidney's door was usually locked because Noelle was a half-knock-before-she-was-in-your-room-without-actual-verbal-permission kinda person.

"Nope. It can go to the answering machine. I am already reading your paper. I have hit my monthly quota of doing boring shit. He's fuckin' wack as hell. You know I don't like talking to him. Why. Does. He. Talk. So. Slooooow? How on earth do you have conversations with him without falling asleep in the middle?" Noelle asked, following her through the kitchen and living room.

Meeting Nelson coincided with Sidney's decision to buckle down on her life, so he just slid right in. Their relationship went on for eight months before Sidney decided to return to the States. Her daughter, Nadia, was entering her freshman year of high school, and she wanted to be present to help her navigate this last bit of her childhood before she sent her out into the world. Although Sidney had been stationed aboard for eight years, they were very close. Nadia spent nearly all her summers with her, and they hopped all over Europe together. Nadia was insatiably curious about everything and everyone.

But transferring back to Virginia meant she'd have to break up with Nelson. He had eight more years left until retirement, and he planned to spend them in the Med. He wanted to live in Italy after he retired. He didn't like coming back to the States. She even had to guilt him into going to Mississippi for one of his grandmother's funerals.

Sidney was still sorting out her feelings about their impending breakup when he announced he was also transferring to Norfolk. She was surprised at how disappointed she was that their relationship wasn't over, not realizing until that very moment that she was absolutely fine with ending the relationship. Her disappointment grew when she didn't follow through on her feelings and continued the relationship.

And *then* she introduced him to Noelle... Nelson could be patronizing when he wanted to be, and Noelle was highly sensitive to that. Sidney had a feeling that they might not like each other, and she was right. There was a bristling animosity between them on sight. In the five-minute meeting, he also managed to belittle their twelve-year friendship by feigning polite shock and surprise that they had been friends for so long. Sidney remembered watching him study Noelle's cut-off shorts and a tank top with no bra on (because she only wore one under duress), and he must've surmised that she and Sidney somehow didn't run in the same circles.

Noelle rounded in on her the second he left, demanding to know why she brought *that* back with her from Naples. Weren't there any lovely, coiffed Italian men who needed a green card that she could have brought back instead?

"We could have taught him English, made him cook for us, and we would have even let him leave his chest hairs out tangled in his gold chain," Noelle had shouted at the time.

To her, anything was preferable to *that* man. He wore khakis with front pleats and brown loafers with tassels, for God's sake! And his insult did not pass over Noelle. After that, she went on a personal one-woman campaign to break them up. To make matters worse, no one else liked Michael Nelson either. Nadia avoided him, and Wade kept his opinions to himself, but she instinctively knew how he felt. Shoot, now that she thought about it, her adopted family in Naples disliked him too.

Yet, she still stayed.

Sidney had also hoped that when she announced she was moving in with Noelle and Celia that he would've taken offense because he actually already had an apartment. It would cause a huge argument followed by an inevitable breakup—easy passive-aggressive peasy.

It didn't happen. Nelson just asked her to keep an eye on his apartment when he was out to sea. His command, the USS Dwight Eisenhower[8] —the Ike—an old aircraft carrier, had recently come out of the shipyard and was doing shakedowns to test for readiness. Nelson hated going out to sea, and for the life of her, Sidney didn't understand why he chose to come back to Norfolk. But his absences suited Sidney just fine. She avoided the fact that they had a horrible relationship, and she had time to do her schoolwork in peace. But the closer she got to completing her master's, the clingier and more patronizing he became.

Irritated with her intrusive thoughts, Sidney shrugged as she opened the door to the stairs leading to her bedroom. "I find conversations with himsoothing. Especially after talking to you."

"Hmmm." Was all Noelle said as she followed her up the flight of stairs.

"Hmmm, what, Noelle?" Sidney took the brushed silver ball studs out of her ears as she crossed the threshold to her bedroom and put them in the small ceramic dish on her dresser. She should have told her that she wanted to be alone. But she doubted that Noelle would have listened anyway.

"Wellll..." Noelle began. She flopped down on Sidney's bed, wrinkling her white comforter and grabbing one of the decorative pillows to lay on while knocking the rest of

---

8. USS Dwight D. Eisenhower (CVN-69) (known informally as "Ike") is a nuclear-powered aircraft carrier currently in service with the United States Navy.

them askew. "I'm just thinking like I always do when Nelson is brought to my attention—"

"No, ma'am." Sidney walked over to Noelle and snatched the pillow from under her head. "Get off my bed Noelle, and please don't start it up again." Her right eyelid twitched as her OCD kicked in. She didn't sleep with her comforter. She rolled it down to the foot of her bed and used her blanket like a civilized person, and her decorative pillows never touched her head. They were for decoration only, and she placed them on the chair in front of her vanity. Noelle knew this.

Why is Noelle so damn ornery? Jesus, be a Prozac pill for my nerves.

"Why are you with him? I keep on asking you that, and you never tell me why." Not missing a breath, Noelle folded her arms underneath her head and rested her chin on them. "Girl, you're back in the States, at the largest naval base on the East Coast. It's a Black man with benefits—not that you need them—candy store. Big dicks, little dicks, marshmallow, caramel, coffee-brown, pecan, toffee, walnut, Bombay mahogany, curly hair, nappy hair, hair with ramen noodle waves—It's like *Crazy Eddie's*! It has me straight trippin' that we have everything here at our fingertips, and you settle for beige-ass Nelson, and that's in color *and* in spirit. He's a walking pair of orthopedic shoes with the velcro. You know the ones with the thick-ass soles? Yeah, that's him."

"Trippin' over the fact that I'm in a steady relationship? I know it's an unfamiliar topic for you to comprehend, so take your time with it." On the defense, Sidney took a dig at Noelle's flight risk status when it came to men. She was 5:1 to Sidney in the two years they'd been stationed together.

"Better to have a relationship with a quicksand foundation than be in a relationship with a man like Nelson. Besides my long list of complaints, which you have not addressed in a timely manner, he seriously thinks he's deep. Deep as the deepest ocean and every word, opinion, theory, the judgment he spits out is profound and earth-shattering, and we should be grateful that he graced us with his fucking *Snapple* bottle knowledge. Get the fuck outta here with that shit. You got his head gassed up and—again—I don't know why. And until you tell me, I will keep on asking questions." Noelle sat up and threw a pillow at Sidney's head.

Sidney caught the pillow in midair and put it on the chair behind her. "And I don't know why you're messing up my bed," was all she could manage to say. Taking a deep breath, she blew it out slowly. She wanted to argue and defend herself, but she couldn't. Every word Noelle said was painfully accurate, and that wasn't the worst of it.

Nelson critiqued everything she did. From the way she made the bed, if there were water spots on the faucet in *her* bathroom (God forbid she did that at his place) if her cooking wasn't the best, but still, he didn't bother to do it. He made sly remarks about her weight even though there was nothing wrong with it. She has always been within BMI standards. He tried to buy clothes he thought would look good on her, and by good, he meant to hide all her curves. She had over a dozen tunic tops hanging up in her closet that she needed to donate to Goodwill. He even tried to go to the hairdresser with her, and when she refused, he made sure he let her know how much he loved her long hair and to not let the hairdresser cut too much of it off.

For the life of her, Sidney couldn't remember him being like this in Naples. He was boring as heck, yes, but this controlling and manipulative, no. Maybe he suppressed it, or maybe she just ignored it. She didn't form really close friendships overseas, and the few people she hung around with were married with kids, so he had her all to himself. He started changing when she got around Noelle and Celia, and there was the potential to have a life that didn't revolve around him.

"Sidney Rosemarie Pascal, why did you ignore his phone call?" Noelle sang out.

Feeling overwhelmed as she always did when dealing with conversations about Nelson, Sidney pulled the scrunchie from her ponytail and ran her hands through her shoulder-length dark brown hair. It was dry. She needed deep conditioning and a change of topic. "Nothing. Like I said, I'm tired."

"Tired of Nelson. I understand."

"I didn't say that."

"You alluded to it. It's all over your body language." Noelle waved her hands in the air. "I be reading that shit you give me about body language and mirroring the client, reflecting and reframing, except for the active listening. I am not doing that shit. But anyway, you're feeling insecure."

"I am not!" Sidney protested even as she folded her arms over her chest.

"Now you're in a defensive posture." Noelle looked pointedly at Sidney's arms.

Sidney groaned, dropping her arms. "Get out of my room so I can take a shower."

"You know what I miss—" Noelle began. She stood up and made a show of smoothing Sidney's comforter and fluffing and straightening the remaining pillows. "—the woman who laughed when Bernard ran over her foot with his car so she wouldn't transfer to Spain. Now *she* was exciting! I'd like her back, please, and thank you."

"Oh my God, no. Uh-uh." Sidney shook her head slowly. "Only you would think that possibly going to Captain's Mast for dereliction of duty and maybe having to hire a defense lawyer for your boyfriend was *exciting*. It wasn't. I was laughing out of shock and self-denial of my predicament."

Noelle put her hands on her hips and rolled her eyes. "Whatever. I was there. You enjoyed the crazy. I saw it in your eyes."

"No! You saw the fear of losing half my paycheck for forty-five days and reduction of rank," Sidney shot back. Since Noelle showed no sign of leaving, Sidney took her dungarees off and tossed them into the wicker hamper in the corner.

"What I now fear is that you're going to let that man keep touching your no-no place. I know that you fake your orgasms." Noelle held up her hand when Sidney opened her mouth. "Don't try to deny it, I hear you. Newsflash: we can hear you in the living room. You're just over the garage, not in a whole 'nother house. I have been traumatized by his grunts followed by your 70s porn star moans. What the hell is going on up there? Never mind, I don't want to know. But bad sex aside, and underneath all that patronizing pomposity, Nelson is nothing but breath and britches."

Completely exhausted by the conversation and the feelings it brought up, Sidney felt like her whole body frowned along with her mouth. "Noelle, what does that even mean?"

Noelle put her hands on her hips. "It means he's nothing but the air he breathes and the pants he's wearing. That's it. He's just occupying space, ain't worth shit. I know he doesn't support you getting your master's because it'll show the world that he ain't on your level, never been on your level, and never will be. Not only are you too damn pretty for him, but you're also smart and empathic and people respond to you because you listen to them, and they know you care about them. You got a big-ass future ahead of you, either in the Navy or as a civilian. The *only* thing that negro has going for him is that he has you on his arm, and he knows it. So anything he can do to dim your light, to keep you in place–he does. I see how he treats you. Don't ever expect me to co-sign your relationship with him because I will always want more for you."

"I know," Sidney said softly. She was taken aback by the seriousness in Noelle's tone. They had conversations about Nelson before, but never like this. She was always able to deflect Noelle's nagging, but she was in rare form today. Noelle had an uncanny knack for peeling back layers of your emotions and letting light into all those dark places you wanted to keep hidden. She didn't do it often, but when she did, it was with surgical precision.

"Good, because you deserve someone who wants you to shine and then bask in your light. And," Noelle started, wagging her finger at Sidney,

"Oh boy." Sidney braced herself. By the way, Noelle said, "and" she knew she was about to say some mess.

"*And* you also deserve someone who's gonna dick you down on demand. Look at you. Look at your body! Do you even look at it? I look at it. Not in a sexual way. Just outta pure jealousy. You should be on one of those velour paintings where the woman is lying naked on a bear rug, straddling a tiger or something. All you're missing is the afro. And Nadia is like twenty-one—"

"She's fourteen," Sidney interjected, "Just fourteen."

"But you don't even look like you had a baby. Titties still perky, with no stretch marks. Who has a thirteen-pound baby and gets no stretch marks? You don't even have them on your big ole ass. My ass is two times smaller than yours, and I have them. You have no cellulite, no nothing. You barely have crow's feet, and you're almost fifty."

Sidney narrowed her eyes. "First of all, Nadia was six pounds and three ounces, and I am only forty-one."

Though Noelle was right, she did have a fantastic body. Her 36C's hardly changed even though Nadia nursed for eleven months. She had a tiny waist to complement her full hips, maintained her diamond gap between her thick thighs, and had that big homegrown Texas booty that drew attention no matter what she wore. Her dark brown eyes were always twinkling. She had eyes like a damn Disney princess. Noelle said that's why people were always trying to talk to her and her full lips were always ready to smile. Her flawless, dark brown complexion, which she was teased about when she was younger, glistened when she put some shea butter on it. It took her almost all her adult life to fall in love with and be comfortable in her skin when society and her fellow Black people valued light skin. She had made it one of her missions to uplift any little brown-skinned girl or woman who came across her path. Sometimes she wished her nose wasn't so big, she was teased about that too as a child, but since she wasn't going under the knife, she embraced that as well.

"*Whatever*," Noelle said, tossing her head dramatically. "Forty-one, fifty, close enough. The fact remains that you're willingly sharing your brickhouse body with Nelson. And that's just *nasty*. And not nasty in a good way. Nasty in a South Bronx sidewalk kinda way."

"Now that's just doggone rude. So, again, for the third time, get out of my room." Sidney pointed to the open door.

"Aht, aht, I am not done. You goan get these words today. Sidney, c'mon we're in our prime, and not to mention you're an old lady, so your hormones gotta be outta control, so we should be having the best sex of our lives. You need a man who ain't gonna care if you washed your ass before he fucks you, just be happy that you bring him that pussy, dirty and all, girl. Then bust a nut, roll over and go to sleep, wake up, and do it again in a pussy that has just been marinating in that shit, so you just slide right in." Noelle ignored the little gag Sidney made and kept on going. "You're wasting your Brazilian on him, 'cause I know he ain't appreciating your smooth butthole. And by appreciating it, I mean licking it, because what else is a smooth butthole for if not for licking? I mean, keep the bunny tail on if you ain't getting it licked," Noelle said. Taking a deep breath, she exhaled and dropped down into a curtsy. "On that note, my dear shipmate, I will take my leave because by the look on your face, I have given you enough food for thought. So I bid you a good day, m'lady." She gave her a sharp nod and left, shutting the door behind her.

Food for thought, indeed. Sidney stared at the door, listening to Noelle thud down the carpeted steps. Sighing, she turned and studied her reflection in her vanity mirror. Indeed, her brickhouse body was being wasted on Nelson or, rather, Breath and Britches.

Not to mention the example she was setting for Nadia by settling for a man that she knew wasn't worthy of her. Especially when her daddy was such a good man. Her momma was a sad, sad woman.

Noelle was right about everything she said, especially the part about Sidney needing a man who was gonna tear her Precious up. Not bring it to him dirty, though, and she was also iffy on the booty licking because that didn't sound very sanitary. But she did have a soul craving for a man that would make her do things she'd be ashamed to admit to her friends—even to Noelle and Celia's nasty behinds—but keep on going back for more because she knew that he could make her come anywhere, anytime. A *girl could only dream...*

A man popped up in Sidney's mind, but she shook her head, clearing the image away. Now that one *definitely* ain't happening.

However, something *did* need to be done about Nelson. She did not want him meeting her on the peir when they came back First, though, she needed to get her thoughts in order. She always made better decisions after a long, hot shower. The water washed all confusing, muddled thoughts away and left everything pristine and crystal clear. She quickly finished undressing, tossed her clothes in the wicker hamper, and headed into the bathroom.

Chapter Nine

Lt Quentin Jacobs

*I*t's *about damn time.* Quentin looked down the refrigerated aisle in the 7-Eleven and finally saw the woman he couldn't get out of his mind. It had been four days and nine hours since Noelle drove away from him. He felt damn foolish coming back to the store multiple times a day. He swore the cashier was starting to look at him crazy. He was always diligent about not letting his gas tank go below half a tank, but it stayed on full over these past few days. What if this had just been a random stop for her? He'd been debating with himself on whether he should just get a part-time job here when he walked down the aisle—and there she was.

Noelle looked like a totally different woman today. Her bushy hair was now curly, and it looked soft to the touch instead of dry and brittle. In all his years of dating, he'd never been with a woman who rocked her natural hair. All of his women had hair down their backs, whether natural or from the beauty supply store. Replacing her Navy sweats were a pair of light-wash baggy Levi's with a frayed hole on one knee. They looked well-worn and comfortable. Her orange halter top showed off her toned arms and back muscles—he loved a woman who worked out, but the little pooch that poked out under the hem of the shirt was in contradiction to her upper body. He didn't mind a soft center, though, he wanted to touch it. Or bite it, to be more precise.

"Do I need a six or twelve pack, hmmm?" She said as he came up behind her.

"Do you always talk to yourself in public, Noelle?" Quentin asked.

"Sonovabitch!" Noelle jumped, then glanced back over her shoulder. Her eyes narrowed when she saw who he was. Cutting her eyes at him, she turned back around and continued her search. "You always try to holla at a girl when you got another one waiting for you in the car, *Quentin*?" She opened the cooler door and bent over to pick up a twelve-pack of Corona.

Quentin knew she was going to bring that up, and he was ready. "That was Cynthia, my ex-wife. Her car was in the shop, and I was just taking her to work."

"Umph." Noelle straightened up and spun around so quickly that Quentin didn't have a chance to step back. She stumbled against him, and he grabbed her waist to steady her. Her curls tickled the skin underneath his chin.

"First of all, somehow you're way taller than I remembered. I'm not sure how I feel about that. And seriously, you gotta come a little better than that." Frown in full effect, Noelle leaned back to look up at him.

Eyes wide, Quentin nodded. "It's da truth. I swear on mi madda." In his attempt to express his earnestness, he defaulted to patios.

"Well ya maada goan be dead den cuz pure lies you ah tell," Noelle answered. "And mi think there's ah lickkle bit of miscommunication between da two auh you because the look she did gimme cudda knock mi down dead!"

Quentin was more than a little surprised when Noelle

switched from standard American English to patios as well. But even so, the accent wasn't strong. Her parents were probably West Indian. That information gave the whole 'sacrificing chicken' question a bit more context. Shit! He always seemed to attract West Indian women. It didn't matter where he went, he would always seem to find the one in his vicinity, usually to his detriment. Because ninety percent of the time it didn't work out too well for him. That was something to mull about later, but right now, he just needed to get back in her good graces.

"I know, it's totally my fault. I know how Cynthia is, but when I started talking to you, I simply forgot all about her. Can you blame me? It's not every day I get to buy gas for a woman who wants me to sacrifice a chicken for her."

Noelle rolled her eyes, but she was smiling. "You keep on bringing it up, so I really think you wanna do it." She laughed and then sobered up quickly. "I am standing way too close to you."

Quentin's hands reflectively tightened around her waist. "I disagree. I think you're still a little bit too far away."

Noelle sighed, her eyes swept over his face, lingering on his lips before meeting his eyes again. Tilting her head to the side, she said, "You know we have gotta stop meeting in the 7–Eleven like this."

"We're inside this time, so I feel like we're making progress." He squeezed her waist again, pleased when she didn't object.

"Yeah, as long as no woman is lurking in the aisles waiting to scratch my eyes out." Noelle leaned to the side and peeked around him, then back at his face.

"I promise you that will never happen again." Quentin watched the indecision play across her face by way of furrowed eyebrows and pursed lips. His story sounded thin even to him, but she hadn't asked him to let her go. Nor had she stepped back. *And* she remembered his name. "You smell good."

"I know." A small, satisfied smile replaced Noelle's frown.

Quentin leaned down and rested his cheek against her temple, and inhaled the scent deeper this time. "Do you, now?" he murmured in her ear. He felt her shiver against him. Noelle slid her hand up to his chest, and it was his turn to shiver. She rubbed her temple against his cheek, her curls tickling his skin. He couldn't resist touching her hair and twirled a short lock around his finger. It was as soft as it looked. He was this close to burying his face in her hair.

"My cousin made it for me. She gets the oils from down 125th Street and makes her own perfumes out of them. This one is honeysuckle, sandalwood, and Egyptian musk, I think," Noelle said, softening against him.

"She should bottle it and sell it," Quentin said. He remembered the stands lining the blocks on Harlem's 125th Street during the summer festivals selling the little brown bottles of oils, incense, artwork, and literature. Had he known the oils smelled like this, he would've bought them out. He wondered if she smelled like that all over.

"Heck no, this is my signature scent," Noelle slapped lightly at his chest. "I don't want anyone else smelling like me. When you smell this perfume, you'll know that Noelle has been here."

Quentin straightened up. "I doubt you need perfume to leave an impression."

"Facts. But scents hold memories. You smell something and remember where you were and what you were doing and more importantly, who you were with," Noelle said.

"Again, I don't think you need all the bells and whistles to be remembered," Quentin said.

"I didn't ask you if I did." Noelle's smile was tinged with ice around the edges.

"I was just offering my opinion," Quentin said in a soothing tone. He tucked away Noelle's sensitivity to people's opinions along with her accent for further evaluation later.

"Well, offer something else." Her smile was a touch softer, but not by much.

"Dinner," Quentin quickly offered. "Will you let me take you out to dinner, Noelle?"

Noelle sighed deeply. "It's only fair since you promised to kill a chicken for me." She lightly pushed at his chest.

Quentin reluctantly let her go. He immediately missed the softness and the heat of her body against his. His shirt probably smelled like her. He hoped so. "You're really going to make me do that, aren't you?"

"You brought it up again, so I think you want to get back in touch with your roots." Noelle started to laugh but stopped when she glanced down the aisle and frowned.

What the fuck? What now? Quentin followed Noelle's gaze to the brother who stood in the middle of the aisle holding a six-pack of beer, staring at Noelle with his brows raised. What is all this about? He knew this wasn't her man. Her reaction to seeing him wasn't anxiety or embarrassment. She was pissed! Her whole demeanor had changed. Her back went straight, her shoulders tensed up, her eyes narrowed, and her chin tilted out aggressively. By comparison, ole dude's attitude and smirk were relaxed—cocky even, like they shared a secret. And if Quentin asked, he would surely spill it. Noelle left him standing there by the refrigerator aisle and met the man before he reached them.

Quentin couldn't help but note the irony of the situation now. He watched the terse exchange with Noelle and the man who he surmised was an ex. *She* had the nerve to talk about *him.* For a hot second, he considered just walking away because their conversation seemed to be getting a little heated. He wanted her, but he was too old to be out here fighting over a woman. In a convenience store, nonetheless, but the thought was quickly followed by a hell no, go get that woman!

In the end, she made the decision for him. Shoving the six-pack into the guy's chest, she strode past him. He called after her, but she just kept on walking until she exited the store. He didn't follow her, just stared in her direction, his longing and frustration clearly written all over his face. Putting the drinks down on a shelf, he shook his head and went back down the same aisle without even sparing a glance at Quentin. They both just left him standing there like he was invisible.

Wuh da rass? This was the second time he missed an opportunity with her because of outside interference. He wasted over a week coming back to the store in hopes of seeing her, and now he absolutely refused to run after her. Annoyed, he snatched up a bottle of water out of the cooler. His cousin, Paul, who had accompanied him, appeared at his side holding a Slurpee.

"I saw you tryin' to holla at that chick. You losin' your game, old man?" Paul teased.

He better not be. Quentin ground his teeth. He was only thirty-eight. He gave his cousin a withering glance before heading up to the cashier. Chuckling, Paul followed him. He was so angry he didn't trust himself to speak or look around for the man. He was pretty damn sure he'd say something, and then they'd be fighting, and that would solve nothing. Noelle was already gone without so much as a backward glance. Sighing, he paid for his water. He should've changed it for a bottle of gin.

A couple of minutes later, he was backing his car out when he noticed a smudge on his windshield. He pulled the wiper handle, washing fluid squirted up, and the wipers began to swoosh back and forth. A scrap of pink paper went with it. He pulled the car back into the parking space and retrieved the slip of paper. Unfolding the damp paper gingerly, he read the name 'Noelle,' scrawled on it in loopy handwriting, along with a telephone number.

He smiled.

Chapter Ten

LT Quentin Jacobs

"**I** would be totally remiss if I didn't mention the irony of the situation," Noelle said as soon as she heard his voice.

"Because I'm a gentleman, I wasn't going to mention that, but since you brought it up, was that a recent or an old ex?" Quentin wasted no time calling Noelle; by the way their interactions were going, she might get abducted by aliens if he waited until the next day. Besides, he was a grown man, there was no reason to play those cool man games. He knew what he wanted, and he was going to get it.

"Old-*ish*, I guess. I wouldn't even consider him an ex, really. I really shouldn't have even acknowledged him. So I sincerely apologize for..." Noelle's voice faded.

"For running away the second time?" Quentin suggested. He really wanted to ask her, if he was so unimportant, why didn't she just ignore him? He also wanted to know if this guy was going to be an issue in the future, but that could wait. He leaned against the headboard on the bed in his parents' guest bedroom. He could hear them yelling at the contestants on *Wheel of Fortune* downstairs.

"Hey, hey now," Noelle protested. "That first time was all you, man."

"But if you had stuck around, I would have explained

everything to you. I might've even introduced you to Cynthia." Quentin couldn't help but laugh at that last part. That would have never happened.

Apparently, Noelle thought it was funny too, because she laughed. "Uh-uh, now you're getting *all* outta pocket because I don't think it would've gone over well with that one. She looked highly upset with you."

"She's cool. We had a talk after you ran away." Quentin smiled into the phone. He liked her laugh. It was quick, bubbly, and unpretentious. "Anyway, how's that attention span been treating you?"

"Issa mess! Jesus! I am literally thinking of four different things right now. I have to get my summer uniforms from the cleaners, get an oil change, rotate my tires, call my mom—she called me two days ago, and I forgot to call her back, *and* I need to buy cinnamon because I used the last of it yesterday!"

Oh damn! Quentin made a face at the phone receiver. Noelle was not kidding when she said her mother diagnosed her. Something indeed was going on in her brain. "That was five."

She harrumphed. "Yeah, I added that last one because I'm eating like my third cinnamon roll of the day."

"You know that sugar makes you hyper right?" Quentin said cautiously.

"It doesn't do that to me. It never has. I'm just always hyped. Sometimes I wonder if I should take a sedative to go to bed tonight because I just be wide awake thinking of how to take over the world."

Quentin was torn between groaning and laughing. "You just might, Brain. Or I could come over and teach you some of those methods I was telling you about before you ran away."

"First of all, Pinky, my flight risk status is not up for discussion anymore. Secondly, I can literally feel the blood running through my veins right now. What can you do for me right now, Doctor?"

I can give you some of this dick. That'll calm your ass down. But instead, he said, "I can show you better than I can tell you. I don't want anything to get lost in translation." There was a moment of silence, and Quentin wondered if he pushed too fast too soon.

"Oh, yeah I forget your methods are intensive, aren't they?"

Quentin relaxed at the soft curiosity in Noelle's voice. "Very."

"*Well*, I guess I ought to at least give you the chance to work on me then. In the name of science, of course," she added in a serious tone. "You got a pen and paper handy? I need to give you my address."

Quentin chuckled softly. "Of course." Then he hopped off the bed to find a pen and paper. "Oh, and what dry cleaners are your clothes at?"

"Why?"

"Because I'm going to pick them up on my way out to you." Quentin paused. "Unless you don't want me to." There were a few seconds of silence, and he thought Noelle had hung up.

"No, it's fine. Oh, but wait, it's on the base, so never mind."

"Which one?"

"NOB[1]. Can you get on it?"

"I can," Quentin replied, then took a deep breath. It was wishful thinking that she wore those silver earrings be-

---

1. NOB: Norfolk Naval Station, Norfolk, Virginia

cause she liked them and not because she was enlisted. He needed to tell her that he was an officer. "I need to let you know something."

Noelle hissed. "Okay..."

"I'm a lieutenant. I'm getting out this September, but I'm still on active duty."

There was another long silence for a moment, then Noelle said, "I guess I should probably give you my last name as well since you just can't say you're here to pick up Noelle's clothes. It's Bentley."

"Noelle Bentley. I like it." Quentin didn't push further because he didn't live in Norfolk. No one would know he was an officer unless he told them, and he was getting out anyway. If she was cool with it, then he was cool with it.

"I'll make sure to tell my mother when I talk to her later ," Noelle quipped.

Quentin chuckled. "You do that."

After she gave him her address, they chatted for the next few minutes; their conversation veered towards their commonality of having parents and what it was like to grow up as American kids raised by West Indian parents. She was a first-generation American, and he spent his youth in St. Croix before moving to New York City during junior high school. They both had lived in New York City though he lived uptown and she was in the South Bronx. They both had favorite aunties who would throw house parties, and they would sneak in and dance with the grownups. They both used outhouses and the village shower when they visited their relatives on the islands. He was okay with using public facilities. However, Noelle had been completely horrified.

"I was ten when we first to St. Kitts for summer vacation. I used the outhouse once. I pooped in a bucket after that.

I feel like no one told me there were no indoor bathrooms at my great-grandmother's house. We had a kitchen but no bathroom. But the village shower was the highlight of my trip. Me and one of the village girls peeked at this guy taking a shower, so the trip wasn't completely a wash," Noelle said with a laugh.

Quentin also laughed. "You were fresh, eh!"

"Yeah, I was. I am so glad my great-grandmother didn't bust my bad ass because I'm pretty sure she saw me. Man, I was terrible. Oh, you know what? Before we get off this phone, what's your sign?"

"Why?" Quentin frowned at Noelle's business-like tone. He liked astrology, but he didn't put any stock into it. It was just something fun to do.

"Because I want to know."

"If I tell you, are you going to judge me without actually getting to know me?"

"Judge is such a harsh word. I prefer to think that I am doing my due diligence."

"Is that what you call it?"

"Absolutely. So what is your sign?"

Quentin exhaled. "I'm not gonna tell you just yet." He continued talking over Noelle's loud objections. "Let's be in each other's company for at least five minutes without some weird shit happening, and then I'll tell you."

"So, like, do you think that's possible? I feel like you're setting me up for failure."

"Whoa, dial back your optimism. I wouldn't want anyone to think that you're a Pollyanna or anything like that."

Noelle huffed. "Shut up. Well, I guess since you're coming to my house, we should be okay. But you gotta tell me before you leave my house."

"You have a deal. Now—" Quentin started, only to be

interrupted by Noelle.

"Ooh, that's my Mommy on the other line. See you in a few...?"

"Yup, around six."

"'Kay. Bye."

Quentin didn't get a chance to say goodbye before she hung up. Shaking his head, he put the phone back on the base. Another interesting conversation. He wouldn't have imagined that they'd be talking about outhouses and horoscopes. Not that he should be surprised since they spoke of sacrificing a chicken at a gas pump. The most exciting thing about her was that she seemed totally at ease with her eccentricity, although he wasn't sure if that was a good or a bad thing. He figured that he'd find out soon enough.

What he did know for sure was that he loved her voice and the way she laughed, the heat of her body when she leaned against him, her smart mouth, and the roll of her hips when she angrily walked away from him. She had the same walk that Bob Marley said of his wife, Rita—she walk an' she roll. In just this short conversation, she had more in common with his upbringing than Cynthia, whose family was upper-class and involved in politics in St. Croix. His family were shopkeepers and farmers.

Quentin felt the familiar stirrings of irritation that came along with thoughts of Cynthia. He'd been so busy thinking about Noelle he hadn't processed their conversation. He was going to have to see her in a whole new light and accept his part in what had gone wrong because things didn't happen in a vacuum. He didn't know how long it was going to take him to adjust. He spent the past sixteen years blaming her for everything, and the backwash of their relationship always managed to sneak its way into his current relationships, especially if they shared a Caribbean background.

He usually found a way to compare them to Cynthia and, not surprisingly, often found similarities between them. Once that happened, it was only a matter of time before he stopped seeing them.

With Cynthia's admission, he was going to retrain his traumatized brain so it could stop asking the usual questions: What if she was like Cynthia? And more specifically, would she try to trap him in a relationship? Now those questions no longer held the same weight. So he had to figure his shit out because wanted the same strong and loving and sometimes annoying relationship his parents had for the past forty-two years.

But that was an issue for another time. Shaking his head, Quentin looked at his watch. He'd better get moving, he needed to take a shower, run some errands for his parents, and go all the way across town to the base to pick up Noelle's dry cleaning. He wouldn't dare be late; he didn't want to anger the dating gods.

Chapter Eleven

PHI Noelle Bentley

T he second Noelle got off the phone with her mother, she booked it to Celia's room and burst in without knocking.

"One of these days, you're gonna walk into someone's room unannounced and see something you can't unsee," Celia warned, putting the book she was reading on the bed.

"As long as you hold that position so I can run and get my government-issued camera so I can do unauthorized shit with it, I'm cool with it." Noelle flopped down on her stomach next to Celia. "Anyway, listen, Quentin is coming over later."

"Over to where?" Celia asked incredulously. "Here?"

"Yes, here. To this house. Where do you think 'here' was referring to?" Noelle rolled to her side.

"*Oh.* You just never invite anyone over. We've lived here for two years, and no one's been here. Sidney and I joke about not wanting to sit in the backseat of your car because that's where you must have sex. Your avoidance issues about bringing someone into your home should be discussed in your next counseling session."

Noelle narrowed her eyes at Celia. "I don't have a counselor, Celia."

"But you should. *You should*," Celia pressed.

"Only if you come with me. 'Relationship Avoidance' is track number one in the *You About To Fuck Up Your Life* soundtrack. There's like ten songs on it."

"Ummm, I didn't know there was a soundtrack," Celia said dryly.

"Oh yes, honey! Participating—nay, actively running and back flipping into unhealthy relationships, is the second hot track, titled 'Firestarter' with a rap by Lil Kim. Number three is 'Staring at the Phone' in parentheses' waiting for it to ring. Track four is 'Lonely Holidays'. Number five is 'You Know I Love You But My Kids Need Me'. Number six is 'How Do I Know If This Is My Baby?', and the DNA remix version is with Foxy Brown because we can't forget the Ill Na-Na. But I'm not all up in your bed to talk about *your* life. What should I wear?"

"I hate you. You are *literally* the worst person I know." Celia grabbed one of the pillows from behind her head and threw it at her. "Okay, let's go back to the beginning. Why is he coming here? You don't even, like, *know* him. You picked him up at the corner store. What song is that? 'Bodega Boo'?"

"It was a 7-Eleven, okay."

"It's the white people's bodega."

"You right." Groaning, Noelle buried her face in the pillow Celia threw at her. "I don't know why I wanna let him come over." Her voice was muffled. Taking the pillow off her face, she sat up. "And he's picking up my dry cleaning. He offered, and I said yes."

"I don't understand. What's happening here?" Celia reached over and felt Noelle's forehead. "Are you sick or something?"

Noelle swatted her hand away. "No, I'm not sick. I don't know why I invited him over. All he did was smile at me. He ain't even tell me I was pretty, but he did say I smelled good. Does that count?"

Celia squinted at Noelle. "I don't know what you want me to say."

"I don't know either. And he won't even tell me his sign. He's all like *'Get to know me first'.*" Noelle sucked her teeth.

Celia threw her hands up in the air. "Imagine that. He's trippin' fo' real."

"I feel like you're mocking me."

"That feeling is correct. You base way too much on people's horoscopes. You judge them without even getting to know them."

Noelle tapped a finger against her lip. "That's what he said, but if you can tell me a time when I have been wrong, I'll stop. Santiago gonna lock you up in one of those Boatswain's Mate lockers; just watch and see. And I ain't gonna save you. So what should I wear?"

Celia rolled her eyes. "Wear the denim dress, the sleeveless one with the snaps. It shows off your arms, and it makes your ass look good. More importantly, it's easy access, should you require it."

"You're right. One quick tug and it's titties for sale. Panties? No panties?"

"I'm gonna say panties, preferably with a liner. Because all he did was say you smelled good, and now you're inviting him over to our home, so you might bust a nut if he holds your hand, and I don't want you to ruin my sofa. Oh, and make sure you take him to your room."

Noelle scooted off the bed. "First, you were all super-supportive, and then you say shit like that."

"And since he has not been vetted in any way, shape, or form, I reserve the right to send him away if he gives off stranger danger vibes. What time is he coming? I need to find my mace."

"You don't need your mace. Just have the phone close by. Oh, and he's an officer too. He said he's getting out soon, though."

Celia grunted. "An officer? What rank? What command?"

Noelle shrugged. "I don't know. I didn't ask. He said he was getting out in September."

Brow furrowing, Celia shook her head. "This is so very irresponsible of you, Noelle."

"I know. It's crazy, right? Are you still making margaritas tonight? I might need some libations to get through this because I am so nervous," Noelle said as she walked out of the room.

"Not nervous. *Insane.* Yes, I am making them, because the man I want is at home with his wife and family, so what the hell else have I got to do?" Celia said.

"Track number seven!" Noelle said quickly and shut the bedroom door avoiding the second pillow that flew through the air.

What was it about Quentin that had her all giddy? Noelle thought as she made her way back to her room to search for her denim dress. He had her feeling like a sixteen-year-old waiting for her date to pick her up and hopefully fuck her in the back seat of his car. (She *did* have a thing for back seats.) None of that ever actually happened in her teenage years because she rode the New York City transit system. She didn't go on her first real date until she got to her first command. So she supposed this is how she might have felt had any of those boys she chased after in high school said yes.

Right now, she was all flushed, and her tummy was bubbling. She wasn't sure if she needed to eat something or go poop. It was all so confusing. This is why she didn't let men make the first move; it threw her completely off balance. Quentin approached her twice, and she was doubly confused. All that confusion usually sent her into interrogation mode. Like, why was he here? What did he want from her? In the back of her mind, she knew all her neurotic questions were ridiculous, and that was why she was going to end up alone with nothing. Not even with cats because she didn't like them.

Giving up control over how she wanted things done and simply trusting someone was something she just couldn't do. She was constantly amazed that she stayed in the Navy for this long since she had minimal control or even the pretense of control over what happened in her life. She always teased Sidney about her love for structure and organization, but Noelle secretly liked the structure the military provided. She still didn't make proper lists and check things off like Sidney did—wooooo, Sidney loved her planner a little too much, but the Navy gave them both what they needed: monotony. She would never admit that the wild child of the South Bronx, who rebelled against everything for no damn reason, actually enjoyed her boring-ass rate. It took a lot of pressure off her overactive brain. Having a real job that required her to have a good work ethic and still have a life was something she couldn't even imagine. She was quietly panicked about the afterlife that some call retirement. She really had to study for the Chief's exam this year.

However, that was not today's problem. Today's problem, or rather a mystery, was why in the heck did she have this man coming to her house after only meeting him twice at a damn gas station? That was worse than the club. Lawd ah mercy! She found her dress and threw it on her bed.

I just hope he's not a serial killer, Constance muttered in her head.

"He's not a serial killer. Name one Black serial killer," Noelle said out loud and waited for Constance to answer while she undressed.

"Exactly," Noelle said when Constance was silent.

"*Esta loca*," Celia called out as she walked past her bedroom door.

Noelle made a face at the empty doorway and went to take a shower.

Chapter Twelve

LT Quentin Jacobs

Four hours later, Quentin stood outside Noelle's front door waiting for her to answer. After what felt like an eternity, he pressed the doorbell again. The second time was the charm. She opened the door, drink in hand. Judging by the sparkle in her eyes, she had already had one or two.

"I'm sorry. I was in the kitchen. Celia's making margaritas, I didn't hear the door over the blender. Were you out here long?" she asked, stepping aside to let him in.

"Just about thirty minutes. I thought you gave me the wrong address," Quentin shut the door behind him.

Noelle sucked her teeth. "Stop lying. It only takes, like, seconds to blend the ice. Why would I give you my number and then give you the wrong address? That's dumb. Besides, I wanted to see if you were actually going to get my dry cleaning." She took the uniforms he held out and draped them over her arm.

"Why would I say I would and not do it?" Quentin asked.

"Why would you think I gave you the wrong address?" Noelle returned.

"Touché." Quentin tipped his imaginary hat at Noelle. "I got you something else." He held a small brown paper bag.

"What is it?" Noelle eyed the bag suspiciously.

"Just take it and see, maybe?"

"I'm not really a gift-receiving kinda person. I know they say all women want gifts bu—"

"Mi rass, woman, take the bag!" Quentin shook it at her.

"When you say it like that, how can I refuse?" Noelle scrunched up her face and took the bag gingerly. Opening it, she peeked inside, squealed, and then peaked inside again. "You brought me cinnamon powder *and* cinnamon sticks?" She reached in and pulled out a bottle. Holding it up, she looked at the label. "Oooh, these are fancy too. I take back everything I said about you."

Quentin shot her a wary look. "You didn't say anything."

"It was all up in my head." She tapped her temple. "I had so many words for you. C'mon, let's go to the living room. Celia's gonna think you kidnapped me if we don't get back there."

Laughing, Quentin shook his head at her and followed her down the short hallway, admiring the way her denim-covered bottom swayed in front of him. She really did have a nice ass. Not too big, not too small. A nice handful. His gaze dropped down to her shiny, toned calves, slim ankles, and the smooth back of her heels.

"Have a seat." Noelle patted the top cushions of the brown leather sofa. "I need to go put these clothes in my room. Would you like something to drink?"

"Do you have gin and tonic?"

"I have no idea. I don't like making drinks. Celia does. I'll ask her." Noelle disappeared down the hall.

Whoever Celia was, he figured he'd meet her soon enough. Quentin sat back and glanced around the contemporary-style room. Everything was in neutral tones, from the brown leather furniture to the cream curtains. The only pop of color was the set of orange throw pillows. It almost looked like no one ever used the room.

"Celia's making your drink." Noelle came back into the room and sat down on the other end of the sofa, tucking one leg underneath her. "It feels like you're in a hotel lobby, doesn't it? We never actually sit in here. We're always in the kitchen or in each other's rooms."

Quentin nodded. "A little bit, but it's nice."

"Quentin said this living room décor is boring. It's like we are at the Days Inn or something," Noelle said the second the attractive Hispanic woman walked into the room carrying two drinks. "I keep on telling her to let me decorate."

What the hell? Quentin straightened up, ready to object, but the woman spoke first after handing him his gin and tonic.

"Yanno, I can make it so that you are actually living in the Days Inn, right?"

Noelle made a face and shrugged. "At least I'd have someone to clean my room."

"Yup and probably crabs. And no, you are not redecorating. For the one thousandth and third time, glitter and paisley on everything is not a design style." Celia handed Noelle her drink.

"It's not glitter on *everything*, just glitter on some things. What you got against glitter? And paisley is awesome."

"Everything. Shush." Celia held a finger over Noelle's lips when she opened her mouth again. Noelle swatted her hand away.

"Since Noelle has no manners, I'm Celia, one of her roommates and long-suffering best friend." Smiling, she held out her hand.

"Quentin." He stood and towered over Celia. He didn't realize how short she was until he stood up; her poise made her appear taller. He took Celia's hand into his. She had a surprisingly firm grip for such a dainty hand. "How long have you been best friends?"

Celia perched on the arm of the loveseat across from them and smiled at Quentin. "Before we get into that, quick question: Our cars are in the driveway, I'm not gonna find our tires on flats, and our windows busted out or nothing like that?"

Oh, so we're just gonna jump right in? Quentin glanced at Noelle, who was sipping her drink and wearing an innocent expression. "I'd be more worried about someone doing that to my car."

"¿Que?" Celia's eyebrows rose as she turned her gaze to Noelle. "What is he talking about, Noelle?"

Crickets.

Just a moment ago, Noelle was telling lies. Now she was suspiciously silent. Since she didn't seem as though she was going to voluntarily tell on herself, Quentin took the lead. He proceeded to tell on Noelle with relish, completely ignoring her soft teeth sucking, noncommittal signs of disagreements, and grumbling.

Celia clicked her tongue. "I assume that was Harrison?"

"Affirmative," Noelle said nonchalantly.

A slight tension in the air as the women stared at each other. Harrison was a bone of contention between them, Quentin realized. *Interesting.* He wondered if he'd learn how big it was right now. He sat there quietly sipping his drink, curious to see how the scene played out. Glancing at Noelle, he saw her lips pursed as she swirled her straw around in her drink. Finally, Celia broke the silence when she said, "This is the perfect beginning to a hood rat love story. What's the theme song for that, Noelle?"

"I don't know, Celia. I was really feeling 'Bodega Boo,'" Noelle said. "It brought me back to my roots."

"Yeah, but there's so much to your story, a single's not

gonna cut it. Wouldn't you agree?" Celia took a dainty sip of her drink, her eyes never leaving Noelle's.

Noelle's head dipped into the classic 'bitch, oh no, you didn't' head tilt, and she squinted and leaned forward.

Okay, enough of this. With that, Quentin knew he wasn't going to learn anything tonight other than that he couldn't spend time normally with Noelle. He should have known they wouldn't just be able to have a drink and talk. Whatever they had going on was going to have to wait until after his date with Noelle.

"So now that we've determined that none of y'all tires will be slashed, but mine might be, how long have you known each other?" Quentin asked.

Celia swung her hazel eyes over to him. Her gaze was calculating as she ran it over his body and then back up to his face. She shot a glance back over to Noelle, who sucked her teeth again softly, then she gave Quentin a wide, satisfied smile. "Gosh, since the 10th grade."

Quentin blinked. A tingle went down his spine. *This one here is nah easy ah'tall*, he thought, mentally shaking himself. She might be able to fit in his pocket, but that was the only thing small about her. No doubt, she was fine, but there was something underneath her pretty smile that made him feel...he didn't get to finish his thought because Noelle touched his knee, drawing his attention to her.

"Don't look her in the eyes. That's how she gets you," Noelle said, shaking her head. She removed her hand and leaned back into the cushions while Celia laughed softly, telling Noelle to stop it.

If he were a superstitious man, Quentin would have bolted out of there because he really did feel like if he stared at Celia too long, something would indeed go missing. He just didn't know what, and he wasn't trying to find out. He covered his small frown by sipping his drink.

"Anyway, I found her wandering the halls of Washington Irving High School and took her under my wing," Noelle said.

"Hey! I wasn't lost. I was on my way to class. And since your ass didn't ever go to class, you didn't know where I was going!" Celia said. "I was a straight-A student before she accosted me in the hallways. I ended up having to go to summer school day *and* night school to graduate, and *then* she dragged me to the recruiter's office."

"I was just trying to broaden your perspective and show you the world. I—"

"You are not Aladdin."

"—think you were still going door to door when I met you. She's an excommunicated Jehovah's Witness. She was like this weird introvert when I met her," Noelle said.

"I knew I should have gone to the Air Force," Celia said, shaking her head.

Noelle gasped. "You're so ungrateful. You'd probably be married now with twenty kids and *still* knocking on doors if not for me. Sidney's my new first best friend. You are now demoted to Friend Number Two."

"Who's Sidney?" Quentin asked, grateful that the mood had lifted.

"Our other roommate. And my new number one best friend!" Noelle said.

Celia tutted and shook her head at Noelle. "Oh no, I don't think so. You made me read those damn Harlequin novels you and your mother read. So I have earned my place as Forever Number One Best Friend. I had my fill of widowed, emotionally unavailable Viscounts being taught how to love by the twenty-one-year-old poor virgin governess who was watching his kids so she could afford college."

"Bonus points if she was fat and got teased by all the skinny people." Noelle held up her drink.

"*Disgusting*." Celia wrinkled her nose. "And on that note, I will take my leave." Celia stood up. "Quentin, it was nice to meet you. I thought she made you up to get attention."

Quentin laughed. "It was nice to meet you too."

"Those disparaging remarks are why you're Friend Number Two," Noelle said.

"I'll remember that when you want me to make drinks again. Have a good night, Quentin. Don't let Noelle get you into too much trouble," Celia said.

"I feel like I've been in trouble since the moment I laid eyes on her," Quentin said, and he meant it. She came into his life like a flirty breeze, but on the days that he went back to the 7-Eleven and didn't see her, the breeze turned stormy and started to whip into a frenzy. He was old enough to know there are certain people you meet who will change your life, and Noelle was one of those people. He didn't even want to think about where he'd be if he hadn't noticed the smudge before he pulled out. What if he'd been driving, and the paper got too wet or flew off? He got tense when he let his mind stray to the what-ifs for too long. Yeah, this woman was going to give him all the damn troubles.

"That sounds like our girl." Celia said, ignoring Noelle's indignant, "Hey!" With a wink for Quentin and a pointed look for Noelle, she left the living room.

"I'll be right back." Noelle handed Quentin her glass and followed Celia. A few moments later, she returned wearing an enigmatic expression.

"Everything good?" Quentin asked, handing her back her drink as she sat down, curling her legs beneath her. He had no doubt they were talking about him.

"Umm-hmm. She thinks you're nice."

"What if she didn't?" Quentin set his glass down on the end table next to him.

"She does, so…" Noelle gave him a small smile as she took the straw out of her glass and raised it to her lips. When she finished her drink, she did a little shoulder shimmy before setting the empty glass on the coffee table. "Those were so good. But I need to get me something to soak up this tequila. Or else I won't be good for nothing but my bed. Come with me." Noelle stood up and held out her hand.

Quentin took her hand and allowed her to tug him to his feet and lead him into the kitchen. He trailed behind her, admiring the sway of her hips. He could watch her walk all day. He was disappointed when they made it to the kitchen.

"Do you want to eat with me? I made lasagna yesterday." Noelle opened the refrigerator and pulled out a Tupperware container.

"No." Propping his elbows on the top of the kitchen island behind him, Quentin leaned back on it. "I ate before I came."

"Oh, what did you eat?" Noelle scooped the lasagna out on a plate and stuck it in the microwave, and leaned back on the counter herself while it heated.

"Some oxtails and rice and beans."

Noelle narrowed her eyes at him. "Come again? You had oxtails and rice and didn't think to bring me none? Dang."

Oxtail and rice were one his favorite dishes, along with fish stew and Quentin's mother always made them when he came home to visit. Other than seeing his family, her cooking was one of his main reasons for coming back.

Noelle nudged him in the shin with her foot. "And you didn't think to bring me none?" she repeated and sucked her teeth. "I don't know how to feel about that."

"As I took the first bite, I did think maybe I should ask you.

But by the second bite, I forgot." Quentin laughed. "Next time. I promise."

"Ima hold you to that."

"You definitely can. I always keep my promises." Right after Quentin spoke, Noelle crossed her arms over her chest. "What did I say?" he asked.

"Why did you get my dry cleaning?"

"And the cinnamon," he added with a slight grin, hoping to lighten the mood again.

Noelle nodded tersely. "*And* the cinnamon. Why did you do that?"

Quentin tilted his head to the side, studying Noelle. She went from being an open house that he wanted to explore to spiking a no-trespassing sign in the front yard with the alarm system turned on. He took a few seconds to mull over his answer as the microwave ticked down, but there wasn't anything he could say but the truth.

"I wanted to make sure you had what you needed."

"Why?"

"Why?" Quentin repeated.

"Yeah, why? You don't even know me," Noelle said.

"Yet, I find myself having a vested interest in making sure your needs are met. I wanted to be the one who got you what you needed. Even if it was only your dry cleaning and cinnamon. You wanted them, so I got them." He pushed off the counter and walked a couple of steps to her. "Would you like me to take your car and get your tires rotated?" Without touching her, he leaned over and whispered in her ear, "And get your oil changed. You need that done too, right?"

"Yes." Noelle leaned forward and brushed her temple against his chin.

"How are your windshield wipers—they good?' Quentin

lightly kissed her temple.

"I don't know. I think so," Noelle said with a sigh and closed the last bit of space between them so they were chest to chest.

"I'll change them out too. Just to make sure." Quentin ran his hand up her back as he trailed light kisses down the side of her face and along her jawline. "Do you need your car cleaned? Would you like me to do that?" His lips brushed against hers.

"Yes, please," Noelle whispered, grabbing a handful of his shirt and going up on her tippy toes.

"I can do that." Quentin wrapped an arm around her and hiked her up against him so they were eye to eye. "Is there anything else you need?" Noelle's lids got heavy at the word need, and a surge of victory ran through him. He found her sweet spot. He squeezed her tighter against him.

Noelle let go of his shirt and wrapped her arms around his neck. "No, I think that'll do for now." Then, she kissed him.

Quentin quickly took over the kiss. He sucked her bottom lip into his mouth and was rewarded with a soft moan from Noelle. Her tongue teased the inside of his upper lip, and he met it with his. She started slipping down, and he wrapped his free arm under her bottom and almost lost it when he felt bare skin on his arm.

"Where are your panties?" he murmured against her lips.

"In my dresser. Would you like me to go put some on?" She massaged his earlobes as she nibbled his lower lip.

"Absolutely not." Chuckling, Quentin kissed her again, enjoying the little noises she made as they kissed and her warm, naked skin against his arm as she continued to rub and squeeze his earlobes. That shit felt amazing. He wanted her to do it while he was inside her, but it wasn't going to be tonight. The microwave beeped as if in agreement with his thoughts.

"Your food is ready."

"What?"

"The microwave stopped. Your food is ready."

"You want me to eat now? Right now, right now? Like at this moment?"

No. Quentin tilted his head back with a deep sigh. "Yes."

"It definitely doesn't feel like you want me to eat." Noelle sprinkled kisses along his throat.

The feeling Noelle was referring to was Quentin's hard-on pressing against her belly. "Ugh, no. I don't want you to, but I can't stay for too much longer."

"Why not?" The kissing stopped.

Quentin rested his forehead against hers before loosening his hold on her. He closed his eyes for a split second as she slid down his body. Damn, she felt good.

"Because I have to be up early to help my father out. If we start something now, it's gonna have to be rushed, and I don't want to rush anything with you. I just wanna take my time, then take a power nap and then take my time again. But if I'm not up and ready by 6 a.m., Daddy's gonna be on his roof without me, and I can't have that. He don't listen when I tell him not to do stuff. He almost broke his damn hip. He won't go sit down somewhere and relax. He's a stubborn man."

Noelle sighed sharply and smoothed his shirt out before stepping away from him and getting her food out of the microwave. "My father is also a stubborn West Indian man, so I gets it." She set her plate on the kitchen table. "Will you stay long enough to watch me eat?"

"I was planning to." Quentin pulled her chair out and settled her in before sitting down across from her.

"So, can I ask you a question?" Noelle asked after chewing a mouthful of food.

"You can ask me anything you want." Quentin leaned back in his chair. He had a feeling he knew what she was going to ask.

"Are you still involved with your ex?"

He was right. "I was."

Noelle nodded slowly as she chewed her next mouthful of food. "When did you stop?"

"The day I met you."

"Oh!" Noelle's eyebrows shot up.

"Yup."

"But you didn't know if you'd see me again."

Quentin braced his elbows on the table and set his chin on his folded hands. "True, and I was pissed that guy interrupted us and caused you to run away—"

"I didn't run away. I left gracefully."

"—but it wasn't about you. It was about us and the damage we were continuing to inflict on each other. After our son was born, our marriage slowly unraveled. We both knew why but never talked about it until that morning. I realized how tired I was of all our shit, so we had an initial talk about it. I'm not sure what we can do to repair our relationship, but since we'll be in each other's lives until one of us dies, we gotta figure something out," Quentin said with a shrug.

Noelle nodded. "So y'all were just 'grudge-fucking' as I like to call it. It's pretty horrible. But I think we've all been there, so trust, I am not one to judge. Thank you for explaining it to me."

"You're welcome. I thought you should know."

"Why?"

"I don't know yet. All I know is that I needed to keep on going back to that 7-Eleven, hoping I'd see you again."

Noelle smiled sheepishly. "I went back like every day too. Sometimes twice a day. My gas tank stayed full for the first time ever. In my life. And I made sure I was super cute because I looked a little itchy and scratchy when you saw me that first time."

"I liked you then, and I like you now. And I'll make sure your gas tank stays full from now on."

"Oooh wee, I was hoping you'd say that. It's exhausting keeping up with that."

"You're a mess, woman," Quentin said with a chuckle. He glanced at his watch. "I need to get going."

"Ooookay." Noelle stood and offered him her hand again. "Let's go, Daddy's boy."

"You got jokes?" Quentin also stood and slid his hand into hers.

"Always. That's how I roll."

"I like holding your hand," Quentin said.

Noelle looked up at him. "Well, I must admit I like you holding it. Or else I wouldn't keep on giving it to you."

Quentin pulled her closer. "A "me too" would have been the appropriate response."

"I am a very inappropriate woman." Noelle rose on her toes and brushed her lips against him, and danced away when he tried to deepen the kiss, then dragged him with her out of the kitchen. "But you'll find out another time. We must make haste and get you to your father!"

Quentin shook his head at her and allowed her to lead him to the front door.

"Can I call you tomorrow?"

"I was going to say call me when you get home, but I guess tomorrow's fine."

"How about I do both?" Quentin gently cupped her face with both hands and kissed her forehead. He wanted to kiss her lips, but he didn't want to drive home with a hard-on. "Have a good night."

Noelle smiled and covered his hands with hers before opening the door. "Drive safe. I would hate to use your expensive cinnamon on rolls for someone else to enjoy because you're dead and can't enjoy my delicious baked goods."

Quentin was still laughing when he started his car.

Chapter Thirteen

MMl Sidney Pascal

Walking down the pier, Sidney looked up at the dark clouds in the distance and pulled her ball cap down more firmly on her head. Virginia was taking this April showers brings May flowers a bit too seriously for her liking. She hoped the rain held off until she got home. She was wet enough with the sweat that started the moment she stepped on the flight deck for duty section[1] turnover, and the hot, sticky air smacked her in the face, almost making it hard to breathe. Without the A/C of the ship, she felt her roots starting to puff out.

Dangit, she just went to the hairdresser two days ago. In vain, she wiped her brow and grimaced at the moisture left on her fingers. Nelson better be waiting at the gate for her when got there. She wished she hadn't lent him her car yesterday. His car didn't start after work, and since she had duty last night, there was no reason for her not to. But when she got to the end of the pier, Nelson and her car were nowhere to be seen.

Sugaredhoneyedicedtea! Where is he? Sidney glanced at

---

1. Duty Section: the group of sailors assigned to 24-hour duty at a command.

her watch again. It was almost 0830. Nelson should have been here already. He knew she hated to wait. But knowing him, he only gave himself *just* enough time to get here on time, not anticipating the weather. She could have just taken Celia's car because her duty section assumed the watch, but Celia also wasn't at muster[2] this morning. Actually, quite a few people were missing. She rolled her eyes. There couldn't have been an accident already? Norfolk was filled with drivers from all over the country, and it seemed like most of them shouldn't be on the road because almost every morning there was an accident. It didn't make sense to her; didn't they all have to pass a driving test? Groaning, she glanced at her watch again when four happened consecutively. Lightning cracked, thunder boomed, the sky opened up, and her pager went off.

"Sonvabiscuit!" Sidney hissed. She was reaching into her backpack for her pager when a black umbrella appeared over her head.

"Why are you still here?"

Startled, Sidney looked up at Engineman[3] Second Class Nicolas Kaneko. She'd been secretly crushing on him since she asked to come aboard two years ago. He was on the

---

2. Muster: taking attendance of the members in a division or department.

3. Enginemen: they operate, maintain, and repair engines, main propulsion machinery, refrigeration, air conditioning.

quarterdeck[4] watch[5] , completely irritated with the young E-3 who tried to cross the quarterdeck was pissy drunk, and it was only 1900. But when he got to her and learned she was checking aboard for the first time, however, his manner completely softened. He smiled at her and welcomed her to the Puget Sound. His dark brown eyes were suddenly warm and friendly, and he had the best crinkles from his laugh lines. She was a sucker for laugh lines on men. He offered his hand out for a shake, and she took it. His palm was warm but not sweaty, and his grip was strong and confident as he shook her hand. A good handshake was another thing she was a sucker for. Some men gave the dead fish handshakes, and other men tried to exert dominance and crush your fingers, but Kaneko's hand was perfect. She was surprised at how disappointed she had been when he let her hand go.

Ever since then, Sidney clandestinely studied Kaneko. He moved throughout the ship as if he didn't have a care in the world, blending in with whatever group she saw him with. He had dap for the Black and Hispanic crew members and played dominos on the mess decks[6] underway with them. He had a seat with the Filipinos during chow, and she had even seen him out on liberty with the known gay crew members. More importantly, however, he had a beautiful

---

4. Quarterdeck: the shipboard area connected to the brow where personnel arrive and depart the ship.

5. Watch: the time an individual is assigned a specific, detailed responsibility.

6. Mess or Mess Deck: a designated area where military personnel eat and socialize.

smile for her every time they crossed paths. It always left her flustered and aroused. Definitely aroused.

No one knew how she felt about Kaneko. Sidney kept it to herself because he was Asian. Now he was a handsome lil thing with the sweetest-looking lips, but what the heck was she going to do with one of them? She couldn't see it happening even if his main liberty buddy was a Black woman, MM2[7] Natasha Simon and she knew that they'd been friends before the Sound. So he could be considered Black adjacent. Maybe. Regardless, she stayed conflicted over her desire for him because it felt wrong— like she was betraying her people. She hoped it would just go away. It hadn't. It just simmered underneath the surface, bubbling up every time she was near him.

And it was Kaneko who came to mind when Noelle informed her that she needed some good sex. She just knew that would be so good. And she loved his accent. She didn't know where he was from, but it reminded her of the soft, rounded lyrical Creole accent from New Orleans. Once, she heard him say the word *baby*, and she almost lost her mind. He wasn't even saying it in a flirty way; he was congratulating a shipmate on the birth of his second child, but instantly, visions of sweaty, writhing naked bodies came to mind. More specifically, she saw *herself* naked, sweaty body tied to the bedposts, bent over a chair, spread-eagled on the floor, sitting on his face... Even now, she had to suppress a shudder running through her when he casually questioned her.

"I was waiting for my boyfriend," Sidney forced herself

---

7. Machinist Mate: are responsible for operating and maintaining ship propulsion machinery and outside machinery.

to say calmly. "But he just paged me from his house so I'm pretty sure he's gonna tell me he's stuck in traffic." Excusing herself, she darted through the rain to the phone booths and called Nelson. She groaned when he told her that there was a huge accident on I-264 E that shut down both lanes. He had managed to turn around in time before he was stuck in traffic. Already comfortably at home with her dang car to boot, he said he'd call her when he was on his way. When she hung up the phone, she found Kaneko waiting outside the booth when she pulled open the door.

"I would have walked you over. You didn't have to get wet," Kaneko said.

Still standing in the booth, Sidney shrugged. "There's an accident, of course. So I'm gonna get wet walking back to the ship anyway. Ugh, I just wanna go home." She stared down at the tips of her boots, trying to ignore the jittery feeling in her body that made her want to twitch. This was the longest conversation she'd ever had with him.

"I understand what you mean."

Sidney heard the sympathy in his voice but didn't look up. Even the most dedicated sailor didn't want to be on the ship when they didn't have to.

"Are you hungry?"

"Huh?" Sidney's eyes shot up to his face, confusion evident in her expression and in her voice. "What? Am I hungry?"

Kaneko smiled at her. "Yes. Are you hungry?"

Sidney frowned. Was she? And why was he asking? "A little bit I guess. Why?"

"I'm starving. I was going to make breakfast when I got home. You can join me if you'd like. I can drop you home after. The traffic should be cleared up by then," Kaneko said.

"Oh." Sidney nearly stopped breathing. Alone with him in his house? Her stomach clenched with nervousness. There was no way she'd be able to sit across the table from him and have a meal with him. "No, thank you, but if you don't mind, could you walk me back to the ship so I don't get soaked?"

It was Kaneko's turn to frown. "Pascal, you'd rather sit on the ship for God knows how long, than have breakfast with me? Unless..." He frowned even harder before continuing. "You're attractive, but not attractive enough to make me risk my career. Just in case you're worried about that."

Horrified, Sidney's mouth dropped open, and she shook her head quickly. "Oh God, no!" He thought her hesitation was because she thought he might try to push up on her in private. "I wasn't thinking that! *Why would you say that?*"

"It felt like a correct assumption," Kaneko said with a shrug.

"It wasn't. Believe me. That was not even a thought in my mind." His expression is still suspicious. She felt terrible; however, there was no way she could tell him the real reason. But she also couldn't let him think she thought he was an undercover rapist. God, why did she lend Nelson her car? She'd rather be stuck in traffic than have this conversation. Clearly unimpressed with her response, Kaneko stared down at Sidney for a moment and then shrugged again.

"Well, I'm gonna get going. Like I said, I'm hungry. See you later."

"Wait!" Swallowing down her fear, she stepped out of the booth and grabbed his umbrella rod, stopping him. She looked up at him. "I *would* like to have breakfast with you if the offer's still open?"

"It depends on if you think I'm using this as a way to take

advantage of you."

"Seriously, I do not. I promise you I don't." Sidney placed a hand over her heart.

Kaneko's eyes narrowed as he studied her face; apparently satisfied with her contriteness, his own expression softened. "Then it is."

Inwardly, Sidney exhaled. That was crazy. "Then I graciously accept your offer for breakfast. I have to call back my boyfriend and tell him not to come." Kaneko nodded, and she ducked back inside to call Nelson, who didn't even bother to ask her who was driving her home. He just told her he'd bring her car by later. *Hmph, that was odd.* She frowned.

"Everything okay?" Kaneko asked.

Sidney shook that feeling away. She'd mull over Nelson's response later. "Yup, I'm ready." She stepped back underneath the umbrella with him, and the breeze picked up. She got a whiff of his musky cologne. It was mixed in with cloying humidity in the air and probably the sweat on his skin. He smelled so good; it almost made her swoon. Lawd, she wasn't going to make it through this breakfast.

They walked the distance to his Nissan Pathfinder without saying another word. Sidney used that time to get her composure back. She was thrown off again when Kaneko opened the passenger door for her. He even held the umbrella over her until he shut the door. It was a first for her, and she felt pleased and sad at the same time. None of the men she dated ever held the door open for her. Not even Wade. She really needed to upgrade her men. She really did.

Sidney was still marveling over his chivalry when he slid into the driver's seat and started the engine. Instantly, the truck size seemed to shrinkwrap around them, and the hot air blowing from the A/C vents didn't help. It blew around his cologne *and* her craving back into her face. He drove a stick, and she watched his hand operate the gearshift. His nails were clean and nicely trimmed. She enjoyed the way his dungarees tightened around his thighs as he switched between the clutch and gas pedal. She sighed and fidgeted in her seat. She was so turned on right now that she literally wanted to pull out his Johnson and give him head on the way to his house. She didn't even like giving head! She could count the number of times she'd done it for Nelson. His semen was so bitter, it made her want to gag. She mentioned it to Noelle, who actually gagged. After recovering, Noelle said it was because 'Nelson was trash—hence trash nut.' Then Celia added it was Nelson's diet that was probably trash because you are what you eat. It was most likely both reasons. Sighing again, she turned to look out her window, watching the rain zigzag down. She should have gone back to the ship.

"So, what do you want to eat? I can make you just about anything you want. I have a taste for Belgian waffles. I have sausage and bacon."

Caught up in her conflicted emotions, Sidney didn't hear him until he softly called her name. "Pascal?" Kaneko's voice was like a hand tuning her face towards his. "Sorry, I didn't hear what you said."

The light turned red. Kaneko slowed the car to a stop and looked at her. "I asked what did you want for breakfast."

Sidney stared at him. She didn't want food. She wanted him to make her cum until she couldn't cum anymore. Just leave her a used mess in the middle of his bed. Get her some Gatorade and a banana, and then start all over again. Her breath quickened, and she licked her lips. She didn't know if she'd get this opportunity, or rather, the nerve to be alone with him again. Did she dare ask? What if he had a girlfriend? He did say he found her attractive, but what if it was just pretty "for a Black girl" but not someone he'd sleep with? *And* what if he was terrible in bed? She would have to see him and be trapped with him every day, plus on duty days.

What if…what if…For fuckssake, just do it! A voice screamed in her head that sounded suspiciously like Noelle's.

Sidney took a deep fortifying breath. "Can we…" She stopped and cleared her throat. "Can we have sex first and then maybe eat later?" she asked in a rush.

When he didn't answer right away, she reached for the door handle, not caring that she was in her working uniform off the base. Heck, she didn't know where they were, and it was pouring outside, but she'd find a pay phone and make it home somehow. Before she could open the door, the light changed, and they were moving again.

"I'm sorry, Pascal, were you going somewhere? Because I *thought* you asked if we could have sex before we had Belgian waffles. Was I mistaken?"

Sidney wanted to crawl into the pothole he just swerved to avoid and die. *Oh my God! Why did I open my mouth?* Wishing cushions could swallow her, she leaned her head back on the headrest and closed her eyes for the rest of the ride. She didn't even open them when she heard his garage door. It wasn't until Kaneko turned the ignition off that she opened them. The whirl of the garage door going down was the only sound.

"Pascal."

"Yes, Kaneko?" Sidney stared at her reflection in the windshield.

"Pascal, look at me please." Kaneko's voice was soft and

coaxing.

Begrudgingly, Sidney turned her head and looked at him. His expression was enigmatic, and that unsettled her even more. She had no clue what he was thinking. Meanwhile, she was about to be sick.

"Are you sure?"

Sidney's mouth turned down. "I was," she mumbled.

Kaneko laughed softly and took her hand from her lap. Bringing it to his mouth, he rubbed his lips on the soft skin of her inner wrist. "I just want you to be sure about this. Are you sure?"

Sidney's body pulsed, and she shivered when he nipped at her skin and then followed with a light flicker of his tongue. "Yes..."

"Ask me again," Kaneko murmured against her skin.

Sidney stared at him from under heavy lids. "Kaneko, can we have sex before you make me breakfast?"

"We can have sex as many times as you want before I make you breakfast, and then we can have sex after if you like." He kissed her palm before settling her hand back in her lap.

"Thank you. I would like that." Sidney said.

"So would I." Kaneko slid from the car, and Sidney didn't move until he opened her door. He held out his hand, and Sidney took it and allowed him to lead her inside.

Chapter Fourteen

MM1 Sidney Pascal

Out of all the things she thought she'd be doing today, staring at Kaneko's back as she followed him to his bedroom was not one of them. The photos lining the hallway walls became a blur as she tried to calm the rise and fall of her chest. She swallowed, moving her jaw and tongue around, trying to build moisture in her suddenly dry mouth. She needed water badly, but one of Celia's notoriously strong drinks would be even better. All she would have needed was a swallow, and then she would have blamed it on the alcohol. Well, at least she took a shower this morning instead of waiting until she got home. The OCD in her would've stopped all progress and demanded a shower.

When they got to his bedroom, Kaneko shut his blinds, darkening the room. The dimness of the lighting helped soothe her nerves as she stood next to his bed. Her head tilted to the side as she closed her eyes.

"Can I get something to drink, please?" She heard Kaneko's muffled footsteps as he walked over to her. He traced a finger around her ear and down her exposed neck. She shivered but didn't open her eyes.

"Of course. I have orange juice, apple juice, water, ginger ale—"

"Just water please," She interrupted, surprised at the breathlessness of her voice.

"Be right back." He was only gone for a moment before a light tapping her on the shoulder got her attention. Sidney took the glass he held out to her and downed the room-temperature water. It was just how she liked it. Everyone thought it odd and gross that she didn't like ice water, or even ice in her drinks for that matter, and usually brought her drinks filled with them despite knowing her preference. But not Kaneko. Clearing her throat, she handed the glass back to him.

"You were a little thirsty, huh?" Kaneko placed the glass on his dresser.

"Just a little," Sidney said.

"Sit down," Kaneko said, gesturing to the bed behind her.

"I can't sit on your bed in my outside clothes," Sidney said with a shake of her head.

"That's an easy fix." Kaneko's hands went to the top button of her dungaree shirt. "May I?"

Sidney swallowed. They were really doing this. "You may."

Kaneko smiled and unbuttoned her shirt and slid it down her arms slowly as if giving her a chance to change her mind. When Sidney stayed silent, her white undershirt was whisked over her head and tossed on the floor. Suddenly she remembered that she had on her plain everyday work bra, but his fingers brushing against her bare stomach as he undid her belt buckle quickly diverted her attention.

The only noises in the room were Sidney's raspy breathing and the sound of her dungarees hitting the floor. She stepped out of them and kicked them to the side. She was also wearing her very comfortable granny panties and apparently, she was the only one concerned with her old lady underwear. He gently turned her around and undid her French braid, combing his fingers through her hair and massaging her scalp. Then he moved down to work on her neck and trapezoids.

Purring with pleasure, Sidney's head fell forward; her body tingled when his fingers at her traps found the knots in her shoulders and back. He gently kneaded them out one by one. All the tension drained from her body. She was so lethargic she didn't realize he had removed her bra until he was cupping her breasts, rubbing his palms over her nipples in a light circular motion.

Every brush of his palm had her belly quivering and sent sharp pangs through her Precious. She arched her back, trying to get more, but he didn't change the pressure or the speed of his hands. It was almost as if he were creating static electricity between them. She looked down at his hands and swore she saw sparks. Or maybe it was the lightning flashes outside?

Kaneko's hands slipping underneath her panties put a halt to her wandering thoughts. His fingers slipped inside her panties and formed a V on her bare mons. His thumbs stroked her smooth skin in an almost questioning way, and her button jumped in response. She tilted her hips up with a question of her own. He responded by sliding her panties down. While Sidney wiggled out of them, Kaneko reached around her to yank the comforter down, then he gently pushed her down to lie on her stomach.

Sidney laid her forehead on her folded arms and tried to ignore that her booty was just all out in the open. She fought the urge to reach over and grab the comforter to cover up. *Just relax girl,* she told herself when she heard the rustling of his clothes, but the sound brought on a fresh wave of anxiety. She started breathing hard again. The air in the room suddenly became stifling, but maybe it was carbon monoxide she was inhaling because she couldn't lift her head. She was going to hyperventilate and pass out before they even started.

"Are you nervous?" Kaneko asked softly.

"Well—I—umm," Sidney's voice cracked. She cleared her throat and tried to speak again. "Nuuuhhhyeah," she admitted sheepishly.

"Relax. It'll only hurt a little, and you'll like it. I promise." Kaneko laughed and tickled the soles of her feet and then ran his hands up her calves and thighs, massaging the muscles.

"Wait, what?" Sidney's voice was breathless. Was he joking? He sounded like he was joking. She was going to question him more, but she got distracted by his hands gliding over her legs. When did he get the oil out? She groaned softly. Those hands were just magical. She could lie here all day while he massaged her. When he got to her bottom, his touch changed. It became almost reverent.

Sidney's breath hitched, and then she gasped when he started kneading her behind like he was a master bread-maker. He slowly ran his palms over her skin, his thumbs dipping into the crease, teasing her puckered hole. She'd never been happier in life that she was such a thorough cleaner of her behind. Eyes rolling, she drummed her feet against the mattress as his fingers gently prodded her. Her breath caught in her throat when he spread her cheeks wide and...

"Oh my goodness," Sidney moaned. Arching her back, she lifted her bottom closer to his tongue. Nelson's never done that before. Correction: no man has. She'd gone her whole sexual life without having a man tend to her backyard. She wanted to find every one of them and smack 'em to the floor.

Kaneko seemed more than happy to unknowingly make up for her lack of booty-loving. The man reveled in her behind. His tongue rimmed her hole, and she was simultaneously appalled and wetter than she'd ever been in her whole entire life! Then everything stopped, and she felt him move away from her. Before she had to question his absence, she felt his slick finger massaging and then probing her tight muscle before slipping inside. She whimpered when she felt him smear more lube on her and a second finger joined the first. He held his fingers still while she got used to him and waited until she stopped reflectively tightening around him then he started to slowly move his fingers. The sensation was... She mewled into the pillow and squirmed on the bed, unsure if she was trying to get away or get closer. Ever so gently he spread his fingers just wide enough for his tongue to strum along her stretched rim. She exhaled in a rush when he pulled his fingers out.

"You smell so good." Kaneko kissed the two dimples at the base of her spine and nuzzled her cheeks.

Sidney shivered. "Noelle's cousin sent her this oil from somewhere down in New York. I don't know what's in it. I just like the way it smells so I asked her for it and she gave me the whole bottle." She felt his smile against her skin. *There I go again with the mindless blather...*

"Okay. But that's not what I meant."

"Then what did you...oh—oh!" Sidney rolled her eyes. Kaneko meant her body scent. No man had ever said that to her either. What has she been doing with her life?

Kaneko reached over her head and grabbed a couple of pillows. "Lift your hips."

Sidney did what she was told, and he stuffed them underneath her hips. If she felt exposed before, she was on center stage now. He palmed her checks and rubbed them before nuzzling her Precious and pressing the outer lips together like a soft taco, nibbling on them. Then he spread her lips open and continued to lick every crease and crevice except for the one thing she really wanted him to lick.

Sidney quickly concluded that he was trying to torture her. Every time his tongue came close to her button, she tensed in anticipation. But he kept on skirting around it. After the fourth time, she couldn't hold back the cry of frustration. "Kaneko!"

"Yes?" Kaneko said, then slid his tongue inside her.

Sidney whimpered. *Ooooh, he's got a long tongue.*

"Was there something you wanted?" Kaneko asked, then continued to use his tongue to her

Sidney's answer was a little jerk of her hips. Her train of thought disappeared when his tongue entered her Precious.

"No answer?" Kaneko rolled her over and tugged her body and the pillows down until her butt was at the edge of the bed. Kneeling between her legs, he threw both legs over his shoulders. Using his nose, he parted her lips, exposing her button to his warm breath. The exact place where she wanted his mouth to be. "Is this what you want?"

"Not exac—ooooh!" Sidney's words ended with a gasp when Kaneko's lips closed around her button and sucked. Her gasp ended with a low moan when he abruptly stopped.

"Was that what you wanted?" Kaneko asked. He kissed her inner thigh.

"Kaneko," Sidney wailed. *What was wrong with this man?*

"Tell me what you want, Pascal," Kaneko whispered against the inside of her thigh. "Or else I won't do it."

Sidney knew he wasn't lying, but she just couldn't say it. *What more does he want from me?* She was here, wasn't she?

She might as well put her dang clothes on and call a cab because he was asking too much from her. Then why did she hear a voice that sounded just like hers give Kaneko a direct order to suck on her button? He echoed her command with a whispered "your button" and a little chuckle, and then he obliged. She didn't have time to ponder her sudden burst of courage because her thighs were squeezing his head, and she was grinding her Precious against his face. Vaguely, she wondered if he could breathe, then decided she didn't care as long as he didn't die before she came. His lips and tongue had her body running amok. Every time she got close to coming, he would change the movement of his tongue and throw her off.

Becoming more and more frustrated, Sidney found herself involuntarily speaking again. "Please."

"Please, what?" Kaneko stopped licking and nuzzled her again.

"Oh, my word!" Sidney hissed, slapping an open palm on the bed. "Would you just—" She lost her train of thought again as Kaneko's tongue slid inside her while he flicked his fingers quickly over her button. *Oh yes, do that...* In no time, she was on the edge again. She tried to hide it, but he knew and stopped again. Clearly, he wanted her to beg, and right about now, she was more than willing. She took a shaky breath. "Engineman Second Class Nicolas Kaneko, can you please, *please* let me come?"

"Oh, you said my full name and rank. Now say pretty please with sugar on top?" Kaneko kissed the top of her mons.

Sidney laughed weakly. This man. "Engineman Second Class Nicolas Kaneko, will you pretty please with sugar on top and whipped cream, cherries, nuts, hot fudge, pineapples, and strawberries just let me come?"

"How can a man say no to a request like that?" Kaneko responded huskily.

If Sidney thought what Kaneko was doing earlier felt good, then what he proceeded to do to her Precious now was nothing short of spectacular. He slipped two fingers inside her and made a hook with them, pressing against a soft spot inside, and began pulling roughly against it hard like he was trying to drag something out of her. At the same time, he sucked and flicked on her button. She could hear herself letting out a flurry of moans—they went from deep and guttural to high and whiny. They sounded like they were so far away, as though they weren't coming from her.

Suddenly a feeling she had never felt before came over her. A huge wave started from the soles of her feet and worked its way up her ankles, cramping her calves and thighs. When the sensation got to her Precious, she pushed at Kaneko's head frantically. "Stoooooop, I have to pee!"

Kaneko ignored her cry and put his forearm over her midsection, holding her in place while his fingers moved at a quicker and rougher pace.

Unable to move and not having the strength or the real inclination to do so, Sidney dug her fingers into his thick, silky hair and held on tight as the wave crashed over her like a tsunami. It hit the shore and pulled back deep inside her and rolled up the rest of her body. Her nipples tightened so painfully she cried out and continued to cry out weakly as water from God knows where flowed from her onto the sheets. He didn't stop moving his fingers until her wildly jerking hips slowed to simply tapping against his face, and the water dried up. Exhaling, she slowly released the vice grip she had on his hair. Her legs twitched, and her breath hitched when he soothingly licked her softening button and tasted her.

"I...I think I peed the bed..." Sidney said weakly. And she didn't care. She felt Kaneko's chuckle against her lips.

"You didn't. That was a g-spot orgasm." Kaneko kissed her mound before grabbing his T-shirt off the floor and wiping his face off.

"Oooooh," Sidney breathed. Still caught up in the after-glow, she stared at the white ceiling overhead. So that was the *formerly* elusive g-spot orgasm. Noelle and Celia spoke of those often while she sat there like a dumb dummy because she'd never been close to having one. They claimed it was indescribable, but it was as close to an out-of-body experience as one could get. She'd been jealous every time they spoke of having one. There was such awe and rev-erence in their words and definitely pity in their eyes be-cause they knew she couldn't relate. However, they failed to mention the extra body fluids. She should've guessed it from the word squirt, but again it was out of her scope of reference. Now she was floating in a small puddle of her own bodily fluids...and still not caring one bit. But this pillow was destroyed.

"You're going to have to buy new pillows, and I hope you have a mattress protector," Sidney said.

"Later. We're not done yet. It'll be wetter than that," Kaneko said. He got up and went to a drawer on his night-stand and pulled out a condom.

"Oh." Lord, there was more? She didn't know how much help she would be. She felt as limp as a rag doll. She turned her head to the side and studied his body as he rolled a condom on his erection. He was always running in the material handling passageway[1] while they were underway. But he wasn't just long and lean; he had a well-developed chest and a six-pack, strong-looking thighs and calves, and a cute little firm booty. Her eyes dropped to his sheathed Johnson.

Kaneko was bigger than she expected. Granted, she didn't know what to expect. She was completely sexin' blind. He wasn't long, maybe around five to six inches, and she was totally okay with that. The only thing childbirth did to her body was drop her cervix lower. If she weren't fully aroused with Nelson—which was often—his coveted nine inches would be highly uncomfortable, often bordering on pain. She suspected Kaneko's size would fit in there just right, and she was no mathematician, but his girth more than made up for his length.

"How are you doing?" Kaneko asked, sitting on the bed next to her. Gently, he brushed her damp hair off her cheeks and forehead. Running his fingers down her cheek, he traced her lips.

Sidney took a deep breath. She could smell herself on his fingers, and she loved it. For the life of her, she couldn't remember ever smelling herself on a man. "I could use a nap, but I'm still in the game."

"That's the spirit," Kaneko said.

"Go Navy..." Sidney said, laughing.

Chuckling, Kaneko leaned over and nibbled her lower lip. Her scent was on him like aftershave, but it was mixed with another smell. Something sweet and earthy.

"What's that smell?" She murmured.

---

1. Material Handling Passageway: A long corridor that has outside access so that large items can be brought on board.

"Coconut oil. That's what used when I had my fingers in your ass."

And your tongue was in there too, Sidney finished in her head. *And now you're all up in my face...* She wrapped her arms around his neck and pulled him closer. She didn't know why she wasn't grossed out and pushing him away instead maybe because she smelled so good on him. Her tongue darted out tentatively, licking his lips, tasting herself on them before Kaneko opened his mouth and gently sucked her tongue inside. It was at that moment she realized that they hadn't kissed. And he was a great kisser. He took his time learning the shape of her mouth. His lips were pressed against hers, but he wasn't smashing her teeth against her lips. His tongue wasn't wild in her mouth, trying to knock her teeth out or reach her tonsils. It swirled and danced around with her tongue before releasing it to suck on her bottom lip.

They kissed lazily for what seemed like an eternity. When he pulled away, she felt bereft. Before she could protest, he re-stuffed the pillows under her hips and then hooked her legs over his arms.

"You ready?" he asked, nudging her entrance with the tip of his Johnson.

Sidney nodded quickly. Boy, was she ever! If he started teasing her like he did with his tongue, they were going to end up fighting instead of having sex because she was pressed to have his Johnson inside her. Her eyes fluttered as he slowly slid inside her until he hit bottom.

"I knew you would feel good but not like this. You're so tight. Goddamn," Kaneko murmured.

Sidney smiled lazily and tightened her muscles, enjoying the groan that came from deep in his throat. Her one and only personal claim to sexual fame was her tightness.

She attended Lamaze class during her pregnancy, and she believed her instructor when she said Kegels are essential for sexual health and more importantly, to stop her from peeing on herself when she sneezed because simply the thought of that was a nightmare.

Kaneko stopped her wandering thoughts when he gripped her thighs and started thrusting slowly. Her body tensed, still expecting to feel the pain when he went in deep. But there was none. The tip of his Johnson just touched her cervix, and it felt good, too. For the first time in four years, she enjoyed penetration and not just waiting for the man to be done. He moved her legs over his shoulders, and that changed the angle and depths of his thrusts so he was hitting her g-spot again. The pressure was even more intense than his fingers. In no time, she was sweating, moaning, and bucking against him helplessly, wanting to pull her own hair out because she couldn't reach his all over again. The fact he could see her mewling embarrassed her, and she reached overhead and grabbed a pillow, and held it over her face.

Kaneko pulled the pillow out of her grasp and threw it aside. "No, don't do that. I like to hear and see the appreciation of my work."

Self-conscious all the same, Sidney grabbed the sheets to prevent herself from covering her mouth and bit her bottom lip in a vain attempt to stop the sounds bubbling out of her. When she dang near screeched at his next thrust, her hands were flying to her mouth—Kaneko's words stopped them in midair.

"If you cover your mouth, I'll stop." To prove his point, Kaneko stilled his hips.

"Nonono, don't do that..." Sidney lowered her hands and grabbed the sheets again. Kaneko rewarded her by palming her breasts. Every time he hit her g-spot; he would squeeze and tug at her nipples. The added sensation interrupted her whimpering, wailing, and moaning. Her throat was dry and scratchy when a sound that she never thought she could make came from her soul.

It was the sound of complete and utter satisfaction. Every molecule in Sidney's body vibrated when she came the second time. It was like the extended version of an already three-hour movie. She just kept on coming and coming and coming. If her first orgasm was an out-of-body experience, then this time, she was reborn in yet another warm stream of liquid. She was still floating down the river back down to her body when Kaneko leaned over and kissed her softly, murmuring a question against her lips. She wasn't sure what he asked, but she replied, "Do whatever you want."

"Are you sure?" Kaneko pulled out and stared down at her.

"Yes." Sidney stared into his eyes, her body responding to the need written on his face. She couldn't remember the last time someone looked at her with such desire. As long as he continued to stare at her like that, she'd give him whatever he wanted.

"You're so beautiful." Kaneko smiled and reached underneath her hips and grabbed a butt check in each hand and spread them apart.

Sidney melted. No man had ever called her beautiful either, but she felt it when he looked at her, in the revered way he touched her. She was still caught up in both the afterglow and the awe of him when she felt the lube again, and then the tip of his Johnson gave a light but insistant knock at her backdoor. Whoa! She told him yes to *that*? She tensed up at the feeling of him trying to squeeze past her threshold.

"You need to relax," Kaneko coaxed.

"Really?" Sidney squealed and did the exact opposite around his tip in response. He took a deep breath and bit his lower lip. Dang, he looked sexy. Even in her shock at what was happening, she couldn't help but appreciate the look of his concentration. But it was what he was concentrating on that had her a little beside herself. "I don't think that's possible. It's a restricted zone."

"It's very possible." Kaneko stilled his hips. "But do you want me to stop?"

Sidney frowned. Oh dear, did she really want him to stop? She didn't expect to be in Kaneko's bed this morning, didn't expect to have not one but two miraculous orgasms—but anal sex wasn't even on her list of curiosities. Wait, did she even have a list? *You should definitely have a list*, she heard Noelle say in her head.

"No, but I've never had..." Sidney couldn't get the words out even though his Johnson was nudged in there.

Kaneko smiled. "I lubed you up good and I'll be as gentle as I can." He leaned over her and the tops of her thighs pressed against her stomach, opening her up wider. "Just bear down; it'll make it easier. And breathe."

Sidney huffed. "I can't believe I'm letting you do this."

"Don't worry, there's more you'll be letting me do," Kaneko said. "Now do what I said."

Sidney took a breath in and bore down on the exhale. She gasped sharply at the popping sensation before he slid all the way in. Her sphincter pulsed around his shaft as her body got accustomed to him.

"Are you okay?" Kaneko asked. His eyes were almost closed, and his voice was low and heavy.

"I guess so." Sidney grimaced. "I'm not sure."

"You feel so fucking good...God," Kaneko said through

clenched teeth.

Good? Sidney was glad Kaneko couldn't see her confused grimace because he was too busy staring at their joined bodies. She wondered how it looked. Having something in there as opposed to coming out was completely messing with her head. She felt really full and but the emptiness of her Precious was confusing her senses. But the feel of his Johnson against her stretched skin every time he moved did feel wonderfully different.

Kaneko's eyes lifted and locked onto hers. "Play with your button."

Sidney couldn't help but smile when he said *button*. She slid her hand between her legs but hesitated. She never touched herself while someone was watching. The absurdity of her thought almost made her laugh out loud. He was in her butt, and she was worried about touching herself while he was looking at her? Her priorities were all askew. But she still couldn't look at him while she was doing it. Eyes fluttering shut, she slid her hand between their bodies and rubbed her button.

"No. Open your eyes and look at me," Kaneko ordered.

This man...Sidney's eyes popped open and locked on Kaneko's.

"Tell me when you're gonna come, okay?" Kaneko's hands moved to her knees, rubbing them at the same slow and steady pace as his hips were moving.

Eyes still locked on his, Sidney nodded. She dipped her fingers in between her lips to wet them and then ran swift circles over her button. Kaneko's eyes flickered down to watch her. She had to admit to herself there was something about playing with her Precious in front of an appreciative audience. He looked like he was having more fun watching her now than she was doing it.

"You don't know how long I've wanted to do this." Kaneko's eyes returned to hers.

"How long?" Sidney's lids lowered. The stark desire on his face made her rub faster and faster.

"Since I shook your hand on the quarterdeck two years ago and stared at your ass when you walked away. I knew I wanted to taste you and be buried inside you—just like this." He punctuated his words with his actions.

Sidney gasped at the feeling of him buried to the hilt inside and the knowledge that he wanted her for just as long as she wanted him. It was just too much. *This* was all just too much. Her orgasm rolled over her, and try as she might, she couldn't keep her eyes open.

On the heels of her orgasm, Kaneko grabbed both of her ankles in a tight grip and spread her legs wide, his hips moving faster and faster. She heard the slaps of his thighs against the back of hers, and then he whispered "Fuck," followed by deep, guttural sounds as he came as well. He ground himself against her bottom one last time before kissing her right ankle and resting her legs back on his shoulders.

"I thought I told you to tell me when you were gonna come."

Sidney sighed blissfully. "I had good intentions. I kinda got lost in the moment."

Kaneko shook his head at her. Leaning back a little, he slowly eased out of her. Looking down, he traced his fingers around the gape that he left behind before it slowly closed up. "I love this."

"That's because you're nasty." Sidney wiggled her bottom. She was so sensitive. "I still don't know how to feel about this."

Kaneko laughed, giving her left ankle a kiss before setting

her legs gently on the bed. "Just give it a moment. We did a lot. It needs to sink in."

A horrifying thought suddenly occurred to Sidney. "Is it a mess down there? I feel like it should be a mess down there." She sniffed the air; all she could smell was sex.

"Just a little on my condom and nowhere else that I can tell. We didn't do the prep, so that's to be expected. Be right back." Kaneko quickly went into the adjoining bathroom.

Before Sidney had a chance to be horrified at *what* was on his condom, Kaneko returned with a pack of baby wipes, a warm rag, and a small basin of water. Frowning, she eyed the items. Was he gonna...Oh yes, he was... Without a word, he propped one of her legs up, to give him access and began cleaning her like it was nothing. Maybe cleaning a grown woman's behind was part of his normal sex routine. He did it so nonchalantly and efficiently and in the correct order—front to back. *Well, after what he just did, maybe I deserve to bathe like royalty.*

When he was done, he took everything back into the bathroom and came out with a tube of.....Preparation H? Sidney watched him squeeze a generous amount on his finger and rub it on and inside her sensitive anus. Her eyes fluttered shut. She didn't know if it was the cool tingles or just him simply touching her, but her body immediately responded to his touch. Then her stomach growled.

"I hear you. I'm going to go start breakfast," Kaneko said. He leaned down and nuzzled her neck.

Sidney couldn't help the giggle that escaped her. She never giggled. This man had her acting like a schoolgirl. "Okay. I'm gonna take a nap." She felt no shame at not offering to help cook.

"That's fine." Kaneko gave her shoulder one more soft kiss before going over to his dresser.

Unabashed, Sidney rolled to her side and watched him pull on a pair of plaid boxers and a white T-shirt. He was such a pretty man. After he left, Sidney scooted up to the top of the bed and got under the covers. She grabbed a pillow that hadn't been under her butt and fluffed it before lying down to mull over what just happened. She had ruined his bedding with whatever came out when she had those wonderful orgasms. She paused on that thought. She had two, not one but *two* g-spot orgasms and played with her Precious in front of a man she barely spoke to. Who apparently wanted to get all up in her booty since she left him standing on the quarterdeck.

Meanwhile, her boyfriend of four years barely managed to give her an orgasm orally, so finding her g-spot was totally out of the question. Did he know where the area was? Did he even care? That was a bigger question to answer another day. Today anal sex took precedence. It was not as messy as she thought it would be, and the little bit of mess he had handled with aplomb. And now she was lying in his very comfortable bed while he made breakfast for her. And...*and* she didn't jump in the shower after or demand that he take one before making breakfast. Did he even wash his hands before cooking? Did she care? Her OCD was strangely quiet. Was good Johnson the miracle cure for OCD? She neatly folded the question and packed it away in her information suitcase for later.

Sidney yawned loudly. It was time for a nap. But first, she needed to pee. She dragged herself out of bed and went to the bathroom, and then flopped back in bed. Her eyes were already closing when she pulled the comforter up to her neck. *Whew*, she was a woman down! She drifted off to sleep to the sounds of Kaneko in the kitchen.

Chapter Fifteen

BM1 Joaquín Santiago

This is a drill. This is a drill. Fire, fire, fire. Class B Fire in unrep station starboard side. Crane Deck. Away the fire party to the boat deck portside.

Joaquín stepped into the empty gym just as the bells went off. He just made it! Ten seconds later, he would have been stuck on the mess decks[1] until the drill was over. He had gotten a heads-up that they would be running a fire drill, so he quickly changed and made his way down so he could get his workout in. In port, he only worked out on his duty days, but underway he was here all the time along with the rest of the crew. It was packed at all hours of the day with sailors using weights to make the time go by faster while also combating sexual frustration—which he knew he was going to have a lot of this cruise, especially if Navarro kept her sights on him.

After their unexpected encounter in aft lookout, followed

---

1. Messdecks: The part of the ship where the sailors eat and play dominos.

by the heated exchange in Admin, he was unsure what to do. No, that wasn't true. He knew what he *should* do, but it wasn't what he wanted to do. He was left with a weird state of anticipation and dread at the thought of seeing Navarro. What if she answered his question and told him exactly what he wanted to hear? That she was serious, and all her focus was on him? What was he supposed to do with that? She hadn't approached him when she saw him throughout the ship—only smiled. But her smile...it held all the answers he ever wanted to know. All he had to do was ask the questions.

If only he had quit smoking last month as scheduled instead of procrastinating, he would've never been in the smoking area. He would have been saved from this temptation and inner turmoil. Sighing and shaking his head, he lifted up two thirty-five-pound dumbbells and started his bicep curls. He was on his second set of curls when he realized he wasn't alone. There was someone doing aerobics in the crew's lounge adjacent to the workout room. Just as long as they kept the door closed, he didn't care. He finished doing his sets of bicep curls and was just about to do overhead presses when the crew's lounge door opened. He glanced up and froze. Navarro stood, wearing a puzzled expression.

"Did they secure the fire drill?"

"No." Joaquín shook his head quickly. His eyes traced over her body. A light sheen of sweat covered her forehead and cleavage, and her neon pink sports bra and black biker shorts left little to the imagination. Not that he needed to use his imagination; her naked, sun-tanned body was burned into his memory. Unable to look away, his jaw clenched as he felt arousal stir in his body. Dammit. "What are you doing here?"

Navarro tilted her head to the side and vigorously fanned her face with both hands. "Doing my Tao Bo. It's my Saturday morning routine. I try to stick to it."

Joaquin caught a whiff of her perfume. Of course, she would have perfume on while she worked out. "No, why are you here on the ship—it's not your duty day. I didn't see you at muster."

"Oooh, I didn't make it to muster. I was stuck in traffic. And as far as the duty day, I swapped duty days before I..." her voice trailed off.

"Before I became worthy of your gaze?" Joaquín said sardonically.

"Worthy of my gaze?" Navarro's smile was impish. "I wouldn't put it like that."

"Then how would you describe it?" Joaquín put the weights back on the rack. He crossed his arms over his chest and shut down the voice in his head that asked him why he was starting this conversation.

"Well..." Navarro began and dropped her gaze to the deck and then back up to his. Resolve shone in her eyes. "As I have already stated, my focus was indeed elsewhere, and for that, I do apologize. It was my egregious error to overlook you, especially when you made it so obvious that you wanted my gaze on you."

Jaoquin's eyebrows. "Did I?"

"You did." Navarro walked the short distance over to him and stopped an arm's length away. "To be more specific, you only did *one* obvious thing: our weekly meetings. They were totally unnecessary. We don't have enough First Class matters to discuss that require a follow meeting —sometimes two every week. So, upon further reflection, it leads me to believe that you wanted my undivided attention. Is my assumption correct?"

"It is." There was no use in denying it. Joaquín clenched his jaw, and his gut clenched as he looked down at Navarro's upturned face. Her hazel eyes were even more beautiful up close. Her pupils dilated, and her lips parted slightly when his eyes dropped down to them. Her lips were so close. All he had to do was lean down slightly, and he could taste her.

"so do you still want it?" Navarro reached up and lightly traced his bottom lip with her forefinger, then down the center of his chin and his throat. "Do you still want my undivided attention?"

Joaquín closed his eyes for a second, relishing in her touch even though it was ever so light and brief. "Yes. Yes, I do."

"Good. When I saw you looking at me and how hungry you were—as if given a chance, you would consume me—flesh and bones, heart and soul. It felt *so good.*" Navarro paused. "I want more of that feeling." She placed her hand on his chest. "You're hungry Joaquín, let me feed you."

Joaquín's body lit up. Covering her hand with his, he held it tightly against his chest. "I want all of it."

Navarro's words were quick: "It's yours."

Joaquín's heart pounded from Navarro's response, and he knew she could feel it. The certainty in her voice made him want to roar with victory. How many days did he watch her, enjoying her in silent agony, never once believing that he would have a chance? Now she was unabashedly offering herself to him. He would take it all and leave her ruined for any other man *or* woman. He wanted to be all she thought about; the only person that mattered to her. He wanted to mark her so that everyone knew she was his and his alone. Now that he had her, he had no intention of ever letting her go.

They were both startled by the 1MC announcement securing the fire drill. He heard male voices coming down the ladder well and reluctantly let her go. She rubbed his chest before quickly going back into the crew's lounge and shutting the door. He picked up the weights again.

"Hey Santiago, what's up?" Lamont greeted as he and his workout partner went over to the workout bench.

"Sup," Joaquín replied with a head nod. He wasn't in the mood to finish working out, but his body was tight with arousal. He glanced down and saw the small tent in his shorts, taking a deep breath in and out. That needed to go down before he walked back to the berthing[2].

Trying to put Celia out of his mind, he began to do some overhead reps. He glanced over to the crew's lounge and saw Navarro take her tape out of the VHS and shut the TV off. Her face was completely neutral and pleasant when she opened the door. She greeted Lamont and the other sailor first and then him. Without a backward glance, she disappeared through the hatch, leaving Joaquín to listen to Lamont talk about how fine she was, that she had nice tits and ass, and how he might try to holla at her during the upcoming cruise since she wasn't fucking with Kendrick anymore. She was on everyone's radar now.

Fuck that shit. Joaquín gripped the handles tightly to stifle the rage that swept through him at the mere suggestion that Lamont thought he could try to take what was his. Not another man on this ship was touching Navarro. He'd make that motherfucker disappear first. *Cuz ain't no way in the fucking wor*—he cut his thought short, suddenly aware of his possessive thoughts and the dangerous path he was setting himself on. He needed to get out of here. He took a

---

2. Berthing: living quarters aboard a ship.

deep breath and put the weights back on the rack instead of throwing them at Lamont. Saying "Peace out" to the other two sailors, he left the space.

"Man, who pissed in your coffee this morning?" Ingram asked as they sat down in the mess decks for lunch.

"What?" Joaquín said.

"You've been grumpy and shit since I saw you this morning. That's why I ain't been around you. You were damn near tearing off your seaman's head when I went up to the boat deck earlier, so I left. I ain't want no parts of that."

"Nothing's wrong. I'm cool," Joaquín said. He thought he was presenting a calm facade after speaking to Celia, but he'd been on edge all day. He had already apologized to Gaines. He didn't like being an asshole supervisor; he'd had enough of them in his career.

After Joaquín showered, he went up to the boat deck and started thinking about what happened between him and Celia, as well as his reaction to Lamont. At that moment, he could have actually done Lamont harm. His rage was cold and absolute. He hadn't kissed her, felt her walls squeeze his dick, tasted her juices...nothing. Yet, he was ready to fight another man over a theoretical relationship. What the hell was going to happen to him once he got inside her? Would he lose his mind?

"I wouldn't say cool. Something's got you fucked up," Ingram said. "Oh, never mind, I see what's going on."

Joaquín followed Ingram's gaze to the other side of the mess decks to where Celia was just sitting down with another female crewmate, Macklin. As if feeling his stare, she turned her head and smiled at him. He nodded back then returned his attention to Ingram, who was staring at him.

"She's been here all day?" Ingram asked.

"Yeah, she took the duty from someone," Joaquín said, dropping his eyes to his food in an attempt to avoid Ingram's knowing stare.

"You talk to her?"

"A little," Joaquín hedged.

"What about?" Ingram pressed in a neutral tone.

"Nothin' much."

Ingram made a noncommittal sound and picked up his taco. After taking a huge bite, chewing slowly, and swallowing, he added, "I overheard that cat Lamont saying he was gonna try to holla at her. As a matter of fact, now that she's back on the market, I heard a lotta guys saying they are going to try to hit that. Her roster is going to be full, but by the looks of that smile, you're the first draft pick. But you know the second starter is always waiting..."

Ingram's suggestive tone had him looking back in Celia's direction. Sure enough, Lamont magically appeared and was gesturing to the empty seat next to Celia. He clenched his jaw as the slow burn of jealousy swirled in his gut.

"Man, if you could just see your face right now." Ingram's lips pursed in a silent whistle. "You look like you're ready to kill somebody."

"I'm cool," Joaquín said for what felt like the twentieth time. He took a deep breath and let it out slowly. As a man who prided himself on not only controlling his emotions but also concealing them from the outside world, he was embarrassed that all it had taken was merely seeing Lamont talk to Celia to break through his mask of indifference. It was one thing to feel jealousy, but to have it show on his face—shit, he was going to have to figure out how to regain control.

"Tell that to your face. 'Cause if that's cool, I don't wanna know what heated looks like," Ingram said. Joaquín shook his head. He needed to pull it together. Thankfully, Ingram said no more about Joaquín's breach of coolness and changed the subject to the upcoming NBA game playing that night.

Forcing himself not to look back over to Celia, Joaquín half-listened to Ingram, nodding appropriately and interjecting when necessary, but his mind was on Celia. She had the power to undo him if he allowed it. It would be done so effortlessly on her part, and that was what gave him pause since this morning. She made him want to be undone and wild and live without consequences. Involvement with her would be so much more than just sex. He knew himself well enough to know there'd be no half-measures; he would go all-in with her. He would lose himself. Maybe blow up his life. *I can't do that to Marisol and my kids.* Feeling the burden of his life weighing on his soul, he finally allowed himself to look at Celia, but she was already gone.

Chapter Sixteen

MM1 Sidney Pascal

"**W**ake up, sleepyhead. Breakfast is ready."

Sidney's eyes fluttered open to see Kaneko standing beside her, holding a bed tray. Blinking the sleep away from her eyes, she sat up, pulling the sheet over her breasts and tucking it underneath her arms as he placed the tray over her hips. She glanced to her left and found an identical tray already on the bed. How did she sleep through all of this? She usually heard a pin drop.

"Oh my goodness, this is a lot of food. How long have I been asleep?" Sidney yawned and rubbed her eyes, then picked up her fork. Kaneko did indeed make her Belgian waffles. They looked so fluffy and delicious. Next to them were sliced strawberries accompanied by a creamy white dip, a mini frittata, perfectly crisp bacon, sliced cantaloupe, and honeydew melon. There was even a carafe of coffee with accompaniments. *What in the world...?*

Kaneko glanced at his watch. "Hour and a half, give or take a few minutes."

"And you made all this in that time? Boy, stop, you got this from the IHOP down the street," Sidney teased.

"What, a man can't cook?" Kaneko huffed. He climbed into bed next to her and repositioned his tray over his outstretched legs.

"No, y'all can cook. It's just..." Sidney trailed off, not wanting to admit that she couldn't recall a man ever cooking for her. Not even Nadia's father when they were married. To be fair, she didn't cook for him either because she loath cooking. They ordered so much takeout during their marriage, she was surprised they didn't die from a heart attack or a stroke- or end up in the Fat Boy Program[1]. They must've spent an entire year of their meager wages on fast food. As for Nelson, he also never offered to cook, but he seemed satisfied with whatever she threw together or whatever of Noelle's cooking she could sneak into his house. The latter she would take to her grave because Noelle would kill her if she found out.

Kaneko shrugged one shoulder. "I love to cook. It's one of my favorite hobbies."

"What's your other favorite?" Sidney asked automatically.

Kaneko just smiled at her and put a piece of bacon in his mouth and chewed.

Sidney felt her cheeks flush. After all they'd done—he had put his face in places where she thought the sun would never ever shine. She didn't know why she was embarrassed, but she was. Thank goodness the only light in the room came from the gray sky outside the window because her face was on fire. "This all looks so delicious. What is this?" She used her fork to point to the dip.

Kaneko chuckled, clearly aware of her discomfort. "I made the aforementioned Belgian waffles. The dip on the side is made with mascarpone cheese mixed with crème

---

1. Fat Boy Program: stigmitized weight-control program of nutritional counseling, exercise, and humiliating monthly weigh-ins.

fraiche, whipped cream dip, sugar, and vanilla. Taste it." He picked up a strawberry slice, swirled it in the dip, and held it to her mouth. "You'll love it."

Sidney swallowed. His voice had dropped an octave speaking those last few words, and she flushed for another reason. "You sound pretty confident about that."

"I am."

Kaneko dabbed the strawberry on her lower lip. Reflectively, her tongue darted out and licked the cream. It was freaking delicious. She opened her mouth, and he slid the cream-covered strawberry inside. When the sweetness of the cream and the tanginess of the fruit hit her tongue, she couldn't suppress the small mewl of pleasure that escaped her. "Ummm, this is good!" She made another small sound of pleasure as she swallowed.

"I'm glad you enjoy it. Try it with the waffles. But there's syrup there also. Real maple. I don't do the fake stuff."

With a roll of her eyes, she responded, "I would expect nothing less." Sidney scooped some of the sauce and dropped it on her waffle, then added some strawberry slices on top of it. She took a bite, and her eyes rolled again for a different reason. Noelle's greedy behind would be in heaven over this. She was in heaven. She reached for her coffee and almost dropped it when Kaneko said, "I already put two teaspoons of sugar in it and a splash of creamer." Then he picked up his knife and fork and started to eat his waffle. As if his words didn't just rock her world.

Sidney paused with the cup in the air. "You know how I like my coffee?"

"I do."

Sidney let his answer linger in the air. Not knowing how to respond, she took an experimental sip of her coffee. He wasn't lying. It was perfect. She took another sip. Kaneko knew how she liked her coffee. Why did he know how she liked her coffee? Nelson couldn't even remember what side of the bed she liked to sleep on, and they'd been together for almost four years. Yet Kaneko, a man she had barely spoken to in the past three years they'd been stationed together, knew how she liked her coffee.

WhydoesKanekoknowhowIlikemycoffee?! She jammed that panicked question away with all the other ones. Right now, she just wanted to eat. In comfortable silence, they began to eat in earnest. The only noises in the room were the thunderstorm outside and Sidney's occasional murmurs of pleasure. By the time they were done, the heavy rain had subsided to a drizzle.

"Okay, I'm stuffed. Can you pack the leftovers in a to-go box, and I'll take some home with me?" Smirking, Sidney leaned back against the headboard.

"Ha-ha," Kaneko said as he moved their trays to the floor.

"I do amuse myself sometimes," Sidney said. She wasn't sure what she was supposed to do now. Maybe she should just call a cab because Kaneko looked in no hurry to move. He laid back down and rolled to his side. Propping his head on his hand he looked at her from under heavy lids. He looked sleepy. He confirmed her thoughts, saying, "I am going to take a nap for a few. I had the mid-watch."

"That's fine. I'll call a cab," Sidney said, glancing around for her clothes. She was trying to figure out how to get to them without having to remove the sheet. Again, with the needless modesty but she couldn't bring herself to just whip off the sheet and walk around him naked.

"No, I said I'd take you home. Come take a nap with me..." He held his hand out.

"I already took one."

"So take another one."

Sidney stared at his outstretched hand. Sex with him was one thing, but spooning and sleeping with him was a completely different story. That was so couple-like, and they were not a couple. They were almost strangers who had sex.

Kaneko beckoned with his fingers and then patted the empty spot next to him. "Stop thinking so much, Pascal. You're going to ruin breakfast by giving yourself indigestion. C'mon. I'll let you be the big spoon."

"Ewww, I don't want to be the big spoon," Sidney said, laughing softly. *Oh what the heck, why not?* She slid down on the pillows behind her, rolled onto her stomach, and closed her eyes. "I sleep on my stomach anyway."

"Well, can I rub your booty 'til I fall asleep?"

"No, you've done enough to my booty for one day," Sidney said but didn't object when she felt his hand massaging her bottom anyway. When his hand slipped down between her legs, she protested with the barest of grunts. "I thought you wanted to take a nap."

"You're still so wet." Kaneko's fingers parted her lips and teased her opening.

Not still wet. Sidney was dry while she was sleeping. Her wetness started the second he rubbed her butt. She made a noncommittal sound and spread her legs to give him more access.

She pushed back against his hand. "I guess no nap, huh?"

His hand disappeared, and she heard him rustling around for a condom. Then slid his arm underneath her and used his free hand to guide her hip backward so she rolled against his chest. She felt his hardness against her bottom for a second before he hooked his arm under her knee and raised her leg high. He nudged against her lips before sliding inside her. She sighed. *Lordy*, this man felt so good inside her.

"After this, I promise," Kaneko whispered in her ear.

Chapter Seventeen

PHI Noelle Bentley

T he phone was ringing! *Quentin!* Without bothering to turn the shower off, Noelle jumped out. She almost slipped on the wet tiles on the way to her bedroom, then dove across her bed to grab the cordless phone receiver on the nightstand.

"Hello?" Noelle answered breathlessly.

"Hey, it's Quentin. You okay?"

Noelle couldn't stifle the contented sigh that came as his deep voice filled her ear. The goosebumps on her skin had nothing to do with the ceiling fan cooling her damp and quickly drying body.

"Yeah, I just almost died trying to get the phone. Speaking of which, let me go turn off my shower." Noelle rolled off the bed and went back into the bathroom.

"Wait, were you in the shower?"

"Yes."

"And you got out to answer the phone?"

"Yes," Noelle said. She pulled her red terry cloth robe on, grabbed a towel from the small linen closet, and dried the floor with her foot.

"Damn. What if it wasn't me?"

"Then my blurb on the *Tom Joyner Morning Show* would be: 'Desperate but cute thirty-four year old woman with a few gray hairs dies trying to answer the phone believing it was the man she picked up in the 7-Eleven a week ago.'"

Quentin chuckled. "I didn't see a single gray hair."

"They're not on my head," Noelle said before she caught herself. *What the fuck, Noelle? Why are you telling him you got an old lady coochie?* Yeah, it was only a few gray hairs. She turned into an acrobat, trying to pluck them all. If there was a pube hair-plucking sport in the Olympics, she'd win the gold medal.

There was silence on the other line for a moment before Quentin spoke. "You sound a little embarrassed. There's nothing to be embarrassed about."

"Do *you* have gray hair down there?"

"No."

Noelle grunted. "Umph. When you get them, let me know. I am quite sure that your feelings are going to change just a little bit. It's like all of your youth is suddenly gone, and you need lube to make everything go in smoothly."

"You won't need any lube, Noelle," Quentin said.

"I don't know about that. I have gray hairs in my pubes. I have been traumatized ever since I found them. So—" Noelle started.

"You won't need any lube, Noelle," Quentin repeated slowly and firmly.

"Hmph," Noelle responded. She went quiet and mulled over his words. What did he mean by—Ooh! *Oh!* Okay! She wasn't gonna need lube because *he* was going to make her wet! Well, goddamn, she really needed to be quicker on the uptake. She exhaled silently; a strong tremor slid past whatever gray hairs might be wanting to regrow around her lips. She slid a hand between her legs and felt the light moisture. "Damn." She didn't realize that she had whispered aloud until Quentin laughed softly.

"As much as I want to continue this intriguing conversation, that's not why I called. I was calling to see if you want to catch a movie and get something to eat," Quentin said.

"I don't know. I think I have some plucking to do. Unless you want to do it," Noelle said.

"That is a very generous offer, and I'd be more than honored to do my part in keeping up the illusion of your youth. But we can do it after."

"Ha-ha!" Noelle cackled and clapped her hands. "Yes! Okay, so what do you want to see?"

"*The Crow*. I love my kung fu. Dolemite is my name…"

"And fuckin' up muthafuckas is my game!" Noelle finished. They could watch all the Dolemite movies together! Could this man be any more perfect? She sighed and then giggled. "Fuck it. Let's just hop on a flight to Vegas and get married. There's no need to play all these games anymore. I think you're my soulmate."

"I agree. Let's do it. We could bounce and be back by Monday morning if we leave soon. I'll even buy the tickets," Quentin said.

Noelle pulled the receiver away from her ear and looked at it blankly. Then two of her all-too-familiar voices were babbling inside her head.

Do it! Gurl, ain't you been waitin' for someone to jump off a cliff with you? This man is motherfucking serious, and you know it! Reckless Rhonda said. *He gonna marry you girl! Doooo iiiitt! Bitch you old, do it! He don't mind the gray hairs on your pussy. He probably got a big dick, and you know he knows how to use it! Doitdoitdoitdoit!*

Then Constance came through with the bucket of water. *No Noelle, you are not doing that. You're just bored. Take your ass to the movies, get some food then come home and maybe have sex if you want. But you should probably wait, if you ask me, and then send him right home.*

Yeah, Constance was right. Noelle nodded. She was probably just bored and starvin' like Marvin. She needed some Chinese food to go along with her karate movie, not Elvis marrying her and a weekend in Vegas.

But an all-expense-paid weekend in Vegas does sound nice, Rhonda said, nudging Constance to the side in Noelle's head.

Ma'am, it's Saturday, and you have work on Monday. Just take your ass to the movies. Please and Thank you, Constance countered.

"You good?" Quentin asked. "You're awfully quiet over there."

"I'm fine!" Noelle blurted out. Nope, that didn't sound weird at all. She rolled her eyes. "I was just thinking. What time is the movie? Can we make it to the matinee? Can we have Chinese after?"

"Hmm okay," Quentin said after a slight pause. "And yeah, we can do both those things. Can you be ready in thirty minutes?"

Noelle pouted when she heard the disappointment in his voice. Wow, was Quentin sad that she didn't say yes? Was it that crazy to consider eloping? Maybe they should talk abo—

Bitch, not today, Constance interrupted.

Ugh fine! "Yup, Sure can. See you in a few. Bye." Noelle rolled her eyes as she ended the call.

"So do you and your crazy ex have kids?" Noelle asked Quentin as she dished out white rice onto their plates.

Instead of eating at the restaurant, she suggested they go back to her house and eat out on the patio enjoying the warm spring day.

"Yup. We have a son. Trevor. We call him Tre. He's almost sixteen, and he's a good kid. An Eagle scout," Quentin said proudly. He returned the serving favor by scooping out some General Tso's chicken on Noelle's plate and then his own. "Have you ever been married? I'm not sure if we need your divorce paperwork for Vegas," he added innocently.

Noelle scrunched up her face. "No siree. The closest I've come is my proposal to you."

"I find that hard to believe."

"Believe it. I have never been trapped."

"You consider marriage to be a trap?"

"A right proper gilded cage, yes."

"Hmmm, I see," Quentin replied, then took a bite of food.

Noelle followed his lead and stuffed a piece of broccoli in her mouth. That felt hella awkward. Or at least to her because she knew she was lying her ass off. She'd been close to marriage several times over the years. But as soon as she got a whiff that he might want something more permanent, suddenly she would remember that she had a pie in her oven and run home to take it out. And that was the last he'd see of her.

"Do you have children?" Quentin asked.

"Nope, and I don't want any. To be honest, I would have had my tubes tied years ago, but I learned my body belongs to a man I don't even know yet." Noelle said sarcastically.

"How so?" Quentin put his fork down and leaned back in his seat.

While Noelle was grateful he stopped talking about marriage, she didn't want to talk about having kids either. This is not a conversation they should be having right now.

They hadn't even had sex yet. What the fuck? She sighed inwardly.

"When my doctor found out I wasn't married and also didn't have kids already, he denied my request. He said, and I quote, 'What if the man you marry wants kids?' So my imaginary husband's wants and needs overrule my own. So, I make sure to double up with birth control and condoms. I don't want kids. The world needs more aunties. I am content to be that."

"Fair enough. I already have a son, so I'm all set," Quentin said teasingly and smiled.

"Noted," Noelle said. She bit her lip to contain the big smile she felt coming on. He was about to get all her teeth with that response. There was no "Our baby would be so pretty with your curly hair," or "Who's going to take care of you when you get old?" He just accepted her decision without trying to change her mind first. *Whew, chile...this man right here...*

The topics stayed light for the rest of the meal. They discussed their mutual love of kung fu and karate movies, the tragedy of the Lee family, their favorite scenes in the Dolomite movies, how the juice from the almond fruit trees back in the islands stained their fingers as kids, and the incredible amount of sugar cane Noelle could eat in one sitting. Before she knew it, the sun was setting behind the house. Together, they gathered the plates and the empty cartons and headed into the kitchen.

"I need something sweet and we didn't get any dessert," Noelle said after she shut the dishwasher door. She went over to the freezer and opened it. She might have some butter almond ice cream left.

Quentin sighed and glanced at his watch. "It's okay. I can't stay for much longer anyway."

Frowning, Noelle shut the freezer door and turned to him. "Why not?"

"I am father's errand boy and servant. I think he's making up for all the time I've been gone. But I do have time for this," Quentin said, walking over to her.

"Oh yeah," Noelle said, allowing Quentin to slowly back her up until she was against the refrigerator. "What you got time for?" She leaned her head to the side as Quentin grabbed her hips and buried his face in her neck.

"You smell good," Quentin said.

Noelle lightly scratched the nape of his neck. "I always smell good." She felt the heat of his breath, followed by the wetness of his tongue when he licked her neck. She hummed and rocked her hips against him. She loved a good neck nuzzling. The side of her neck was even more sensitive than her nipples. She dug her short nails into his scalp when his teeth grazed her skin, followed by his lips pulling at her skin. Is he trying to give her a hickey? They just met. *Fuck it, I might just let him.* She wrapped her arm around his waist and rubbed herself against him.

Quentin braced one hand by her head, and the other slid from her hip to underneath the skirt of her sundress. They both groaned when his palm met the bare skin of her behind. "Do you ever wear panties?"

"When I remember. Why? Is that a problem for you?"

Quentin kneaded her cheek with one hand, and the other moved to the junction of her thighs. "You know it's not. But knowing that makes things easier and harder at the same time. Babe, spread your legs a little for me." He slipped his hand between her legs and cupped her pussy. Rubbing it, he leaned back and looked down at her. "See I told you, you wouldn't need any lube."

"Yeah, she's a little moist..." Noelle's eyes fluttered shut as

Quentin chucked and dipped his fingers between her lips. She could feel his eyes on her face, and for a split second she felt self-conscious but shit, it felt so damn good. She knew she was making an ugly ass face, but hon-*ney* dem fingers were doin' thangs…

Then he did something unusual. Instead of continuing to rub her clit or even fingering her, he made a V with his fingers, straddling her clit, and firmly rubbed the soft skin to either side. The sensation was like him rubbing her clit directly, but it felt deeper if that were possible. She gasped, and he kissed her lips once before returning to the crook of her neck. The movements of his fingers never missed a beat as his lips made their way to the soft, sensitive skin behind her earlobe before sucking the naked lobe in his mouth.

"Shit!" Noelle's breathing hitched, and she tried to rock her pussy against his hand but stopped when she realized it interfered with his fingers, and she couldn't have that. She bit her lower lip, but she couldn't stop the whimpering that escaped her mouth nor the surprised squeal when she came and then gushed just enough to run down the inside of her thigh. Did this man just make her squirt standing up in her kitchen? Whoa! She was gonna have a conversation with Celia about this one. Not Sidney though, she'd never eat in the kitchen again.

"Sir, what in the hell just happened?"

"What do you mean?" Quentin cupped her pussy and rubbed his fingers between her lips. "God, you're so fucking wet…I wish I could stay." His fingers stopped rubbing and then started up again.

"I mean, like how did you make me cum so fast? I even did a mini gush," Noelle mumbled the last words into his chest. She didn't know why she was embarrassed about squirting since that is always her ultimate goal when it came to sex, but she was. Maybe it was because he did it so quickly. A man usually had to put in a little bit of work for it. He didn't even finger her.

"A magician never reveals his secrets." Quentin chuckled and rubbed the back of her head soothingly.

"For what it's worth, I can see why your ex wanted to fight me, horrible relationship or not. Shit, I'd wanna fight everybody from your momma to the cashier at the supermarket for just looking at you."

Quentin straightened up. "Nah, I'd keep you cummin' all day. You wouldn't have the strength to fight. You come so fast."

"I usually do but not the gushing though. That's a surprise." Noelle looked up at him and smiled.

Quentin kissed her forehead, the tip of her nose, and then her lips. "Well, you do now."

Noelle wrapped an arm around his neck and slid her tongue into his waiting mouth. With her other hand, she traced his erection through his jeans. Reckless Rhonda was correct. He did have a big ole dick. She felt a slight moment of panic. She needed to see what she was working with so she could mentally prepare herself. She was unbuckling his belt when his pager went off.

"Ugh, goddamn!" Quentin said. He rested his forehead on hers.

"I don't think I like your daddy," Noelle said with a pout. "I really don't."

"I'm beginning not to like him either." The pager went off again, and Quentin sighed.

Noelle buckled his belt and massaged his erection through his jeans. "I guess you should go."

"I know but first…"

Oh my! Noelle gasped when Quentin dropped to his

knees and flipped her skirt up. She grabbed his head when he buried his face in between her legs. She felt his tongue slide in and taste her then flicker a few times over her clit before rising back to his feet. Still in shock and aroused completely again, she stared at him with her lips slightly parted.

"I only saw one gray hair," he said and licked his lips slowly. His pager went off again. He wrapped his hand around her neck and pulled her towards him for a long kiss. Noelle held on to the waistband of his jeans and melted against him until he broke away from her lips. He trailed small quick kisses along her jawline and down the side of her neck. "I'll call you later."

"'Kay." Noelle sighed. Taking his hand, she led him to the side door. He gave her one more kiss before walking down the short flight of stairs to the garage door.

I think he's a really good man, Noelle. Like really, really good, Constance said.

I know, Noelle replied. For the control freak part of her to admit that a man might actually be good for her instead of shoring up her walls was a rare moment indeed.

So try not to fuck it up, Constance warned.

Noelle sighed and shut the door.

Chapter Eighteen

EN2 Nicolas Kaneko

The unfamiliar heat and softness roused Nicolas from his sleep. He opened his eyes to a face full of hair. Pascal. Sidney Pascal was in his bed. And *she* asked him to be there! He gently pushed her hair away so he could see her profile. Unbelievable. He would've thought he had better chances of winning the lottery. He couldn't say that he was focused on her. She was more like in his peripheral vision. He'd catch a glimpse of her as she passed him; she was on the edge of conversations but never the full topic. It wasn't that she wasn't attractive. Quite the contrary, she was pretty as hell. She just stayed out of the limelight and out of the drama that was so prevalent on their ship. But every time he saw her, he'd get a hit of desire but then back to the peripheral she went until the next sighting.

Plus, she had a man, and there was something about that cat he didn't like. He was what his momma would call siddity. He smiled too much; a little bit too loud, especially when other men were around—he always wanted everyone to know that they were together. As if they could ever forget, he was around every duty day. But he could see why now. If he were her man, he wouldn't let her too far out of his sight either. But he would make damn sure she didn't want to be away.

Pascal stirred and turned her head towards him. She cracked open her eyes. "Why are you staring at me?"

"Because I can."

Pascal laughed as Nicolas buried his face in her neck and then moan softly when he nibbled on her skin. He slipped his hand under the comforter and ran it down the warm curve of her hip. He could do this all day. Yeah, he would definitely be haunting the ship every duty day. Hell, he'd even try to bribe the detailer to station them together. She'd be so sick of him.

"Are you hungry?"

Pascal combed her fingers through his hair. "Not yet but I will be soon."

"Ok, go back to sleep and I'll make us something to eat." Nicolas kissed her neck one last time. Pascal mumbled in agreement and rolled over. He gave into the urge to rub her butt before rolling out of bed and heading to the kitchen.

Nicolas got his love of cooking from his Uncle Chauncey who took him under his wing when he was young and awkward, feeling misplaced in his mother's family. Chauncey, being the family outcast, sympathized with his young nephew's plight. His uncle always told him to marry a woman with a healthy appetite; it meant she had a zest for life. If you married a woman who picked at her food, she'd feed off of you and leave you an empty shell of a man. He also said she'd be really good in bed too. Nicolas had been too young to grasp that concept, but as he got older, his advice turned out to be true indeed.

So what was he going to make her? He glanced at the clock on the microwave. It was too late for lunch, and they also had a big breakfast. He opened the fridge and stared inside. A light supper would do. He didn't want her to go back to sleep after eating, they had things to do. He could make some shrimp po'boys or a quick etouffee, soba noodles, or gyudon since he had some shaved steak. He also had salmon but he wanted to save that just in case she stayed. He was going to do his best to convince her. He opted for the gyudon and got to work.

"Do you know you hum when you really like something?" Nicolas asked after he heard Pascal hum again. They were eating in bed again because neither one wanted to leave it.

"I don't hum. What are you talking about?" Pascal ate another forkful of food.

Nicolas knew the exact moment that the flavors hit her tongue because she started to hum happily. "That right there. You didn't just hear yourself?"

"Nope." Pascal shrugged one shoulder. "I didn't hear anything, but this is delicious. What is this called anyway? It tastes like Chinese food."

Nicolas shot her an incredulous look thinking she had to be joking, but her face was completely straight. Maybe she really didn't know. She'd been humming ever since her first bite of Belgium waffle this morning. It was the cutest thing ever. But how could she not know?

"It's called gyudon and it's Japanese. I was going to make some po'boys but I didn't want the place to smell like fried shrimp."

"Japanese to Creole food. That's quite a combination," Pascal said.

Nicolas heard the confusion in her voice and realized she

didn't know about him. "Well, my father is Japanese but my mother's Black. She's from New Orleans."

"I know you lyin'!" Pascal's head reared back as she squinted at him suspiciously.

"No, I am not. My mother is just very light-skinned—like passing for white light skin. And she could've passed if she really wanted to which she didn't. Her family wanted her to get married, but she joined the army in 1960 instead of going to college. She was the rebel of the family, and she met my father when she was stationed in Japan. You thought I was Chinese or Filipino, didn't you?"

Nicolas wasn't surprised. His racial identity wasn't something discussed. It always felt awkward and forced to announce his mother was Black like he was trying to prove something to the people around him. So he just let it happen organically after years of struggling to find a place in his mother's family and coming up short.

"More Filipino I guess. They're more common in the Navy. But definitely not Black. You don't look like you have even one drop of Black blood in you. Like none. Zero. I don't even know what to say," Pascal said.

"I get it," Nicolas said. He was almost a carbon copy of his father, Hikari. While his mother's almond-shaped eyes blended perfectly with his father's, they didn't create the double eyelid that his sister had. Maybe if one looked hard enough, the bridge of his nose was not as sharp and a little bit flatter than the average Japanese, and if he grew his hair out, the thickness of his waves might prompt a question or two. His father's genes almost completely overrode his mother's. It was only when he tanned did his mother's genes make an appearance. By the end of a summer deployment to the Med, his skin was a nice deep, almond shade that quickly faded in the mild Virginia winters. His sister, the other hand, was naturally a couple of shades darker than him and completely favored their mother with only a slight uptilting of her eyes. It made her look exotic and mysterious—two words he hated when they were used to describe her when they visited the States when they were young.

"So Creole huh?" Pascal's gaze turned from suspicious to inquisitive as she continued to stare at him. "So that's where your accent comes from. I just thought you had picked it up from being around Black people. Wowzers! Can't say, I was not expecting to hear this. Gimme a minute while I process because my mind is like..." She pantomimed her head exploding.

"Take your time." Nicolas nodded. "I know how I look. I took most of the Japanese genes, and my older sister Natalie took most of the Black and white ones. DNA is funny with how selctive it is. Whenever we visited New Orleans everyone thought she adopted this poor little Japanese boy, and my sister was the only biological child. And then they were so apologetic to my mother, not because they made a mistake but because she had an Asian-looking child."

"Awww, poor baby." Pascal tsked. "I am sorry you had to go through that. Remind me to give your inner child a hug later."

"Only if I can suck on your nipples while you do it," Nicolas said to lighten the mood. He heard the sympathy in her voice, and while appreciated, it wasn't what he wanted from her.

"I don't think your inner child needs that."

"No, but my inner teenage boy does."

"I bet your inner teenage boy needs a lot of things," Pascal said dryly.

"He actually does," Nicolas said with a small smile. He was

surprised at how much he meant that. His wistfulness must have been reflected in his voice because Sidney looked at him curiously.

"Don't get me wrong, I had a great childhood. But I wasn't always this gorgeous piece of man meat you have sitting before you tantalizing your taste buds. I was an awkward teenager. I had acne so bad—it was a nightmare. Had it not been for my high school friend Sarah, who was even more awkward than I was, I would have stayed a virgin until I joined the Navy."

"But could you cook back then too?"

"Yup. My uncle taught me. I've been cooking since I could hold a knife without cutting my fingers off."

"And you didn't try cooking for them?"

Nicolas sent her a dubious look. "What teenage girl wants gyudon and po' boys?"

"Probably just Bentley." Pascal tilted her head from side to side. "But I'm not saying that's all you would've had to do but it;s a start. Anyway, they missed out on all this good eatin'." She punctuated her sentence by sticking a piece of steak in her mouth.

"Is that all they're missing out on?" Nicolas said, looking at her profile while she chewed. He saw her glance at him out of the corner of her eye and smile, but she didn't respond. He didn't push for an answer because he wasn't sure how she would take it or where the conversation would lead. Apparently, she was missing out on a lot of things which led her to his bed on a rainy Sunday morning. She'd always been friendly enough, but she had never shown any interest in him professionally or otherwise. He knew she had a man and he wasn't one to get caught in drama. So other than on duty days, they didn't interact with each other. He didn't have a reason to visit main control[1], so he never went down to her space. The mess decks[2] were where he saw her the most. He came upon knowing how she liked her coffee when he overheard her giving her coffee order to Bentley one morning, and it just stuck in his brain. He never thought he'd have a reason to use the knowledge.

Speaking of Bentley, Nicolas wondered about their friendship and even Navarro's for that matter. He was friends with both women; he and Bentley were assigned to the same General Quarters station. They joked around with each other, even lightly flirted, but Bentley was a firecracker, and he'd had enough explosions in his life. Navarro, he'd met at his first command here in Norfolk back in '82. Even then, she made the hair on the back of his neck stand up. There was something about her...Plus, he was an ass man, and neither woman came close to Pascal.

Personality-wise, Pascal was also the antithesis of both women. Her demeanor was calm and collected. She was warm and approachable. When she spoke, the people around her quieted down to listen to her soft Texan accent. Her big, brown eyes just drew people in. The few times she directly looked at him, the world faded around him. She made you feel as though no one else existed in the world but you and her at that very moment. She even did the attentive lean-in. He occasionally watched her do it with everyone, from the E-1s to the Captain of the ship. She was sweet, and she sprinkled fairy dust everywhere she

---

1. Main Control: controls the propulsion system of the ship.

2. Messdecks: the part of the ship where the sailors eat and play dominos.

went, enchanting people along the way. She was like a fairy godmother, only showing up when you needed her.

Nicolas already knew he was going to need a sprinkling of her every day. Hands down, today was some of the best sex he'd had in at least five years. Everything about her was amazing. Her pussy was so tight; it felt like she was gripping him with her hand. He almost came after a few strokes before he calmed himself down. She tasted like a dream, he could spend the day with his face between her thighs. She had those big nipples and areolas that he loved, and they were so sensitive. He could also spend all day sucking on her nipples and playing with her titties.

And she let him do anal! Never in a million years would he have thought she'd let him do that. It was also not something he did the first time around. He usually waited before asking about that, but he didn't know if he'd get another chance with her. So he had decided that before she left his bed, he'd have his fill. He was going to try to fuck her in every way she'd let him. He wanted to make sure he left a lasting impression on every part of her body, make sure he came in every hole. The next one was her gorgeous mouth. He wanted to feel her soft lips on his cock and his balls in her mouth. Would she let him gag her? Could she deep-throat? What was her hand game like?

"Why are you so quiet?" Finished with her meal, Pascal put her fork down and with the sheet still tucked under her arms, leaned back against the headboard.

"Just thinkin'." Nicolas set his tray on the floor next to the bed.

"About what?" Pascal grabbed her glass of sweet tea before Nicolas removed her tray and placed it on the floor next to hers.

"About how good you taste. I dare say it's refreshing."

"So I'm thirst quenching?" Pascal smiled as she took a sip.

"Better than Gatorade." Nicolas gave the sheet a tug, but Pascal squeezed her arms tight.

Eyes wide, she shook her head. "No, I need to take a shower."

"A shower? For what?" Nicolas gave a sharp pull, and the sheet jerked from her body causing her to spill her drink. He tossed the sheet aside and licked the droplets of tea from her breasts while his hand slid between her thighs.

Pascal trapped his hand with her thighs. "We've been having sex."

"And?" Nicolas said around her nipple.

"And I'm funky." Pascal's voice was breathless.

Nicolas sucked her nipple and ran his thumb over her mound until she loosened her grip. Then he spread her legs and buried his face between her thighs. He slid his tongue inside her, sampling her wetness, before replacing it with his fore and middle fingers. Straightening back up, he rubbed his lips against hers and whispered, "You smell like you've been fucked. It's the best smell in the world." It was even easier to find her g-spot in her semi-reclining position, and he pulled roughly against it roughly in a continuous beckoning motion Now that he knew he gave her her first g-spot orgasm, he was going to give her one every chance he got. He was still shocked she never had one before but damn happy he was the first one to give it to her. She'd never forget it—or him.

"You're so nasty." Pascal pulled her mouth away and threw her head back against the headboard and bucked against his fingers. "Oh, my God!"

When the pressure became too much, she tried to get away like the first time. But instead of loosening her, he threw one of his legs over one of hers to keep her in place while he fingerfucked her roughly. Tangling his hand in her hair, he pulled her face down back to his and kissed her. The mewling sounds she made against his mouth made him move his hand faster and faster until her body went taunt, and a guttural sound came from her deep within her throat, and she groaned in his mouth. He felt the release of fluid from her orgasm flow over his fingers. He didn't stop until she was empty and her head flopped back on the headboard.

Nicolas sat back on his heels and stared at Pascal's sated body. Her legs were splayed open, one was on her stomach, and her breasts sloped to the sides. And she somehow managed to hold on to her glass.

"Those g-spot orgasms are so much…Is this why you have me such a big glass of sweet tea?" She asked lazily.

Nicolas laughed. "Yes. I gotta keep you hydrated. Can't have you fallin' out mid-nut."

"This tea might not cut it. My goodness, I can't believe I held on to this glass." Laughing softly, Pascal took a big gulp of tea. "Sir, I think you're trying to turn me out."

Indeed, I am. "I will, if you let me," Nicolas said.

Pascal swallowed and dropped her gaze to his chest. Nicolas just rubbed her thighs and let her think. He could imagine what was running through her mind. She was in a relationship, and the Puget Sound was about to start a cruise. So if this went south, they'd be stuck on the ship together. He was Japanese presenting, no matter that his mother was Black, and she was Black. Yes, it was the '90s, but prejudice was still a huge issue. But he was more concerned about her getting rid of her guy; they could work out the rest. He kept his thoughts to himself and waited. She took a deep breath, returning her eyes to his. Her gaze was soft and seductive, and he knew she didn't realize how sexy she was. That was also part of her allure.

"Will it always be like this?"

"Be like what?" Nicolas knew what she was asking, but he wanted her to say it. She needed to acknowledge what she was asking for.

"You know you know what I'm trying to say." Pascal rolled her eyes and huffed.

Nicolas just raised his eyebrows.

"Fine." Pascal muttered and then in a louder voice said, "Will I always have really good orgasms every time we have sex? Is that something you can guarantee? I feel like I am asking a lot here."

"Honestly, an orgasm is the bare minimum. There is so much more to sex than orgasms. So what I can guarantee is that whenever we get together it will be an experience like none other. Is that what you mean?"

"Yes, that's what I mean." She smiled slowly.

This smile wasn't like her other smiles. This one was solely created for him and born out of the pleasure he brought her. Nicolas's chest swelled with pride and something he wasn't quite ready to name yet. He leaned over, trapping her beneath while he sucked on her bottom lip. "And I won't let you sleep in the wet spot."

"What! No sleeping in the wet spot? Sold! You actually might wanna change the sheets because they're really wet now." Pascal managed to wiggle out from underneath him and scoot over to his side of the bed, taking the comforter with her.

Laughing, Nicolas rolled off the bed and went into his bathroom to grab a towel. Laying it over the wet spot, he felt another surge of pride at the size of it. "Yeah, finish off that tea. I might have to stock up on Gatorade because I don't have any IVs handy."

"Listen, I don't like needles, but if that's what it takes to keep this going, I might have to switch my rate[3] and become a HM[4] so I can just hook myself up and keep it moving," Sidney said and finished off her tea and handed him the empty glass.

"I like your initiative. That's some 3.0 evals." Nicolas clapped and rubbed his hands together.

Pascal gasped. "3.0! I am offended."

"Calm down, now. You didn't read my write-up." Nicolas pretended to hold up a piece of paper. "It said: MM1[5] Pascal has improved in all areas that require improvement. She has shown great initiative. She picks up things quickly and is able to emulate whatever is shown to her. But for her next evaluation, MM1 must show improvement in her fellatio skills as she has yet to demonstrate them. Once that is completed, she'll be a 4.0 sailor." He then folded his imaginary paper and put it in his imaginary shirt pocket.

Pascal sat up against the headboard and crossed her arms over her chest, tapping her fingers against her biceps, and said stubbornly. "I don't do that."

Nicolas nodded slowly. He wasn't surprised. Some of the Black women he'd been with over the years started out not enjoying giving head. He suspected it was the type of

---

3. Rate or Rating: an enlisted sailor's job or job description.

4. HM/Hospital Corpsman: assist health care professionals in providing care to Navy personnel.

5. Machinist Mate: are responsible for operating and maintaining ship propulsion machinery and outside machinery.

men they were messing with. He saw firsthand how some of these sailors lived, he wouldn't want their cocks in his mouth either. But because he liked receiving almost as much as he liked giving, he made sure his sperm tasted as good as he could make it so she had no complaints.

"Well, MM1, if you are willing to hook yourself up to an IV to keep on squirting in my face, you're going to have to learn to take my cock in your mouth."

Pascal made an ugly face. "Not if you use that word."

Nicolas' brows rose. "Cock?"

Hand flying to her chest, she made a silent gagging motion. "Yes, I hate that word. It's so hard. It's vulgar."

"You'd rather I say take my dick in your mouth?" Nicolas was confused. That word was just as bad.

"Absolutely not!" Pascal grimaced and shook her head vigorously.

What the hell? This was a first. Nicolas had never had anyone complain about the word dick before. *Oh yeah, she doesn't curse.* Suddenly he remembered one of the peripheral conversations about Pascal that he had with Bentley during general quarters[6] about their favorite childhood snacks Cracker Jacks and the fact that it was one of Pascal's replacements for bullshit. Pascal didn't curse and if she did—watch out. Shit was about to go down. So what was her name for cock? He decided to ask her.

"Don't laugh when I tell you," Pascal warned, pointing a finger at him.

Nicolas smothered the chuckle that almost escaped. "I won't." He held up his right hand. "I promise."

---

6. General Quarters: announcement made aboard a naval warship to signal all hands must go to their assigned battle stations as quickly as possibl

"Johnson. I call men's…" She gestured to his groin. "Johnson."

"Oh, that's not bad. It's like you gave my guy here a name. Johnson was very pleased to make—" Nicolas gestured to Pascal's pussy. "What's her name? I assume she has one."

"It's Precious."

"Well, that's just…" Nicolas' voice trailed off when Pascal rolled her eyes. He couldn't stop the small chuckle that escaped. She was so damn cute sitting there, torn between embarrassment and determination. "Johnson was thrilled to make Precious's acquaintance. I think they are going to be best friends. Don't you think? Oh!" He tilted his ear up, pretending that someone was whispering in his ear. "Johnson also just told me that you're gonna really like the taste of cum."

"No." Pascal shook her head adamantly. "No, I didn't hear that."

"I eat well, and we exercise. It's full of nutrients. It'll be just like taking a vitamin. I've been told that my come is delicious and nutritious."

"Vitamins are gross. I choke them down."

"You might choke, but I assure you, it won't be because of my taste."

Pascal sighed. "I definitely didn't think I'd be having this type of conversation ever. In life. And especially not with you."

"Don't question God's plans," Nicolas chided as he climbed into bed with her.

Pascal burst out laughing and slid down on the pillows and rolled to her side. "You're going straight to hell for that one." She yawned. "Matter of fact, I'm taking another nap because I wanna be asleep when he comes for you. Keep your hands to yourself," she added when Nicolas spooned her.

"I'm just trying to get comfortable." Nicolas threw his arm over her and discreetly smelled her hair. It smelled like flowers and sex.

"Stop smelling my hair."

Nicolas chuckled and pulled her closer to him as though he'd done it a million times before. She felt good up in his arms with her naked ass pressing against his cock. He felt himself stir when she wiggled her ass, trying to get comfortable. He kissed her shoulder.

"No, sir. Go to sleep."

Nicolas smiled and closed his eyes.

Chapter Nineteen

YN1 Celia Navarro

T he visor from Celia's ball cap shielded her eyes as she watched Joaquín walk across the flight deck for duty section turnover. His expression was pensive, and she wondered what he was thinking. They hadn't spoken since yesterday morning, and she hadn't sought him out. She needed time to think about their conversation and what she promised. She was amazed that she was giving herself away—lock, stock, and barrel—to a man she barely noticed a week ago but now was somehow consuming all her thoughts, wants, and desires as though he was her childhood crush coming back into her life.

She promised herself that she would not get involved with another married person, especially with a man. They were so possessive and reckless. She'd seen so many marriages break up and people go to Captain Mast unnecessarily over cruise affairs simply because the man couldn't let go. On the other hand, women just went back to their pre-deployment lives as though they didn't spend the whole cruise getting their freak on. They weren't about to destroy their lives over cruise dick. It was unfathomable to most of the women she knew. The cruise wasn't real life; it was an interlude, sometimes a welcome break from the monotony of everyday life. It didn't replace real life. The ones who thought it did usually end up in a world of hurt.

Between her and the bulkhead, she spent most of the night looking up at from her rack; she didn't fancy men as much as she did women. They usually didn't incite this level of attraction for her. She enjoyed men, but they were just too complicated. There were all these rules they wanted to put down in the relationship. Her ex-fiancé was a typical machismo Puerto Rican man. She enjoyed the domesticated life for a while, but that shit got mundane and boring soon enough, then he had the nerve to cheat when they were on deployment. She learned how to make her mother's beans and rice for that man. She was livid for weeks after they broke up. But here she was, chasing after a Columbian man from Miami.

Celia wondered if he had not revealed how much he wanted her, would she want him? Was this a case of borrowed emotion? Did she want him simply because he wanted her? Was she willing to upset her life? There was a possibility she'd be over this man before the cruise even started, and she'd be stuck trying to avoid him for six months.

She was still lamenting when she saw him on the mess decks[1] for chow. The moment their eyes met; all her previous thoughts evaporated under the heat of his stare. The need to touch him, smell him, have him inside her- it gave her pussy a throbbing heartbeat all its own. She wanted to clench her thighs together and savor the moment. Then Lamont appeared at her table, fucking up her vibe.

However, she perked back up when she caught a glimpse of Joaquín's expression. It was so mouthwateringly pos-

---

1. Mess or Mess Deck: a designated area where military personnel eat and socialize.

sessive and angry. She'd be lying if she said she wasn't positively thrilled by it. He knew why Lamont was at the table. She had so many men hitting on her since she broke up with Kendrick; she wondered if it was in the POD[2]. It wasn't as though it would stop when she got together with Joaquín because she was going to try her best to keep their relationship on the down low. This was going to be an interesting cruise.

Out of the corner of her eye, she spotted Lamont walking towards her, so instead of going to join her department, she moseyed over to where Ingram and Joaquín stood. "Good morning, sunshines! How are we doing this fine, fine Navy morning?"

Joaquín, wearing a neutral expression, just dipped his head at her. Celia's eyes discreetly searched his face. She wondered what he was thinking.

"It'll be *fine* when I get the fuck off this damn ship," Ingram complained. "I hate Saturday duty[3]. It kills your weekend. I guess I can just grill today or something."

"Sundays are a good day to grill," Celia agreed then laughed when Ingram shrugged.

The announcement to muster[4] for duty section[5] turnover came over the 1MC[6] and sailors began to move into their departments. She was turning to leave when he asked to have a word with her before she left. She smiled and told him they could go to Admin. After duty section turnover, they both bid adieu to a grumpy Ingram, and Celia

---

2. POD/Plan of the Day: command's schedule for the day.

3. Duty: Responsibilities given to a group of people for 24 hours.

led the way to the Admin office. They were the only two people in the passageway, and neither one of them spoke as she unlocked the door.

Once inside, Celia turned on the overhead light, then locked the door and leaned back against it. Joaquín moved further into the space to put some distance between them. They stared at each other for a moment before he spoke.

"Celia, I've wanted you since the first time I saw you, and it's been driving me crazy. Before this, I have never, ever been tempted to cheat on my wife. I've kept it in check by making up reasons to be alone with you without you realizing the reason." He shook his head. "I was able to keep this under control because you never wanted me back. But—"

"But now I do," Celia interjected. She pushed off the door and walked over to him. She framed his face with her hands. "I want you too. So much. Honestly, the intensity of it has caught me by surprise. You went from being nobody to somebody mighty quick. I don't understand it. I can't explain it, so I am not even going to try. It just is. I feel consumed by the need for it." She brushed her thumbs lightly along his bottom lip. "By this need I have for you."

Joaquín sighed and closed his eyes. She felt his body slump, and his head got heavy in her hand. He shuddered when Celia combed her fingers through his hair and raked her nails lightly down the back of his neck. She smoothed out the furrow between his eyebrows and ran the backs of her hands over his cheeks before framing his face again and lifting his head.

"Shhhh." Celia placed two fingers over his lips when he opened his mouth. She trailed her fingers across his lips. "Listen, I want you to take some time and really think about this. There is no rush. Because right now you look..." She shook her head and tsked, her eyes sweeping over his face. "You would hate yourself after and probably hate me too." She pulled his head down and kissed his forehead gently, inhaling his scent, and she rubbed her thumbs over his cheeks. "And I don't want that for you."

Joaquín grabbed her wrists when she tried to let him go. "I could never hate you, Celia."

Celia's hand tightened on his face for a split second. "You don't know that, and I don't want to risk it." She brushed her thumbs over his lips one last time before tugging her hands away and stepping back. She wanted to kiss him, but if they started kissing, it wasn't going to stop with that.

The sound of voices and keys jingling from right outside the door prevented Joaquín from answering. Celia opened the door before it could be unlocked. YN2[7] Ziegler standing in the passageway looked startled when the door opened. He looked from Joaquín to Celia before clearing his throat. "Do you want me to come back?"

Celia shook her head. "No no, BM1[8] was just leaving."

Joaquín gave a quick nod to Ziegler. "Zielger."

"BM1." Zeiglier returned the nod and went over to his desk. Looking uncomfortable, he sat down and busied himself.

Joaquín turned his attention back to Celia. "I'll talk to you tomorrow, *si*?"

Celia gave him a faint smile but didn't respond as Joaquín left the office.

---

7. YN/Yeoman: administrative and clerical worker

8. BM/Boatswain's Mates: crew members who train, direct, and supervise personnel in ship maintenance and boat seamanship.

Chapter Twenty

YN1 Celia Navarro

"Awww, you look like a disappointed Poobear. What happened?" Noelle asked, setting her grocery bags on the counter.

Sighing, Celia looked up from the *Ebony* magazine she was listlessly flipping through. Despite reading the page twice over, she couldn't even begin to tell you what the rumor about Toni Braxton was even regarding. To take her mind off Joaquín when she got home, she did a couple of loads of laundry and cleaned her bathroom, but he might as well have been handing her the scrub brush because her thoughts never strayed from him.

"Santiago had duty yesterday. I didn't even know that when I switched with Rios 'cause, yanno. So anyway, we got stuck in the gym during the fire drill, and then we had a talk after turnover." Celia closed the magazine. Now that she had Noelle, she gave up the pretense of reading.

"Oh, do tell." Noelle quickly put all the refrigerated groceries away and left the rest in bags. She washed her hands and then grabbed a rectangular Tupperware container. Popping it open, she took out a cinnamon roll, plated it, handed it to Celia, and then got one for herself. "They're still warm. I woke up way too early and couldn't go back to sleep so I made them."

"Well…" Taking the plate, Celia considered how much to tell Noelle. If she told Noelle verbatim what he said and then what she said in response, Noelle would tell her to stop before she got in too deep. But it would be like trying to stop breathing.

"It was that much, huh?" Noelle said when Celia didn't speak.

Fuck it. Celia took a deep breath and told Noelle what happened.

"Oh dear, and y'all didn't even kiss yet, and you've given him the key to the chastity belt? Ooof, I don't know, girl. This is a bit much, don't you think? I know I get over-whelmed easily, but those were strong, meaningful words. I would never say that. And if someone told me what you told Santiago? I would run quickfast in a hurry."

"Which words?"

"The consumption of each other. Or you of him. You're just offering yourself up like you're the dessert table at Shoney's lunch buffet. It's too much. I simply cannot!" Noelle threw her hands up in the air.

"Yeah, I didn't expect to say all that. But I had to give him some of his power back. I think he feels helpless about how he feels about me," Celia said.

"In light of him being married and all, I can see how it might be a sensitive subject," Noelle said with an eye roll.

"And when I held his face in my hands and told him I needed him, he put his head down, and it was like some-thing in him broke. As much as I relish the thought of owning his body and maybe a little bit of his soul for at least six months, I want him to give it to me in full awareness. There are no take-backs. So, I told him to think about it."

"What the fuck!" Noelle grabbed her face in her hands. "A little bit of his soul? I'm already stressed. I don't even know where to begin. There's so much wrong in that entire statement."

Celia shrugged. "You know how I am."

Noelle grimaced. "Ummmm, no boo-boo. This is a deeply hidden side of you that I have never seen. Put it back away. I don't want to know my best friend is moonlighting as a succubus, m'kay. Is this how your titties stay high? 'Cause I really feel like they should have dropped by now."

"No, that's just because nothing but adult mouths are suckling on these nipples. And I do my pilates and tao bo. You should do it with me."

"No, thank you. I'll just get a better bra. I don't like to sweat any more than necessary." Noelle clasped her hands together. "Okay, listen. Somehow this went from 'Ohhh, Santiago wants me' to 'I want to own his soul' very quickly. Upon reflection, I don't think it should have ever gotten here. Yet, here we are discussing transferring ownership of souls. I can't even...so I'm just going to offer a suggestion, is that okay? Are you open to taking suggestions, my dear friend?"

"Sure. You know I always weigh the facts before I make my final decision," Celia said and took a bite of her cinnamon roll.

"True, but you also happen to pick the most subjective facts to base your decision on. That's why we've been able to stay friends for so long. Our mutual love of bullshit bonds us together like a glue that shouldn't work—but it does. I think that maybe you should find another guy's soul to steal. What about Evans? He's been just waiting in the wings for you to stop eating coochie. I don't think he'd have any difficulties or barriers that would prevent him from putting his soul on your altar."

"Nah." Celia wrinkled her nose. "It tastes better when

there's a little bit of resistance left mixed in with a smidgen of guilt."

"Goodfuckingnight!" Noelle slammed her palms on the table. "I need a goddamn drink instead of this cinnamon roll. Remember what I said about your counselor; please go ahead and book a session in advance. And a baptism; you need Jesus back in your life."

"It'll be fine. You worry too much."

"I think 'it'll be fine,' and 'what's the worst that can happen,' are phrases that usually herald disaster." Noelle broke off a piece of the roll and popped it in her mouth. "Oh, I forgot to tell you, I went to the movies with Quentin yesterday, and afterward—hey, chica."

"Hey." Sidney strolled into the kitchen and went over to the phone. After pulling a piece of paper out of her shirt pocket, she dialed a number. Turning her back to them, she whispered something and laughed before hanging up.

"I am sorry about yesterday," Celia said after Sidney hung up the phone.

"Don't worry about it. You can't control the weather." Sidney took a cinnamon roll out of the container and took a small bite. Then, humming softly, she took a plate from the cupboard.

"I hope you were calling Breath and Britches and letting him know you're home now. He called the house phone right after you called to say you weren't gonna be coming home. I told him that you had a migraine and were lying down."

"Thank you," Sidney said.

"You're welcome. And sooo, where were you all day yesterday?" Noelle asked, glancing at the watch on her wrist. "And half of today?"

Celia studied Sidney. She had gotten the message that

Sidney had gotten a ride yesterday, but she didn't realize that she hadn't gone home. That was interesting. Where had she been all this time? She sent Noelle a quizzical look, but Noelle was too busy staring at Sidney to notice. In silence, they both watched Sidney pour herself a glass of milk. Then with a big smile for the two of them, she left the kitchen.

Stunned, Noelle looked at Celia. "Shut the front door! Did she just sashay out of here?"

"Uh-huh." Celia nodded her head. "I think it was more like floating." She swayed her arms in the air.

Noelle drummed her fingers on the table. "And correct me if I'm wrong, she was humming 'Darling Nikki'?"

Celia squinted as she thought for a moment and then nodded again. "I believe she was."

"Okay. Well then." Noelle clapped her hands and stood up.

"Where are you going?"

"Oh, she got fucked last night and she's lookin' like how I wanted to look yesterday. So I need to know who put it on her. Because you know she ain't hummin that Prince song for Nelson's limp-dick ass. You comin'?"

Celia jumped up and grabbed her plate. "Of course I am."

Chapter Twenty-One

MMI Sidney Pascal

"Ahhh, don't you knock?" Startled, Sidney spun around at her door flying open. She was tossing her clothes in the hamper when her door opened. She glared at Noelle and then at Celia, who just peeked out from behind Noelle while nibbling on her cinnamon roll. "I'm going to need you to knock. I don't just barge into your room without permission."

"I did knock. Three times! I thought you were in the shower, but apparently, you couldn't hear me over your new theme song. It's 'Darlin' Nikki'...amirite, Celia?" Noelle asked.

"Yes, you are," Celia said through a mouthful of food.

Sonavobiscuit! Sidney had called Kaneko 'Nicky' at some point during their sex-a-thon, and she found herself humming Prince's song during the cab right home. She looked around for something to cover up with; her robe and towels were in her bathroom. Turning on her heel, she darted into the bathroom, snatching her robe from behind the door. "I don't know what you're talking about. Shut my dang door."

"Well, did you know that your gorgeous melanin that glows in the dark when you put shea butter on it—of which I am highly jealous of due to my lack of it—is not dark enough to hide that hickey on your left butt cheek?"

"What!" Sidney flipped the edge of her robe up and craned her neck over her right shoulder, trying to see her behind. She spun around in a circle like a dog chasing its tail before she got frustrated.

"That's the right butt cheek you're looking at, but there's one on there too. You have *matching* hickeys on your butt cheeks!" With that last exclamation, Celia and Noelle walked into her room and shut the door so Sidney could see her reflection in the mounted mirror. "Look!"

Modesty gone, Sidney ran over to the mirror and dropped her robe to the floor. Turning turned around, she looked over her shoulder at her reflection. Sure as sugar, there were two symmetrical hickeys on her butt cheeks. Oh, so that's what he'd been doing back there.

"Oh chile, and also have two bruises right at your lower back, over your hips. It's like they wrapped around...are those...fingerprints? Oh, my gawd!" Noelle gasped and clutched her pearls. Swooning, she fell dramatically onto Sidney's bed. "My nerves can't take this! Jesussomebody pass me the smelling salts!"

"Fluffnutter," Sidney whispered. Those were indeed fingerprints. The other four were on the front of her hips. He left those sometime during the night when she rode him reverse cowgirl (another first for her) so he could look at her butt. Again, he was telling her how much he loved her Precious. That really got her going and then he got going. It was a good thing they reversed on the bed so she could hold on to the headboard when he vice-gripped her hips and took over. She thought she was going to break the headboard loose from the frame. She couldn't stop the soft smile that appeared.

But what other marks did Kaneko leave on her? Her eyes traveled up her back, where she found a bite mark and another hickey on her right trapezius muscle. He did that one in the early morning hours (how many times did they have sex?) before they took their nap the first time. Every time he hit bottom, he would bite and suck on her and whisper something dirty in her ear. That man was nasty with a capital N. She could call him Mr. Jackson.

Her dizzy spell apparently over, Noelle sat up on the bed. "Who were you with? Tell me now. I must know!"

Sidney bit back a smile, picked up her robe, and put it back on. It felt good to finally have a secret. And this was a good secret, too. She wasn't ready to talk about it; her information suitcase was still in baggage claim.

Noelle scooted off the bed, stood in front of Sidney, and folded her arms. "Don't be trying to ignore me now, Brown Cow. You've been gone since yesterday morning, and now you lookin' all dewy-eyed, hickeys all over, and fingerprint- ed up, hummin' 'Darlin' Nikki' as you enjoyed *my* delicious cinnamon roll. I'm finna reach down your esophagus and into your stomach and take it all back if you don't tell me who has been smackin' on ya ass for over twenty-four hours?"

Celia cleared her throat delicately. Both Sidney and Noelle looked at her expectantly.

"Ummm, I thought I should mention," Celia paused and stared at Sidney's throat. "That I believe you have marks around your neck as well. It's very light. It's just a little darker than your skin. As though it was gentle choking. I could be wrong, but that's what it looks like to me." She took another bite of her roll.

"Your neck! *Your neck!*" Noelle leaned in and studied Sid- ney's neck. "Sidney, what the fuck girl! Did this nigga choke you?"

"Not, a choking per se. I just think I bruise easily. I might have a vitamin deficiency." Remembering what Kaneko said about vitamins, she giggled.

"Bitch,are you giggling? Who were you with?" Noelle asked again.

Sidney shook her head. "No. I'm not ready to share just yet."

"Oooh Ima choke you and it's not gonna feel good at all!" Noelle flung her hands up in the air. "Oh my, God! You suck!"

Sidney popped her tongue. "That's the only thing I *didn't* do last night."

"Wait!" Noelle froze. "You were fucking by the looks of your body—a lot—and you didn't give him no head? A hand job?"

"Nope." Sidney gave a toss of her head.

Noelle gasped and slapped a hand over her mouth. "You made him do all the work? For hours and hours? I am so proud of you girl." She wiped a fake tear from the corner of her eye.

"Thank you." Sidney preened under the compliment. She was proud of herself too! Since Kaneko was so vocal in his enjoyment of her body and feeding her, she hadn't realized that she sure did just lay there and get her needs taken care of for a day and a half. After he mentioned head, he didn't press for it. He didn't try to coax her head down, put her hand on his Johnson, nothing. He just treated her body like it was his personal playground and explored every nook and cranny of it. He definitely knew how high to pump his legs to get the swing to go over the fence...She lost track of how many orgasms she had, from g-spot to clitoral. Hell, she even had a little orgasm just by him playing with her nipples. Her body was still humming.

Noelle made a show of taking a deep breath and slowly

exhaling. "Okay, I am a little bit calmer now. And as much as I hate to wait because you take forfuckingever to tell me shit because you're an annoying ass Virgo, and I don't understand why you—"

"Focus, Noelle," Celia reminded gently and shot Sidney a wink.

"Thank you for the redirection, Celia. I was about to go on a tangent." Noelle put a hand over her heart and took a deep breath. "Now, what I was going to ask is did you finally have a g-spot orgasm, because after alll of this you better had had one and then I'll leave you be."

Sidney folded both hands over her heart and nodded solemnly. "Numerous. We joked that I was gonna have to get hooked up to an IV."

Noelle put her hands up. "Blessed be! I'd hug you, but I don't know if you have any residue on you."

"I probably do."

"I'm grossed out and overjoyed at the same time." Noelle's expression matched her conflicted feelings.

"Aight, let's go." Celia put a hand on Noelle's shoulder and steered her to the door.

"This interrogation is not over. You will tell me his name," Noelle vowed over Celia's "*Felicidades*," as she shut the door behind them.

"Gracias!" Sidney yelled at the closed door. She could hear Noelle fussing at Celia for dragging her out. Tired but happy, she sat on the edge of her bed, contemplating if she still wanted to take a shower. She had taken one at Kaneko's place, but they had sex in the shower and continued after so that one probably didn't count. That man's stamina was ridiculous! How he got it up so many times was beyond her. Her Precious ached; the poor baby wasn't used to all this activity. But it was a satisfied ache. She didn't feel rubbed raw because he made sure she was wet every time either with her own juices or with lube *and* he also cleaned her up after. She felt exquisitely used exactly how she imagined it would be with him. She sighed in contentment. No shower. She was going to bed. But first…She cleared her throat and coughed a few times to make her voice as rough and scratchy as possible. When she was satisfied that her voice sounded sick and sleepy enough, she called Nelson.

"Where have you been?" he demanded. "I have been calling and paging you since yesterday. I was coming over this morning if I didn't hear from you."

At the worry in his voice, Sidney tried to muster up some concern, but she really could not care less about his feelings right now. "I think the weather gave me a migraine. Celia gave me her car, and I just came home after they cleared the accident and took my migraine medicine and a sleeping pill. I stayed in bed all day. I'm just getting up now."

Occasionally, she had debilitating migraines that required bed rest either at home or on the ship. They didn't happen often, but she'd had a couple since they'd been together, so Nelson knew what they did to her.

"Why didn't you call me? I would have come over and taken care of you."

With the Navy's 800 milligrams of Motrin, no doubt. Sidney rolled her eyes and stifled an irritated sigh. "It's okay. I am about to grab something to eat and just go lay back down."

"Do you want me to bring something over?"

"Umph-um. I am okay but thank you," Sidney said.

"Are you—"

"Yes, I am sure." Sidney interrupted. *Gosh, shaddup man, and hang up.* His voice was like dirty water on her afterglow.

"Well, okay, just call me if you need anything. I love you." Nelson didn't sound convinced.

"Mmm, my head is starting up again. I'll call you when I get up. Bye." Sidney couldn't bring herself to say 'I love you' back and was too tired to care. Hanging up the phone, she crawled into bed. She could smell Kaneko's Ivory soap on her skin. She didn't know what she was going to do about the hickeys and the rest of the marks on her body. Not that she was entertaining the thought of having sex with Nelson after Kaneko. There was no way in this world or the next that would happen. She was going to have to do something about him, but later. Her eyes fluttered closed. She'd think about that later.

Chapter Twenty-Two

EN2 Nicolas Kaneko

"What was that about?"

"What was what about?" Nicolas sat down and looked across the table at his best friend, MM2 Natasha Simon.

"You do know that when you answer a question with a question, it's a dead giveaway, right?"

Of course, he knew. But that didn't stop him from trying to avoid answering. He stared blankly at Simon. Dammit, when he saw Pascal sitting there without her coffee, he automatically went and got it for her, despite the fact that she hadn't said one word to him in the two weeks since they had sex. By accident or by design, he had barely seen her throughout the ship. The had duty last night, so he saw her briefly during duty section turnover, but she didn't look in his direction so he left her alone. Had he not met Simon for breakfast, he doubted he would have seen her again today or the rest of the week for that matter.

After their night together, she adamantly refused to let him drive her home. They debated about it for ten minutes, but she wouldn't back down. Nor would she answer the question as to why not. So he reluctantly called her a cab after making her promise him that she would call when she got home. She did, and that was it. Unsure of what to do, he decided the best course of action was to fall back and let her come to him. Again. He just hoped it wouldn't take too long. He wanted her back in his bed, but he didn't want to rush or pressure her. But knowing that she had been thinking about him too gave him the patience to wait her out. The cruise was starting soon, and he'd have her all to himself for six months. He was a patient man, and he didn't mind twiddling his thumbs until then.

"Man, why did you take Pascal coffee? Staring at me is not going to make me forget," Simon said.

"Oh, *that*. It was nothing." Nicolas picked up his fork and started to eat his scrambled eggs.

Simon narrowed her eyes. "Um, I have known you for six years. You doing something for nothing is *not* in your vocabulary. What are you up to?"

What am I up to? He wasn't sure himself. Nicolas took a bite of his toast and chewed while he thought about how much he wanted to reveal. He and Pascal had sex. It was some damn mind-blowing sex, and he wanted to do it again, but there wasn't much more to it than that, really. He didn't know why he hadn't told Simon, as he usually did a cross-check with her when he met someone new. She was an excellent judge of character, and she had steered him away from many a crazy woman. She knew all of his clean *and* dirty secrets. But Pascal was different. He wanted to keep her to himself for a while.

"Oh, so we're not sharing now? Well, thank you for the memo," Simon quipped, followed by her sucking her teeth loudly.

Nicolas leaned back in his chair and stared at Simon. If he wasn't mistaken, she sounded jealous. She looked like a petulant Black Betty Boop, right down to the little curls framing her face. It had been almost six years since he had met Simon at his last command and although he thought about pursuing her, she was dating someone else, so he settled for friendship.

After they had gotten close and she trusted him, Simon revealed that she was a lesbian and the chief she'd been dating for ten years was gay. She played his beard, and he played her skirt. They continued the ruse even after "Don't ask, Don't tell" was introduced into law this past February. Had the Navy found out Bishop was gay, he would have never made Chief, and Simon wanted to be a Warrant Officer, so they decided it was better to be safe rather than sorry. Currently, Simon was single, but Bishop was in a long-term relationship with another Chief stationed on shore duty.

"It was just a cup of coffee, Simon. It wasn't an engagement ring. No one is going to replace you, so just simmer down there, little lady." Nicolas had to stop himself from laughing when Simon inhaled sharply.

"Little lady..." Simon narrowed her eyes at him. "That was the furthest thing from my mind, but since you brought it up, *are* you planning to replace me? Are all Black women interchangeable?"

"No one could ever replace you. You're my unattainable dream. You will forever hold a place in my heart," Nicolas said, placing a hand over his heart. "If not in my bed."

"Never in your bed, my friend."

"That's a shame. You don't know what you're missing."

"I guess I can just ask Pascal. Be right back since you wanna be a smart ass." Simon put her fork down and started to stand up.

"Fine, you win." Nicolas held his hands up. "Just sit back down."

With a small smirk, Simon settled back into her chair. "I wasn't really going to go over there. What would I say to her anyway? The fact that you haven't told me about her says something about it. Though she does fit your type, though, so I am not surprised."

"My type? I didn't realize I had a type," Nicolas lied. Pascal was his type. She was the prototype.

"Big asses, Nicky. That's your type. Big ole badonkadonks." She held her hands out about a foot apart. "The bigger, the better. That's the Black in you, shipmate." Simon glanced over to Pascal, who was joined by a couple of sailors. "She does have a nice ass." When she turned her gaze back to Nicolas, it was thoughtful. "You don't have to tell me if you don't want to. It isn't really any of my business."

Nicolas made a noncommittal sound as he ate his scrambled eggs. "You're right. But it's not that I don't want to tell you. I just don't know what to say." He shrugged one shoulder.

"I see." Simon peeled back the foil lid from a small packet of grape jelly. "So did you have sex with her, or are you trying to?" She used her butter knife to spread some jelly on her wheat toast.

"Yes, and yes," Nicolas said.

Simon's toast paused before it hit her lips. "Oh! She let you hit it?"

Nicolas frowned. "I'm not sure if I should be flattered or offended at the complete and utter shock in your voice."

Simon took a bite of her toast. "Both. Now, I could understand if you said Bentley 'cause she's all 'I'm from New York,' and she's just intentionally weird and shit. But you went after a *strong* Southern woman. A Texas woman. Her ancestors' blood is in that soil. Her people were part of the Juneteenth release party. She talked about it during

Black History Month—that's how Southern she is. Those types of women only date Black men, and usually Southern Black men at that. You have some of the southern parts but basically, you're a Japanese boy from Japan. If I were a betting woman, I would have never placed my money on you because the odds are none."

Nicolas pursed his lips together and exhaled through his nose. "I am a Japanese and Black *man* and," he held a finger up and then pointed it at his chest, "...and she came for me. That's why you'd lose; your instincts are off."

Simon's head reared back slightly. If her eyes got any wider, they would fall out of her head. Before she could turn her head, Nicolas told her not to look at Pascal. Her expression would have been a dead giveaway. He didn't want Pascal to suspect they were talking about her, especially on the mess decks[1] where someone could overhear them.

"Oh my God! When did that happen?" Dropping her toast, Simon gripped the table and leaned forward.

Content that he had humbled her, Nicolas took a sip of his cooling coffee before answering. "Two weeks ago."

"Two weeks ago? You had sex two weeks ago?" Simon mouthed.

Nicolas smiled, nodded slowly, and mouthed back, "Yes."

If pure amazement were a person, it would be Simon. "You gotta start from the beginning because I cannot believe this shit. But wait, doesn't she have a boyfriend? I overheard Bentley talking about him one day. I don't think she likes him."

"I don't think Pascal likes him either to be honest. But I

---

1. Mess or Mess Deck: a designated area where military personnel eat and socialize.

don't know the status of their relationship right now." Nicolas lowered his voice because some sailors took the table behind them. "We can talk about this later, somewhere other than the mess decks."

"Are you done? Because I am ready now."

"No." Nicolas shook his head. "Didn't your parents tell you not to waste your food?"

"Nope, we're wealthy. Fraud, waste, and abuse is a lifestyle for us."

"I don't like to waste food, and I'm hungry, so I'm going to eat. Come to the shop after muster[2]." Nicolas glanced at Pascal. She had a full table now and was laughing at something one of the guys said. Damn, she was effortlessly pretty. She wasn't wearing any makeup, save for the mascara he had noticed earlier, and her hair was pulled back again into a neat French braid. The memory of him undoing it made him clench his jaw. She glanced at her watch and then started to clean her area up. She swung her legs around and stood up facing him. They made eye contact, and her expression went soft while still being slightly guarded. It brought him back to the stoplight when he asked her to repeat what she wanted from him. She started to smile, but it was cut short by the guy at the table grabbing her wrist.

"Now what the hell was that shit? I was feeling a bit uncomfortable watching y'all. That was some serious eye-locking," Simon said. "Let me find out you put it on her."

"Are you gonna let me put it on you too?" Nicolas joked in an attempt to deflect.

"Man, by the way, you two were looking at each other,

---

2. Muster: taking attendance of the members in a division or department.

even if I finally said yes, it wouldn't matter."

Simon was right. Nicolas just smiled and concentrated on finishing his chow before muster.

"Okay, I am ready," Simon stood in the hatch of Nicolas's shop.

"Did you even go to muster?" Nicolas said from his stool. Afternoon muster[3] just secured. He hadn't even turned on his computer yet.

"Yes, but I ran up here right after. Look, I have work to do, and I can't wait until lunchtime. So give me a tightly condensed but packed with all the pertinent information version. Starting with how she stepped to you. Go!"

The condensed version was fine with Nicolas; he didn't want to go into the details about Pascal as he did with other women. They both traded tales of their sexual escapades and their lives in general. Simon jokingly referred to him as her work wife because while he wasn't much of a gossiper, she was notorious for it and he was always present and accounted for when she had something to share. Other times, Simon was like one of the guys, and they sat around watching porn while underway[4] with zero sexual contact between them.

---

3. Muster: taking attendance of the members in a division or department.

4. Underway: laymen's terms: the ship is out to sea. Nautical definition: the vessel is not at anchor, aground, or secured to the shore or dock.

"This is amazing!" Simon leaned back against the door. "So this came out of nowhere? She never said anything. You never said anything?"

"I was totally caught off guard. I was just going to make breakfast as usual and then take her home after the traffic died down. That was the plan." Nicolas tapped his fingers on the metal desktop. "But I guess it explains why she never really spoke to me unless I relieved the watch."

"Has she talked to you since?"

"No."

"Hmmm," Simon murmured and then frowned.

"Hmmm, what?" Nicolas didn't like that frown and what it might imply. From Pascal's silence, he'd been wondering if she regretted being with him. It was one thing for him to speculate about it but to have someone else think it as well was embarrassing.

"You don't think she regrets having sex with you?" Simon crossed her arms over her chest.

"Why would she regret having sex with me? Because I look Japanese?"

"You *are* Japanese."

"But I'm also Black," Nicolas protested.

"Only on the inside." Simon patted her chest. "On the outside, boo, you look like you know all the noodle and rice dishes and how duck sauce is made. Or in your case teriyaki. Okay wait, lemme reword this, she might may not regret it, perhaps she's just wondering about her next move. Because how many Black women and Japanese men much less Asian men do you see out here? I have seen a few Filipino women with Black dudes but that's it."

"I can't say that I've had." Nicolas exhaled sharply. "Fuck. Do you really think that's a possibility?"

"Anything is possible." Simon shrugged. "I've had quite

a few women want me in private but God forbid anyone knows about us. Civilian and Navy women. They ignore me out in public but be sneakin' trying to get some when no one is around. I still fuck them but it's out of spite, and the fun is taken out of it. I would hate for her to do that to you. She doesn't seem the type to do that, but I don't put shit past folks."

Nicolas stared at his friend. Simon was right. No matter how connected he felt to his Black side, he was basically Japanese on the outside. As much as he didn't want to, he trusted Simon's judgment, and he quietly stewed over the same thought. When situations like these came up, he felt like the teenager who sat in his grandparents' living room watching them ignore him and praise his sister. That sense of inferiority was not something he ever wanted to experience with Pascal. She never gave him an indication that his race was an issue before he told her about his mother. If it was, why would she bother to fuck him in the first place? There were plenty of Black men on the ship and out in town she could dally with. However, if that was the case, then fuck it, they both got their rocks off, and there was nothing more to say. Undoubtedly he'd be disappointed because other than the bomb-ass sex, it was really nice just being with her. Easy like Sunday morning so to speak. Now if she was embarrassed, he couldn't be Simon and still have sex with her. That didn't sit right with his spirit, as his mother would say.

"Guess anything is possible so I just have to wait and see," Nicolas said.

"Umph." Simon frowned and pushed off the door.

Nicolas had heard that 'umph' many times. It was usually followed by an argument. "Natasha, *do not* say anything to her." He stood up. "I mean it. Just leave it alone. Whatever is gonna be, will be."

Simon narrowed her eyes at him.

"Promise me." He pointed at her.

"Nope." Simon dashed out of the room.

Chapter Twenty-Three

LT Quentin Jacobs

"Aye, did you ever call that girl that left her number on your windshield?"

What the fuck? Quentin turned to glare at his cousin Paul before dropping his hammer down. They were at his parents' house repairing the back deck with his father, who, unfortunately, picked that moment to join them outside.

For the past couple of weeks, he had managed to keep his family out of his business. It helped that he was hardly ever at his parents' house. When he was there, he shut down all questions of his whereabouts, despite the fact there were questions every time he walked out and returned home. For years after the divorce, his parents tried their best to reunite him and Cynthia. Quentin Sr., or simply Jacobs as he more commonly got called, believed that the junior Quentin had made a terrible, stupid mistake breaking up with her. Not once had he asked his son how *he* felt about the divorce; he just automatically blamed him for it.

During one of their more intense arguments, Quentin snidely suggested that his father divorce his mother and marry Cynthia, since he was so concerned about her well-being. Jacobs paused in mid-speech; a quick expression flashed over his face and revealed the truth. Quentin had always suspected that his father harbored a crush on Cynthia. His father's behavior wasn't inappropriate—he didn't flirt or anything—but a person can always sense when someone wants what they have.

After that, his father left him alone and dialed back his comments until Quentin said he was moving back home. It wasn't like the incessant arguments of the past, but he would still sneak in his unsolicited opinions whenever he saw an opening. Apparently, Quentin's dating was an opening.

"So that's where you've been sneaking off to, eh?" Jacobs asked.

Quentin sighed and glared at his cousin, who smiled apologetically. "I'm thirty-eight. There's no need to sneak around."

Jacobs took a seat in the patio chair. "If you're not sneaking around, why are you keeping it a secret? What's her name?"

Quentin picked up another nail and hammered it down. He wanted to ignore his father, but he would keep on until he got the information he was seeking. "Her name is Noelle."

"And?" Jacobs asked.

"And?" Quentin reached into the box and got out another nail. "What more do you want to know?"

"What does she do? Who her family be? Is it serious? You've been out every night. You even took some of your mother's oxtails to her. She told me, yanno."

Quentin cast another blistering look toward Paul. He was going to gut-punch his cousin when he got him alone. He sat back on his heels and looked at his father. With a sigh, he said, "She lives about 30 minutes away. She's in the Navy, and I'm just trying to get to know her, Daddy. That's all. You satisfied?" He left out that her family was from St. Kitts because that would start a whole new line of questioning that he wasn't prepared for.

Jacobs sucked his teeth. "If you're moving back home, I just don't see why you don't get back with Cynthia. She is still lookin' nice and slim."

'Nice and slim' was his father's bar for women; it didn't matter if they were demons or not. Granted Quentin didn't consider Cynthia a demon anymore, but he still wasn't getting back together with her. He closed his eyes and counted to five. He knew the moment he decided to move back home, his father would try to push him and Cynthia back together. "Yup, she looks great, Daddy. Always does. But no, thank you. Mi duh wid dat and she has a man." He looked at Paul for assistance, but he was staring at the deck, sipping his Heineken wearing a troubled expression. What the hell was wrong with him? He started this. He didn't have time to contemplate because his father started another round of questions.

"What do you mean you're done with her?" Jacobs said. "How can you be done with her? You have a son together."

"Tre is sixteen years old, and we have been divorced for eight years. There is no getting back with Cynthia. Mind you, she has a life yanno. She's not waiting for me to come back here and be with her. Is that what you think?" Quentin asked with a shrug. He started working on the deck again.

Jacobs shook his head. "This, ah—what is her name again?"

"Noelle."

"Noelle. Are we going to meet this *Noelle*?" Jacobs asked.

"No time soon," Quentin answered. He was still trying to get to know Noelle. She was skittish enough without bringing his family into the mix. His father was correct; he'd been out with her every night since their first phone call. His day always started with a good morning page from her and then various phone calls throughout the day when she was in between doing whatever a photographer's mate does on the ship. Which wasn't much, he assumed, due to the number of pages and calls he got during the workday. A page letting him know she was off work. A call telling him to come over. A call asking him what he wanted to eat for dinner. A call telling him to stop by the store on his way because she forgot something. Calls throughout the day just because she was bored at work.

Although they spent every day together except for her duty days (and even then, they talked on the phone until the morning) for the past two weeks, it still felt like he was on day one with her. Their conversations were engaging and vast—Noelle could literally make watching mold grow sound newsworthy —but she kept her cards close to her chest. If not for the way she responded to him whenever he touched her, he would have thought she didn't want him. But want him she did.

And he took pleasure in denying her. Sometimes he slipped his hand underneath her skirt and fingered her, and she'd already be wet and ready. Other times he'd just grind himself against her while tonguing her down and playing with her breasts. He always made her come, and then he left promptly, denying her requests to stay. It was hell on him, but it was the only thing under his control in their burgeoning relationship. Other than that, he had none. When she called, he picked up. If she said come, he ran. A little bit out of excitement but mostly out of fear that in the time it took him to get to her, she'd be gone.

Sometimes he'd catch her looking at him with an odd expression of suspicion and wonderment on her face. He never questioned her about it; he just pretended not to notice. He took her blithe mention of being a flight risk very seriously. She could be prickly at times, and her tongue was quick, especially when she thought he was trying to undermine her autonomy. So he let her take the lead, from inviting him to come over to deciding what they did or ate. It didn't matter to him as long as she kept calling him. He wasn't in any rush. He had all the time in the world to contain and domesticate Noelle.

His second interview had gone well. So well, in fact, he put an offer on a house—close, but not *too close* to his parents. He only had to pack up his home back in San Diego, and he'd be ready to settle down to live his post-Navy life. Preferably with Noelle.

Quentin had absolutely no doubt that she was going to drive him crazy. She was full of theories and ideas, and very willing to share them. He'd never met someone so comfortable with expressing her opinions on everything. Yet, she couldn't tidy up her bedroom or sweep the floor in one go without getting sidetracked. She left all these little piles throughout the room. He actually helped her put away her laundry last week after listening to her complain for eight straight days that she couldn't find any underwear. It was all in her basket. He took her car to get gas twice a week and even had the oil changed because it was a thousand miles overdue. If he had a dollar for every time she said, "I need to get that done," he'd be a rich man. But then she had moments when she hyper-fixated on implementing an idea, and he couldn't coax her away from it. She vacillated between trying to do everything all at once and doing nothing at all. He didn't mind being the weighted tether to her floating in the clouds balloon. He'd give her a long string so she could feel free and then yank her back down when he was ready.

The pager on his hip beeped. Speaking of his little tumbleweed…He unclipped his pager and read the number code from Noelle: 423.

Call me.

Yes ma'am. Quentin re-clipped the pager back to his belt and stood up. Unsnapping the knee pads, he took them off.

"I guess we're done for the day?" Paul said with a grin. Apparently, whatever was bothering him had been forgotten because he was back to his jovial self.

"No, *I'm* done. It's 6 o'clock, you just sat there and watched me work. You can finish up," Quentin said and threw the kneepads over to Paul.

Paul pushed them away with his foot. "Nah, I don't want to mess anything up."

Quentin scowled at his cousin. "Can you manage to put everything away without messing anything up?"

"That I can do," Paul said graciously.

Quentin shook his head and went into the kitchen to call Noelle.

"Hey babe," He said when Noelle answered.

"Quentin," Noelle moaned. "Why didn't you stop me?"

Quentin frowned. "Stop you from doing what? You didn't tell me I needed to stop you from doing something today. What did you do?"

"I did Tae Bo with Celia after work, and now I'm dying. Everything hurts," Noelle whined.

Quentin tsked. "Poor baby. Why did you do that?"

Before Noelle could answer, he heard Celia in the background.

"You're not dying. She's fine. You're just lazy and weak. She's weak, Quentin!"

Quentin bit back a laugh when he heard scuffling and Noelle shouting: "Get out of my room, you demon!" A door slammed, and Noelle was back on the phone. "I think she's trying to weaken me so she can kill me. She's always been a terrible friend."

The laughter he was holding back burst out. "You want me to bring you some food when I come over later? How about some lamb vindaloo with a mango lassi and butter almond ice cream if I can find some, Rocky Road if not? Would that make you feel better?"

"Yes." Noelle sighed. "And a massage. I really need a massage, Quentin. Can I have a massage too?"

Quentin swallowed. Noelle's voice went from drained and weak to soft and seductive in the same sentence. "Yes, babe, I'll give you the best massage you've ever had in your life."

"You're the best. Don't be tryna slip one in. I just want a massage."

Quentin just grunted. They both knew Noelle wanted more than a slip-in. If she had her way, they would've had sex the first night. He hadn't intended on dragging it out, but he found himself enjoying the slower pace and sexual tension it created between them. The main bonus was how much it frustrated Noelle, who was clearly used to getting her own way. She was a bossy little thing, and she would not control him no matter how much she wanted to. Every time he left her with a wet pussy—whining and annoyed in her foyer, the front seat of his car, or standing in her kitchen—it strengthened his resolve. Granted, he might have to go to jerking-off rehab since he was developing a two-or-three-times-daily masturbation habit. But they'd both suffer until he'd broken down Noelle's walls completely.

Despite her living in a fort surrounded by a moat filled with spikes, he already had her figured out. She used sex as both a shield and a distraction tactic. She liked him and enjoyed his company, but she didn't want him to get too close. She wanted to remain this big, unsolvable mystery. Though, she was only a mystery to herself. She wanted what everyone wanted: to be loved, seen, accepted, and ultimately, understood.

When she talked about herself and her accomplishments, it was self-depreciative. It was almost as though she was afraid to admit to herself that she was capable. She would talk about her failures freely, but then Quentin would have to pull her victories out of her. She attributed getting her master's degree to being mad at one of her professors instead of her own intelligence and hard work. She had created an alternate persona of being carefree and light, maybe a little ditsy, but she was far, far from it. Everything she did was well thought out and calculated. She might not appear to spend a lot of time on contemplation, but he knew from being around her damn near every day that it wasn't true. She woke up thinking about whatever decision she had to make and ruminated over it until she reached a suitable conclusion. Noelle was both levity and gravity. A complete contradiction. And he loved it.

Quentin froze and stared at his reflection in the glass patio door the weight of his insight settling over him. He was falling in love with Noelle Bentley. *Damn, already?* Closing his eyes, he inhaled slowly and deeply and then exhaled all the air out of his mouth until his abs contracted. He repeated it two more times until he felt his body relax. He knew he liked her a lot and was extremely attracted to her, but he thought he'd make it to the Fall before deeper emotions entered the picture, not mere weeks. He probably started falling the minute he saw her standing, looking perplexed at the gas station pump.

Women thought men didn't fall in love as quickly as they did, but that wasn't true. They did all the time. Sometimes they did it even before the woman; they just hid it better. Black men, in particular, were not allowed to show their emotions so freely. It wasn't manly to admit a woman had them by the balls and heartstrings. They were taught by society to keep their feelings hidden, not to show any weaknesses, lest they be taken advantage of. He was grateful that his father publicly showered his mother with love and affection, teaching his son it was okay to love and be loved—that it wasn't a weakness to show it. So, he had no problem telling Noelle when he thought she was ready to listen and accept the words. He had only just gotten her comfortable with him doing stuff for her. However, even though he told her that he would take her car to be serviced, he read the struggle all over her face when he asked for her keys. They both exhaled when she handed them to him.

Well, I guess this is what I'm doing. Quentin shook himself, found the menu for the Indian restaurant, and called to place an order for pick up. With one last look at his reflection, he gathered up his wallet and keys from the counter and left.

Chapter Twenty-Four

MM1 Sidney Pascal

"I thought you were staying at Breath and Britches' place tonight. It's six o'clock. You're missing the boring-ass weekend edition of the PBS *NewsHour*," Noelle said when Sidney walked into the kitchen where she was making a drink with a shaker.

Sidney set her heavy overnight bag on the floor next to the kitchen table and took a seat. "The PBS *NewsHour* is very informative without all the bias and BS. You should watch it."

"Hard pass. If we ever went to war, I don't want to know about it until the Captain announces it. You want a drink? Did you eat?"

"No, I was busy. Why?"

"Quentin is bringing us Indian food later because Celia tortured me with Tae Bo earlier."

"You should have known that was going to happen, and Quentin is bringing dinner for *you*," Sidney corrected.

"If Quentin is as smart as I think he is, then he knows to bring dinner for *us*," Noelle replied, making a circle in the air with one of her fingers. "Sundays are for family gatherings. I am quite sure he knows this."

Sidney squinted at Noelle, wondering why she thought Quentin buying dinner for the roommates of the woman he's been pursuing for only two weeks made perfect sense to her. It didn't make any sense, but she wasn't about to argue with her. She'd had enough arguing for the night. "Are you making whiskey sours?"

"Of course, it's Sunday evening. What else would I be doing?"

It was Whiskey Sour Sunday. Noelle made them every Sunday religiously when they were in port. It was one of the only drinks she could make. She said it prepared her for the work week. Actually, Noelle drank a little every day except for her duty day. Sidney frowned. It was usually just wine, but maybe she needed to talk with her friend. "You figure out how to make a virgin one yet."

"You know I forgot as soon I said I would try. And I wasn't expecting you to be here." Noelle gave the metal tumbler one more shake and then took two tumbler glasses from the cabinet. She poured herself a drink and garnished it with a wedge of sugared lemon. Then she quickly made Sidney a glass of fresh lemonade poured and also garnished it with a wedge. "What were you busy doing earlier? I know y'all weren't having sex. It's too early. You can still see each other with the lights off."

Rolling her eyes, Sidney took a sip of her drink, smacking her lips at the tartness. Perfect! "Busy breaking up with Nelson."

"*Biiiiitch!*" Noelle's glass stopped halfway to her mouth as though someone yelled: *Freeze!* "That should have been the first thing you said when you walked in the kitchen! Now say it again."

"I broke up with Nelson."

Wearing a dazed expression, Noelle took a gulp of her drink and gasped loudly. She took another sip after clearing her throat. Topping her glass off again, she took a seat across from Sidney. "My brain literally *can-not* handle all these goings on. Firstly, I picked up a man from the 7-Eleven, proving you're never too old to get your Freaknik on. Ducely, Celia stopped eating coochie and went straight for a married man. She didn't stop, take in some new dick that had been waiting in line, just to take the edge off. Nope, she went straight to the unattainable. And you—you, my dear friend, got some organic, Grade A strong, prime Black dick. Just strong. Your naked body is burned into my retinas. And now this *coup de grace*! It's a goddamned good day to be alive."

Sidney winced at the words *Black dick*, but Noelle didn't notice. "Why are you so dramatic?"

"Because I have dramatic-ass friends who won't admit they're dramatic, so I have to wear the crown all alone. It's heavy, but someone's gotta represent. So, what did he say when you broke up? Don't tell me." She held up her hand. "I got this. I bet he just dismissed you at first, perhaps suggesting that you had a bad day or that you were hormonal. And then when he saw you were serious, he sobered and turned the TV off, gave you his undivided attention while trying to offer you words to placate you, and *then* when he realized that none of that was working, attacked you. Not physically, of course, because he's not that stupid and because also in the back of his mind, he still thinks that he can shut this rebellion down. Am I right?"

Sidney's jaw dropped. Did she have her bugged? "That you are."

Noelle tipped her imaginary hat. "Of course I am. *Flippin the Script* is one of the sacred tomes of the *L eve Nigreoes* fraternity. It means trifling Negroes in Latin. It's a secret fraternity filled with insecure Black assholes who blame their mommas and the unfortunate women who get involved with them for their problems."

Trifling Negro indeed. Sidney scowled. "He had the nerve to say that this was happening because I was doing my master's. Apparently, I spent too much time on my schoolwork and not tending to our relationship, i.e., him. That ninja doesn't even have an associate degree. His education stopped at A-school. He doesn't even have his ESWS[1] pin and he's been on two other ships besides the Kennedy. And he's been an E-6 for four years. What the heck?" She took a bigger sip of her lemonade and stared at Noelle, who was suspiciously quiet. "Go ahead and say it."

"Say what?" Noelle asked with wide eyes. She licked some froth off the rim of her glass before continuing. "Say that Nelson is a nugatory, solipsistic, parsimonious, extemporaneous, and superfluous man, innately filled with unsubstantiated and egregious illusions of grandeur further reinforced by beautiful and intelligent Black women such as yourself who provide him a buffer and deflection for his inferiority complex by devaluing their own self-worth and shrinking themselves down into teeny tiny insignificant versions of themselves so that he can feel as though he's extraordinary and relevant when in reality he is of little consequence or value to anyone but himself? Is that what you want me to say?"

Sidney rolled her eyes. "You didn't have to use so many words."

"Every so often, I like to remind you hoes that I am a Philologist, and I love my words. Y'all be sleepin' on a sister bit I stay woke!" Noelle said with a small neck roll.

---

1. ESWS (Enlisted Surface Warfare Specialist): Personnel trained and qualified to perform duties aboard surface warships.

Sidney rolled her eyes again. She needed to stop before she gave herself a headache. "It's one of the reasons Nelson didn't like you. You deliberately overwhelmed him."

"Honey, *One Fish Two Fish Red Fish Blue Fish* by Dr. Suess would have overwhelmed him. The man is dumb as a goddamn bag of bricks. I still don't know why you gave him the time of day. But it's all. Over. Now. *Hallelujah!* I was wondering when you were gonna break up with him because you're not a cheater. I'm still surprised you slept with the Mystery Man. I was going to give you one more day before I started questioning your thought process."

Kaneko… She'd been unconsciously but still somehow consciously avoiding him, she realized. She needed time to think. Noelle was right about her; she wasn't a cheater. The first and last time she did, she was married. Both she and Wade were discreetly cheating on each other while trying to maintain a happy front for their daughter. She put off getting divorced for five years because she didn't want to be another statistic: A Black single mother. And Wade, bless his heart, didn't want to be a weekend dad.

It wasn't until she saw Wade out one night with the woman he would finally end up marrying after her—witnessing how he looked at Tamika, the smile on his face, and how much they laughed together—that she put aside her fears and ego and asked for a divorce. They both deserved happiness, and Nadia would be fine as long as they were. Tamika might not be her birth mother, but she loved Nadia just as much as she loved the two children she and Wade had together. Nadia even called her mom—and that was something Sidney never thought she'd allow. Ever. But when Nadia asked her with all her seven-year-old innocence if she could, reassuring her momma it didn't mean that she didn't love her any less, *and* she also loved Tamika too, Sidney agreed.

After her divorce, Sidney never cheated again. If she felt herself wanting to stray, she just broke up with the man. Cheating was too damn stressful, and she didn't like multiple men inside her. Youth got her pH balance through it the last time, but she was too old now for all that extracurricular activity. Thank goodness she started her period and Nelson left her alone, so she didn't have to make up excuses for not wanting to have sex.

"I made the decision after my duty day rendezvous. I just needed to make sure I was doing it for the right reasons and not a reaction to—"

"That dirty, delicious sex?"

"Yes."

Noelle laughed. "What made you decide, other than the obvious?"

Sidney had gotten up early enough to have breakfast that morning, and after getting her usual scrambled eggs with cheese and two slices of bacon, she sat down at the table and stared at her tray. This was not the food she wanted to be eating. She was trying hard not to think about the breakfast she had with Kaneko for the eighteenth millionth time when suddenly he placed a mug down in front of her, gave her a slight tilt of his head, and left without saying a word.

Wondering if the last time he had made her coffee at his place was a fluke, she picked up the cup and took a sip. It was perfect yet again. *Cheese and crackers!* She discreetly glanced at Kaneko, who sat three rows away on the other side of the mess decks[2]. He was talking to Simon. She took another sip of her coffee and made her decision.

Later that evening, after she cooked Nelson what would be his farewell dinner, she reminisced about the dinner Kaneko cooked her. As he ate, she went into the bedroom while watching television and quietly packed up all the stuff that she had over at his place. She didn't so much as leave a bobby pin behind.

"How do I like my coffee?" Sidney asked suddenly.

"Let me see, two teaspoons of sugar and enough creamer to make it light-skinned like the men you like," Noelle added cheekily.

"Would you staaaahhhp saying that!" Sidney shook her fists at Noelle. "Enteeways, I have been with Nelson for four years, and he doesn't know how I like my coffee. And if I'm correct, any of my drinks."

"Nelson probably doesn't know where your clitoris is, so how can you expect him to know how you like your coffee or anything relevant about you? You were wanting too much from Breath and Britches, girl."

Sidney rolled her eyes. "You're right. But this guy knew how I liked my coffee."

Noelle leaned back in her chair. "Well, that's interesting. So—"

Before Noelle could ask her who he was, Sidney interrupted her. "And my goodness, the man can cook! You're gonna be so jealous." She gave her the rundown on all the food Kaneko made her. "I didn't leave his bed all day, except to pee and take a shower. He wore my tail out *literally*, and

---

2. Mess or Mess Deck: a designated area where military personnel eat and socialize.

then he would take *his* tail back on to the kitchen and fix me some yum-yums, honey!"

"Hmph." Noelle cocked her head to the side and narrowed her eyes at Sidney. "I'm gonna get back to the getting served in bed because psssh, that shit is awesome. But I first wanna focus on the part of the sentence when you said, and I quote: 'He wore my ass out literally.' Because something about the way you said *literally* feels to me like it wasn't hyperbole, but he *literally* wore your ass, as in *hole*, out. And it's in bold, capitalized italics, underlined twice, highlighted, and circled." She leaned forward. "You let that man get in your booty, didn't you?"

Sidney scrunched up her face and folded into herself. She meant to leave that part out, but it just slipped out as easily as he slipped in, which was actually remarkable when she thought back on it. "Yes."

"OH MY GOD," Noelle shrieked and did a dance in her seat that shook the table. "Who is this man?"

"Why are you always yelling, Noelle?" Celia asked as she walked into the kitchen. She went over to the sink and washed her hands before grabbing a glass.

"You would be yelling too if Sidney told you that the man that was slapping her ass also got in her *boo-tay*. I am literally—" She looked pointed at Sidney. "—besides myself." Noelle fanned her face. "Whew, honeychile, I am flushed! Oh my goodness...Lord..."

Celia stopped rolling her rim in salt and looked at Sidney. "No."

"Yes!" Noelle hollered for Sidney.

"Noelle, hush. Seriously, you're impossible." Celia finished making her drink and sat down at the kitchen table. "So, how was it? The way Noelle is acting, it must've been your first time. It's amazing when it's with the right person, and they take their time and get you all ready. Ummm, it's so good."

Sidney unfolded herself, took a fortifying breath, and straightened up for her salacious interview. Now that the booty part was out of the bag, the rest should be easy. "Okay, let me just say from the beginning, he was all about my booty. And when he parted my cheeks like the Red Sea and went straight for the booty hole, I was not prepared. But girl..." Her eyes closed, and she shivered a little bit at the memory.

"Ohohoh, there she goes again." Noelle snapped her fingers. "I didn't scotch guard this fabric. Pull yourself together and focus on the story."

"Sorry." Sidney's eyes popped open, and she continued her story. "He was down there for a while; just doing this thing with his tongue and his fingers, which also felt really dang good. But in the back of my mind, I'm like, this my booty?"

"It's definitely a complicated feeling. I didn't do full-on anal before Julia. I had only done light butt stuff. I think I just didn't want a man to have all of me. Julia got every hole and then some. God, she was a nasty woman." Celia shook herself, not even realizing she had said *nasty* with a hint of a sigh. "Anyway, I think it's because it's so forbidden. You feel dirty and turned on, then you go back to feeling dirty, and then somehow you're even more turned on because it's so dirty. Nasty, dirty sex is the best sex, in my humble opinion." She lightly placed her hand on her chest as she spoke.

"That's because you're the epitome of nasty, Celia," Noelle quipped.

"Bitch so are you," Celia shot back. "I learned how to give head from you. You started way before me."

"Well, the student has surpassed the teacher. 'Cause I

don't do butt stuff. I mean I totally support y'all and y'all's nastiness, but I do not do that. I cannot believe you let him in your booty, and you squirted—all in one weekend. You, dear Sidney, have *also* surpassed me for sure! It's always a teacher's greatest joy when her students achieve greatness. So I salute you both," Noelle said. She sharply saluted Celia, then Sidney.

Sidney laughed at Noelle's mock seriousness and Celia's exaggerated eye roll. Noelle was so *very*. "It wasn't even the weekend. It was 29.5 hours. If it was the whole weekend, I would have probably moved in with him. I thought when I squirted, I was peeing the bed. It was so intense! And then he just kept on going and kept on going and kept on going, and when I came, it was like…"

"…like you're floating, and then a cherub comes by playing the harp, and a fairy flies offering you the sweetest grapes, while another one fans you with perfumed peacock feathers, and another one is massaging your scalp and your feet…" Noelle continued.

"…and when you finally float back down and open your eyes, your body feels like tall grass swaying in a gentle summer breeze and everything is perfect and in harmony," Celia finished. The three women were quiet as their words resonated.

Sidney sighed blissfully, breaking the silence. "Between feeding me and the sex, he had me in perfect harmony all morning and night, then the next morning."

"Okay, who the fuck is he? Seriously!" Noelle said, staring at her over the rim of her glass.

Biting her lip, Sidney smiled. Lord, if Noelle hollered at the anal sex, she would probably do a death roll when she told her it was Kaneko.

"No, no, wait. Let me guess. This is gonna be my

one-thousand-dollar pyramid question on the Atlanta Freaknik special edition. Do I know him?"

"Yes." Sidney kept her face neutral as she answered.

"He's in your duty section because you went home with him."

"Yup."

"The men in your duty section…Who could it be?" Noelle tapped her lips as she thought.

"It's Kaneko," Celia said confidently.

Sidney jumped, barely managing to keep her mouth from dropping open. She stared at Celia. How the hell did she guess? She barely admitted it to herself.

"EN2 Nicolas *Kaneko*? Kaneko! Nu-uh, you're wrong. He ain't a Black boy, Celia. You know Sidney don't do nothing but them high-yella Black guys. He's yellow but that's a different yellow. Right, Sidney?"

Sidney pointed at Noelle. "Don't make me fight you." Then she turned to Celia. "How did you guess?"

"Kaneko? Kah. Ne. Ko! And butt stuff! Sweet baby Jesus, you *are* trying to kill me today," Noelle gasped, falling back in her seat.

Sidney ignored her and waited until Celia finished swallowing her drink.

"While Noelle was talking, I was going over the men in your duty section. It wasn't Allen: he's a ho. Not King: he's actually happily married. Not Baker: he's in the closet. Not Rueben; he's dating Macklin. But then Kaneko's name suddenly just popped up, and I knew it was him. He's the kinda man to remember how you like your coffee. He's a good guy. If I remember correctly, he's Japanese right?"

"And Black!" Sidney exclaimed.

"No! Where?" Noelle said. "In his dreams?"

"Girl, his mother is from New Orleans. She's Creole. She's

even lighter than you Noelle. That's why he doesn't look it. His sister though, is browner not by much though. I saw pictures."

"Well, I can't say I saw that coming," Noelle said. "Did you know that Celia? You've known him the longest."

Celia's face screwed up as she thought then she snapped her fingers. "Oh yes! His mother visited our command once and everyone was so confused. But that was so long ago, I forgot."

"That would explain his accent though. It sounded familiar but you know how we pick up things from other people. Like you do, Noelle. I never put it together because I would never in a million years thought his people came from NOLA. I thought he was lying and I felt bad when he pulled out the family album," Sidney said.

"Okay, time to recap because too much has been said." Noelle drummed on the table. "Kaneko is Japanese and filtered Black—"

"Just like you," Sidney cut in.

"—and apparently a damn freak of the week. What the fuck? We have General Quarters together, and he stopped me from fighting with Martin last cruise. I was just drunk enough, and that bitch was talking shit as usual. But he started dancing with me, and he kept the rhythm too. He did the snake, and I almost peed my pants. So if I had to choose a sorta Black man to deflower your butthole, it would be him," Noelle finished.

"Thank you." Sidney scowled at Noelle. "I guess."

"So, what now?" Celia asked.

"I don't know. I do know that I didn't break up with Nelson just to be with him. Now, he was definitely my springboard. The last man that catered to me even remotely was Bernard. But—"

"Bernard was a lot of crazy," Noelle interjected.

"Yeah…but if he did all this, I might've had to look past the crazy. I could have never imagined the possibility that there is someone out there that would bring me breakfast in bed with freshly squeezed orange juice and fluffy Belgian waffles, and international cuisine." Sidney ticked off with her fingers as she spoke. "He knows how I like my coffee—you know I am particular about my coffee—asked me questions about myself and has excellent conversational skills. I just couldn't go back to Nelson. I just couldn't. He doesn't even remember what my degree is in even though I told him multiple times."

"That is so fucking sad." Noelle tsked. "I knew he was shitdick, but I didn't know he was that trife. Well, just keep them eyes right. It's all behind us now." She reached across the table and covered Sidney's hand with hers. "When are you getting fucked and fed again?"

Sidney grasped Noelle's hand and shook it lightly. "I don't know. We haven't spoken since. I think I put out 'don't talk to me' vibes because I don't know what to say, but he did bring me my coffee this morning. So we shall see." She shrugged. "I am in no rush."

Noelle raised her finger. "One last question, if I may?"

"You may," Sidney answered with a regal nod of her head.

"Who approached who?"

"I did." Sidney quickly explained what happened above Noelle's enthusiastic applause. "I have always been attracted to him. I never allowed myself to go there because he wasn't Black. I mean he is now sorta kinda. But I'm still a little *grrrr*, I mean, I dunno what to do."

"Yeah, you are kinda closed-minded so I get it," Noelle said. "I mean not anymore. Apparently, nothing's closed now," she added with an exaggerated wink at Sidney when she sent her a dirty look.

"Why are we even friends?" Sidney asked Noelle.

"Because until now your life was pretty damn boring without me. But you're way more exciting than me now. You're doing butt stuff. Please continue with your story." Noelle blew her kiss.

"I don't want your kisses." Sidney swiped at the air. "Anyway, I started thinking about what you said the other day, Noelle, although I shouldn't give you credit because you are being so ridiculous, and I asked him if we could have sex before breakfast. He took a moment to answer, and I wanted to die. But he asked me if I was sure, and I said yes, I was. And the rest is history."

"I know I said this before, but I am so fucking proud of you. Just when I think that the surprises are done, you just keep on giving me more. This is like the beginning of an epic saga. My heart is bursting with joy," Noelle cried out and clutched her heart as she spoke.

"Then your heart is going to explode out of your chest with this last one."

"Like in *Aliens*?" Noelle asked breathlessly.

"Yes! After we had dinner in bed, I said I need to shower because we'd been having sex and I'm funky. And he spread my legs and buried his face in my Precious and said I smell like I have been *fucked*." Sidney mouthed the last word.

"Fucked! I got you girl," Noelle hollered with glee as she threw back her head.

"And he said it's the best smell in the world. And *then* he ate my funky Precious, and that's when I peed the bed the second time." Sidney squealed and buried her face in her hands before throwing them up in the air.

"Ooooh girl!" Still wearing a huge smile, Noelle raised her glass. "Here's to good eating and 4.0 orgasms. Ladies, may your coochies stay wet, your limbs flexible, and your assholes tight." She clinked her glass against Sidney's and added for Celia, "Yours needs to stay extra tight 'cause you extra nasty."

"Shut the hell up," Celia said. The clinking of her glass against Noelle's coincided with Quentin knocking on the back door.

Sidney was closest to the door so she let him in. True to Noelle's words, Quentin appeared to have brought enough food to feed them all. He was setting the bags down when Noelle came up behind her and whispered in her ear.

"Don't ever doubt me again, newbie freak."

Chapter Twenty-Five

YN1 Celia Navarro

"I see Kendrick is still in her feelings, though y'all broke up like ten years ago. And I'm not sure she can still be mad while having chow with Allen. I mean, what in the actual fuck! I do know if she keeps on mean-mugging over here, I am going to give these chicken heads something to squawk about." Noelle plunked her tray of spaghetti and broccoli on the white tabletop and then sat down in the seat that was bolted to the *deck.

"It was two weeks ago. And don't be startin' no trouble, Noelle," Celia said. "If your ass wasn't perpetually running late, we could have gone to base galley like we planned. So eat your spaghetti and soggy broccoli and behave." She also hated eating on the mess decks[1] when they were in port. She glanced over at Kendrick, who was now thankfully paying attention to Allen. It had taken two weeks for the gossip around Kendrick to start to die down, and Celia wasn't in the mood for it to start up again.

The Puget Sound was an old ship, and with an old ship came pests, from mice to roaches. It was like living in a

---

1. Mess or Mess Deck: a designated area where military personnel eat and socialize.

floating project building. The forward and aft mess decks sat around a hundred and fifty sailors, but after serving fourteen hundred sailors for thirty years, it was only clean on the surface. She almost stopped eating there altogether last year after she saw the enormous pile of dead and dying roaches swept in a pile in front of the scullery. Yeah, she grew up in the South Bronx, but she didn't think her immune system was strong enough for that. Neither was the sailor that was cleaning; she somehow contracted hepatitis A from mess crankin' in there. She was constantly amazed that more sailors didn't get sick from food poisoning or other food-borne illnesses while serving aboard the ship.

The only perk to eating on the mess decks today was the possibility of seeing Joaquín, which is why she didn't just grab her tray and eat in her office. Other than the flight deck, the mess decks were one of the biggest gathering places on the ship. She canceled their useless weekly meeting, and he didn't object, so she hadn't seen him since their talk. She wanted to seek him out, but she still wasn't sure what to say to him. The more she sat with the idea of having an affair with him, the more it felt like she wasn't going to be left unscathed when they got back home. She was waiting for the rest of her self-preservation to kick in.

"If I see a roach, I'm gonna have a fit. We shoulda just gone up to Admin or the Photo Lab." Noelle sucked her teeth. "Oh, never mind. I know why we gonna contract scabies. You still stalkin' your prey? Girl, you could give the alien from *Predator* a run for his money, honey."

"I am not. We wouldn't be here if you had been on time." Celia narrowed her eyes at Noelle. "You literally went to the 7-Eleven for a week just to see Quentin again."

Noelle used both hands to make air guns at Celia. "On your advice, remember. And we could've gone to McDonald's. So, Stalker Mommita, have y'all spoken since the last time?"

Celia rolled her eyes. "Two weeks ago. I canceled both 1st class meetings after parties and sent out emails instead. I saw him in the material handling passageway[2] yesterday, and he looked like he wanted to talk to me, but he was with King and Glass, and those are some gossipin' ass mofos. So I did a complete about-face and ran back to Admin."

King and Glass were 2nd classes who worked under Joaquín on the boat deck. Both 1st and 3rd divisions[3] were a mess. As the biggest department on the ship, it was the ship's eyes and ears, and mouth. If you wanted information about anyone or anything, find someone in Deck, and you'd have the scoop and then some. It consisted of the first division that took care of the maintenance of the ship, and the third division where Joaquín worked, which ran the boat deck and the cranes. A lot of the sailors were E-3s and below, and the sheer amount of trouble they could get into during a cruise was astounding. She definitely didn't want them in her business.

"So wait, you're *avoiding* him now? After you just threw the coochie at him and hit him in the face with it? This

---

2. Material Handling Passageway: A long corridor that has outside access so that large items can be brought on board.

3. Deck Department: consists of two divisions. 1st division maintains the outward appearance of the ship and specific areas throughout the ship, and 3rd division runs the boat deck. Together they are responsible for the safe navigation and operation of the vessel, both at sea and in port.

is exactly why he's gonna lock you in one of the storage rooms. You play too much," Noelle said with a shake of her head.

Celia ignored her. She wasn't playing—at least not intentionally. She meant every word she told him. He was too conflicted, and she didn't want him to hate her. In her experience, the main reasons people cheated were physical attraction or an emotional connection. If the latter was the dominant reason, that's where everything went to shit. If Ingram was right about Joaquín's wife, their affair would be tinged with revenge. She didn't need all that drama in her life; she wanted a clean cheat. It already felt chaotic, and it hadn't even started yet.

The subject of their conversation stepped through the hatch leading to the forward mess decks[4] , followed by Ingram. Her heart skipped a beat. She hoped that he hadn't gone off the ship for lunch or eaten before she came. He hadn't seen her yet because a sailor grabbed his attention before he looked in her direction. She didn't take her eyes off Joaquín as he stopped to chat with a few of his friends. He wore his dungarees today. They fit him just right, not crossing over the too-tight line as some of the sailors aboard the ship seemed to do with reckless abandon. The sheer amount of moose knuckles she'd witnessed during her time in the Navy made her wonder if the country's birth population would soon be on the decline due to sperm getting cooked in the sacks. She was grateful Joaquín let his balls breathe. He must have felt the weight of her stare because he began to look around as the sailor talked to him.

---

4. Mess or Mess Deck: a designated area where military personnel eat and socialize.

When he finally locked eyes with hers, he held her gaze for a few seconds that felt like an eternity before he gave a quick upward tilt of his chin and made his way to the chow line with Ingram in tow.

Celia let go of the breath she wasn't aware she was holding. God, she missed being caught up in the intensity of his gaze.

"I take it he's here," Noelle remarked. Her back was facing the hatch. "You're wearing your stalker eyes from the Lifetime Channel special edition of *Obsessed Other Woman Mrs. Potato Head Doll*."

Celia rolled her eyes so hard she almost gave herself a headache. "And you're wearing the sneaker feet from the 'I'm just gonna complicate shit unnecessarily' edition made for the BET. Because speaking of playing games," she said, wiggling her fingers at Noelle. "What are you going to do about Quentin? Have you had sex yet? You've been out with him every night, and the cruise starts in *two weeks*. Does he even know we're leaving?"

"Good deflection. First of all, I am vigorously throwing the pussy at him every moment we're together and when we're not together. I haven't masturbated this much on the phone since I was a teenager. I'm about to get tennis elbow. And no, we haven't. I do not know why. Quite frankly, it's a bit disturbing. Is he gay? I don't think he is, but what if I'm his beard? And yes, I know I'm running out of time. And no, I haven't told him."

"He's not gay, Noelle. He might be actually trying to set a foundation for a relationship with you that doesn't just focus on sex. Can you imagine?" Celia placed a hand delicately over her mouth with feigned surprise.

"No, I cannot!" Noelle hissed, rearing back in her seat. Her mouth gaped open and closed like a fish out of water. "Oh

God, you think so? That's not good."

"Why not? You're thirty-four years old; don't you think it's time for a real relationship?"

"No, actually, I don't." Noelle shook her head adamantly.

Celia looked incredulously at her friend. "Why the hell not?"

"Why the heck not what? And why are we eating here?" Sidney appeared suddenly, setting her tray down and taking a seat next to Celia.

"Why the hell is Celia playing duck duck goose with Santiago?"

"Why hasn't Noelle told Quentin we're leaving soon?"

Celia and Noelle answered at the same time.

Sidney looked back and forth between the two women. "Oh."

"Yeah, *oh,*" Celia said. "I have been telling her to tell him. Maybe you can convince her to do it."

"Or maybe you could convince Celia to stop starting shit she can't finish with men who are going to lock her in closets," Noelle shot back.

"Or maybe I could just leave you two alone because I hate being on the [5] mess decks?" Sidney shrugged and started eating.

"And how are you lovely ladies enjoying this fine, fine Navy chow?"

Celia scowled at Noelle before smiling up at Ingram, who stopped beside their table with Joaquín. "It's just as tasty as always. Just like momma makes it."

"Then your momma is a horrible cook, hate to say it,"

---

5. Mess or Mess Deck: a designated area where military personnel eat and socialize.

Ingram said with a laugh.

"Navarro," Joaquín said by way of greeting.

"Santiago." Celia greeted him back.

"And hello to you too, BM1[6]," Noelle said cheekily.

The corner of Santiago's lips lifted in a half smile. "Bentley." He turned to Sidney. "Pascal."

Sidney nodded absently; she was looking in the direction of the port side[7] hatch[8] leading to the forward mess decks. "I'll see you guys later." She abruptly stood up, grabbed her tray and utensils, and headed to the scullery on the other side of the mess decks while ignoring Noelle's, "But you just got here."

"Well, I guess we'll sit here if you ladies don't mind." Ingram sat down next to Noelle without waiting for an answer. Santiago slid into the empty seat next to Celia.

"You've been avoiding me," Joaquín murmured in Spanish.

"What do you mean?" Celia answered back the same way. Trying to quell her onset of nervousness, she picked up her green mug and took a sip of her fruit punch. The almost candy-sweet liquid hit her tongue, and she smacked her lips. One of the Black crankers definitely made this batch. If she finished this cup without adding water, she'd be bouncing off the walls like Noelle.

---

6. BM/Boatswain's Mates: crew members who train, direct, and supervise personnel in ship maintenance and boat seamanship.

7. Port: left side.

8. Hatch: A watertight opening to a deck. If it goes through a bulkhead, it's a regular door.

"You did an about-face the other day and canceled our meeting." Joaquín picked up his fork and twirled spaghetti around it. He spread his legs so one of them pressed firmly against Celia's underneath the table.

"Yeah, I did," she responded as they both continued in Spanish, Celia bit the inside of her bottom lip. Immediately her leg lit up, and a flush spread over the rest of her body, settling between her thighs. She resisted the urge to wiggle closer and massage the side of her breast on the arm resting on the table next to hers. Or slip her hand underneath the table so she could rub his thigh, or shit, rub herself. All from his dungaree-covered leg touching hers. This man had her like a cat in heat. Hells yes, she was avoiding him.

"Why?" Joaquín asked. He put some food in his mouth and turned to look at her while he chewed.

His tone was so casual. Celia turned her head and stared at him. How was he sitting there so calmly when she was about to combust? How dare he be so unbothered by her presence? The last time she spoke to him, he looked absolutely tortured, and now he's all 'You've been avoiding me.' What the fuck was going on here? She couldn't have him thinking he could just sit at her table and throw her off her game. Although she had to admit, she hadn't been completely on it either since she caught him staring at her. She vacillated between her desire for him and her moral compass, trying to reorient itself. That was confusing enough. She didn't need him irking her with his damn nonchalantness in her presence. Not today. *Not on her watch!*

"It's just that I've been thinking that maybe we should go back to how it was before," Celia said, her voice somber. She even added a sympathetic head nod and apologetic shoulder raise.

Joaquín stared at her with slightly narrowed eyes. "You

mean you're going to start dating women again and go back to pretending I don't exist." He put his fork down.

Oh, you don't look so chill now, do you? Celia felt a perverse sense of satisfaction at his mood change but kept the gloating from her expression and voice. "I'm not going back to women…"

"Now see, I don't think that's gonna work, Celia," Joaquín began.

*Whew, chile…*Celia repressed the shiver at the slow way her name rolled off his tongue. "But I do think it's for the best."

"So now you're making decisions that involve me without consulting me." Joaquín leaned towards her. If anyone were looking at them, they would think he leaned in to hear something because the forward[9] mess deck was almost to capacity with people and ambient noise. But if they could see his eyes and the storm waging within them, shipmates might have told her to run for cover.

That's more like it. Celia dropped her eyes demurely for a second while she reveled in her victory. When she raised them back to his, she was all wide-eyed innocence. "I didn't know I had to consult you first, Joaquín." His eyes darkened when she said his name. She was grateful that her bra, her white cotton T-shirt, and her dungaree shirt covered her breasts because her nipples were so hard they were painful, and a shock went through her pussy. She wanted to curl into herself and writhe, but she was on mess decks. She inhaled his sandalwood cologne. Joaquín's eyes dropped down to the slight parting of her lips when she exhaled slowly.

---

9. Forward: the front of the ship or a space.

His eyes slowly rose back to hers, pinning her once again with the determination and indignation in his gaze. "You don't get to decide what's best for me, mami. I'll decide that for myself."

Celia matched the determination and indignation in his stare with a subtle satisfaction. She bit back her smile. She was about to poke at him further because why not, when Noelle's voice interrupted her.

"This is better than watching *Telemundo*," Noelle said in awe. "You don't even need to know Spanish because the body language is so intense!"

"I agree. *Muy caliente!* You can cut the tension with a knife! What will happen? Find out on the next episode of *Playing with Fire*?" Ingram added in a fake and exaggerated Spanish accent.

These motherfuckers! Celia's head whipped around, and she glared at Noelle and Ingram, irritated and amused at the same time. She had forgotten they were there. Shit, she had forgotten they were on the *mess decks. Once Joaquín had looked at her, everything faded until all that was left was him. Joaquín cursed under his breath and sat back in his chair.

Celia mouthed "I hate you" to Noelle, who mouthed, "I love you" back, immediately followed by a flinch when Celia kicked her foot under the table.

"Hey babe, you got anything going on after lunch?"

Celia felt a hand on her shoulder and looked up at BM2 Derek Evans, who appeared next to her. Evans had been trying to get with her since they sat next to each other during indoc, but he took the constant rejection lightheartedly. It was an ongoing joke between them. Every month, he'd ask, "Is it my turn yet?" And every month, Celia would hit him with a firm no. It wasn't that Evans wasn't attractive.

No, he was fine; he was North Carolinian country boy fine. He was what Noelle liked to call a Food-Shelter-Water man. Some of them still weren't 'bout shit, but the ones that were—well, those were the men you brought home to meet the family. Noelle wanted Celia to date him simply because he knew how to barbecue, which meant they would have all the free food she could eat. Evans was definitely still on the roster. Had Celia not seen the way Joaquín looked at her, she might have pulled Evans from the bench to play. Aside from their flirting, they had become good friends, something else that Kendrick had hated. He was another one of the reasons they argued so much. So if Joaquín didn't pan out, Evans was getting a uniform.

Celia smiled at Evans. "No, I'm good. Do you want me to come up to the flight deck, or are you coming by Admin?"

"I'll come by Admin," Evans replied. He nodded at Santiago and Ingram, then winked at Noelle.

"Man don't be winking at me unless you have a plate of barbecue in your hand. Are we having a cookout before we leave?"

"You know I got you, girl. It's already planned. I got everything together while I was on leave. I had my aunt make the sauce, and I brought it back."

Noelle's eyelids fluttered as she placed a hand on her heart. "You got me tearing up over here. I feel the love. Can you guys feel it?"

"No, we can't. Because we don't cry over food. We're normal," Celia said dryly.

"Since you feel that way, you're not invited to the barbecue."

"It's not your barbecue."

"It doesn't matter. Your presence will spoil the meat, bruja," Noelle accused with a straight face. Ingram snorted and then hung his head to hide his grin when Celia glared at him and swatted Evans' hand when he whispered, "Not the meat. Say it ain't so, girl." Even Santiago managed to snicker before he smothered it with a frown.

"You know what!" Celia tried to kick Noelle again but ended up playing footsies with her in an attempt to find her shin. After a few moments, Celia gave up and looked back up at Evans. She had forgotten he'd been on leave for fourteen days. No doubt he had questions about Kendrick. "I'll see you after chow[10]."

"Aight." Evans pointed to Noelle. "Behave."

Noelle gave a small shake of her head and mouthed No.

Santiago glanced at his watch. "I'm out too."

"Yeah," Noelle drawled, and her eyes darted over to Celia's. She picked up her fork.

Celia narrowed her eyes, and she gave a little shake of her head. What the hell was she about to say? She was always saying some off-the-cuff shit, whereas Celia's fire-starting was very nuanced and targeted.

"Yeah," Noelle repeated, suddenly engrossed with the task of twirling her spaghetti around her fork. "You *should* go before the bruja gets you too."

Celia heard Joaquín's soft grunt. Apparently, Noelle heard it too and paused in her twirling. She looked at Joaquín, and her smile was a mixture of amusement, regret, and pity.

"My bad. It's too late. She's already got you."

---

10. Chow: to sit down and eat.

Chapter Twenty-Six

EN2 Nicolas Kaneko

"Hey Kaneko, are you busy?"

Finally. Nicolas smiled to himself before putting down the TV remote and spinning his chair around to face Pascal. She stood in the hatch[1] of his shop, wearing her usual warm but reserved expression. When he made eye contact with her as he passed through the mess decks, he had hoped she'd come and talk to him. He was tired of replaying their time together over and over in his mind. If it were a VHS tape, it would have worn out and jammed the machine.

"No, I was just sitting here waiting." Nicolas stood up and leaned his hip against his desk.

Pascal's brow wrinkled. "Oh, you're waiting for someone. Well, I can—"

"You. I was waiting for you, Pascal," Nicolas said with a smile.

Pascal's back straightened up. "Oh, I see."

"Do you?" Nicolas asked.

Pascal took a deep breath and relaxed against the bulk-

---

1. Hatch: A watertight opening to a deck. If it goes through a bulkhead, it's a regular door.

head. "I do."

Nicolas nodded, satisfied with her answer because although she didn't elaborate, he knew she understood that he was letting her set the pace. Just from their short time together, he knew she was a thinker, chewing over her thoughts and words so they were digestible before she made a move. He didn't know if what happened between them was a plan just waiting for an opportunity or an impulsive decision that she now regretted. He was about to respond when one of his coworkers stepped through the hatch carrying his lunch tray. He greeted them and sat down at one of the desks.

"Come with me," Nicolas said and walked past Pascal to the climate-controlled space next to his office where the ship's fuel injectors were stored. He was so glad his other coworkers went out to Micky D's for lunch leaving only him and O'Neil who had *duty in the shop.

"So, how have you been?" Nicolas hopped up on the long desk they sometimes used a bed while Pascal stayed next to the closed hatch.

"I've been good. I've been doing a lot of thinking and making important decisions as a result. How about you? What have you been doing?" Pascal asked.

Nicolas took note of her last question. There was a definite difference between asking someone what they were doing instead of what they've been up to. The former denoted a possessive familiarity, and he welcomed it. He wanted her to settle on the idea of them, to claim him first so she wouldn't put up so much resistance when he staked his claim on her, which he planned to do as soon as she let him. He prayed it was today because he didn't know how much more waiting he had left in him. He missed her presence in life. It'd only been one day, but that was enough to know he wanted more.

"I've been just chilling. Bought a new cookbook I've been wanting for a while. I was about to start trying some recipes out, but I realized that I didn't want to cook for just myself. So I have been just twiddling my thumbs." *Waiting for you* hung in the air between them.

Pascal's smile was cheeky. "That's a shame because you're such a good cook."

"Just good?" Nicolas teased, enjoying the replay. "I distinctly remember the noises you made when you ate my cooking."

Pascal laughed, and there was something about sound the sound of it that made him study her a litter deeper. *Wait a minute...*

"Did you break up with your boyfriend?"

Pascal's smile froze, then she frowned at him. "Who told you?"

"No one." Nicolas shook his head. "Who would tell me? He's not even stationed with us. You're just lighter. More relaxed. Well, you were."

Pascal took a breath and blew it out between her lips. "I didn't do it because of...of this." She gestured to him and then back to her. "I just want that to be clear. But being with you just highlighted some of the things that I just kept on trying to ignore."

"He never bothered to learn how you took your coffee, did he?" Nicolas said. *Or anything else, for that matter.* He really wanted to add, but that was already apparent. No need to rub it in.

Pascal shook her head slowly. "No, amongst other more important things."

"I see. So am I allowed to take advantage of your newly single life?" Nicolas casually asked the question, but he was anything but. It was a good sign that she sought him out, but she could be just trying to clear the air between them so there wouldn't be any awkwardness during the cruise.

Pascal visibly softened at his words. She leaned back against the hatch. "Do you want to?"

"Aye aye, ma'am, I do." Nicolas hopped off the desk and walked over to her. Reaching behind her, he dogged[2] the hatch[3] and then pressed his body against her softness. "But the question is, do you?"

Through heavy lids, Pascal looked up at him. "Do you think I'd be here if I didn't?" Pascal grabbed one of his belt loops and pulled him even closer.

"You're full of surprises, Pascal." Nicolas' eyes swept over her face. Damn, she was so fine. That man was a fool when he let her get away. "So I'm going to need to hear the words just to be sure." He lightly kissed her lips, pulling back when she tried to deepen the kiss, moving his lips along her jawline to whisper in her ear. "Tell me what you want Pascal. Do you miss my tongue licking your asshole? Do you want to ride my face again? Drip your cum down all over me? Do you miss me fucking you? Tell me."

"I..." Pascal inhaled shakily when he slipped his leg between hers and ground it against her crotch. She grabbed the front of his coveralls and wrapped an arm around his neck, burying her face as she rode his leg. "I miss all of that. I want you so bad Kaneko. It's all I've been thinking about."

Fuck! Nicolas groaned against her shoulder. "Can I taste you? I need to taste you." He didn't wait to hear her answer.

---

2. Dog: to close or "dog down" a water-tight hatch.

3. Hatch: A watertight opening to a deck. If it goes through a bulkhead, it's a regular door.

He just dropped down to his knees, and Pascal offered no resistance as he quickly undid her belt buckle and yanked her dungarees down enough so she could spread her legs a little. Pulling the gusset of her panties aside, he felt the bristle of new growth on his nose when he parted her lips with his tongue. He wondered if she let it grow back during the cruise. All thoughts were forgotten when his tongue found her wetness. The taste of her made him hum in agonized pleasure. He pulled at her thighs, bowing her legs as he tried to bury his mouth deeper between them. Pascal grabbed his hair and arched her back when he began to suck on her clit. She started to whimper, and then she went almost quiet. He glanced up; she muffled her voice with one hand. He also saw the clock on the bulkhead next to her head. Chow was almost over.

Quickly standing, he replaced her hand with his mouth, and his tongue with his fingers. "I want you to come for me, sweetheart. We don't have much time. Okay?" Pascal nodded and rocked her hips against his hand as his fingers moved fast over her clit. He swallowed her moans and squeals when she came and held her as clung to his shoulders, collapsing against him. Dammit, he wanted to fuck her. He almost came in his coveralls when she did; that's how hard and ready he was.

"That was your reward for breaking up with Nelson," Nicolas said against her lips.

Pascal laughed. "I would have done it sooner if I knew I'd get all this." She rubbed her nose against his. "You smell like me."

"If it didn't smell like you, then I wouldn't be doing my job," Nicolas said.

"You're a mess. Lordy, *I'ma* mess. I need to go to berthing[4] before I go back to *main control." Pascal pushed lightly at his chest.

"Lord bless this mess," Nicolas said, trying to laugh when Pascal sent him a horrified look.

"I might have to bump my tithes up to twenty percent messing around you." Pascal's tone was scolding, but she was also trying not to laugh before giving in. After straightening up her uniform, she sniffed the air. "Oh my goodness, this whole room smells like me."

Nicolas took a deep breath and used his hands to waft the air to his nostrils. "Ahhhh, it smells divine."

"I cannot with you." Pascal shook her head at him. "I simply cannot."

Nicolas chuckled. "I promise you, you can. Remember when I told you that there's so much more we can do."

Pascal smiled. "Yes."

"I say it was long past time we got started, don't you think?" Nicolas saw Pascal's throat move as she swallowed hard. She was nervous, and she should be. The plans he'd been dreaming up were going to take her so far out of her comfort zone she'd never want to go back. He held his hand out to her, and with a small, exasperated smile, she took it.

---

4. Berthing: Living quarters aboard a ship.

Chapter Twenty-Seven

MM1 Sidney Pascal

"**A**nyone else in here?" Sidney asked as she walked into the photo lab. After a quick trip to the berthing to clean up the mess that Kaneko made, she went to find Noelle so she could finally unpack her mental worries suitcase.

Noelle looked up from the negative she was holding. "No, just me. What's up?"

"Okay, so Kaneko just ate me out in their engine repair room," Sidney said in a rush and sat down on one of the stools. Her body was still tingling.

"Where the hell is that? And I was wondering where you ran off to. That man done turnt you into a jezebel!" Noelle slid the negative holder into the machine, looked at the small screen above it, and pressed some buttons.

"It's on the boat deck. But it's an engineering space. Never mind, " Sidney said when Noelle gave her a blank stare. "Anyway, I think I agreed to have a relationship of sorts with him."

"A relationship of sorts? So y'all gonna be fuckin'? Is that what you meant to say?" Noelle asked.

Sidney winced. "Yes, we're gonna be doing that. But it also feels like I agreed to more than just that. But I *just* broke up with Nelson—what the heck am I doing?" She was starting to panic. It was good and well to agree to something in the afterglow of an orgasm but now she felt so unsure of herself.

"I am not even discussing Breath and Britches. I refuse. " Noelle sliced a hand in the air. "But let me tell you what you're doing since you seem to be unclear. For the first time in years, you're going to be getting your sexual needs met with a man who's intent on bringing you pleasure. And someone else will know how to make your coffee beside me."

Remember the need in Kaneko's voice before he dropped to his knees, Sidney closed her eyes and hugged herself. "He did act like he was starvin' for reals." Her eyes popped open at Noelle's snort. "But I mean the cruise is about to start and so does this mean that we are going to be a thing?"

"Do you want to have a thing with him?" Noelle asked patiently.

"I don't know!" Sidney shrieked. The panic was full-blown now. She took a deep breath before continuing, "He put his hand out and I took it so it's like a gentleman's agreement but I do not flip people the way you do. I don't move fast on anything."

"Yes, yes, I know you're as slow as cold molasses. And we all know I'd rather go hunt for my own food than wait for him to decide what we should eat." Noelle sat up and slapped her hands on her thighs. "But Ima need you to stop tryna to act like you're so different from me. You let that man get in your booty on the first night okay? So don't be actin' like you got the Miss Purity award at the debutante ball and I be out here hoein' down the town."

Sidney squeezed her eyes shut in chagrin this time. She did have a habit of getting on her high horse when she was afraid. "You're right. I'm sorry."

"Apology accepted. Now say you're a dirty girl because you are." Noelle ordered.

"I will not," Sidney said. "Okay so we've established that he makes my Precious very happy but—"

"No, no, no, NO! Don't even start with that shit," Noelle cut her off. "The one-drop rule applies. Ya'll both would be on the auction block. He'd just be in the house and you'd be in the field. But enslaved nonetheless."

Sidney huffed. "I don't know about that analogy. I feel like he would have been a freeman. Maybe if he looked like his sister I wo—"

"Enough! Even if he was pure Japanese you better let that shit go! All these Black guys be out here just running through them white, Filipino, Spanish, whatever they can get their dicks into and we're supposed to just wait for them to finish with their any-other-girl-but-Black-girl-phase and choose us. Fuck. That. Shit. It's the fucking '90s! You betta live your fuckin' life girl. And besides I think he knows karate. He almost made it to the Olympics, I believe, so he can defend you if some shit pops off in dem streets. That's my main concern."

"It's aikido and judo," Sidney corrected automatically. In the middle of the night, they had a conversation about his childhood in Japan and his attempt to get into the 1978 Olympics, among other things. It felt so natural to be laying there naked and talking to a man she avoided for over two years. She never even felt that comfortable with Bernard and she knew him for years before they dated. Taking another deep breath, she exhaled forcefully. "Would you date him?"

"C'mon now, you know I don't offer advice on shit I wouldn't do. So hell fucking yes, Sidney! I'd fuck that boy down port and up starboard, forward and aft." Noelle directed her hands like an airline stewardess as she spoke.

"Why haven't you then? I know all types of guys have tried to talk to you. I *have* seen them."

"Look here now, I am not interested in the boys that only date Black girls. It feels so weird to me. Date me because you like me and we actually have things in common, not because I season my food and remind you of delicious toffee candy. I would rather date a white boy who listens to Metallica than a white boy who listens to Jon B. because suddenly it's cool to be a white boy that likes Black girls. If that makes sense."

Sidney's head rocked side to side as she took in Noelle's words. "But what if he's like embarrassed or something for people to know his mom is Black and he wants to creep around with me on the down low."

"Just because *we* didn't know he momma's was Black, doesn't mean other people don't. It just wasn't on our radar." Noelle stood up to get the prints from the tray. Inspecting them, she added, "But at the end of the day, you have to do what you're comfortable with. If *you're* not comfortable with being seen out with him in public, then leave him alone Sidney. Personally, I don't think he's a bad dude. Celia has also confirmed this, and she's known him longer. I haven't heard any rumors about him, he's got outstanding dick, his head game is strong, he licked your butthole, finally made you squirt, cooked for you, can carry a conversation, *and* just ate you out on your lunch break. Is there anything else you actually need from him right now other than that?"

Sidney sighed. Yes, those were all fantastic and amazing things, but what if people stared? There was no 'what if' about it. They were going to stare at them. Noelle might not mind, but she didn't know how she would handle it. "He's got this fascination with my butt, though. Isn't that the whole big-ass Black girl fetishizing thing?"

Noelle looked up at the overhead lights and muttered under her breath what Sidney imagined to be her version of prayer before answering. "You're just gonna grab at all the straws huh? Newsflash: I fetishize your ass. I just wanna smack and motorboat your butt cheeks, and I ain't gay." She pretended to smack and grab an imaginary ass and motor-boated the air.

Mentally putting the straws away because Noelle was right, Sidney laughed. "You do be smacking my booty. A lot. And for the record, I hate it."

"I wouldn't have guessed from recent events. Look, all jokes aside, I just want you to have fun. Your soul needs this. Your Precious needs this. Especially after Breath and Britches, you deserve to have your Precious cleansed every afternoon by Kaneko. It's like he's sucking out the poison with his mouth, and his dick is the antibiotic. So stop borrowing trouble and just enjoy some duty-free dick during the cruise. The future will deal with itself, Sidney. Oh, and how could I forget this gem? I know he ain't fucking with you because he thinks that he's doing you a favor because you're a dark-skinned sister, and he's the coveted light-skinned brother with the good hair brother and light eyes."

"Yeah, that…" Sidney's lip curled up, and she shook her head. She looked around Noelle's photo lab as the reality of her previous relationship draped her like a smallpox blanket. She willingly dated a man that hated Black women. No, just dark-skinned Black women. He only dated her because she took care of him. She guessed that's what a mammy was supposed to do.

Noelle's smile was full of sympathy. "Don't beat yourself up about it. We all do stupid shit. But you're almost fifty, so you should probably stop." Noelle sat back down on her stool and pressed some buttons on the machine.

"I am only forty-one. Would you cut that out please?" Sidney slouched. "I honestly don't know what I was thinking. I really don't."

Noelle sighed. "You don't? Seriously? Really? Since you want to beat yourself up instead of letting it go and move on like I want to, let me clarify some things for you then, yeah. You're lazy, Sidney, and like me, you're also scared to invest in people. If me and Celia like crazy, you and I are runners, so it was easier to stay with Nelson because you knew what to expect from him. That's it. *Voila!* Mystery solved. So there's no need to keep on searching and—" she paused dramatically, "*Taint* your afternoon with thoughts of Breath and Britches."

"That's such a terrible word," Sidney said, grimacing.

"But it does feel good when it gets licked though."

"Indeed it does...." Sidney shuddered at the memory of Kaneko doing just.

"There you go with that look on your face. You *nasty*."

"But you brought it up!"

"But I ain't all hot in the crotch about it. *Nasty*," Noelle whispered the last word.

"You know what!" Sidney blurted as she jumped up.

"What? That EN2 released your inner freak? Hallelujah!" Noelle waved her hands in the air.

"I feel like you're using that hallelujah in the wrong context," Sidney said walking over to the door. Both Noelle and Kaneko were the same with all their blasphemy.

Noelle shrugged one shoulder. "Probably, but you can't save my soul now, my spot in hell has been reserved since the summer of '82. But I think anal sex is the sexual 666, so it does bring me comfort to know I'll see you there."

With her hand on the knob, Sidney stared aghast at her friend. "You think so?"

"How the hell would I know, Sidney? C'mon now! The only part of the Bible I remember is that woman riding on the six-headed dog. Which personally, I think is cool as shit. But I do think she's a demon, and it's the revelation, and we're all gonna die, so...welcome to hell...and have a nice day. Let me know what you want for dinner. Ta-ta for now."

"Ugh. Thanks. I guess. And I want some smothered pork chops and mashed potatoes with peas," Sidney said quickly and shut the door on Noelle's laughter.

That damn woman is the absolute worst, and she probably is going to hell. I am not going to hell, Sidney griped to herself as she made her way back to Engineering. *Because I am already in hell*, she added when she saw Nelson cross the quarterdeck.

Chapter Twenty-Eight

MM1 Sidney Pascal

W ithout saying a word to Nelson, Sidney walked past main control and headed to aft[1] lookout. Picking a corner away from the other sailors smoking, she turned to Nelson. "Why are you here?"

"Why am I here?" Nelson shook his head. "I have been trying to call you, and you're not returning my calls. So I wanted to check on you."

"Hmm, I'm good. Thanks for checking on me. How are you?" Sidney asked before she could catch herself. *Fudge.*

"I don't know. I'm still kinda fucked up over you wanting to break up with me. I thought we should talk about it..." Nelson let his voice trail off as he held out his open hands.

Quietly disgusted, Sidney studied Nelson. He was doing his humble man shuffle again.

"I did break up with you, there's no wanting about it, and there isn't anything we need to talk about. We said everything last night. At least I did, but I have about—" Sidney glanced at her watch. "I have about ten minutes before I have a meeting, so what do you need to say that wasn't said last night?"

---

1. Aft: rear of the ship or a space.

"After four years, all I get is ten minutes?" Nelson said incredulously.

"Or you could have waited until the end of the workday." Sidney could feel all her repressed anger starting to bubble up. To come to her job to discuss their relationship was so manipulative because he knew she wouldn't cause a scene.

"This is fucked up, Sidney! I don't know why you're acting like this. One day we're cool, and the next day you're like 'I'm breaking up with you', and I just gotta be cool with that shit? We can't even talk about it. I love you. I still want to marry you despite all this, but you *gotta* keep your friends out of our relationship," Nelson said.

Sidney narrowed her eyes, refusing to take the deflection and triangulation bait along with the 'I'm just gonna dismiss your autonomy and disrespect your decision-making skills just the heck because.' And the marriage card? She guessed that was the 'get a girl back' final defense play. Why did men think that was all they had to say to turn things in their favor? Never once had they discussed marriage. Shoot, they barely discussed their boring relationship.

The thing is though, she couldn't even get mad at Nelson. She was a fully present and active participant in this tomfoolery. She had allowed the mediocracy to run amok with only a few half-hearted attempts at improvement. Because like Noelle said, he was safe. So there wasn't anything to improve because they were never compatible. He just wanted someone to take care of him like his momma did. He dang sure didn't encourage her to pursue higher education, be it her master's degree or her studying for the Chief's exam. He downplayed the fact that she was 1st class, saying it was easy to advance in the Machinist Mate[2] rate because they needed women and Black women at that unlike the Boatswain's Mate[3]. He acted as if he was a doggone Nuke[4]. The man was so sorry.

"Nelson, you're right. I did just drop this on you, but it didn't just come out of nowhere. It was slowly creeping up on me. Maybe I should have spoken to you about how I was feeling instead of just staying quiet, so I do apologize about that. But that being said, this relationship should have ended a long time ago," Sidney said.

"Why?" Nelson threw his hands up in the air. "Why are you saying that? And why are you saying this now? Is there someone else?"

Ugh, she hated when he repeated himself. A movement over Nelson's shoulders caught her eye. Hudson, one of the BM's she was cool with gave her the thumbs up. She gave him a tiny nod. He sent her the 'I'm watching you' hand motion, and she had to smoother her grin before turning her attention back to Nelson, who of course didn't notice because he was too busy riling himself up.

---

2. MM/Machinist Mate: are responsible for operating and maintaining ship propulsion machinery and outside machinery.

3. BM/Boatswain's Mates: Crew members who train, direct, and supervise personnel in ship maintenance and boat seamanship.

4. Nuke: Navy's Nuclear Program consisting of various rates/jobs.

4. Nuke: Navy's Nuclear Program consisting of various rates/jobs.

"No, there isn't anyone else." Not really. And shoot, even if she was breaking with him to be with Kaneko, she dang sure wouldn't be telling him. Mattie didn't raise no fool. "This is about me and what I want. Do you know what my master's degree is in?" Sidney went silent, patiently waiting for him to answer her question. After about five seconds of them staring at each other, she spoke again. "So even though I've been doing this for almost two years and I'm almost done with it *and* you complain about it constantly you don't know, do you?"

Nelson finally opened his mouth, but Sidney silenced him by holding up her finger. "Something so important to me, you couldn't bother to remember even when I've told you multiple times. Moving on, do you know how I like my coffee? Or even my regular drinks? Do you know what my favorite book is? My favorite color? Do you know why I joined the Navy? My family history? Do you remember *any-thing* about me other than my duty days because that's the only time I wasn't able to be with you and you had to fend for yourself? And now you want to talk about marriage? For what? One, we never discussed it. And more importantly, why do you want to marry me?"

Nelson dared to look contrite when he had yet to answer even one of Sidney's questions. "Because I love you. We've been together for four years. And—"

"Full stop!" Sidney waved a hand in front of her. "You drink your coffee black with four sugars. You hate peanut butter and jelly sandwiches but love fluff and peanut butter together. You think grape soda is gauche, but you're fine with orange soda. Your favorite food is Maryland-style crab cakes. You like the right side of the bed and only use Irish Spring soap, which I hate by the way. You poop every morning between 0530 and 0600. You brush your teeth for three minutes and gargle for sixty seconds—you like to push past the burn of Listerine. Your fixation with the waves in your hair borders on obsession and you constantly steal my head scarves when you can't find yours without even asking me. You think your hazel eyes and light skin along with your beloved waves give you a superpower over women. They don't. You are spoiled rotten by your parents and you take them for granted because of that. You never invited them to Naples and when they asked to come and you made some lame excuse for them not to. You barely visit them now and they are a four-hour drive away. But you do make sure you see them for Christmas and your birthday. But if I didn't tell you to call or send a card you would forget their birthdays. You had no intention of returning back to the States because you complain about everything so I still don't know why you came back here. In the same way, I don't know why you want to be with me because clearly you have no interest in me other than my long hair and that I cook your dinner."

Nelson looked shocked as she ran off his information. "Look, I know I messed up, and I'm sorry. I promise I will do better. But everything you mentioned are small things, and we're not breaking up because I don't know how you like your coffee. That's crazy, Sidney. You gotta admit that it's crazy."

Sidney shook her head. "But it's not *crazy* because those things are all about *me*. What's crazy is that they seem so small and insignificant to you. There is nothing to repair between us. There is no one whispering in my ear; it's simply the fact I don't want to be in a relationship with you anymore, and because of that, our relationship is over." She made sure her voice was kind but firm. A part of her wanted to rip him a new one, but she didn't want to give him a reason to keep arguing with her. She really did have a meeting with one of her E-3s. And they were on aft lookout. This must be the ship's break-up spot. Not to mention, she was pretty sure Hudson would fight him because he was a known brawler.

Shocked, Nelson stood there staring at her. Then his demeanor started to change when the realization set in that she wasn't budging on her decision. The Humble Man was replaced by the Scorned Man. She felt the heat of his anger in his gaze. His scowl twisted his pretty boy looks into something ugly. Sweat dotted his forehead, and he clenched his fists a few times while taking some deep breaths.

Sidney tensed up and surreptitiously glanced over his shoulder again. Hudson pushed off the railing and was slowly heading their way wearing a smile. Lordy. She shook her head but Hudson didn't stop until he was a fist throw away. While she appreciated his concern, it was unwarranted. Nelson wouldn't lay hands on her even if they were alone. He didn't value her career, but he did value his lackluster one. But had they been at his place, he would have tried to intimidate her with yelling and stomping around when his rational, dismissive approach didn't work.

What in the world had she been thinking, or rather not thinking, for the past four years? Sidney was not about to waste any more of her time playing the staring game; she was done. Just when she was about to send Nelson back to where he came from Hudson said, "Hey MM1, you got a minute?"

Nelson open his mouth but Sidney cut him off. "Nelson, take care of yourself."

The glare Nelson sent her before he left was designed to scorch her soul. Sidney exhaled when he stepped through the hatch. She hoped he had gotten it through his thick, self-entitled skull that their relationship was over, but probably not. She might have to show her tail, something she hadn't done since Bernard, and remind that man and herself that she was from Fort Worth, Texas.

"MM1, what was that all about? I thought I was gonna have to knock a nigga out!" Hudson bounced lightly on the balls of his feet.

Sidney laughed lightly. Woah, he was way too excited at the prospect of beating Nelson's behind. She was too actually and she was totally shocked by how much joy she felt. "Calm down killa. It's all good. I appreciate you though." She really did. It's been a while since a man stood up for her and it felt great. She wondered how Kaneko would've handled it and immediately the song *Fung Fu Fighting* played in her head. She couldn't wait to tell Noelle.

"You know I'm 'bout it. So you let me know if you need me now," Hudson offered.

"I will. I promise." Sidney linked an arm with his and led them to the hatch[5].

---

5. Hatch: A watertight opening to a deck. If it goes
    through a bulkhead, it's a regular door.

Chapter Twenty-Nine

BM1 Joaquín Santiago

"**A**re you sure you don't want to come out with me? It's not too late to get Anita's daughter to babysit." Marisol said, adding the ingredients for her dirty martini into the tumbler.

"No, I'm good," Joaquín replied and took a sip of his cognac. Settling back into his recliner, he watched Marisol as she shook the tumbler. She bartended her way through college, and he loved the way she deftly handled the bottles as she made drinks. She could still do all the tricks that were used to get her the big tips.

"If you'd said yes, I'd have to go play the lottery!" Marisol laughed. She opened the mini-fridge beneath the counter and cursed. "I didn't bring the olives down. Be right back."

Joaquín laughed, and his eyes followed her naked ass as she dashed past him and up the stairs to the kitchen. As always, Marisol came down to the basement in her underwear and shared a drink with him before going out. Tonight she wore one of his favorite sets: a lacy red push-up bra and matching thongs that completely disappeared between her cheeks. When they first met, she complained that he had nothing to hold on to even though he reassured her that he had more than enough to grab. But skinny or thick, he was satisfied with Marisol. Now two children and fifty pounds later she had what she called her 'grown woman's weight'. Her breasts were two cups larger, and her thighs and hips had filled out and rounded. But her apple-shaped ass was her prize possession. She loved the look and feel of it probably more than he did—and he did love it. It was perfect for either lying on or smacking. She even loved her tiny pouch. He offered to get her a tummy tuck if she wanted one, but she refused; she liked it when he held it when they made love.

Marisol's dark caramel skin and voluptuous curves were a complete contrast to Celia's fair skin and lean body. They both exuded sensuality. Celia delicately wove her web around you until you were hopelessly ensnared. Marisol hit you with a force that knocked you to your knees, leaving you gasping for air.

"I don't know, papi, you might enjoy yourself," Marisol said upon returning. She dropped three olives in her martini glass and then poured her drink.

"Mari, I am never going out with you and your friends." Joaquín took a sip of Henny before continuing. "Besides you need time away from me and the kids and your girls are too messy. They talk too much, and they can't hold their liquor. Anita gets a little too touchy-feely, Megan gets white girl wasted, and Tamika is just mean. I am surprised you all haven't been arrested for lewdness and/or disorderly conduct."

Joaquín didn't add that he enjoyed having the house to himself sans their sleeping kids until she returned home around 2 or 3 A.M. At the end of the workweek, he always needed time to decompress from being around so many people. But he suspected she knew, as they were both Scorpios, and they both needed their dark corners. She would have hers tomorrow when he took the kids out to the movies.

"I'm surprised. You wouldn't think these women were teachers, nurses, and lawyers during the daylight hours." Marisol drained her glass and set it on the counter. She daintily picked an olive out of the glass and popped it in her mouth. "So, Anita got all touchy-feely at the BBQ, huh? I knew she was crushin' on you."

Joaquín groaned. "You knew and you left me alone with her? That's sadistic. I had to keep on slapping her hands away. Isn't she married?"

"Yup, but I don't think she and hubby have sex. Or even have fun. Nor do Megan and her husband. Or they are having bad sex because when we talk about sex and I tell him how we get down—"

"Mari!" Joaquin exclaimed. "*Hay Dios mio!* Why are you telling those women about our sex life?"

"Not all of it. They couldn't handle it. I give them *un poquito,*" Marisol teased, smiling as she walked over and placed herself between his knees. Running her hands through his hair, she sighed. "I just feel sorry for them."

"You feel sorry for them?" Joaquín very much doubted that. Marisol didn't get mean, touchy, or wasted. Her messiest quality was that she wanted to be admired, and she wanted her friends to be jealous.

"Yes, I do. They don't have the kind of relationship where they can whip out a tittie and say, 'Papi, are you hungry?' like I can." One hand stayed tangled in his hair while the other pulled her bra down and freed her breast. "Come nurse." She pulled his head to her.

Joaquín grabbed her hips as his mouth closed over her nipple and as much areola as he could. She tugged at his hair and he bit her nipple then suckled and bit again, a little harder the second time, biting hard enough to leave an indentation on her nipple the third time. She hissed and shuddered against his mouth as he freed the other breast and repeated the action on the other nipple. He slid one hand up her thigh to tug at the scrap of fabric covering her pussy. Not surprisingly, she was wet.

"They can't say—or won't say—leave your teeth marks on me, tie me to the bed, fuck me hard, make me scream, slap me, come all over me, inside me. They wish they had this. They wish they had you." Marisol's last word ended with a moan because Joaquín slid his fore and middle fingers around her clit and squeezed hard enough to make the average woman cry out in pain. But she just got wetter and wanted more.

"Take off your pants," Marisol ordered softly.

Releasing her nipple, Joaquín did what he was told. Thoughts of Celia were forgotten as Marisol straddled him. The tip of his dick replaced his fingers as he grabbed her hips and guided her down slowly. She loved the feeling of him stretching her out one inch at a time. She also liked to be in charge when she was on top, so he let go of her hips and let her take it. There were so many things he let this woman do.

Rocking her hips, Marisol took his face into her hands and kissed him. Joaquín bit her bottom lip, stopping before he drew blood. Then he opened his mouth, and her tongue slid inside, dueling with his. As the kiss became deeper, the teasing and retreating more forceful, so did her hips. Marisol let go of his face and grabbed the back of the chair for leverage as she rode him. He grabbed her ass cheeks, dug his nails into the firm flesh, and pulled them so wide apart his fingers rimmed her asshole. If they were in the bedroom, she'd either have a plug or a string of pearls in there for him to pull out when she came. But for now, he'd use his fingers. When he felt she was close to orgasm, he pulled her closer, dipped down to her wetness, and jammed two fingers inside her hole. Marisol covered her mouth with one hand to keep from screaming, but she didn't stop riding him until shudders racked her body and her face was buried in his shoulder.

"Oh no, *papi*, you're still hard. Why didn't you come?" Marisol's voice was muffled.

Joaquín eased his fingers out and kissed her sweaty temple. "I wanted to make sure you came first."

"I taught you well," Marisol said and then yelped when Joaquín smacked her ass. Laughing, she scooted off his lap, turned around, and wriggled out of her thong. She playfully stuck out her ass, and he gave each cheek an open-palmed slap. Then she went down on her knees and slid her arms forward until her chest was flat against the carpet. "Whichever hole you want."

Joaquín wrapped his hand around his dick and rubbed it while he stared at her ass, taking a second to admire the view and contemplate. Before Marisol, he'd never done anal sex and what he considered freaky was breaking out the chocolate syrup. Marisol changed all that for him. She wanted to try everything—on her and on him and he let her. She was damn near insatiable in her pursuit of pleasure. The doorbell rang, interrupting his musings.

"Fuck!" Marisol groaned and pushed herself to her knees. "Shit, run and tell them to give me twenty minutes."

"No, it's okay. I'm good." Joaquín could feel himself already getting soft. He reached for his T-shirt and put it on.

Marisol stood up and faced him. She put her hands on her hips. "You sure? They can wait or go without me. I don't care."

Joaquín smiled because he knew she meant it. "No, go out

and have fun. I'll still be up when you get home."

Marisol grabbed his face and kissed him. "I love you. Okay, can you tell them to gimme ten minutes then?" She picked up her discarded thong before heading upstairs to their bedroom.

Joaquín pulled on his shorts and answered the front door relaying Marisol's message. He invited the three women inside, but they opted to wait in the car. He shrugged and closed the door. He didn't want them in the house anyway, especially Tamika. Aside from being mean, she was constantly staring at him—but not in a sexual way. He had mentioned it to Marisol in the past, but she just brushed it off, so he let it go.

Precisely ten minutes later, Marisol met him in the living room, where he had waited for her. Her thick, curly hair piled on top of her head in a high ponytail. She was wearing a shiny blue halter top and pair of his old light wash jeans that she claimed for her own, along with a chunky black belt and large gold hoops in her ears. Resting on her breast was a heart-shaped pendant. It was the size of a quarter, made of soft 18-karat gold, delicate and intricately designed. A little over a year ago, it suddenly appeared around her neck, and she only took it off when she went to bed.

"We'll finish up later. I won't be too late. Love you." Marisol reached up and pressed her cheek against his as they stood in the foyer.

"Love you too. Have fun and be safe. Call me if you need a ride home." Joaquín opened the door for her and watched her get into Megan's car. The overhead light turned on, and he saw Tamika turn back and greet Marisol. She was still wearing the smile when she faced forward again. Her smile tightened a bit when she saw Joaquín looking at her.

That woman is fucking odd, Joaquín thought as he closed

his front door.

Strangely enough, Joaquín was still thinking about the pendant when he hopped in the shower. The appearance of the pendant would have been a small thing on its own. It was beautiful, and he could see why she wanted it, however, it coincided with the change he sensed in her. She was already a moody woman, but her bouts of quietness began to come more frequently, and when she didn't know he was watching, she would sometimes be wearing a forlorn expression as she looked at the kids. As if to say, "Is this my life?" Whenever she looked that way, she was always playing with the pendant. Then in a flash, it would be gone, and she'd be back smiling again.

The pendant and her melancholy mood tied to it was what sparked his suspicion. Marisol only wore earrings, her engagement, and wedding rings. She claimed to have brought it while visiting her family in New York City, but it was completely out of character for her. What jewelry she did own, he bought her. He asked her if the design represented something. She said she didn't know.

One night while she was sleeping, he took a picture of it to research it at the library. Turned out it was the symbol of Oshun, the Yoruba goddess of love. They both were Catholics, but Marisol grew up with a mother who mixed Catholicism and Santeria, and she still burned candles and left offerings. Marisol sometimes did the same. He wasn't a staunch Catholic; he went to Catholic school growing up, so the religion was somewhat ruined for him. As a result,

Marisol's occasional Santeria practice wasn't an issue. Just the pendant. Because in his gut, he knew she wasn't wearing it because it was pretty.

But did that mean someone else bought it for her? Was he just reaching for a flimsy excuse to justify Celia? *Your honor, I cheated on my wife because she bought a piece of jewelry.* Joaquín shook his head at the absurd thought. Turning off the shower, he stepped out and grabbed a towel.

Marisol had been his rock for fifteen years. They met at Hampton University's Homecoming weekend in 1980. She felt so familiar to him, especially the way she moved as he watched her interact with her friends. They had a whirlwind romance. By the fifth date, he knew he wanted to marry her, much to his boys' dismay. So many young enlisted men and women were caught up in homesickness and married the first piece of ass they got in an attempt to cure it.

But not him; he loved Marisol. He loved her laugh and her witty comebacks—she always had an answer for everything. But not in a condescending way; she was just intelligent, way smarter than he was—and he didn't mind. She took his own occasional moodiness in stride because it matched her own by acknowledging they both needed space sometimes. She was proud he was a sailor and never made him feel guilty that he was gone out to sea six to eight months out of the year. She just held it down. She had also kept her last name when they married, despite the pressure from their families to take his, or at least hyphenate. She even went by her middle name in her professional life because she thought Marisol was too flowery. She kept her work and home life completely separate because she never wanted to bring any issues from the hospital home with her.

Beyond Marisol's strength and personality, their unique sex life added so much to their relationship. Or at least it was unusual to him back then. Now it was commonplace, though never dull. He still remembered his shock and confusion when she came home one night from nursing school and sat him down on the edge of the bed and handed him a paddle.

"Are we going to play ping-pong?" Joaquín asked, glancing around the room.

Marisol took a deep breath and then sighed. "I want you to use that on me."

Joaquín looked at the paddle in his hand then back at Marisol, and back at the paddle again. "You want me to—what? *Why*?"

"Never mind." Marisol went to grab the paddle, but Joaquín held it out of her reach.

"I asked you why."

Marisol closed her eyes, and when she opened them again, her gaze intensified. "Because I *need* it. Are you going to do it or not?"

Joaquín stared at his fiancée. Although her voice was very calm, he could feel the tension and the insecurity rolling off her. He knew this was a turning point in their relationship. What she wanted him to do went against everything he was taught. Men didn't abuse women. It was wrong. Then, he remembered a short piece of a porno they had watched about a month earlier. Most of it was regular sex, girl-on-girl, a gang bang, the usual shit. But there was one part where the man had the woman tied up and bent over a chair, and instead of a paddle, he used a belt. Marisol quickly turned it off and climbed on top of him, so he thought nothing of it. She had been extra aggressive that night. Now he knew why.

Joaquín stared at Marisol. She wanted him to spank her, to cause her physical pain because she needed it. He loved this woman more than he thought was humanly possible, and if she wanted this...

"Bend over the dresser."

That introduced him to a whole new world and a deeper level of intimacy between them. His wife was a masochist. Pain translated differently for her. It brought her relief. Sometimes he left such deep bruises that freaked him out. But Marisol soothed his nerves when she told him that she liked to feel the twinges of pain throughout the day, and the marks he left on her body made her feel claimed and loved.

The role of sadist was not something on his radar, but after a short period, he found himself enjoying it. If he knew she had a particularly rough day at work, he'd break out the rope and flogger for her later that night when the kids went to bed. Sometimes there wasn't even sex involved. She just needed the release. He made sure she got exactly as much as she needed. She was his wife, teacher, confidant, mother of the only children he'd ever have, and an insatiable and possessive lover. She was the sun to his moon and complimented him in every single way. She was, for all intents and purposes, perfect.

Until Joaquín saw Celia, he had never wanted another woman. Many had crossed his path, mistaking both his need for privacy and his marriage as a challenge. He shot them all down, but Celia was different. He wanted her with the same all-consuming intensity that he wanted Marisol. Maybe she was a witch, like Bentley hinted at because he shouldn't feel this way about her. But she was underneath his skin, quietly whispering in his ear, a phantom voice slowly rising until it became a shout. He was a hypocrite for still questioning Marisol's commitment after what happened with Celia. Yet the question remained: if she was having an affair, then what? He still loved her, and he damn sure wasn't any better. Despite Celia telling him to think about it, he knew he was going to have an affair with her. At this point, would it matter who cheated first? Suddenly weary with all these questions, he rubbed his forehead. Damn, he needed a cigarette, but he threw them all out. Even the emergency pack in the garage. He sighed. This was going to be a long night.

Chapter Thirty

PH Noelle Bentley

"**A**lrighty now, y'all listen up." Noelle clapped her hands to get her friends' attention. They were having their last monthly game night at the house before the cruise started. While a lot of people she knew played spades, Noelle stuck to UNO because she'd never learned how to play spades. It made her anxious. She'd seen people damn near get into fistfights over a card game in which zero money was involved. Where's the fun in that?

"Don't mention to Quentin that we're going on the cruise, please, and thank you," Noelle said once everyone quieted down.

"He doesn't know?" BM2 Raquel Monroe asked. The shock was evident in her voice and on her face. Besides Celia and Sidney, Noelle had exactly five other close friends on the ship that she trusted with her business: Monroe, who she went to boot camp with; SK1 Allison Williams; BM1 Gerald Montgomery, who was a former lover from her first command; SH2 Gary Brown, and PN1 Kimberly Brooks, both of whom she met on the Sound during Indoc.

"You haven't told him? Why not?" Williams asked.

"For reals?" Brooks asked. "You gon be in trouble."

"Girl, you trippin," Brown said.

"We have two weeks left. C'mon now, girl," Montgomery

"

chided with a shake of his head.

"I have already gone over this with Celia earlier—"

"And I can confirm that she ignored my advice," Celia interjected.

"—so y'all just don't say anything. I got this." Noelle held up a hand to stop further questions and then headed into the kitchen to get drinks.

No, she didn't have this. Not even fucking close. She had no idea when she was going to tell Quentin. They hadn't even had sex yet. It had been a month, and she was dying! Who voluntarily goes this long without sex? Not her! They had done some seriously heavy petting, and he ate her out at the most random-ass times. Sometimes he stopped right when she was about to come; other times, she was squirting all over the damn place. If Sidney knew all the places her ass has been, she'd probably move out. She was frustrated, intrigued, and confused. Mostly she was confused because she didn't know what to do with Quentin, much less what he was thinking.

"Babygirl, what are you doin'?"

Noelle visibly cringed when she heard 'babygirl'. Not because the endearment irritated her, but when Montgomery called her that, she knew a lecture was coming. She and Quentin had run into Montgomery while waiting to be seated at the same restaurant last week. When he saw her the next day on the ship, he bombarded her with questions for which she had no answers.

"You know that man is into you, right? I saw how he looked at you. He did the 'she's mine' arm around the shoulder, made sure I knew he was a part of the conversation, and I peeped him out playing with your hair, too, while we talked. I know you love that."

Noelle sure as hell did love that Quentin's hands stayed

up in her hair. If they were driving, watching a movie or television, or walking, it didn't matter—if she was in arm's reach of Quentin, his hands were in her hair.

"I got this under control, Monty, don't you worry. I'm good." Noelle poured the strawberry margarita Celia made into a glass pitcher.

"Really? You just told us not to not to tell the guy you're dating that we're leaving. So I don't think you do. Maybe I should've asked you when you're gonna stop running?"

"Never. Because then I'll get fat. I don't want to be in the Fat Boy program," Noelle quipped, while inwardly, she groaned.

Montgomery scoffed. "Or in a good relationship, apparently. Do you remember what you did when I told you I loved you?"

Of course, she did. It was not one of her finest moments. Montgomery was the first relationship she had after boot camp. She was a young hot-to-trot E-2 stationed here in Norfolk, and Montgomery took to her like a bee to honey. They were both just fucking like rabbits, enjoying life, and then everything came to an abrupt halt when he told Noelle he loved her. She immediately panicked and broke up with him. She transferred a week after his admission. She didn't see him for another five years, and by that time, he had forgiven her. But it didn't stop him from reminding her about her faux pas from time to time.

"No, Montgomery. It was a very long time ago. You know my memory is shitty."

"More like selective. Let me refresh it for you. You broke my little nineteen-year-old heart when you went into the bathroom, threw up, and then you broke up with me the next day."

Noelle started shaking her head. "I threw up because

I was drunk off the Bacardi and Kool-Aid, which was a disgusting concoction. I don't know why I drank it."

"No." Montgomery held up his hand. "You threw up because you were scared, and then you transferred to Jacksonville two weeks later. I didn't even know you were up for transfer. We were together for a year and you just bounced out on a nigga. You didn't even say goodbye. You just weren't at quarters one morning, and that was that. Does all this sound familiar?"

For fuckssake! The muscles in her back and neck started to stiffen up, and her shoulders began to creep up to her ears. Inhaling deeply, she drew them down. She didn't want to talk about her emotions or her fear of them. Or why she wouldn't stay in a relationship, have her mail delivered at her residence and not to a P.O. Box, own a pet, not even a plant, and why at the age of thirty-four she was roommating with her two best friends instead of living on her own. Nope, she just wanted to get her a drink, play UNO and whatever games people brought, avoid being called out for not telling Quentin she was leaving, and hopefully, finally have sex later. Was that too much to ask for?

"No, it doesn't. Not at all. I am not transferring; just going on a cruise. We'll be back. Apples and oranges." Noelle picked up the pitcher, intending to head back into the living room, but Montgomery blocked her path.

"How many relationships have you been in since us?"

"You want me to go back almost twenty years?"

"Yes."

"Can we do this later?"

Montgomery crossed his arms over his chest. "Can I blurt out we're leaving June 7th and tonight is May 26th?"

With a heavy sigh, Noelle set the pitcher down. "Fine. I have been in—excluding Harrison because that shit was a nightmare—fifteen mini relationships and two extended ones. I took a year off after you and then after number four and number eight. Now can we go play UNO and get drunk?"

"Fifteen mini relationships! What the hell is a 'mini relationship'?"

"A mini relationship lasts for about one to three months."

Montgomery shook his head. "That's not normal, baby girl. You know that right?"

"And just because I don't want to be in a relationship, or married with kids, or just have kids, in general, does not make me abnormal. I am quite fine being single and independent."

"If you're so fine with being single and independent, why are you always dating men who want to settle down and marry you? I know that we should have been celebrating our eighteenth anniversary and about to be sending a kid off to college or some shit like that. And I know for a fact that Charles, Perkins, and Matthews were also marrying men, and by the way Quentin acts around you, I can guarantee he is too. So you are choosing men who are stable, reliable, and ready to commit, then you dump them when they actually make commitment moves. Does that sound normal to you?"

Noelle put her hands on her hips. "Oh hell, the fuck naw. First of all, I didn't choose you. You came for me. And I didn't choose any of those other men either. They all came for me. I will not be responsible for other people's actions. So let's quit making it sound like I need to have an FBI profile and be on the watch list. Y'all need to take some responsibility. Did I ever talk about marriage and kids when I was with you? Because I know for a fact, I did not with those other men. And what is so wrong with letting someone go when you're not compatible with them? Was I supposed to marry them because they loved me and they wanted to marry me? No, I broke up with them because I didn't want that. So now you want to throw that in my face? Get the fuck outta here with that bullshit, Montgomery. Seriously."

"No one is saying that you should marry someone if you don't want to. What I am saying is don't tell me that you don't know who these men are and what they want by week three. You are too smart to lie about that. See, I've been watching how you move all these years—"

"That doesn't sound creepy at all."

Montgomery ignored Noelle and kept on speaking. "And I have come to the conclusion that you love that they love you and want to be with you. Because deep, deep, deep down inside you really want it. So you take it all in, and you learn how to cook their favorite foods, take care of their needs, have them around your friends, and maybe take them home to meet your family. Noelle, you make them a part of your life, and then for whatever reason you break up with them. And when you end up with niggas like Harrison, who ain't about shit, then you mad. That's what's not normal. That's what ain't right. And don't you dare try to tell me it is."

Noelle stared at Montgomery. The shame of her relationship pattern caused by her fear of commitment and anger at being called out each fought inside her to be the dominant emotion. She wanted to apologize to him again and mean it this time, find a counselor, fling the pitcher of daiquiri in his face, and kick him out all at the same time. Because how dare he? In the end, her pride trumped them all.

"Well, Montgomery, aren't you glad you dodged a bullet?"

Montgomery sighed and shook his head. "No, I am not,

babygirl. I wish you had taken me out, but I had no choice but to let you go. It took me a while, but I did. Or else I wouldn't be able to tell you this without shaking the shit out of you. But I'm worried about you. I want you to let someone love you, even if it isn't me."

Noelle sighed. This was too much to think about right now. Quentin was due any minute; she'd think about what Montgomery said later. Or never. She was leaning towards never because she'd rather not ever think about this conversation again.

Nonetheless, she gave him a small but appreciative smile. "I really don't know what to say to all this. But thank you for still being my friend."

Montgomery pulled her into a tight hug. "Always."

Noelle rested her head on his chest and relaxed into the hug. Montgomery did give the best hugs; they used to turn into really good sex. She wrapped her arm around his waist and returned the hug. Now, he just made her feel so safe and cared for.

Montgomery gave her one more squeeze before he let her go. "Yup, I wanna be there when you figure your shit out."

Yeah, she wanted to be there too. Wherever "there" was. Noelle laughed and picked up the pitcher. "Hopefully, I'll be there before we get dementia."

"My granny has dementia, but she still remembers that I stole five dollars from her purse when I was seven. I'll remember this," Montgomery promised.

"Well, that's great." Noelle's tone implied it was not.

"Babe, where do you want me to put this?"

Noelle looked over to the doorway, and Quentin was standing there holding two paper bags filled with blue crabs. As happy as she was to see the bags of blue crabs, she was absolutely delighted at the way he looked at her. His eyes were all soft and brown and focused completely on her. Yup, she loved it. Fuck!

"Oh, just put them on the counter behind Mont. You remember Montgomery, right?" Noelle said, hoping Quentin didn't hear Montgomery's soft humph. He must've caught the look too. Man, she just wanted to play UNO.

"I do." Quentin held his hand out. "How you doin'?"

Montgomery shook his hand. "I'm good. Ready to kill Noelle at this UNO game. I'd kill her at spades, but she don't wanna learn. I keep on telling her to be open to new things. She'd enjoy it."

Noelle narrowed her eyes at Montgomery's double entendre. He smiled at her innocently.

"Spades is a good game." Quentin laughed, rubbing the small of Noelle's back and she had to stop herself from purring.

Even when it wasn't playing with her hair, he was always touching her. It surprised Noelle that it didn't annoy her. She usually didn't like people touching her too much, but she couldn't get enough of his hands on her body. They held hands everywhere they went. He rubbed her feet, shoulders, back, even her damn scalp. He seemed to enjoy giving as much as she enjoyed receiving. She found herself constantly touching him, too, and smelling him. She had to stop herself many a day from burying her face in his armpits. She usually settled for the crook of his neck. He smelled like life. She would have buried her face in his neck, her usual way of greeting him, but Monty was standing there watching her. Judging her. The bastard.

"Okay fellas, we didn't gather here to talk in the kitchen. Y'all came to get ya asses handed to you in UNO. So let's go!" Noelle challenged. Taking Quentin's hand she led him and Montgomery into the living room.

Chapter Thirty-One

LT Quentin Jacobs

"**U**NO, bitches!" Noelle yelled and slammed her last card. "Now y'all get the hell outta Celia's house!" She pointed to the front of the house.

Quentin laughed at Noelle's antics while her friends groaned. He spent the last hour and a half drinking, watching Noelle eat crabs because he didn't like them—much to her horror—and cracking up at her and her friends playing UNO. Then they switched it up to Sorry!, Win, Lose or Draw, Old Maid, and even Memory. He remembered playing these games with his son years ago and never thought he'd be willingly playing them as an adult, much less with a bunch of drunk adults. But here he was and enjoying the hell out of himself. He thought Old Maid was never going to end because hardly anyone could remember who had what cards. Celia might've traded the alcohol for water a little too late.

"I think you cheated!" Raquel accused, throwing her cards at Noelle.

"Nooooo ma'am. You just suck. What the hell did you do when you were a kid? I know you're white, and you probably didn't play UNO the right way, but you suck at Old Maid too, and that's the whitest game evaaaaa!" Noelle sang out that last word as she picked up the cards that Williams threw at her and the rest of the deck off the coffee table.

Raquel rolled her eyes as if she'd heard all this before. She was the only white person in the small group—all the rest were Black, except Celia. "We played UNO, but y'all got all those damn house rules, so don't blame my whiteness because we read the rule book."

"There's a rulebook? To UNO? And you read it? That's the problem right there," Gary said.

"Shut up, man. I'm gonna stop playing with y'all 'cause y'all always are picking on me," Raquel grumbled. Then she yawned, stretched, and flopped back on the couch.

"C'mon drunken sailor, it's time to go home," Gary said, pulling on Raquel's arm to give her a little tug. He was the designated driver for the night.

Monroe allowed Brown to help her to her feet. "No, we gotta help clean up, and then we can go."

"Psssh, me and Quentin will clean it up. Y'all go home." Noelle waved her off and stood up. She took a moment to gather her bearings before looping her arm through Monroe's and leading her to the front door. They were whispering and laughing as they walked.

"You've been volunteered for clean-up duty," Gerald told Quentin.

"Apparently so." Quentin expected it. Noelle had been running him back and forth to the kitchen to fetch things for people all night, so clean-up duty was the natural course of things. He started going around gathering up glasses and small plates, saying bye to people as they began to trickle out.

Gerald was an interesting character. Quentin could tell that he and Noelle had a history together. Their conversation was too smooth, too nuanced. He wondered if Gerald still had feelings for her. Quentin caught him observing him a few times but didn't let on that he noticed. Noelle, for her part, made sure he was included in all of the conversations, so he never felt uncomfortable or out of place. She spent most of the night sitting beside him on the couch, rubbing his thigh or his back in an almost absent-minded way, or she sat on the floor between his legs while he played in her hair. When she did leave, she was never gone for long, boomeranging right back to his side before he had a chance to miss her.

After all the daps were given amongst the men and hugs exchanged between the women, Celia bid them goodnight and disappeared down the hall. He and Noelle were left alone in the quiet, and now tidy, living room.

"I like your friends," Quentin said as Noelle snuggled up against him on the couch.

"Me too," she replied, then suddenly jumped up and told him she needed to use the bathroom. Instead of leaving him on the couch, she took his hand and led him down the same hall to her bedroom. A room he'd been trying to avoid for weeks. He'd only been in there for a few moments at a time before he escaped from the temptation that was Noelle's round bed.

Before going to her private bathroom, Noelle turned on the hanging lights over her nightstands. Geometric patterns painted the ceilings and the walls. She then lit a stick of incense, and a light flowery fragrance floated in the air.

"Be right back," Noelle said before going into the bathroom.

Quentin nodded and sat on the edge of the overstuffed armchair while he waited for her to come out. Her bedroom was just as vibrant and colorful as her personality. If he suddenly woke up in her room, he might panic for a moment, thinking he'd been kidnapped and taken to Marrakech. Or more precisely, a harem—well, that part might not be so bad. Her custom-made round bed had about a thousand pillows on it, and it was pushed against an intricately carved five-foot headboard.

"I love the look on people's faces when they first see my room," she told him when he initially saw it. "Welcome to my sultana's chambers. When we went to Spain last year, I hopped on a ferry to Morocco, and I fell in love with everything I saw. I shipped the headboard, textiles, lamps, and pillows. Hell, I almost bought the man who was selling them—oh, he was beautiful. It cost an arm and both my legs, but it was worth it. The shit you can spend your money on when you don't have to put it into a college fund."

Quentin half-listened to her after he heard the "look on people's faces" part. Whose faces and when? He was not a jealous man, and *of course*, she'd had other men in her life before him, but the flare of jealousy that sparked at the thought of someone else sharing her bed took him by surprise. He had to stop himself from asking exactly just how many others had *seen* her room, however, she answered his unspoken question for him.

"And by people, I mean my momma and them. I don't have people over. This is my space." She said that last part very nonchalantly, though Quentin knew her statement was anything but. It was a big fucking thing that she was letting him into her space. Noelle was like a book on display for everyone to look at, but when you picked it up to glance through it, you'd find it to be vacuum sealed.

Noelle's return to the bedroom interrupted Quentin's musing. She'd taken out her large hoops and exchanged her jean shorts and tank top for a long, white silk robe loosely tied at her waist. Bathed in the light, she looked soft, ethereal, and sexy. He held out his hand, and she came over to him. Wrapping his arms around her waist, he pulled her closer, nuzzling the bare skin on her chest that peeked through the robe.

"I don't think I put deodorant on today after I showered, but I don't think I smell. And I used my bidet to wash my butt just now cause I'm too lazy to take a shower. Shout out to visiting Egypt. Bidets are amazing!" Noelle said as she rubbed his head.

"You're so romantic." Quentin leaned back and looked up at her. He smelled one of her armpits. She smelled earthy. "You don't stink, but you're right; you didn't use deodorant today." He sniffed her other armpit. He detected another scent underneath the earthiness. It was sweet and musky and so enticing. "Are you ovulating?"

"Ummmm." Noelle rubbed his head as she thought. "Yes, I think so. You wanna make a baby?"

Quentin inhaled again. His hands moved down over her bottom, and he rubbed her cheeks in time with her hands on his head. A baby? With Noelle? An image of her belly swollen with his baby flashed in his mind. She was beautiful, and she was his.

"Yes." Quentin untied her robe, and spread it apart, baring her breasts.

Noelle took Quentin's head in her hands and guided his mouth to her nipple. "Then let's get to it. These eggs won't hang around forever."

Quentin chuckled against her nipple before sucking it into his mouth. He rolled her nipple around his tongue then blew on it, turning it into a stiff peak before sucking on it again. From earlier make-out sessions, he learned that Noelle loved prolonged nipple play. He had almost made her come by playing with her nipples while they watched a movie. Replacing his mouth with his hand he kissed a trail to her other breast and gave it the same attention as its twin.

He only stopped when Noelle began reaching down to pull up his T-shirt. He finished pulling it over his head and threw it on the floor. He slipped her robe off her shoulders and admired her stiff nipples, the slope of her breast, the soft mound of her belly, and the flare of her hips. Her hair was just as curly between her legs as it was on her head, and it was just the way he liked it—long enough that he could comb his fingers through it but not long enough to interfere with his breathing.

"I love your body."

Noelle scrunched up her face. "I think I need to lose about ten pounds. I'm getting cellulite on the backs of my thighs."

Quentin ran his hands down the backs of her thighs. "I don't feel anything. You just feel soft and nice—womanly." He kissed her belly.

Noelle made a noncommittal sound. "That's the cellulite. Just look at me with the lights on. Texture for days."

"I'm not worried about that. I'm focused on this." Quentin cupped one breast, recaptured her nipple, and Noelle's response turned into a hitched breath. As he sucked on her nipple, he trailed his fingers down her belly and twirled them in her damp hair, ignoring the fact that she spread her legs for him to get further access. The scent of her arousal mixing with the fragrance of the incense almost made him lightheaded. She was definitely fertile. She nudged against his hand and spread her legs a little bit wider.

"Go sit on the bed," he ordered softly. He fully expected Noelle to protest, but she went over to the bed, flipped the comforter aside, and sat down patiently. This was the most submissive he'd seen her in the seven weeks they'd known each other. He liked it. He rose and went to stand in front of her. Noelle looked at him and smiled. He brushed his knuckles down the side of her face. This woman did something to him; there was no doubt about that.

It was Noelle's turn to run her hand down the back of his thighs, and then she came around and traced his hard-on through his jeans while she held eye contact with him, smiling lazily. "You sure you wanna be makin' a baby with me?"

"Absolutely." Quentin leaned down and kissed her. Noelle reached for his belt buckle, but he stopped her.

"Quentin..." Noelle said with a groan.

"Wait. Let me do this first."

"Do what?"

"Do this." Quentin gently pushed Noelle so she could lay back on the bed. He knelt between her knees, and his lips brushed the stickiness on the inside of her thighs as he slowly worked his way up to her lips. He was already acquainted with them, by touch if not by sight. Many nights he went home with the smell of her on his fingers. She complained about being too lippy, but he loved them. It gave him more to play with. He sucked and nibbled on them, also using his tongue to find the right wishbone of her clit while using his fingers to massage the left one. He rubbed and licked until she arched her back and came, with a long gasp followed by a heavy sigh. Giving her a moment to catch her breath, he threw her legs over his shoulders, then palmed her cheeks and sat back on his heels, dragging her up with him.

Using the tip of his nose, he parted her lips to fully unveil her clit. The other thing he learned by touch was how big her clit was. He never had to search for it because it was impossible to miss. He gave it one long swirling lick, and her body jumped. He teased her like that until she swatted the top of his head. Chuckling, he sucked on it and reached up to tug and pinch at her nipples. It didn't take her long to come again. He knew she was at her peak by her moans and the way she grabbed his head. When she came the second time, it was with a low wail that was music to his ears. He stopped playing with her nipples, grabbed her ass, and kept on sucking, alternating between her clit and her wishbones. She tried to get away, but he held her there tightly.

When she came the third time, her hips bucked wildly in his hands. He felt the soft spray hit his chin before she squealed, "Oh my God" before grabbing a pillow to bury her face in to stifle her shrieks. He stopped sucking her clit and stuck his tongue inside as far as it would go, drinking her in. Her body was still trembling when he gave her clit one last lick before sliding her legs off his shoulders. Mewling, she scooted back on the bed and then curled into herself.

"We're not done," Quentin said and laughed when Noelle weakly waved him away. He stood up and grabbed his T-shirt, using it as a towel for his face. Damn, he couldn't wait to get inside her. He was so worked up that he thought he would come right along with her that last time. He threw his shirt back on the floor and unbuckled his belt. He unsnapped his jeans, kicking out of them when they hit the floor. His hands were on the waistband of his boxers when he heard Noelle exhale. It was a long, slow, steady exhale. One that usually indicated only one thing.

Awww, nah man, this woman did not fall asleep! Quentin threw his hands up in the air. He walked over to the side of the bed that Noelle was turned to and looked down at her. Her lips were slightly parted as she breathed steadily. She was knocked the hell out.

Unfuckingbelievable. Quentin put his hands on his hips

and stared down at the sleeping Noelle. She still managed to control the situation even without knowing it. He shook his head and threw his hands up in the air again. He wasn't sure what to think or feel. He was proud that he put that ass to bed with just his mouth. As if in agreement, Noelle stirred and reached for the covers that were out of reach. Sighing, he pulled the comforter over her. Yeah, he was definitely proud of that, although his dick was still making a big top tent in his boxers and feeling left out of all the excitement. He could almost hear the sad closing song of *The Incredible Hulk* playing in the background as his erection began to shrink.

Sorry bruh. This was not how he planned to end the night either. He was damn ready to make a baby with this crazy woman, even though she zealously followed astrology, had too many thoughts in her head, maybe drank a little bit too much, and was a 97.9% flight risk. He was reasonably certain their relationship was going to be the emotional equivalent of off-road racing. He was probably going to blow out some tires, tumble the truck down a hill, and hit a damn boulder head-on, but it would no doubt be exhilarating.

Quentin yawned. The abrupt letdown caused an adrenal crash, and he was suddenly ready to crawl into bed with Noelle. After snuffing out the incense and opening up a window so he didn't wake up with swollen eyes and a sinus infection, he turned the lights off and slid into bed beside her. Kissing her shoulder, he inhaled the spicy earthiness of her skin and the lingering scent of her arousal before shutting his eyes.

Chapter Thirty-Two

YNI Celia Navarro

The moment Celia shut her bedroom door; she dropped her happy façade. Sitting in her small slipper chair, she sighed so deeply it was almost an anguished moan. The funk she'd been hiding was finally allowed to take over. She would have rather hidden out in her room all day. But had she done that, Noelle would have been knocking at her door asking what was wrong. There was no way in hell she was telling Noelle that she had been dreaming about Julia again for five nights straight. She dreamt of Julia often, but it was always worse when the anniversary of their breakup was near. It didn't matter that she spent a decent amount of her waking time continuing to struggle over what to do about the Pandora's box she opened with Joaquín. Her nights were filled with Julia.

She'd made the mistake of mentioning it last year, and Noelle gave her the sad panda face, sat her on her bed, and got ready for Celia to emotionally vomit all her feelings out while Noelle held the bucket. That best friend of hers was always willing to be the bucket-holder and keep your hair out of your face while you did the deed, whether it was literal or emotional. But Noelle never was the regurgitator. She swallowed her emotions more impressively than an anaconda swallowed a wild pig. Not Celia was the poster child for emoting, but she did process and deal with her feelings accordingly, to avoid all the emotional backwash that Noelle found herself swimming through on the regular.

Celia always did an exceptional job of gathering herself back together after a breakup. Until Julia. She was still as in love with her tonight as she was when Julia had ended them. The wound was still just as fresh. She wanted to march up to Julia's front door every other day and interrupt her dinnertime, demanding that Julia take her back—her husband and family be damned.

Sighing again, Celia stared at her bed, but instead of seeing her empty bed with its rumpled sheets, her dreams replayed before her eyes. Julia's naked curves were covered in the moonlight as she lay on the bed, her fingers lazily trailing across her chest. Nothing about Julia was small. Her personality matched the fullness of her body. Her full lips were the kind models paid for. Her upper lip was darker than her bottom lip, and it was Celia's favorite nibbling spot. Her heavy breasts, with their huge, dark areolas and nipples, gently sloped as she rolled onto her side and rested her head on her arm. Her tummy didn't sink or dip; it stayed nice and round. Her hips were wide, her thighs soft and malleable, and her ass jiggled solidly every time she moved. Even her calves and her short, square toes were cute.

"What are you staring at, *amante*?" Julia asked.

"You. I'm always staring at you," Celia said, leaning back in her seat. She twirled a piece of hair around her finger. They'd just finished making love. Julia's dildo and harness were buried somewhere in the sheets. The vibrator she held on Celia's clit as she fucked her had gotten kicked to the floor.

Before Julia, Celia wasn't a fan of strap-ons. Vibrators and dildos? Yes. She had a collection of those, but when it came to putting on a harness, everything went awry for Celia. It cut into places that it shouldn't. The dildo just seemed to bob around, her strokes were clumsy and awkward, and it made her lower back hurt. She felt like she needed an Epsom salt soak after she was done.

So when Julia whipped one out, she was not very receptive. Julia had to do some serious persuading and generous pourings of Patron before Celia allowed her to use it while they having sex. Even as tipsy and horny as she was, Celia's expectations were low. She was simply entertaining Julia. The first few moments were exactly like intercourse with a man. She lay on her back, and Julia climbed on top of her and felt how wet she was before slowly sliding her dick in.

Then, everything was different. Perhaps it was because Julia was a woman, she took her time to find the right spots, and she found Celia's g-spot almost immediately. She was shrieking and babbling and wetting the bed in five minutes. Her ass was a fan after that. Bonus points for Julia not wanting it used on her. Celia laughed softly.

"Now you're laughing..." Julia said.

Celia laughed again. "I was thinking about when you first pulled out the strap-on."

Julia made a noncommittal sound. "You didn't like poor Julio at first. But you get on your knees, ass up in the air now for him, don't you?"

"*Absolutamente*," Celia said with a nod. "You're the only one who's got me to like it."

Julia only smiled. Celia saw that smile every time she had an orgasm. It was full of pure satisfaction and ownership, and she loved it. She just loved everything about this woman, period.

"You look like a goddess. Like Oshun. All lush and fertile.

Just gorgeous," Celia said.

When she was a child, her mother—though a practicing Jehovah's Witness—would sometimes go to the local Santeria shop for stuff she would have to hide from her husband. Secrets and all the things people did in the dark had always intrigued Celia. Santeria became one of those secrets she shared with her mother. When she died, Celia buried her with a lightning pendant for Oya, the goddess of death, hoping it would light her way on her next journey.

"Yes! You gas my head up every time you see me. But you've never called me goddess before." Julia stretched her arm up with a flourish. "I think I like it."

"As you should."

"So, what do you offer Oshun?"

Celia leaned back in the chair, tapping her forehead. "Oranges, cinnamon, pumpkin, sunflowers...and honey." The last word came with a smile.

"Mmmm, come bring me some of your honey." Julia dropped her arm back down to the bed and beckoned her lover.

Celia stood up and untied the belt of the silk robe she was wearing. With a shrug of her shoulders, it fell to the floor. As she walked to the bed, Julia rolled onto her back, and Celia climbed on the bed and straddled Julia's face. "Take all that you want..."

"Don't I always?" Julia kissed the soft skin on the inside of Celia's thighs before cupping her cheeks and bringing her pussy down to her mouth. As in all good sex dreams, though, the scene changed right before the climax, and she and Julia were sitting in Celia's living room; an air of resignation filled the space between them.

"Celia..." Julia began.

Celia held her breath for a second. There was so much

apology in the way Julia said her name. She wanted to finish her sentence but forced herself not to.

"I can't see you anymore," Julia finished.

Celia nodded. She tightly pressed her lips together and remained silent. She had known for a couple of weeks that this conversation was coming. Something had shifted in Julia; it was subtle, but she knew it would damage their relationship.

"I do love you. So much. *Too much.*" Julia's breath hitched. "I knew I would love you, but I didn't think I would love you this much. I...I'm starting to not want to go home. When I leave you, it's like someone, *them*—my husband and my kids—they are ripping me away from my real home. I have to sit in the garage for a couple of minutes to pull myself together before I walk into my house because I don't want them to see how much I am starting to resent them all. Every 'mommy, can you' or 'baby have you' is grating on my fucking nerves."

Julia's fingers flew up to her temples and rubbed them. "I thought I would be able to be with you and keep it separate and contained, but it's slipping out into my other life. And this is killing me. I can't break up my family. I can't do that to my kids. Maybe if they were older, but I still love my husband...I don't know...but I just can't do this anymore. I am so sorry. I'm so sorry." Tears were running down Julia's face as she stared at Celia. "Please say something."

"*Un momento, por favor.*" Feeling her own tears well up, Celia blinked them away. She'd make it through this without crying and stay strong for both of them. Julia was right. Their relationship was all-consuming. She didn't know how they managed not to burn each other up in the two years they'd been together. She'd also begun to feel resentment that Julia had a family to go home to, and a husband that she slept next to every night while Celia slept alone. It was slowly eating away at her, too, but she loved Julia too much, and she was too weak to initiate the breakup. Now that Julia had done it, she needed to support her decision because it was the right thing to do even if it felt like it was going to end her.

Cupping Julia's face, Celia tried wiping the tears away with her thumbs, but they kept on coming. "Mi *amor*, you don't have to apologize. I knew I couldn't keep you. But I am so grateful and will forever be grateful that you were here for me after Mother's death. I would have completely fallen apart without you. You held me down and kept me going. And you loved me. I don't think I have been loved so completely before you. I needed that. I know you wanted to give me everything, but you can't give 100% and still have something left over for your family. I understand. I always knew we were on borrowed time from day one."

"I love you so much." Julia's hands covered Celia's and gripped them tightly. "I don't know how I am going to handle not being able to see you or talk to you. You're my first thought in the morning and my last one at night."

"Honestly, I don't know how I'm going to do it either, because right now, my heart is fucking breaking—but this is the right thing to do, and we will get through this. Your family needs you."

"I need *you*, Celia. What about what *I* need?" Julia asked with a sob.

Celia didn't answer her because Julia already knew the answer to her own question. Sighing, she pulled Julia's head down and kissed her forehead. Julia wrapped her arms around Celia's waist and rested her cheek on top on top of Julia's head. Celia rubbed her back and rocked side to side.

"We'll be okay. Just give it some time. We'll be okay," Celia promised.

"I hope you're right," Julia said. Celia hoped she was, too. She told Julia what she needed to hear, but it was a goddamned, bald-faced lie. They were both fucked. She couldn't imagine that she could love anyone else the way she loved Julia. This was some once-in-a-lifetime kind of love. But she kept that to herself. Julia was having a hard enough time as it was. She tenuously held it together as she watched Julia walk to her car, then Celia proceeded to fall apart when she shut the door.

Exhausted and numb from crying, she was still lying on the floor of the foyer when Noelle came home from duty the next morning. Noelle almost had a heart attack because she thought Celia was dead. Her worried admonishment was the only thing that got Celia off the floor and to the kitchen table where Noelle made her a hot toddy.

"Now don't be turnin' into a sloppy drunk because of this." Noelle's words were sharp, but her face was full of concern. "We're leaving soon, so that should help."

I doubt it. Celia sipped her drink. The warm brandy felt good, sliding down her raw throat. Two years later, she was still quietly fucked up, but functioning. She never spoke to Julia again. They both stuck to their promise of no contact.

When the ache of missing Julia became umbearable, Celia would lurk in the parking lot of the hospital where Julia worked, just to catch a glimpse of her at the end of her shift. She stopped going when she once saw Julia crying alone in her car.

Okay, enough of this. Celia shook herself and drummed her feet on the carpet, shaking off the memories that had ensnared her. Rising from the chair, she placed her hands over her heart, closed her eyes, and sent Julia some love as she always did when she thought about her. Tucking her love back away into her heart, she undressed and headed to the shower.

Chapter Thirty-Three

PH1 Noelle Bentley

U*gh, I need some water.* Noelle smacked her lips, grimacing at the sour and dry taste that filled her mouth. The slight throbbing in her head was, no doubt, due to dehydration. She opened her eyes, and a naked, muscular back greeted her. She stared at it for a moment, then as though someone hit the rewind button on the VCR, then play, the events from last night rolled.

Fuuuuuck! She had fallen asleep on Quentin. She didn't think she'd been that drunk. Underneath her liquor courage, she was beside herself, nervous about finally having sex with him. So she kept on drinking in an attempt to calm her nerves. Then add the weight of the conversation with Montgomery; she was pretty sure she drank a whole pitcher by herself. Tequila and orgasms were more effective than a heavy workout *and* a Tylenol PM. Gingerly, she lifted the comforter and peaked at his ass, disappointed that he was wearing his boxers.

God, please don't let this man wake up till I wash my ass, Noelle thought as she carefully slid out of bed. She froze when her right knee cracked as she stood up. Damnit, that was loud. She loved her low bed except for moments like these. Had her out here just announcing her age louder than the ship's [1]1MC. She stared at Quentin's back, checking for movement. Satisfied he was still sound asleep, she tiptoed into the bathroom.

Before hopping in the shower, she grabbed the Navy cure-all: an 800 mg dose of ibuprofen, downed it with a large glass of water, and set a new toothbrush out for Quentin. She wasn't one of those women who overlooked hot, dragon morning breath just because a man was fine. Then, she brushed her teeth and got into the steaming shower. She quickly washed her body and was just about to lather her hair when she heard Quentin using the toilet. He just straight-up peed like she wasn't in the shower. It felt so...normal. She frowned, unsure how she felt about that. Resisting the urge to peek out at him, she listened to him pick up the toothbrush and turn the faucet on. She knew he was going to get up. He was probably up when she snuck out of bed. Staying silent, she let the water run over her until there was a knock on the glass stall door.

"Who is it?"

"The man you fell asleep on last night."

Noelle slid the stall door open and peeked out. "I truly apologize. That was bad form. I will make it my morning's mission to make it up to you." She slid the door wider. "Do come in."

"I'm gonna hold you to that," Quentin said and dropped his boxers.

Noelle did a slow appraisal of his body. Quentin was not overly cut. He had broad shoulders, and thick arms and thighs, with a belly that was firm, but had just enough give to be comfortable. She never liked a rock-solid man

---

1. 1MC (Main circuit): Loudspeakers.

because it was like trying to cuddle a boulder. His body reminded her of yard work, car washing, power tools, solid three-square meals plus desserts, and a snack along with warmth in the wintertime. At rest, his dick appeared to be *maybe* average length but definitely not average width, but that image was a lie. She knew that he was a grower, not a shower, from trying to get it out of his pants for the past month. She personally preferred width to length, and even though she ain't planning on having no babies, she didn't want her cervix destroyed. And he was going to wreck her shit. She thought she had mentally prepared herself for his size from the first time she felt his erection. But watching him grow right before her eyes, now she wasn't so sure. She thought she had mentally prepared herself for his size from the first time she felt his erection. But watching him grow right before her eyes, she wasn't so sure. His dick was beautiful and terrifying.

"You done?" Quentin held his hands up as he spoke.

Noelle chuckled. "Yes, thank you. I missed this last night. But I didn't miss those orgasms. They were spot on, Lieutenant. You've made your country proud. Just don't tell them, or else you'll be in trouble. But between you and me...can you do it again? And this time, I won't fall asleep after because I've had a good, nay, a *great* night's sleep."

"If you fall asleep again, I'm waking you up." Quentin stepped into the shower and took the shampoo from Noelle. "Turn around." He squirted some on the top of her head.

Noelle closed her eyes and sighed blissfully. She shuddered when he used his nails to scratch her scalp. "After you retire, I think you might have a second career as a shampoo boy. Or this could be your side hustle right now. Fine as you are, I think women wouldn't even want to have sex with you, this is plenty. For them—not for me. You goan give that up today." She faced him and tipped her head back underneath the spray to rinse it. "Did you at least have a good night's sleep?"

"After my hard-on went down, yeah. Your bed is very comfortable. Thanks for asking," Quentin said dryly.

"I detect a little bit of sarcasm in that statement." Noelle maneuvered Quentin around, so he stood under the water spray. She picked up the Palmolive liquid body wash her grandmother sent her from England and squirted some in her hand. She didn't use the loofah because she wanted to feel his skin. She made soapy swirls on his smooth chest, pausing to focus on his nipples, enjoying the feel of his breath deepening with every squeeze and pluck. She learned early that women didn't pay enough attention to men's nipples and all the other sensitive spots on their bodies. Most women just went straight for the dick, and three-quarters of them didn't even do that right. She liked to take her time and explore a man's body, paying attention to all the hidden areas, from the soft skin behind his ear to the sliver of skin between his fingers to the overlooked skin underneath his balls.

"Just a little." Quentin's voice dropped, and his eyelids lowered as Noelle's hands made a slow, soapy path to his groin.

"I'll let that slid because I deserve it." Noelle stroked his growing erection from base to tip and back again while gently rolling his balls with the other hand. Not caring if she got a little soap in her mouth, she leaned forward and flicked her tongue on his nipple, timing it with her hand strokes. When he was at his full length, she stopped and looked down, and took a deep breath. His dick was like a thunderstorm—beautiful and terrifying all at once. She reached up behind him and took the shower head down and sprayed the soap off his body.

"You are really big. Did you know that? I mean, I felt it, but that didn't prepare me for the visual. I hate to break it to you, but I'm not sure it's gonna fit." Noelle hung the showerhead back up.

Quentin chuckled. "Don't worry, it'll fit. I promise."

Noelle's brow furrowed. "Ummm, I don't kn—" Her protest was cut short by Quentin's lips. She sighed when he grabbed a handful of wet hair and tugged her head back to deepen the kiss. His lips though...she could literally kiss him until the water ran cold, provided he shielded her away from it. He backed her up to the wall without breaking the kiss and picked her up, and her legs automatically went around his waist.

Noelle wrapped her arms around his neck and reluctantly pulled her lips away. "You know I have always thought that sex in the shower was a dangerous and reckless thing to do. Did we rinse all the soap out of the tub? What if you lose your footing and drop me? I could break a hip or die or something. I don't want to have to explain to the doctor how I broke my hip. Or to the angels how I died. It would be a funny story, but I really don't want to have to tell it."

Quentin sighed and rested his forehead against hers. "Would you like to get out of the shower?"

Noelle rubbed her nose against his. "Yes, I think that would be for the best. The bed is much more comfortable anyway."

"Okay." Quentin lowered her down and stepped out of the shower. Noelle turned off the water and followed him out, trying not to laugh at his obvious irritation. He stood there, dripping on her bathmat with his hands on his hips. He looked like a beautiful, angry, naked warrior who was stopped from slaughtering her cervix. Her eyes dropped down to his dick. It was even bigger outside the shower. *Oh lord!* It seemed like it was growing even more right in front of her eyes. How was that possible?

"Would you like a towel?" Noelle asked with a sweet smile.

Quentin cocked his head to the side and looked at her. "No, I thought I'd just air dry."

Laughing, Noelle pulled her towel from the rack next to the shower and wrapped it around her. Tucking it underneath her arm, she scooted around him to get a towel from the linen closet. Instead of handing it to him, she started drying his back, his bottom and worked her way down his legs. "Turn around, please." He obliged, and she playfully dried his face, making cooing noises before drying the front of his body. When she was done, she grabbed the jar of coconut oil from the shelf. Before this man impaled her, she was going to have her *Shaka Zulu* moment. She scooped out some coconut oil and rubbed it between her palms. Starting with the top of his head, she slowly applied the oil all over his body. She even had him spread his arms out so she could reach underneath there too.

"I have been wanting to do this since I watched *Shaka Zulu*. But I don't think this part was on Fox 5," Noelle said as she oiled his dick.

Quentin cleared his throat before speaking in a low voice. "No, I don't recall seeing this part either."

"Oh wow, you watched the series too. Wasn't it good? I thought the woman who played his mother was so pretty. And I'm still like those damn British people. I wish—ahhh!" Noelle's sentence ended when Quentin suddenly picked her up and threw her over his shoulder. He headed into her bedroom and unceremoniously plopped her on the bed.

"For a moment, I was gonna say that was some sexy shit

until you dropped me on the bed like a sack of potatoes." Noelle scooted further up on the bed and propped herself up on her elbows.

"Don't worry, you're the good Yukon gold ones."

"Mmmmm, they do make the best mashed potatoes, don't they? Remind me to make you some after this." Noelle bit her bottom lip as she stared up at Quentin. This man...*this man.*

"Is that my apology gift: mashed potatoes?" Shaking his head, Quentin glanced up at the ceiling.

Noelle nodded. "Yes. Because my mashed potatoes are delicious. I make them with real butter. Not margarine. You deserve butter from grass fed cows."

"You don't need to make me mashed potatoes, Noelle."

Noelle's brow furrowed in mock confusion. "Oh, but they are really delicious, though."

"I believe you. But I just want this." Quentin reached down and spread her knees wide and climbed between them. "I see all this talking of food has you wet."

"You know food turns me on," Noelle said breathlessly, lying back on the bed. Her eyes fluttered when he ran his hand over her thighs, his thumbs skimming the sensitive skin on the inside. They closed completely when his hands ran over her lips and took turns quickly circling her clit. She gripped the bedsheet with both hands and rocked her hips. Her muscles clenched as her orgasm began to build. He barely touched her, and she was about to come. This man...Then she remembered a critical piece of the drunken conversation she had with him last night. More importantly, what she asked and then what he agreed to. "Fuck!" She moaned at both the memory and the orgasm flowing through her. Her eyes popped open when she felt the blunt tip of Quentin's dick at her entrance, parting her lips.

Wandering around in the fog of her orgasm and simultaneously being caught up in her thoughts, she missed him stuffing a pillow underneath her hips. She really needed to pay more attention to what was going on around her. She only got the "Que" of his name out before he slid inside her to the hilt. Her mouth gaped open, and she could only stare at him in awe. Never in her whole goddamned life had a dick felt so motherfucking good inside her. *Fuckity-fuckFuck!* And he wasn't even moving. He was just still and letting her body get accustomed to his size, and she was about to bust another nut. This might not have been a good idea. She was just about to tell him that when he laid on top of her. The weight of his body plus his dick inside made her moan softly. She opened her eyes when he brushed his thumb, which smelled like her pussy, across her lips.

"You good?" Quentin's lips replaced his thumb as he kissed her.

Quentin's kisses were ever so soft; Noelle had to stretch her neck to catch his lips. "I think I'll live."

Quentin smiled at Noelle, then buried his face in her neck, hooked her right leg in his elbow, and started to thrust.

"Oh..." Noelle breathed. Hitting the right places, he fit so perfectly inside her. He took care of her body by not thrusting too hard and deep, but she still felt her body stretching ridiculously to accommodate him. With each thrust, she felt her eyes tear up. She could hear herself moaning and squealing uncontrollably, joined by incoherent babbling. She grabbed at his ass and scratched at his shoulders, unsure of whether she was trying to push him away or pull him closer. She was pretty sure she was going to have blood in her nails from his back. She hit the mattress with her fists; hell, she might have hit him because basically, she was losing her fucking mind over Quentin's dick. When she finally came, it was with her whole entire body. It gave her the strength of a thousand women orgasming. She arched her hips so hard and fast that it lifted Quentin's lower body.

Then the cherubs floated in...only to be jostled aside abruptly when Quentin grabbed her headboard and pounded into her. Noelle didn't think she could come again; her second orgasm was so complete. But her pussy had other plans. It was making up for four weeks of lost time. She wanted to scream, but she couldn't catch her breath. Was she going to pass out from pleasure and lack of oxygen? Quentin grunted softly, and she felt his dick throb as he released. Had he been wearing a condom?

Before Noelle broached the subject, she took a moment to enjoy the weight of him on top of her and his kisses on her shoulder and the side of her neck. She rubbed his sweaty head and his back, also enjoying the small hiss when the salt from his sweat touched the scratches she made.

"I think that gave you at least a six-month supply of mashed potatoes. I might have to go to a dairy farm and buy that freshly churned butter. Shit, I might even make it myself," Noelle said, instead of bringing up the "let's have a baby together" agreement from last night. Nor did she want to discuss his lack of protection right now. She was surprised that she didn't want to talk about it. She never played Russian roulette with her cervix. After her one and only abortion at nineteen, she decided that she didn't want kids and practiced extremely safe sex from then on. So why she suggested and then went on to let Quentin nut all up in her good and deep was not something she wanted to think about or discuss. At least for the next two weeks, if her period didn't come.

"Just six months? I think by the way you were carrying on; you'd at least give me a year's worth." Quentin pulled out slowly as he spoke. Then, he rolled off her and took her with him, so she ended up on his chest.

"Okay, nine months then," Noelle compromised and then inwardly cringed when Quentin's fingers slightly paused while twirling her hair. Why the fuck did she say *nine* months? What was wrong with her?

"I'll take nine months. I'm pretty sure I'll do something else during that time to earn more tokens and prizes."

Noelle exhaled quietly. Thank God he didn't bring up having a baby. "I'm gonna get a roll of those tickets they give out at the carnival so I can give them to you when you do a good job. You can save them up and turn them in."

Quentin chuckled. "Do I get to choose my prize?"

"No. You get what I give you. But don't worry, I'm a generous carny." She threw her leg over his and rubbed his chest.

Quentin put his hands over hers and stopped her. "Unless you want me to start earning tickets now, you should stop that."

Again? So soon? Noelle glanced down. Sure enough, his dick was getting hard again right before her eyes. It was a magnificent sight to behold. Hmmm, she knew her pussy was swollen. Not that bad though; she could go another round. However, she was going to need an ice pack *and* a warm sitz bath after this. But that was after. Her mommy ain't raise no quitter. She sat up and gave him a deep kiss, sucking on his bottom lip while she straddled him. Taking his dick in her hand she gently wedged it between her lips. Quentin grabbed her hips. Her eyelids got heavy, and she hissed as she felt the sting of his dick stretching her open again as she slowly slid down. When she felt the twinge of his dick touching her cervix, she leaned forward and flattened her palms on his chest.

"It's never too early to earn tokens..."

Chapter Thirty-Four

BM1 Joaquín Santiago

"When do you guys leave?" Marisol asked. She was performing her nightly ritual of braiding her shoulder-length hair out in front of the mirror. If she left her hair out, she joked that the rasta fairy would visit while she was sleeping.

"June 7th," Joaquín said, climbing into bed.

"Oh, so you're gonna miss Junior's graduation." Marisol started a new braid. "I wasn't sure. You hadn't said anything about it, but I just wanted to double-check."

"Yeah, I already spoke to him about it. He's okay with it." Joaquín leaned back against the headboard and watched Marisol. She wore the soft pink camisole set that hugged her full curves. He always teased that her ass was too big for the shorts. And that's why she wore them, she would respond back.

"Do you still love me the same way you did in the beginning?" Joaquín asked.

Marisol's hand froze in mid-braid. Quickly finishing up the braid, she stared at him in the mirror for a moment before turning around to face him.

"No. I love you more. Why would you ask me that, *papi*? Do I go out with the girls too much? Does it bother you? If it does, I'll stop. I don't need to go out with them. They're not important," Marisol said in a rush.

"No." Joaquín sat up and waved his hand. "I don't care about that. It's about you. You've been acting differently over these past couple of weeks. You're here with us, but at the same time, you're not. And it's happened before from time to time for a couple of years now. I don't know why I haven't said anything, but I'm about to go on this cruise, and I can't leave with this so heavy in my head right now."

With a sigh, Marisol's hand flew up to touch the pendant hanging between her breasts before changing course and landing on her hip. She leaned back against the dresser and crossed her arms over her chest. "You're right. I am kinda out of it. I think things are changing, and I don't know what to do."

Joaquín frowned. "What things?"

"Not with you. But Junior and Esme are growing up. Junior's going to 9th grade, and he'll be driving soon, and Esme's starting junior high school. She has all her little friends now, which I love, but I'm not her best friend anymore, and Junior makes his own lunch. They are growing up, and I don't know what to do with myself." Marisol shrugged.

"You could always go for your Nurse Practitioner's license. I know you put it off because the kids were so young," Joaquín said.

Shaking her head, Marisol sighed again. "I don't want to do that anymore. I don't even know if I want to be a nurse anymore, for that matter. I might be having an early midlife crisis."

Marisol pushed off the dresser and walked over to Joaquín. He swung his legs around, sat up, and she knelt between them. "But that has nothing, and I mean *nothing* to do with our marriage or my love for you. I have loved you since you drove all the way to New York because I wanted a New York slice and brought me back a whole damn pie. You knew me for three whole days, I hadn't even put it on you yet." She laughed softly. "No man, save for my father, has loved and cared for me the way you do. You're a wonderful father; our kids know you love them, and they see how you love me. You have supported and encouraged me through anything I wanted to do. You give me room to breathe, though I know it goes against your nature sometimes. I know if you could wrap the kids and me up in bubble wrap, you would. I love you for that. I love you for always making me feel protected and safe and loving me through two bouts of postpartum depression." She took his face in her hands. "And I have always felt desired by you. We fuck, we make love. No other man knows my body the way you do, and no one ever will. Believe me when I say I will never love any other man besides you. You're stuck with me until I take my last breath, which will be immediately followed by your last breath because I fully expect you to die without me."

"I fully expect I will." Joaquín chuckled and framed her face with his hands as well. The relief he felt at her words flowed through his veins, giving him life. The nights he spent lying next to her in bed wondering about her faithfulness, fearing that he had somehow lost his wife, as well as the mystery of the pendant, were forgotten as he stared into his wife's eyes.

"I am my beloved..." Joaquín began quoting part of the Song of Solomon verse from their wedding vows.

Marisol pulled Joaquín's face down until their lips touched lightly. "And my beloved is mine."

Chapter Thirty-Five

PHI Noelle Bentley

"I love you."

Every muscle in Noelle's body froze as her eyes popped open, only to be blinded by the glaring midday sun. She had just finished basting her body with sun-tanning oil when Quentin arrived. He seemed quiet and pensive, but she didn't mind because she was feeling the same way. Her impending departure was her reason. She wanted to tell him; she really did. But every time she saw or spoke to Quentin, the words got caught deep in her chest, and her throat would literally squeeze shut out of fear. Everything had been so good between them. It was surreal—like a damn romance novel. Never in her life had she been with a man who predicted her every want and need. She'd be just sitting there minding her own business, thinking about rice crispy treats, and he would suddenly just ask if she wanted some. It was impressive and fucking unnerving.

He also kept up with her erratic and constantly meandering thoughts and wild ideas, and he came along on the journey with her, adding his own spin on her ideas, which were usually more reality-based. He always presented them in such a way that it didn't irritate and immediately put her on the defensive. He also understood why she named the voices in her head. Granted, she had never planned on telling because she was well aware that shit sounded crazy as fuck. He caught her talking to herself one day, however, and she had to decide what was crazier: telling him or ignoring the fact that she had a whole-ass conversation with herself while she plucked her eyebrows. He simply said that as long as that helped her, he didn't see the problem and ordered some Thai food. Impressive and unnerving thing number two.

Impressive and unnerving thing number *three* was the sex. Good googly moogly! His agonizing weeks of foreplay were definitely put to good use these past two weeks. He'd managed to learn her body as though they'd been together for twenty years. One look, one touch, and she was a goddamned Slip 'N Slide. And they hadn't used a condom. Not once. That wasn't the wisest decision, but her period came, and she was really trying to remember to take her birth control pills.

The only thing that could bust her happy bubble was her deployment. When she allowed herself to think about their relationship and what it meant to her, she admitted to herself—and herself only—that she was deathly afraid that everything would change between them when she told him that she was leaving. She'd be gone longer than they were together. Were they even really a couple to begin with? They didn't put a label on their relationship, so would they actually break up or just take a break? This was a fucking nightmare.

Eyes tearing up from the sun, Noelle blindly reached for her shades on the glass table next to her. Putting them on, she sat up and turned to face Quentin, who sat underneath the umbrella staring at her with an expression of resigned humor.

"I didn't mean to just blurt it out. I planned for a much smoother delivery. Maybe over dinner or after sex. I'm not exactly sure, but I guess 'I love you' doesn't need an introduction. You just say it. So, Noelle Bentley, I love you. I know we've only known each other for a little over a month, and I admit this is very sudden. I have never fallen for someone so fast, not as a kid and definitely not as an adult. It's a bit nerve-wracking, and if someone else told me this I would think they were lying. But I'm pretty sure you had me from the moment you convinced me to sacrifice a chicken for you."

"Which you still haven't done," Noelle replied dryly. Feigning a calmness she didn't feel, she reached for her glass of lemonade. She was surprised her hand didn't shake as she took a sip because her head was light, and her stomach was queasy as fuck. A million thoughts threatened to implode her brain.

Quentin loved her.

And she loved it. She. Fucking. Loved it!

Yes, we love this! He's perfect for us. He's secure; he understands us. Did he look at you crazy when you told him about us? No, he just rolled with it. He doesn't try to control us, he's patient, he—" Constance began firmly until Anxious Annie finally decided to make her appearance after all these weeks. Apparently, Quentin hadn't stirred her up until his declaration. She drowned out Constance's voice by screaming *What the fuck! We might not be crazy, but this shit is, Noelle. No one falls in love this fast—especially not a man. And he's a MAN! I don't believe it and you shouldn't either. He's playin' us, girl.*

Rhonda was silent. She usually stayed out of these more serious conversations. She usually let the other two battle it out.

Noelle stared at Quentin, but she wasn't really seeing him. She was remembering when she woke up and caught him staring at her, and she wasn't creeped out—quite the opposite. His gaze was like the warmest and strongest hug. She felt seen and protected. Adored.

That feeling didn't stop her from avoiding meeting his family. She dodged going to his parents' house for dinner when he asked last week because, thankfully, she had duty. She'd never stood the midwatch with gratitude before. It was bad enough that she introduced him to her friends, especially after her conversation with Monty. Did she lure him into a false sense of security on purpose? Was she that horrible of a person?

"I'll save the chicken sacrifice for our honeymoon," Quentin said with a small smile.

Bitch! I cannot! Annie yelled and ran around inside her head like a mad woman.

Noelle choked on the second sip of lemonade. Wincing, she tried to clear her throat, trying to speak past the burn. Her throat felt scarred. She opened her mouth to say something, she didn't know what when Quentin raised his hand.

"Noelle, you don't have to say anything. I didn't tell you for an 'I love you' back. I said it for myself. I'm fine with being in love with you. So just relax," Quentin said, holding out his hand. "Come here."

Staring at his outstretched hand, Noelle scowled in confusion. He was so fucking calm and self-assured and comfortable with expressing all his damn feelings. She fidgeted, resisting the urge to wrap her arms around her waist and soothe herself by rocking back and forth. She needed a real drink because this lemonade wasn't cutting it—and a fucking Percocet. She wondered if she still had some left in her medicine cabinet from when she finally let them pull her wisdom teeth last year. Would she get in trouble if she took them? What if they gave her a piss test before they left? Popping a controlled substance out of panic because a man was in love with her would not be excused under the [1] UCMJ. That's [2] an article 135 for sure.

Why. Is. This. Happening? Annie screamed in her head.

I. Don't. Fucking. Know! Bitch fucking ask him shit! Noelle snapped in her head. Oooh, her tummy was starting to act up. She put her hand on it and rubbed it.

Quentin sighed and shook his head. "Get out of your head, Noelle, and come here." He beckoned her with the hand he still held out.

"I'm all sweaty and stuff." Noelle wasn't just saying that as an excuse. The heat was blazing, and she was a nervous wreck now, so that didn't help her personal heat index. The sweat was running down her back, between her breasts, and pooling in the junction of her clenched thighs.

"Your sweat got in my eye last night. Just come here. Don't make me come get you."

*Oh, brother...*Noelle sighed and stood up, mildly distracted by Quentin's eyes narrowing as they swept down her body. She was wearing her favorite bronze—and teeniest—bikini for minimum tan lines. Now, his lust she could handle *and* control. She made a small show of drying the sweat from around her neck, slid the towel down her arms, and over the soft mound of her tummy, patting her cleav-

---

1. UCMJ / Uniform Code of Military Justice: enacted by Congress, contains the substantive and procedural laws governing the military justice system.

2. Article 135: Unofficially, the catch-all article. If there isn't an article for an offense, it goes there.

age. She cupped each breast and dried underneath, then flipped the towel over her shoulders and shimmied it down her back, making her breasts jiggle in the process. His eyes followed every move. *Good.*

Noelle's eyes dropped down on Quentin's hard-on pressing against his thigh. *The titty jiggle gets them every time.* He was already unbuckling his belt when he stopped and looked around the yard.

"There's no one on the other side of that fence, and Mr. Thomas over on that side there is like a thousand-year-old WW2 and Korean War vet. Sometimes I sunbathe topless just to thank him for his service." Noelle loosely wrapped the towel around and tucked it underneath her arm. Reaching under it, she wiggled out of her bikini bottom.

"Only you would do that," Quentin said with a chuckle, then continued to unbuckle his belt.

"Hey, it's better than those fake poppy flowers the DAV gives out. It's more personal, more from the heart. Don't you think?" Noelle stepped out of her bikini bottoms and waited until his dick was out before straddling his lap. She wasn't sure if Celia had sex in mind when she purchased these Adirondack chairs, but they were the perfect width for straddling a man's thighs. They gave outer edge support without being too constricting. Poised over his tip, she took hold of the top of the chair on either side of his head.

"I think you're just fresh, Noelle." Quentin's large hands framed her hips and slowly guided her down.

"Yeah, that too. Don't tell anyone though, it's a secret..." Noelle's voice trailed off as she closed her eyes, enjoying the friction and fullness of Quentin inside her. *This man and his goddamned demon dick.* For the first time in her life, she understood how women got addicted to men and ended up fighting on the *Jerry Springer Show*. Outstanding dick will make a bitch act out of pocket.

"Don't worry. It'll be our little secret," Quentin promised. Keeping one hand on her hip, he helped guide her up and down. He buried his other hand in her sweaty curls and pulled her head to the side, exposing her neck to his teeth.

Gasping at the sharp prick of his teeth on her skin and his dick tapping at her cervix, Noelle grabbed Quentin's head and leaned in closer to him. Holding both the back of his head and the back of the chair, she took over the riding. She felt the towel slip and didn't give a damn if Mr. Thomas watched her ass bounce up and down. The tension built in her body, and she rode him faster and harder. She was about to come when Quentin pulled away from her grasp and framed her face with his hands.

"Noelle."

Noelle ignored him.

"Noelle. *Look at me.*"

Quentin's insistent tone pulled Noelle out of her reverie. She opened her eyes and focused on him. The look in his eyes was so intense as he stared at her. *God, he was so beautiful.*

"I love you."

Staring into Quentin's eyes, absorbing all the love he was giving to her, Noelle had the best damn orgasm of her life thus fucking far! Then spent and overwhelmed with the emotion she refused to name, she slumped against him. He wrapped his arms around her and pumped a few times before coming as well. She didn't know how long they stayed locked together before he released her.

"I think we've thanked Mr. Thomas for his service more than enough," Quentin said. He reached down and picked up the fallen towel from the grass and wrapped it back around Noelle's waist.

"We gave him a damn parade with a twenty-one-gun salute." Laughing, Noelle eased off Quentin's lap. Using the end of the towel, she dried him before he stood up.

Noelle's anxiety slowly started to build again as she watched Quentin as he fixed his clothes. He loved her. He motherfucking loved her! She wanted to fucking vomit and shit, run around the neighborhood like she was on fire as the weight of the responsibility of his feelings and the expectations that were sure to follow settled on her shoulders.

Annie was right. This was too much to deal with. On an average day, she didn't know what to do with her feelings. For as long as she could remember, she had so many kinds of feelings about every damn thing. It bogged her down and clouded her mind, and it made her highly reactive and sensitive. All her life was experienced in 3D. She preferred it in 2D. As the years went by, she found it easier to keep her love reserved for her close friends and family. It kept her sanity in check.

"Noelle."

Startled, Noelle jumped and focused on Quentin's face. Whatever he saw on her face made him sigh and pull her to him for a tight hug. She exhaled the breath she didn't realize she was holding and wrapped her arms around his waist. Damn it, she needed to tell him she was leaving.

"Quentin," Noelle began. She needed to tell him right now.

"Shhhh," Quentin kissed her temple. "Let's go get something to eat."

"Sure! I'm starved. Are we ordering delivery?" Being the emotionally repressed, commitment-avoidant, punk-ass woman she was, Noelle took that reprieve and ran with it. Ignoring Constance's pleas in her head: *Tell him.* She still had a week left before she had to emotionally vomit all over this man, and she needed all seven of those days.

Chapter Thirty-Six

YN1 Celia Navarro

"**H**ey Navarro, did you get my email?"

Surprised, Celia looked over to the Admin helpdesk window to see Joaquín standing there. "Sorry. I haven't checked my email yet." Lies. She saw the email and left it unread.

"Oh, it's okay. It was kinda spur of the moment, but I sent one asking if our usual time was available for a meeting. I just wanted to go over some things. Get everything all tied up before we pulled out."

"Oooh, yeah, no, I don't have time right now. I have an appointment I'm about to head out for," Celia said. "But I can call you when I get back." Another lie. She was just going to McDonald's for the office.

Joaquín nodded. "Yup. Just shoot me a call when you're ready."

"Aye aye, BM1." Celia studied Joaquín. There was something different about him. The last time she spoke to him was during that crazy scene on the [1] mess decks. After that, every time she caught a glimpse of him, he looked

---

1. Mess or Mess Deck: a designated area where military personnel eat and socialize.

all stressed out and tired and weighed down by life. But a brand-new man stood at the helpdesk window this morning. His shoulders were relaxed, his eyes weren't guarded, and he was even wearing a light smile. He looked unburdened and peaceful.

Celia was glad one of them was happy. She'd been in a serious funk since game night that she couldn't shake off. Thoughts of Julia had her head all fucked up, and it spilled over onto her situation with Joaquín. She couldn't deny the similarities between them. They both caused that same instantaneous fire that threatened to reduce her to ashes. But they weren't the same, and she couldn't seem to hold space for both her sudden attraction for Joaquín and her endless longing for Julia. So her feelings for Joaquín fell to the wayside.

Which in all honesty was a smart idea if she wanted to be prepared for the Chief's exam in January. An affair with Joaquín would be too tempestuous and distracting. Things might be different if they stayed in port; he had a family to go home to, and their time together would be limited. Being on a cruise changed all that. They would be living and working together for six months. The only contact with family and friends came from letters and phone calls. Everything important was so far away.

Celia knew that's where the danger lay for her. The danger of forgetting her place in Joaquín's life because they lived in a floating bubble where only the here and now mattered. Chances were high that she would fall in love with him because that seems to be her modus operandi when it came to unavailable people. She wasn't naïve enough to think there would be a happy ending to their story. She had already played pretend with a married lover, and the common sense part of her was warning her not to do it again. But now here he was tapping on her windowpane, and she felt all her hard-earned resolve and good sense start to waiver.

"I'll catch up with you later then," Joaquín said, not giving any indication that he noticed Celia staring at him.

"Ummm-hmmm." Celia nodded in agreement.

Joaquín rapped his knuckles on the windowsill and disappeared from view, only to pop back up a second later. "Wait, are you heading out now?"

Jesus. Celia stifled a sigh. "Yup."

"I'll walk you to the quarterdeck," Joaquín said with a smile.

"Okay." Celia swallowed and rose from her chair, grabbing her black purse. Something about his smile suddenly had her feeling more unsettled. She only knew dark and brooding Santiago, who clenched his jaw and stared silently at her. She really didn't know how to deal with the happy and friendly Joaquín, who seemed like he wanted to hold hands and skip down the [2] passageway.

"So, how have you been?" Joaquín asked as they made their way down the passageway.

"I've been good," Celia responded cautiously. All her prior bravado was completely gone, replaced by nervousness as she walked down the passageway with him. She actually wanted to kick him in the shins with her steel-toed boots and run the other way.

Joaquín pulled her into the corner by the ladder[3] just as she was about to go down. "You said you wanted me to come to you willingly. Do you still want that? Do you still

---

2. Passageway: hallway of a ship.

3. Ladder: stairs

want me?"

Stunned, Celia stared up at Joaquín. The happy-go-lucky Joaquín was gone. The intensity of his gaze burned through the heavy fog that permeated her mind for weeks. She exhaled the breath she hadn't been aware she was holding. On her inhale, she breathed in his desire, and it stoked the fire inside her that had almost died out. The flames roared to life, and her mere seconds ago normal temperature body was suddenly an inferno. Her skin felt prickly as the flames started licking at her skin. The familiar beads of sweat ran between her shoulder blades and down her spine. She was going to combust in the damn passageway.

"*Todavía me quieres?*" Joaquín murmured.

Did she still want him...? Oh God, yes! How did he do this to her so quickly? Celia's lids lowered, and she felt herself swaying toward him only to pull back abruptly when two sailors walked by on their way to the ladder. One disappeared down the ladder well, but the other trailed behind.

"BM1, do you know when the work party is starting?" SK3 Biggins said.

"Probably in about ten minutes or so. You on it?" Joaquin asked.

"Unfortunately," Biggins said, then disappeared down the ladder.

Joaquín turned his attention back to Celia. "Where were we?"

"You asked me if I still wanted you. But that would depend," Celia began.

"On what?"

"On if I have to do guilt triage every time you come."

Joaquín nodded slowly. "Let me start off by saying, I love my wife. She is amazing. She takes care of the kids and me. She holds it down while I'm gone, and not once has she complained. She is everything I could have wished for in a wife. I love my family, and I love my life."

"So if you love your wife and you love your life, why are we having this conversation?" Déja vu swept over Celia as she listened to Joaquín's preamble. It was almost verbatim of what Julia said when they began *and* ended their affair. Just replace 'not complaining about deployment' with 'encouraging her to finish her degree', and it would be exactly the same conversation. Oh my God, what was she thinking? This was a mistake. She needed to get away from him because clearly if he was anywhere near her, she lost her damn mind. As if sensing her thoughts, Joaquín stepped close to her, almost blocking her path.

"It's only because I love my wife, and I know that I am not leaving her that I can do this." Joaquín clapped his hands together and held them up. "Lemme be completely one hundred with you, Celia: I have wanted you since you signed my check-in sheet. You told me 'Welcome to the Puget Sound', and gave me that beautiful smile of yours that you also gave to the other two dudes who were checking in with me—so it wasn't even *for* me—and it didn't matter. It was a done deal for me, and then you basically ignored me for two years. We had a meeting every month that I initiated; we used to have lunch together during the cruise—me, you, Ingram, Bentley, and whoever else was around."

Celia's brow wrinkled. Lunch? When the hell did that happen?

"You don't remember that do you?" Joaquín asked.

"Ummm." Celia tried to recall ever having lunch with him at any given time, and she drew a blank. "No, I don't." She shook her head. She had a feeling where he was headed, but she let him continue.

"That's because you didn't *see* me. I was just another 1st

class. Outside of that, I didn't exist. Then one day, you're like, throwing it at me and expecting me to just catch it. Like I should be grateful or something that you're payin' me some attention. And the fucked-up thing was that I *was* so fuckin' grateful! It was like I had won the lottery. Goddamn, neña, I wanted you to wake up with my dick inside you that afternoon in the gym. To make matters worse, I had spent almost two years thinking that my wife was cheating on me. So wanting you was mixed up in that, and I was all fucked up in the head. I can't even explain how much."

"I knew you were conflicted—as you should be because that is a perfectly normal reaction. At least it should be. So I just left you alone. I wasn't going to drag you kicking and screaming into my bed. That's crazy." Celia crossed her arms over her chest and leaned her shoulder on the bulkhead. "So am I now to assume that you don't think she's cheating anymore?"

"No, I am positive she's been faithful."

Celia pursed her lips. "And now *you* want to have an affair?"

Joaquín nodded quickly. "This is gonna sound loco, but I wasn't sure if I wanted you only because I thought my wife didn't want me anymore. Like I said, I love my wife. I love her even more now than I did 15 years ago when we first got married, and if I had slept with you without knowing if she'd been faithful, it would have been all about her. And I didn't want that. I wanted it to be about you and me."

Joaquín began to lean in even closer then quickly backed up when he heard someone coming up the ladder. "I want the next six months to only be about you and me. I know you're up for a transfer soon, so we're never gonna have this chance again. This is it. Does that make sense?" He asked in a low voice.

Celia searched Joaquín's face and only saw sincerity. This man was ready, but was she? She still wasn't sure despite the inferno raging inside her. "I'm pretty sure my moral compass is off, if not broken, because as fucked up as your reasoning is, it makes perfect sense to me." She sighed. "However, I've been thinking about what's good for me and I'm pretty sure having an affair with you would not be good for me. I've only been with one other married person and it caught me by surprise—"

Joaquín's brows rose. "Kinda like this? One moment you're with Kendrick and the next..."

"Yeah, kinda like this. But it was so hard on me. I didn't stop to think about that when I just threw it at you. And to tell you the truth, I'm worried about this attraction I have for you. It's..." Shaking her head, Celia unfolded her arms and pushed off the bulkhead. "Listen, we both have the Chief's exam in January; I think it would be best if I—*we*—focus on that. I already have one person who's refusing to leave my dreams. I don't think I can handle another one. I'm—I'm- sorry I started this, but I just can't."

"All personnel assigned to the working party
muster on the aft messdecks."

Thankful for the interruption, Celia took a deep breath. "We both need to go." She walked a couple of steps to the ladder. Hand on the railing, she turned back to Joaquín, who was just standing there wearing an enigmatic expression. "We good?"

"We're good. But we're not done, Celia." Joaquín gave her a two-fingered salute and walked back the way they came.

Celia stared at his departing back, excitement and caution racing through her to get to the lead. Goosebumps popped up on her arms, and she shivered. She just told the biggest lie she had ever told in her whole entire life. She didn't mean for it to be a lie. It was not a good idea for them to get any further involved than they already were. She sighed. *Fuck.* Why was she like this? She shook her head and shrugged in defeat when excitement crossed the finish line, leaving caution choking on the dust. Who was she kidding? She was not passing up the chance to have Joaquín all to herself for six months. She indeed was up for transfer next year, and she had plans to leave the Norfolk area. So he was right; this would be their only chance. She fully expected to be completely shattered and sobbing when the ship returned in December, and his family was waiting for him on the pier.

Fuck it. Celia thought. *Fuck. It.* She added with more resolve, and then she headed down the ladder. She'd look for her old counselor's number when she got home and set up an appointment for December. She'd deal with her self-destructive ways then. But until then, she'd enjoy this man in every possible way she could.

Chapter Thirty-Seven

LT Quentin Jacobs

He fucked up. He had fucked up so bad. Quentin lay in his teenage bed staring up at the ceiling. The basketball mark from twenty years ago when he threw his ball at the ceiling in anger and frustration during one of his college breakups with Cynthia was still there. If he had a ball, he would be throwing it up again every time he remembered the look of shock, nausea, and entrapment on Noelle's face when he told her he loved her. For seven days and seven nights, it was his constant companion. He drank with his Earl Gray in the morning and was with his brandy before bed.

He didn't know what made him tell her; because he knew she wasn't ready. Hell, she might not ever be ready if her reaction was any indication of future conversations about his feelings and their relationship. She damn sure never talked about her actual emotions, although could go on and on about her love of food and her thoughts of the moment. She wanted him or more precisely, his dick. He'd woken up to her lips wrapped around him every morning that he'd stayed the night. Maybe all she wanted from him was sex. That was the thought buried in the back of his mind, and he refused to think about it because he thought it was an insecure backlash about his feelings.

After lunch, Noelle pretended she was fine as she led him back to her room, where she claimed she needed a nap after all the sun and sex, and food. But Quentin didn't sleep. He just wrapped his arms around her as she lay on his chest and played with her curls the way she liked until she fell asleep, and worried that he had caused irrevocable damage between them. Why didn't he keep his mouth shut?

"Fuck..." Quentin groaned as he sat up and swung his legs to the floor.

When he left her house this morning, Noelle had been even more distracted than usual, and he didn't want to bring attention to it. The walls that he thought he broke down, or at least climbed, were slowly going back up even taller. He was pathetically grateful when she leaned on him, but there was something melancholy about the way she rubbed and squeezed his arm when he pulled away. Her sigh was deep and long when he kissed her forehead, as he always did before he left.

It was his turn to sigh as he grabbed his pager from his nightstand. There was no 'hey baby, what you're doing', or 'I miss you' code. He would have settled for a 'bring me some lunch' at this point. He debated calling her for a few minutes before dialing the Photo Lab. She picked up on the second ring. He barely got out 'ello' before she spoke.

"I have something to tell you. As a matter of fact, I should have told you already. We're going on deployment soon."

Quentin frowned. "How soon is soon?"

There was mention of something between Noelle and her roommates about their last cruise together. Whenever it came up, Noelle deftly changed the subject so smoothly he hadn't worried about it. When she didn't answer, he felt his right eyelid start to twitch.

"When are you leaving, Noelle?" He heard Noelle take a

deep breath and exhale.

"Monday." Her voice was barely above a whisper.

"Excuse me?" Quentin asked. She couldn't have possibly said—

Noelle cleared her throat. "Monday." She repeated louder. "We're leaving Monday morning."

Quentin's breath hissed out. That's what he thought she said. It was Saturday. He gritted his teeth together and willed himself to calm down. He didn't get mad often, but he felt rage stirring in his belly and rising into his chest. He gripped the receiver tightly. If he started yelling at her, he was never going to stop. "When were you planning on telling me? *Were* you planning on telling me?" Her silence was his answer.

"I don't know, bu—" Noelle began.

"You don't *know*?" Quentin interrupted, barely managing to keep a snarl out of his voice. "What the hell, Noelle?"

"No. No, I was! I just didn't know how and when to tell you. We were having so much fun, and I damn sure wasn't expecting you to say what you said to me last week. That totally threw me for a loop. Had I known that was happening, I would have said something sooner."

"What I said to you?" She couldn't even say the words. Quentin stood up and started pacing around his room. "You mean when I said that I love you? Is that what you're referring to?"

Noelle sighed. "Yes. I'm sor—"

"Stop right there, Noelle. Don't say anything else. I'm on my way over. Whatever else you have to say, just wait 'til I get there. What time is your watch?" Quentin was surprised at how calm he sounded because he was fucking livid. From the sound of blood whooshing in his ears, his blood pressure must be sky high. He held the receiver away from his mouth because he didn't want her to hear how heavy he was breathing.

"I have the 12 to 4 watch."

Quentin glanced at the wall clock. It was 9:30 a.m. It would take him at least thirty minutes to get to the ship. They needed more than an hour and a half to discuss how the fuck she was going to leave without telling him. "Okay. I'll be on the quarterdeck when you're relieved."

"Quentin..." Noelle said with a sigh.

"What Noelle?" he asked tightly.

"Can we talk about this tomorrow?"

Quentin narrowed his eyes at the plea in her voice before asking a question he already had the answer for. "Do you even *want* to talk about anything? Talk about you damn near leaving without telling me? Or the fact that when I told you I loved you, you looked like you wanted to throw up."

Noelle paused before speaking. "I did want to throw up, and honestly no, I really don't want to talk about this because I—I don't have anything to say. I'm leaving. I didn't think you were gonna..." She trailed off.

"Fall in love with you? Or just catch feelings in general? 'Cause I am at your house every day. We be fuckin' raw, and you can't even remember to take your birth control."

"I'm not pregnant, Quentin."

"That's not the point, Noelle. I'm almost forty, and I have a life. If I am spending all my time with you, it's because I want to. I wasn't just there to fuck you. What did you think we were doing, Noelle?" He asked incredulously.

Noelle sucked her teeth. "It hasn't even been two months—I don't know what we were doing. You didn't give me your letter jacket, so I didn't know we were going steady, okay?" Her voice was fast and sharp. She inhaled sharply. "I'm sorry, I didn't mean for this to happen this way."

She was lying. This is exactly what she wanted to happen. Had he not admitted his feelings, she would have just left without a word. Like he wasn't shit—just some dude she was fucking. Quentin sat on the edge of his bed, tapped the receiver on his forehead, and closed his eyes.

Taking a deep breath, he put it back to his ear. "You're right, Noelle; we didn't talk about what we were doing. I made all these assumptions about our situation. I should have known better." He paused, giving her a moment to say he was wrong, that they were in a relationship or at least on the cusp of one. But her silence was damning. He grunted softly as he tried to find the right words, but all he could think about was Noelle leaving him. Not just for six months either. They were done. He knew from the moment he told her that he loved her. It wasn't about the deployment either. That was just a convenient excuse.

What made all this worse was he knew she had feelings for him. There was no way she could deny how well they fit together. There was a rhythm between them that most couples didn't have even after years in a relationship. They were easy. She might not love him yet, but her feelings were there and tangible. There was no way she could fake her smile whenever she saw him, reaching for him when she was sleeping and curling herself around him. Yet here she was, just throwing it all away. If he knew that he could eventually catch her, he would chase her across all seven seas, but he couldn't catch her if she didn't want to be caught. She'd been dropping hints from their first conversation; he just made the tragic mistake of thinking he could change her mind. He could fight with her, but he'd be staying where he didn't belong and wrecking himself in the process.

Or he could let her go.

"Have a good cruise, PH1. Make sure you have a liberty buddy with you when you leave the ship because you get lost in a straight line. We're not in a war right now but just be safe, okay."

There was a slight pause before she answered. "Aye-aye. Lieutenant. Will do."

Quentin took a deep breath and let it out quietly, along with his last bit of hope. "Lata." He couldn't bear to say goodbye even though that's what this was. He hung up before she could reply. He gently set the receiver back in the cradle, fighting the urge to fling it against the wall. If he did that, his mother would be in the room in an instant. He didn't want anyone in his business. He wanted to grieve privately.

There was a knock on his door and his mother poked her head in. "You up? Good. There was a letter in the mail. I forgot to put it on your bed." Walking in, she gave him an assessing look but said nothing. Rubbing his head, she handed him the letter and left.

Quentin glanced at the envelope. It was from Bon Secours. He opened it and shook his head in disgust as he read the generic rejection letter. He had lost his girl and his coveted position all in the same day. What the hell was he going to do now?

Chapter Thirty-Eight

PHI Noelle Bentley

*O*hmyGodohmygodohmyGod! *What the hell are you do- ing?! Pick up the phone and call him back now, dammit!* Constance was losing her shit in Noelle's head.

"I can't," Noelle whispered aloud. Wringing her hands together, she stared at the phone on her desk.

What do you mean you 'can't'? Just pick up the phone, call him back, and apologize. It's very simple, Constance said soothingly, but sternly.

"No, it's not! It's *not*. I don't even know why you're sayin' that," Noelle said, jumping up from her office chair so fast, it flew back and hit the bulkhead behind her and bounced back, almost knocking her back down into it. Kicking it out of the way, she started pacing around the lab. The conversation with Quentin replayed in her head. Or more accurately, the hurt and anger in his voice.

Did you expect him not to be hurt, Noelle? Everything he said was true. You knew he was in love with you. You knew! And you knew you weren't going to commit, and you let him do it anyway. Who does that? Call him back and just explain yourself, Constance said.

"I didn't know he was actually falling in love with me. I knew he enjoyed being around me. Everyone likes me. I'm a fun person, okay? What the fuck!" Noelle stopped in front of the Noritsu machine and slapped her palm on it before resuming her pacing.

Nice try. I am literally inside your head. You can't lie to me. You can lie to Quentin and the rest of the world, but never to me. Ever. That is not how this works, so don't even try. Call him back, Noelle, Constance insisted.

"*Yeah, you trippin'. He's a cool dude. Call him back,*" Rhonda urged.

"And say what, exactly?" Noelle asked, throwing her hands up in the air. "I'm sorry I didn't tell you that we were leaving, but we never put a name to our relationship, so I didn't think I had to tell you?"

I would give you an aneurysm if you said that shit. I would kill us all. Your pressure's already up—you feel that headache already starting. It won't take much. But listen, you can fix this. Quentin loves you. You knew this before he told you. Just tell him you're sorry and tell him why you're this way. Explain yourself, he'll understand," Constance said.

Noelle stopped pacing and stared at the Sixth Fleet formation picture she had taken during the last cruise. But she wasn't remembering how scared she was to be in a helicopter and was still determined to get a good shot. Instead, she was nine years old and back in her godmother Evelyn's small dining room, trying to eavesdrop on her phone call with her mother, Grace. When she hung up, she came out of the bedroom and crossed the short distance to where Noelle stood by the small kitchenette table.

"Your mother is on her way home. She broke up with Harold," Evelyn said with a huge sigh.

"Oh," Noelle said, scratching her head. Her mother went away somewhere for the weekend with her boyfriend, Harold. He was nice to her, but she didn't know him that well. When he came around, her mother was utterly inattentive in her happiness, which Noelle loved, using those times to run the streets of the South Bronx with her friends. Harold didn't try to tell her what to do except for that one time her mother made him help with her math homework. It didn't go well for either one of them. After that, they made an unspoken truce: You leave me alone, slide me a couple of dollars when you stop by so I can buy some penny candy, and I'll leave you alone. She wasn't sure how to feel about Harold. When her mother broke up with her other boyfriend, George, she didn't tell her. He just stopped coming over. She hadn't liked George, so she didn't care. But her break up with Harold felt different.

Evelyn sighed again. Shaking her head, she started taking out her pink foam rollers and dropping them on the table. "Gracie told me that after they broke up, she was walking down the highway deciding whether she should throw herself in traffic. So I'm gonna take these rollers out because Harold's bringing her back, and I don't know how she's going to be when she gets here. I don't want her pulling my hair out if I have to hold her down." She gathered up the rollers and went back into her bedroom.

Noelle listened to Evelyn open and close one of her dresser drawers. Her nine-year-old mind was racing as she tried to make sense of what was going on. Her "love" experience consisted of passing notes to boys in class, avoiding the boys who liked her, chasing the ones who didn't, and listening to her friends talk about their boyfriends. The thought of her best friend Antonia throwing herself in front of the ice cream truck because her boyfriend Hector broke up with her was...fucking crazy! Was her mommy crazy?

She also had limited experience with crazy people. She had a cousin who lived with her grandmother, but they said that someone did obeah on him when he went back home to St. Kitts because he used to beat his wife. Did someone do obeah on her mommy? Because her mom had four other kids besides Noelle—two older brothers and two younger sisters. Her older brothers would be fine, but who was going to take care of them if their mother was throwing herself at cars?

Scowling with what Noelle figured out later was horror and a heavy side helping of disgust, she stared up at the Last Supper portrait that hung over the dining room table. Her mommy *was* crazy! Whatever she was doing with Harold made her...misbehave, rude, wild, bad, and hard-headed—her brain tried to come up with all the words her teachers used to describe Noelle's classroom behavior on her report cards. Her mother would definitely be in special ed if she was in her school.

Everyone always said Noelle was her mother's daughter. She looked just like her, right down to her smile. The only thing that was different about them was their skin color and hair texture. Her mother had light skin, so people thought she was Spanish.

Was she going to be crazy like her mommy? *Nope.* Noelle shook her head slowly, her eyes never leaving the portrait. She was not going to be like her mommy. Whatever *this* was, she didn't want it.

Unknowingly with that thought, Noelle hid her nine-year-old heart away, and for the next twenty-six years, men—some of them were really good and noble men—went on a hero's journey to find it, only to return home depleted of resources, worn down, and hurt.

To her dismay, every year, she looked more and more like Grace Bentley. Her high voice softened down to the same alto huskiness; people often mistook her for Grace on the phone when she visited. Her mother was still with

Harold to this day, and their relationship was still chaotic. But after the birth of her two younger sisters, it was quiet, primarily chaos filled with digs and attention grabs, and passive aggression from both sides.

And whatever *that* was, Noelle still didn't want it.

That's not what you had with Quentin. He understands us. And he would understand this. If you just tell him, Constance said softly. She sounded exhausted like she had returned from her own hero's journey of trying to get Noelle to reconsider.

"You don't know that," Noelle said.

I do. And more importantly, you do. Call him, Constance pleaded.

No. Noelle grounded her teeth.

"*I mean I don't think he's that bad. I'm sorry I overreacted. I think was just scared,*" Annie apologized.

Noelle rolled her eyes. Fuck, now even Annie was having a change of heart.

C'mon Noelle, we deserve to have nice things. Why won't you let us have nice things? Constance said.

"Such is life." Noelle exhaled sharply and steeled her spine. The irony of using that particular phrase was not lost on her. It was the same one her mother used to explain seemingly unexplainable things that really had a logical explanation.

Seriously though, you're not your moms, Noelle, Rhona said.

"And I won't be," Noelle said.

Is she really that bad Noelle or are you just using your mother as an excuse? Constance asked.

"Enough!" Noelle sliced her hands through the air in front of her. This decision was hers. She didn't need to rationalize it with the goddamn voices in her motherfucking head.

Damn, you really are a terrible person. Just in case you were wondering, Rhonda said.

She wasn't. Noelle inhaled deeply and held her breath for four seconds. Exhaling, she silenced Constance. She repeated the sequenced breathing two more times until the only voice left in her head was hers. Thirty minutes later as she stood the quarterdeck watch, no one would ever guess that she just broke her own heart.

Chapter Thirty-Nine

PHI Noelle Bentley

N oelle picked up her Cannon Rebel and focused the lens on a young sailor and his wife hugging him about twenty feet away from her. She snapped a picture before she realized the wife was bawling. She tried to drum up sympathy but came up short. All this snottin' and cryin' rankled her nerves. All these goddamned women were always crying. Well, mostly the young ones were anyway. The older wives had an air of resignation and steadfastness to them and shit. Hell, some of them even looked relieved. There was truth in the saying that deployments saved marriages. They dropped off their husbands with a kiss and a hug and hopped back in their dirty minivans. The same scene played out with the older husbands. But the younger husbands looked lost holding their kids' hands while they cried as their mothers walked up the brow.

To her left, another woman was sniffling; she didn't have any kids with her and wasn't even noticeably pregnant. Noelle rolled her eyes. Come the fuck on. Tighten up. She needed these military spouses to get it together. If they wanted a landlocked person, they had two other branches to choose from. Half of these tears were for show anyway. Some of these folks were going straight to their jump-off's house before sea and anchor[1] was secured. Or worse yet, moving them in for the next six months.

Noelle put her camera down and searched down the pier again for a non-crying couple. Some of these people had to be happy their partners were leaving. At the far end of the pier, she saw a dark-skinned civilian walking. His shoulders were back, head held high, and he had the same confident stride as Quentin. Her heart started pounding, and her bacon, egg, and cheese McMuffin rolled in her stomach. Frozen in place, she stared at the figure. She almost peed herself in relief when a female sailor came up beside him, holding a daughter on her hip.

Now why in the hell would that be Quentin, anyway? You told him you wanted to vomit because he loved you and then you broke up with him, Constance said. *He's definitely not gonna be running down pier twenty-four to see you off.*

Noelle sighed and rolled her eyes. This was the first time Constance popped back up after she shut them all down. Of course, he wasn't coming. She would run away if he did. For the millionth time, she wondered why the fuck did he fall in love with her, of all people? She wouldn't fall in with anyone like her. There was nothing about her that said, *yeah, she's the one. I'm gonna take her home to meet my parents,* which he tried to do multiple times by using his mother's cooking as bait. But she stayed strong despite her inner glutton's cajoling that she didn't have to stay long—she could just pop in and get a-lickkle bitah food and leave.

She didn't tell Celia or Sidney what really happened and

---

1. Sea and Anchor Detail- Sailors are assigned to specific areas throughout the ship so they can attach and release the mooring lines to the pier safely and also pick up and drop the anchor safely as well.

thank goodness they were too busy with their own shit to question her about him—yet. But it was coming, and she still didn't know what lie she was going to tell them.

Glancing at Quentin's lookalike one last time and ignoring the prickle in her chest when he bent down to his wife and took his daughter into his arms, she turned to head back to the ship. That was when another family caught her eye. Santiago was walking down the pier, holding his daughter's hand—his teenage son was next to the girl, and his wife walked next to the son. She was looking down, talking to their son, but when she looked back up to speak to Joaquín, Noelle's eyes narrowed. Even from this far away, the woman looked familiar. She picked up her camera and zoomed in on the wife's face.

"What in the hot fuck!" Noelle said in a loud whisper.

The couple standing close by looked at her sharply.

"Sorry. My camera ran out of film, and I left my bag on the ship. So frustrating." Noelle gave them a fake smile, turned, and ran back to the brow. When she got aboard the ship, she ran to the Admin office to find Celia, but the office was empty. She ran down to the berthing[2]; it was full of sailors stowing their items away, but no Celia.

The announcement came over the 1MC[3] for all hands to muster on deck. Cool. The brow was coming up next. Good. At least Noelle wouldn't run into Santiago and his family aboard the ship. That would have been super awkward.

"Where the hell is she?" Noelle shook her fists in frustration. She stood in front of Celia's empty cube and tried to figure out where she was.

---

2. Berthing: Living quarters aboard a ship.

3. 1MC (Main circuit): Loudspeakers.

"Have you seen Navarro?" Noelle asked one of Celia's cubemates when she brushed past her to enter the cubicle.

"She was here earlier, but I think she said she was going up to find a good spot to man the rails," Heap said as she opened the lock on her rack locker.

"Oh, that's not good," Noelle said, ignoring the questioning look Heap gave her. Noelle wove through the maze of cubicles to the back entrance of the lower female berthing and made her way up to the forward mess decks. She glanced at her watch. They were going to raise the brow[4], set sea and set anchor soon, then the crew would man the rails, and they'd be on their way to the Mediterranean Sea.

Noelle never manned the rails[5] because she was always taking pictures for the cruise book, which she really needed to do, but *first*, she had to find Celia. Where the hell does she like to stand? She drew a blank. Where was she last year? She snapped her fingers. Aft lookout. She wanted to be shielded from the elements since the sailors manned the rail even in inclement weather.

Noelle held her camera close to her chest, and she took off in a sprint to aft lookout[6], not caring if she looked crazy

---

4. Brow: Temporary bridge that connects the ship's quarterdeck to the pier.

5. Manning the rails: Sailors at parade rest, spaced evenly on port and starboard the wing walls, and the aft lookout while the ship leaves the pier and when it returns.

6. Aft Lookout: Covered section extending from the rear of the ship.

running through the mess decks[7] and the engineering spaces to the aft of the ship. She found Celia and Sidney in the same spot where Celia had broken up with Kendrick.

"Girl, why are you running?" Celia asked.

Noelle held a finger up while she caught her breath. She only ran twice a year for the PRTs[8], and this was a panic run in polyester dress whites. She was about to pass out.

"Come," Noelle grabbed Celia's arm and dragged her over to the short port wall. She lifted her camera and searched the crowd for the person she was looking for. As luck would have it, her person of interest was standing in plain sight. Taking her camera strap from around her neck, she handed her camera to Celia. "In front of the brow at 10 o'clock."

"What's going on?" Sidney asked Noelle, who shook her head.

Celia held up the camera and followed Noelle's directions. She gasped and almost dropped the camera, but Noelle caught it and gave it back to her, and she looked through it again.

"What's going on?" Sidney asked Noelle again. "Who are you looking at? Who is she looking at?"

Silently, Celia handed the camera to Sidney. Frowning, Sidney took the camera. When she saw who had Noelle running to them and making Celia gasp, she soundlessly mouthed a slow "wow" and held the camera out to anyone who would take it. But Noelle was looking at Celia, who was breathing heavily, still looking at Santiago and his family on

---

7. Mess or Mess Deck: a designated area where military personnel eat and socialize.

8. PRT (Physical Readiness Test): Done twice a year for all hands.

the pier.

"Is that *Julia*?" Sidney asked, looking at Celia and then Noelle. "I know it shouldn't be, but it looks just like her. But I mean, I think it's her."

"Yeah, it's her. And I don't fucking know how this is possible." Noelle pursed her lips and shook her head. The only thing different about Julia was that her hair was longer. Oh, and the fact that she was Santiago's *wife*. Yeah, that was different too. Well, different to them. She and Santiago looked pretty damn cozy. At least she had solved her own personal mystery of why Julia reminded her so much of Santiago.

The three women watched Santiago hug his son and daughter, and when it came to Julia, he held on to her and buried his face in her hair as her arms wrapped around his waist. They were still cuddled up when the announcement came to finally secure the brow. Santiago kissed his wife and let her go. With a wave, he turned and headed to the brow, but his wife called his name and ran to him for one more kiss. Laughing, they broke apart, and Santiago continued on his way up the brow. How adorable that would have been if the wife had been anyone else.

"Isn't that sweet?" Celia murmured, tilting her head to one side.

"Under different circumstances, it's hella sweet. Under these circumstances, however, it's fuck-shit!" Noelle said. "Celia, how did you not know that Julia was Santiago's wife?"

"I knew her as Julia Peron. She mentioned that she used her maiden name for work but I didn't ask what her married name was," Celia said. She was remarkably calm. The only outward sign of stress was the rubbing of her forehead. "I never once saw her husband, not even a picture. I didn't even know his name. I didn't ask because I didn't want to know about that part of her life. She didn't volunteer anything other than that she was happy with him." She cursed under her breath and rolled her eyes. "I didn't question it. Julia was my lifeline after Mother died, so I didn't care what the fuck was going on in her life when she wasn't with me. I just needed her."

"But why haven't we seen her before today? I don't even remember seeing her. Did she not pick him up when the ship pulled back in last year? Where the hell has she been all this goddamned time?" Noelle said. The Boatswain[9] piped, and the announcement that brow[10] was secured came over the 1MC[11], followed by the commencing of sea and anchor[12].

Sidney snapped her fingers. "I know why she didn't pick

---

9. BM/Boatswain's Mates: Crew members who train, direct, and supervise personnel in ship maintenance and boat seamanship.

10. Brow: Temporary bridge that connects the ship's quarterdeck to the pier.

11. 1MC (Main circuit): Loudspeakers.

12. Sea and Anchor Detail: Sailors are assigned to specific areas throughout the ship so they can attach and release the mooring lines to the pier safely and also pick up and drop the anchor safely as well.

12. Sea and Anchor Detail: Sailors are assigned to specific areas throughout the ship so they can attach and release the mooring lines to the pier safely and also pick up and drop the anchor safely as well.

him up last year. I remember hearing he got a Red Cross message[13] from his wife so I don't think she showed up. I guess we weren't paying attention in '92 because there wasn't a reason."

"True. So I guess you're the "mystery man"," Noelle made air quotes, "that Santiago thought his wife was cheating on him with. Well, ain't that a plot twist we didn't see coming."

They all were quiet for a moment as Noelle's words resonated in the air between them.

Celia gave her a rueful smile. "Julia broke up with me because she said I made her want to leave her husband and that wasn't something she ever thought she would do."

"You two were pretty hot and heavy. And stressful. I was so vicariously stressed," Noelle said.

Celia nodded. "It was too heavy. We both knew it. That's why I didn't fight the breakup."

"You know, if we don't count the non-contact stalking, you did good. And now look at you," Noelle said, then she groaned. "Oh Celia, girl, I thought this kinda crazy shit only happened to me! I feel like I should apologize or something. What are you going to do?"

"What do you think, Noelle?" Celia's tone was bone dry.

Noelle groaned again. "I think you're a sadist or a masochist; I'm not sure which one. Probably both."

Celia rolled her eyes and then narrowed them as she looked at Noelle. "Speaking of one that enjoys pain, where's Quentin? I didn't see him on the pier this morning."

The Boatswain piped again and instructed the sailors

---

13. Red Cross message: confidential emergency communication via the American Red Cross to service members who are on deployment.

to man the rail[14] . She was never so happy to hear that annoying, ear-piercing sound.

"I really need to go take pictures of all of this 'cause it's my job," Noelle said, stepping back as Sidney and Celia took the position of parade rest at the wall.

"You used '92's sea and anchor in last year's cruise book. I was there when you did it, trick," Celia threw over her shoulder.

"First of all, lower your voice. Don't be putting my business out like that. And trick? Such language coming out of your pretty mouth." Noelle tsked. " But I know where that mouth has been, so I am not surprised."

"Whatever ho. As soon as we secure, I'm coming to find you," Celia said.

Sidney chuckled and shook her head. "Y'all stay outta pocket. I'll see ya'll later. I gotta get back to main control[15]."

"She needs to stay in her damn pocket and stay outta mine," Noelle grumbled. She sneered at Celia's back. She was not looking forward to having that conversation with her.

"I can feel you staring a hole in my back. Go take your pictures and think of the lie you're gonna try to sell me that

---

14. Manning the rails: Sailors at parade rest, spaced evenly on port and starboard the wing walls, and the aft lookout while the ship leaves the pier and when it returns.

15. Main Control: controls the propulsion system of the ship.

15. Main Control: controls the propulsion system of the ship.

I will *not* be buying," Celia said.

"Ugh!" Noelle groaned so loudly, some of the other sailors quickly glanced back at her as she walked away in a huff. If she could hide in the Photo Lab for the next twelve days until they hit Spain, she would. She could pee down the drain and take a ho bath in the sink. She had a microwave in there too and fuck it, she'd sleep on the floor. Anything not to talk about Quentin. She wasn't ready to deal with that right now, if ever.

Noelle went to the furthest part of aft lookout[16] and took a picture of the pier as it faded away along with all connections to the people who watched their loved ones head out to sea. Julia's face popped up in her mind. Her mind was completely blown. Julia was Marisol. Marisol was Santiago's wife. *And* Celia was also going to sleep with him too. Were they about to witness a real-life Jerry Springer episode? And little Miss Salacious Sidney? What the hell was she going to do about Kaneko? She hadn't mentioned him after their afternoon delight no matter how much Noelle poked and prodded. But she caught Sidney watching him whenever they were in the same space together. Boy oh boy, this was turning out to be a hella cruise, and they hadn't even made it out far enough to dump trash. She shook her head. She couldn't imagine what the next six months would bring, but they were all about to find out.

---

16. Aft Lookout: Covered section extending from the rear of the ship.

Six Months, Two Couples, One Lonely Heart
&
1,318 Sailors

The Puget Sound is underway! Join the
crew as they travel along the
Mediterranean Coast in

We Were The Puget Sound Series

Book 2

Coming June 2024

About the Author

Danielle Bailey is a Jill of most trades and an expert of some who is finally fulfilling a lifelong dream of being an author. Unabashedly obsessed with the 90s and with a nostalgic love for the Navy, she writes stories of a time when bell bottoms were the uniform of the day, Don't Ask, Don't Tell was the rule, and the only thing you had to worry about was staying out the eyes of the ship.

She grew up in South Bronx and joined the Navy at 17. After spending almost six years in, she moved to the beautiful state of Maine, where she's lived for over 20 years with her mostly-adult three kids and two fur babies.